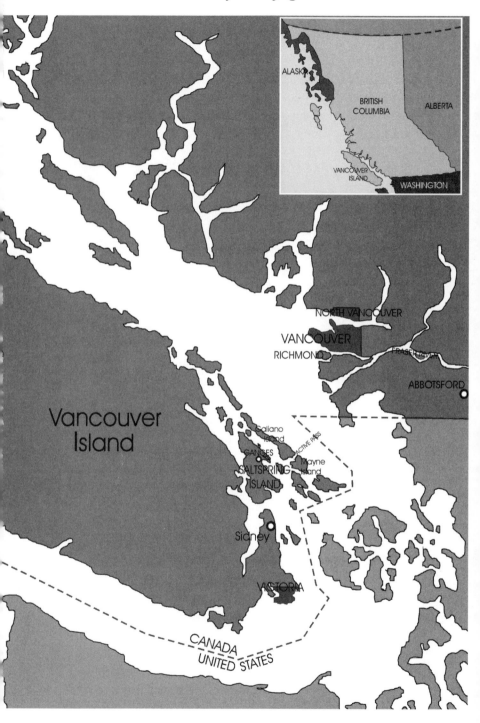

Operational Area - Diplomatic Protection Unit

Also by Anthony Bruce

Fiction:
To Taunt A Wounded Tiger.
The East Wind.

Non Fiction
Railway Surveyors Handbook

A LIE TO COMFORT
THE DYING

A novel by

Anthony Bruce

Copyright © 2001 Anthony Bruce

Canadian Cataloguing in Publication Data

Bruce, Anthony Alexander
A lie to comfort the dying

ISBN 0-9681787-2-3

1.Title
PS8553.R72L53 2001   C813'.54   C00-911020-8
PR9199.3.B738L53 2001

A Glendambo Book
Published by Glendambo Publishing
151 Saltair Lane
Salt Spring Island.
B.C. V8K 1Y5

With grateful thanks:
In Britain, to: Sir Ivan and Lady Gloria Lawrence
                  Andy Bruce
In Corsica, to: Guido Falcone and O.E.
In Canada, to : Deon and the Vortex gallery
                Janice Finnemore
                Laura Thomson
Printed in Canada

For Nick

Rafa said,

"There are three things you should never do: Never piss into the wind. Never lie, unless it's to comfort the dying, and never ever taunt a wounded tiger."

cover design by Irwan Kurnaedy
cover **Wound, Scab, Scar** *2000 - Deon Venter*
back **Casanova in the Leads** *- Deon Venter*

Prologue:

Southern Lebanon – Israel Security Zone

The heat hammered down. The high bright sun, a mailed
fist of midday malice seared the sand-coloured camouflage sheet spread over them. Nothing moved in the
burnt air; even the desert lizard lay supine in what scant
shade the eroded rocks grudgingly provided.

Ignoring the perspiration trickling down his face,
he saw the jeep, a small khaki beetle, trudge over the
distant hill and crawl along the fenced boundary road,
leaving a column of dust hanging in the still air. The
long wait was nearly over. Time passed, and as the
vehicle drew closer he heard the whine of its engine
before it crested the nearest hill. The jeep rolled down
the road on the Israeli side of the fence. It stopped short
of the culvert and dust curling forward obscured his
view for a few seconds before beginning slowly to settle.

Squinting through the Habicht scope into the
harsh sunlight that skidded in shimmering waves off the
rocks, he watched as the driver lit a cigarette. The whip
aerial waved lazily as three soldiers swung down from
the jeep. Dust, fine as talcum powder, lifted in soft
clouds from their desert boots. Weapons held casually,
they lined up to urinate against the high security fence
topped with razor wire. Hearing Hasid beginning to
hyperventilate he slid his hand carefully over the sand
and gripped the younger man's shoulder. He felt Hasid
stiffen, then force himself to relax, as the hard fingers
dug into his shoulder.

Without removing his eye from the scope
Dragovic relaxed his grip, and saw the lead soldier

glance idly at the culvert. The driver called something. The distance was too great to make out the words but the intent was clear: it was time to move on. The other two soldiers yelled at the driver and their words, indistinct, floated on the burnt air. Dragovic marveled: their discipline was certainly as sloppy as he'd been told. No one stood guard, or scanned the rocky hills for possible danger; they must be short-term reservists to be so casual. He focussed on the driver's face, heat from the rocky desert distorting the man's features. With a start he realised he was looking at a woman, a good-looking woman.

"Do they suspect?" Hasid whispered, turning his face away from his own scope to look at Dragovic, his dark brown liquid eyes trying to read from Dragovic's expression what the Bosnian Muslim was thinking.

"Quiet," Dragovic grunted, his eye fixed to the telescope and watching intently as the lead soldier wandered back to the jeep. The soldier leant against the jeep next to the driver and shook a cigarette free from a packet taken from his tunic pocket. He offered the packet to the driver and Dragovic saw her short-cropped black hair sway as she shook her head in emphatic refusal. The soldier lifted his hands in the air in frustration and called to his two companions, who called back. It was obvious they were mocking his attempt to placate the driver. A burst of laughter floated towards where Dragovic and Hasid lay concealed on the Lebanese side of the wire. Finally, zipping up, the two remaining soldiers sauntered back to the jeep and clambered aboard.

With practised ease, Dragovic flicked on the arming switch and moved his thumb over the detonator button. Suddenly he felt weary. How many times had he done this in the past, waiting for Serb vehicles to roll over the remote-controlled mine artfully hidden in the road? These sloppy, unwitting children were not his enemy but a debt to be repaid to the men who had brought him here.

The jeep jerked forward as the driver engaged the clutch without waiting for the soldiers to settle. The front wheels rolled over the culvert and Dragovic pushed down hard on the firing button. For a split second nothing happened, then the road erupted with a roar and the jeep reared up, flipping over in a burning mass of twisted metal. A cloud of dust, shot through with flame, boiled eerily upward in roiling clouds to obscure the scene.

Hasid was yelling in exultation, slapping Dragovic on the back. Savagely Dragovic snapped at Hasid, "Move, damn you, move—the helicopters will be here any second." Without waiting for the Palestinian's response he shrugged off the camouflage cape, collecting his weapon as he ran towards their vehicle, a battered Peugeot pickup, hidden in a shallow wash behind a crumbling outcrop. A thin high-pitched screaming followed them as they ran. Dragovic hoped it wasn't the woman; he'd seen the injuries survivors of a land mine explosion carried to the grave.

Chapter 1

Vancouver BC - Anne

Anne Flett closed the door softly. The patient would sleep now that the analgesic in his drip had kicked in. She waited another minute, listening for any sound, before walking down the brightly-lit passage towards the emergency room of St Paul's hospital. She smiled at an ER nurse who gave her thumbs up. The man should not have survived, the big semi had crushed his little Escort into a mass of twisted metal and it had taken the firemen an hour using the Jaws of Life to extricate him. For three hours she had worked on his broken body, several times nearly losing him on the table. She stretched her shoulders. God she felt tired.

"Doctor Flett—Anne—a minute please." Anne stopped at the call; Sam MacGuire was hurrying towards her. "Before you go, I have some messages. Your husband phoned. He'll meet you at the Pan Pacific if you finish before ten." Anne glanced at her watch. It was 10:30 p.m. MacGuire, noting the movement, nodded "If not he'll go on to the party and meet you there."

"Thank you Sam, was there anything else?" She'd hoped that Mike would have made some excuse for them both. He knew she didn't want to attend yet another film party celebrating some actor's part in a forgettable movie, especially since she'd left a message with his secretary that a Code Blue emergency had just come in.

"Only from Mrs. Olivera asking when you might be home." Mrs. Olivera, their housekeeper, had planned to visit her daughter in Victoria. Anne sighed in frustration.

"Damn, she'll have missed the last ferry."

"Sorry. What?"

"Nothing Sam. Nothing." Anne brushed her hand across her forehead, moving loose strands of hair away from her eyes. Sam MacGuire, like most of the staff in the Trauma Section, liked Anne Flett very much. She was so small; petite and unfailingly gentle that it was hard sometimes to think of her as a very good emergency room doctor. Sam, a homosexual with a partner he doted on, still wanted to put an arm around the thin shoulders and tell her to go home and rest. He thought she looked like a pocket-sized version of his favourite actress, Emma Thompson, but with short dark hair and blue eyes. Hesitating, he waited.

"Can I call you a cab, Doc? I guess you don't feel much like driving."

"No, thank you. The traffic will be light and it's not that far to the party. I must call Mrs. Olivera first though. Did you give her any indication of when I might be free?"

"No, all I said was that it looked like you had a serious one and it might be quite a while."

Anne pursed her lips, "Yes, I see. Well, you were quite right. I'll call her now." She touched his arm briefly then moved down corridor towards the senior staff room where her locker was situated.

After calling Mrs. Olivera and apologising for the confusion she changed into a black dress, split to mid thigh, with spaghetti straps—her universal fall-back uniform for events like tonight's. She pushed her feet into high-heeled evening shoes, brushed her hair briefly, picked up her small black leather bag and remembered to tuck her invisible leash, the cell phone, inside. She passed through the reception area heading to the elevators and waved goodbye to Sam and a group of nurses gathered around the desk.

Ten minutes later, listening to the car CD playing

the 'Andante' from Mozart's Symphony No.40 in G
minor, she swung the green Range Rover off the Lions
Gate bridge and turned west towards British Properties.
The Film Institute was having its party in the home of
Joyce and Dino Caramanlis. The long brick paved driveway, in this, the most expensive of Vancouver's suburbs,
led steeply up the hill toward a huge house, blazing with
lights that turned the approach into daylight. No—
house was the wrong word she thought—this was a
small palace, anchored on the steep slope with a breathtaking view of Vancouver at night. A young man in a
white shirt and red bow tie appeared beside the door. He
smiled, exhibiting perfect teeth in a tanned, rather too
good-looking face. She wondered if he was another of
the many hopefuls who orbited around the glitteratti of
the film world, hoping to impress. He pointed to another
man waiting under the portico who, he advised, would
park her car.

Entering the vast foyer Anne was accosted almost
immediately by Joyce Caramanlis. "Oh my dear, so good
of you to come. Mike told me that you had been de-
tained at the hospital—Paul—Paul, bring that tray over
here, doctor Flett must have some champagne." Surprisingly, for they had little in common except for the fact
that both their husbands were commercial real estate
developers, Anne liked the older woman. Joyce
Caramanlis had a wicked tongue that, if provoked,
could peel the skin off a longshoreman. Never a beauty,
her looks not much improved by numerous face-lifts,
she could still, at 60 years of age, dominate a room of
successful men with her vitality and wit. Her husband's
success in real estate during the boom years of the
eighties when it seemed that every Asian with money
wanted property on the West Coast, and expensive
property at that, had given her a lifestyle that few could

ever hope to attain. She treated Anne like the daughter she'd never had. "Come and sit with me—no Hector." She stiff-armed a gaunt looking film director dressed in fashionably faded denim "Not now, I'm going to have a few words in private with Anne." She pulled Anne over to an alcove containing a curved chaise longe. Patting the seat she indicated where Anne should sit. "He's actually very clever, did a marvelous movie set in the Gatineau. He's busy raising financing for a movie based on that book, I forget the name, by that local author, the one from Salt Spring."

Looking around while Joyce chattered on, Anne could not see her husband. "Is Mike around? I should let him know that I've arrived."

"Oh, don't worry about him. Dino and Mike took a couple of German clients to look at some show houses in North Vancouver they think the Germans might be interested in."

"At night?"

"Oh, you know Dino, something about a view of the city at night from the property. Apparently the Germans are leaving tomorrow."

"Did he say anything about meeting me?"

"Mike? Not to me dear." The older woman looked at her curiously. "I can call Dino and ask when they'll be back if you wish."

Anne felt a brief flash of anger then, startlingly, the prick of tears. Damn him, tonight of all nights. She realised that tiredness was clouding her judgement and making her emotional—but still. She blinked rapidly, then placed her hand on the older woman's arm. "Joyce I'm really very tired. Would you mind awfully if I slipped away"

Joyce Caramanlis gave her a brief hug, "I see so little of you—but of course my dear." Placing her hands on Anne's shoulders and leaning away from the younger woman she smiled. "Even with bags under your eyes you're still the most ravishing thing in this room. Look, why don't I get Gregory to drive you home? One of the boys can follow and bring him back."

Anne shook her head, "I must look awful. That's the second time tonight I've had the offer of a drive home. Thank you, but I'm fine, honestly." She squeezed Joyce's arm; "Thank goodness it's Saturday tomorrow. I'll get a long lie-in."

"Have you eaten? No I guess not. Let me have Marko make you up a couple of sandwiches." Ignoring Anne's protest she beckoned one of the waiters over. "Tell Marko I want a couple of sandwiches made up quickly, and have them put in doctor Flett's car."

"Joyce, you mustn't fuss. I can dig something out of the fridge when I get home."

"Fuss, it's no fuss. Good grief girl, someone has to look after you. I bet you haven't had much all day. Anyway this bunch all nibble at their food. You'd think," she chuckled hoarsely, "that creativity depended on looking anorexic. Tomorrow I'll be sending truckloads to the food bank."

Twenty minutes later, after saying her good-byes and with a mouth-watering aroma coming from the box on her front seat, Anne swung into the underground parking of their apartment complex. After parking the Range Rover in the reserved slot she entered the empty elevator and pushed the button for the 18th floor. As the elevator moved smoothly up the exterior of the building she saw, through the clear glass sides, False Creek and the yacht basin lit up with a million twinkling lights. Even in her tired state the panorama spread below never failed to lift her spirits. For her, Vancouver was still the most beautiful city in the world.

The phone was ringing as she opened the door,

and placing her package on the side table she hurried to reach the instrument.

"Anne? Is that you Anne? It's mother."

"Mother?" Her heart lurched. Her father was recovering from bypass surgery, she glanced at her watch, it was nearly midnight, and it would be past seven in the morning in England. "Dad, is Dad all right?"

"Yes dear, your father is fine, he's recovering very well. I'm afraid it's Sandy." Alex, her older brother, had always been known as Sandy. From when he was very small the nickname had stuck. Now, as a British officer, attached to UNPROFOR, the United Nations Protection Force in Bosnia guarding the fragile peace brought about by the Dayton Accord, everyone simply knew him as Sandy. Not nearly as academic as his younger sister, Sandy excelled in most outdoor sports and from his childhood made it plain that he intended to follow his father's footsteps into the armed forces. He'd climbed Nanga Parbat and K2 with the SAS team, been posted to Northern Ireland, Columbia and Borneo. He loved the life, confiding to his sister on one of the rare occasions that they'd met since she'd left England, that he'd never wanted to do anything else with his life and was terrified at the thought of a desk job. Her mother was saying. "Johnny Johnstone phoned and Sandy has been injured in Bosnia. He assured me that Sandy would be fine after treatment. Apparently their armoured vehicle hit an old land mine. The Army is flying him home tonight." Anne could hear the tears in her mother's voice. Theirs was very close family, almost incestuous— as Mike sarcastically noted when the monthly phone bill from Telus arrived, for Anne kept in touch by e-mail and telephone on a regular basis.

"How badly is he hurt Mom? What did Colonel

Johnstone say were the extent of his injuries?" Mentally Anne was weighing the possibility of getting a locum in to take over her duties and flying to Britain.

"Johnny said it's a leg and foot injury—his left leg. But Johnny is convinced that Sandy will be walking again in a couple of months. Sandy wanted to call but he's been sedated with the other injured in preparation for the trip home, so Johnny promised to call us both."

Unconsciously Anne had been holding her breath. Now she expelled a long sigh. A leg wound—a leg wound—thank God. "Do you want me to come? I can probably get a locum and be in London for the weekend."

"No dear." Her mother's voice was stronger now. "I think it best to wait and see what happens once he arrives back in Britain. I'll let you know as soon as I have more information." They talked for another ten minutes before Anne put the phone down.

Feeling slightly sick after the sudden rush of adrenaline she sat down heavily on the sofa and then, stretching out, pushed her shoes off. Lying with her arm crooked over her eyes she wished that Mike would come home soon. She desperately needed to talk to someone. Why was Michael never around when she needed him? Tiredness washed over her and within a few minutes she fell into a deep sleep.

It was here in the early morning that her husband, Michael Monroe, smelling faintly of White Linen perfume and stale sex, found his wife asleep, and slipped quietly past her still form to shower and change.

Chapter 2

Tehran - The Council of Wise Men

"What has been written is an insult to the faithful!"
Spittle flecked the Imam Basra's beard as he flung the
words at the Council. Albarrasan raised his hand to quell
the flow of rhetoric, thinking that it was a pity such a
pious and clever man could lose control so easily.

"It is true," he said quietly, his uplifted palm
facing Imam Basra to forestall any interruption.
Albarrasan looked around the table at the six clerics
waiting for him to continue. He sighed, "Of course he
must receive the most severe punishment, but tell me
Saidi my friend, what do you think will work this time?
The apostate Rushdie is still alive despite huge sums
and all our resources; do you believe Talawi will be any
less secure than Rushdie once we issue the *fatwa*?"

"We will succeed—even if it takes a lifetime.
Ayatollah Hassan Sanei has said the commitment to
killing the apostate, Rushdie, will only grow stronger
with time. Not imposing a *fatwa* on Talawi will indicate
to all the enemies of the faithful that we have grown
weary." Basra's stern face, hard with anger, stared at
Albarrasan. "Think how little we have heard from
Rushdie, whose name I will not mention again in this
room of holy men, since Khordad 15 increased the
bounty on him. He cannot be seen anywhere without
special protection and those who would publish his
blasphemy know the price of such sin."

"Again, what you say is true, but if we are to
succeed we need more than rhetoric." He watched
Basra's face flush. The Imam was not accustomed to
criticism. A low murmur rose from the table. He looked
at each member in turn, his eyes daring anyone to ques-

tion him. He continued quietly but there was no mistaking the authority in his voice. "If we issue a *fatwa* today against Talawi then he will be protected, as is Rushdie. What I propose is this, that we do nothing for twelve months. We issue no statements of any kind, and we do not respond to the probing of the Western press." He took a sip of water and waited for the outburst but even Basra sensed an important statement was imminent and held his peace. "This apparent lack of interest in Talawi may cause the protection around the other apostate, Rushdie, to relax and perhaps offer our martyrs a chance to get close and carry out his punishment." He brushed drops of water from his beard. "But our primary target must be Talawi. We will issue a *fatwa* in the same hour our agents choose to strike. Our enemies must not be forewarned. His death will cause fear in the hearts of all the sons of sin and all who foolishly guard them from the *Shariah*."

A murmur ran round the table. Sheik Mutawalli, looking down at the table, and speaking softly in a low voice, asked, "You are repeating the saying of the Prophet, *sallallahu alayhi wa salaam*, that this apostasy of the third category renders a person a non-Muslim—even if he does not deem it harmful or a sin as such? And any action we take is sanctioned by this fact?"

Albarrasan stroked his beard before answering. "You bear the name of a great scholar, Sheik Mutawalli, and you also have studied long and deeply. We"—here he indicated all present with a slow arc of wrist movement—"know that the Prophet, *sallallahu alayhi wa salaam*, also said that a person might utter a word he thinks harmless and yet have committed blasphemy. It is not even necessary for him to know that the uttered word is blasphemous to be punished. But this man knows both the law and the punishment for sin yet he makes light of his birthright."

Imam Basra nodded slowly, "It is a good plan." He looked at Albarrasan. " I spoke without thought; passion is no substitute for reason. I beg your indulgence brother."

Albarrasan waved his hand in dismissal, "There is nothing to forgive, passion in the service of Allah, *the Compassionate, the Merciful,* is required of us all. Now let me tell you what the plan entails. We have a man, a Bosnian Muslim, whom our own volunteer mujahideen saved from death when he was wounded during a failed attack on a Serb tank column. This man, greatly skilled in the arts of war, but not of subterfuge, will be sent to a training camp in Europe. When we are ready to strike he will be sent to cleanse the world of the apostate."

"He is trustworthy?" al-Quirny was ever watchful for infiltrators into the PFLP, the Popular Front for the Liberation of Palestine.

For the first time Albarrasan smiled thinly. "Indeed, the attack on the Zionists three months ago at Rumaysh was planned and executed by him."

"Attack, it was not a road accident as claimed?"

The thin smile disappeared, but Albarrasan did not answer the question. "The files that you are receiving--" Albarassan nodded to a revolutionary guard who started passing out black folders, "—give details of the man's background. Once you have read I think you will agree that he is the only possible choice." While the clerics studied the files Albarrasan stroked his beard and stared at the ceiling. He wondered about the Imam Saidi Basra, the man had agreed too easily—yet it was a good plan and had every chance of success. He shrugged beneath his heavy robe. The man would bear watching.

Chapter 3

Mediterranean Sea – Izmir.

While the clerics studied the contents of the black files the *Izmir* slid smoothly through a light swell. The island of Pantilleria was barely visible to the south as the 24-metre motor sailer traversed the Strait of Sicily. Last night the big diesels had pushed her at 12 knots past the island of Malta and soon the skipper would turn north on a direct course for Corsica.

Nico Dragovic, naked but for a pair of faded shorts, lay on the forward hatch cover watching the thin cirrus scratch patterns in the hot blue sky. For the first time in months he began to relax, letting the warm sun soften tense muscles. He stretched luxuriously, absently rubbing the scars on his chest and stomach; ugly scars startlingly white against his deepening tan. A seagull wheeled overhead watching the wake for scraps and he smiled. Then, without warning, memories he'd suppressed for so long flooded back. Startled, he felt the prick of tears. Their child had so loved clouds, especially cirrus, 'mares tails' she'd called them, using the English expression, which had made them both laugh. Shaking his head angrily as if he could scatter memories like a dog shedding water, he sat up, clasping his knees, the muscles on his arms standing out like corded rope. Staring at the wake, a ragged blue and white braid bubbling into the distance behind the boat, he asked himself—why now—why after all this? He grimaced. Perhaps it was time—.

" Some water, *Efendim*, you should drink in this heat." The Turkish term of respect caught him by surprise as the skipper came up the companionway carrying a glass of cold water.

"Thank you." He blinked to clear his eyes. "You

read my mind." He reached across to clasp the moisture-beaded container.

The skipper, a stocky older man in faded khakis, his walrus mustache counterpointing a deeply tanned bald head, smiled as he passed the water over. "You've been on deck a long time, *Efendim*. It is a hot day and the wind also sucks moisture from the body."

Dragovic grunted, "Yes—yes you are right, Captain. Please pass me my shirt behind you." The captain turned and called to a crewman standing beside the rail. Throwing his cigarette overboard the sailor moved to pick up the shirt that had blown back towards the rear of the yacht and passed it to the captain with a comment in Turkish.

The captain growled an answer, lightly cuffing the man alongside the head and pushing him away. Expressionless, Dragovic watched the exchange and lifted an eyebrow to the captain, who handed the shirt over.

"He asked where you had received your wounds and I told him that was a matter for you to offer, not for children to ask." He waited in silence while Dragovic sipped water from the glass. Dragovic knew that the proud old skipper would not ask directly, for he was of the faithful and had made several trips like this, transporting hard-eyed men who called themselves tourists; men who brooked no questions and asked none. He was being well paid for the journey, which had begun for Dragovic on a rusty freighter from Tyre in Lebanon to Famagusta in Cyprus.

After the attack on the jeep, at a pre-arranged spot ten kilometres north of the ambush site, Dragovic had swapped vehicles with a Lebanese businessman and driven the businessman's car to a safe house in Tyre while Hasid and the businessman drove the Peugeot to Sidon. For six weeks, as arranged, Dragovic had waited

in Tyre before boarding the freighter that took him to
Famagusta. Here, Dragovic had waited a month, until
the *Izmir* arrived, the safe house a short walk from the
docks. His cover as a Bulgarian, from the town of Varna
on the Black Sea, travelling to Corsica to investigate a
newly established free zone for foreign businesses, was
sound and could stand all but the most intense scrutiny.

Wiping his lips with the back of his hand he
passed the glass back to the captain. For a second he
was tempted to indulge the old man's curiosity, then
merely said. "An accident." He smiled grimly, "I moved
too slowly." The captain, whose name was Ilyas, nodded. He'd seen bullet wounds before but this man with
the empty eyes should not have survived two bullets to
the stomach and one through the upper chest. He
sucked air through the gap in his front teeth, "You were
lucky, *Efendim*—you were lucky. Allah, *The
Compassionate,the Merciful,* must have been with you that
day."

"Indeed, all praise to his name." Dragovic turned
away. That he'd been tempted to talk to the likeable old
man was a bad sign. Staring over the sea flecked with
flashes of sunlight he tried to regain his mood of a few
moments before but, like the whine of a mosquito on a
quiet evening, the rush of memories would not go. The
Serb machine gunner had caught him as he rose to throw
the grenade. That much he remembered, the rest was a
blur of pain: travel, hospitals, then the long convalescence in Libya. Finally, when he could move again, he'd
asked about the others and was told that they'd been
withdrawn after the Dayton Accord and reassigned. The
Arab doctor smiled when he asked more questions,
answering only, "There is time—rest."

Hussein, his closest friend, and the only one with
whom he could speak French, had come for a brief visit.
He heard then for the first time that his desperate throw

with the grenade had saved them all from annihilation. Even as he was hit, his grenade bouncing off the Serb gunner's chest and falling between the gunner's legs into the tank must have detonated one of the cannon shells being readied for firing. A fluke really, but enough to stop the Serb tank attack and allow their shattered band of mudjahideen fighters to retreat carrying his limp body. The Serbs had halted their murderous attack; apparently believing only a hidden anti-tank weapon could cause such catastrophic destruction. Hussein shrugged when asked why they had risked their own lives for someone who was so critically wounded. "Ah Cedar," using Dragovic's old code name, "Insh'Allah. We could not leave you brother." Hussein rose from his chair in embarrassment to pace the room, pretending to be interested in the view of the sea from the apartment window.

Dragovic smiled sadly in remembrance. A good man, an honourable man, the one who'd kept him sane and nursed him through those terrible early days of the war after Reena and the child were murdered. During the bitter rearguard action to hold the ancient city of Mostar, Hussein had been his right hand. Then, a month after the visit to the Libyan hospital where Dragovic was recovering, Hussein was killed in a stupid traffic accident. A dog running from a child on Abdul el Muchtar Street in Gaza had crossed his path and in swerving to avoid the child, he collided with a parked truck. Dragovic sighed softly, then stood to pull on his shirt and turned to Ilyas.

"I'm going below for a while Captain. You'll wake me at six?"

"Of course, *Efendim*." Ilyas watched as Dragovic vaulted lightly off the hatch cover and made for the companionway. He took a deep breath, thinking there goes a man who is with the dead. As usual he had been told nothing of his passenger's history. Over the past days, as they moved inexorably to their destination, he'd watched Dragovic and, unlike the others he'd carried, this man had no passion, no emotion—his life force a barely flickering ember fanned only briefly to flame by the wind of memories. Ilyas felt a sudden shiver of fear; glad he was not this man's enemy.

Chapter 4

London - The Author

"Damn it, woman, stop fussing!" He pushed her away, knocking the folder she was holding out of her hand to the floor. Red-faced, she mumbled an apology and stooped to retrieve the scattered papers.

"Ismail, Maggie is only trying to help," John Farquarson remonstrated gently. A tall, spare man with a permanent stoop and shock of unruly gray hair, the senior partner in McCallan, Ross and DeJong, Publishers, he found Ismail Talawi a rather unpleasant fellow. Unpleasant even before his latest book, *'Lunch with the Prophet,'* had catapulted him into international prominence. The man was a gifted writer and his earlier books were minor classics but the latest had taken the literary world by storm. Farquarson, a natural gentleman, had learnt long ago to discipline himself when dealing with unruly authors but Talawi taxed his patience to extraordinary limits.

"She's only trying to help, she's only trying to help," Talawi mocked him sarcastically, "Then tell her to stop fussing around me. I don't give a shit what I look like and I'm damned if I'm tarting up for a gaggle of book club buyers."

"Book clubs represent a huge slice of the market, Ismail. It's in all our interests to have them on side."

"In your interest perhaps. I'm getting sick and tired of all this excessive hype. The sales are going well aren't they? Madeline tells me that you're into a third printing. So what's the panic?"

"Fourth printing actually. But the sales curve is dropping. As you know we have only a few months in the public eye and it's important to stay there as long as possible."

Talawi snorted, "My dear John, as I've said before

on many occasions, my function is to write the books that make all the money and yours is to sell them. The technical details are of no interest to me." Talawi looked into the large ornate mirror attached to the office wall, fussily straightening his tie and adjusting his jacket. "Will someone give me a comb for heavens sake? Damn it, I can't go out looking like this. Maggie, stop flopping all over the floor and hand me a comb."

John Farqurson waited until Maggie handed Talawi a comb and waited while the author carefully stroked his already groomed hair into place. Farquarson felt a ripple of distaste at the preening; Ismail Talawi had the physique and looks of a male model and be-haved with the same self-absorbed vanity. Turning to the others in the room Farquarson outlined the travel arrangements. "We will use two pool cars to carry every-one. Ismail, Maggie, and myself will go in the Daimler, and Ross, Dennis, and Heather will follow in the Rover. Now the distance from Clerkenwell Green to Green Park should take us no more than 20 minutes, but I think we should be moving down to the street now." A rumble of assent rose from everyone except Talawi, who was still placing each strand of hair with meticu-lous care.

"Ismail, if you're ready." Farqurson held out his hand as the others trooped out of the dark oak doors heading for the circular stairwell to the street.

"Yes, yes, let's get this nonsense over with."

§

Parked on the corner of Clerkenwell Road and St John Street, its softly idling engine noise drowned out by the midmorning traffic, the heavy Honda Gold Wing touring motorcycle, with its two leather-clad passengers, drew few glances from the passing crowds. Mashood adjusted his motorcycle helmet, settling it comfortably before adjusting the straps tightly. He wiped his hands, suddenly wet with perspiration, on a rag from beneath the seat. He was glad that Ahmed had warned him this might happen; it was the little things that mattered. Ahmed had done this before, in Stockholm two years ago. For Mashood, it was the first time. His skill in handling a motorcycle had come to the ears of Imam Basra of the Judgement committee and they had given him this mission. He suppressed a ripple of fear that bubbled up from the pit of his stomach. This was a great honour and, as Ahmed had said, one day he would tell his children of his part in this day. Behind him Ahmed was checking the saddlebags. The Velcro fasteners would ensure quick and easy access to the weapon in the bag. Mashood revved the engine slightly, listening for any unusual sounds; today the machine must operate perfectly, they must not fail. Imam Basra was not a man who took excuses easily.

Ahmed thumped him twice on the back and Mashood twisted the throttle, releasing the clutch in one easy movement as he brought his leg up to the footrest, accelerating the heavy Honda away from the curb. Out of the corner of his eye he saw Abbas Salameh holding the cellular phone to his ear and realised that their target was moving at last.

Through the clear visor he searched for the silver-gray Daimler that they had followed every day for the past week. Ahead were two cars, then a large furniture van that blocked his view of the street. He hesitated, weighing the risk of a fast run up the inside to pass the furniture van when it suddenly turned into Clerkenwell Green. At the same time the silver-gray Daimler turned out into Clerkenwell Road heading towards Theobald's Road and the turn into Procter Street. Mashood stayed

behind the two cars separating him from the Daimler
and did not notice the Rover that pulled into the traffic
behind him.

As the small phalanx of vehicles turned right past
the Holborn tube station onto the one way traffic of
High Holborn the two cars between Mashood and the
Daimler continued straight into New Oxford Street
while the Daimler followed High Holborn towards
Shaftesbury Avenue. Mashood accelerated sharply to
bring the Honda alongside the Daimler. He felt Ahmed's
helmet bump into his back as his companion bent
forward to extract the compact Heckler & Koch MP5-
PDW submachine gun from its hiding place in the
saddlebag. Time seemed to slow as he held the motorcycle steady alongside the Daimler. He heard the flat
metallic click as Ahmed cocked the submachine gun and
felt the slight twist in the saddle as Ahmed turned
sideways preparing to fire into the rear of the Daimler.

Fifty feet behind the Daimler and motorcycle,
Reg Coombes, driving the Rover carrying the rest of the
publisher's staff, watched in startled amazement as the
Honda roared alongside the Daimler then held it's
position. It was unfortunate for Mashood and Ahmed
that Coombes had spent two tours in Northern Ireland
as an infantry driver before being invalided out of the
service after a nasty crash while chasing a suspected
IRA terrorist down a country lane. Such is fate and
coincidence. Realising almost as soon as the motorcycle
began to move up on the Daimler that something wrong
was happening, Reg floored the accelerator while holding his hand down hard on the horn.

Ahmed, lining up the submachine gun, jerked at
the sound of the horn. He half turned, hesitated, then
swung back to sight in the rear window. As he did so the
Rover smashed into the back wheel of the Honda just

as he squeezed the trigger, causing him to empty the full curved clip of 9mm bullets into the rear, front, and engine of the Daimler. The impact catapulted the Honda up and sideways in an uncontrollable slide that ended when the motor cycle smashed into a lamp standard, shearing off Mashood's head. His leg trapped under the still roaring motorcycle, Ahmed was feebly trying to extricate himself when the wreckage exploded into flame.

The Daimler mounted the curb outside a theatre where it came to a full stop, steam pouring from the punctured radiator. For a long moment there was eerie silence, then someone screamed, and people started running toward and away from the wreckage. A policeman mouthing words into his lapel microphone was first to reach the Daimler. He wrenched open the front passenger door and Maggie Crossley's body slid down to the pavement. Quickly, expertly, the policeman felt her neck pulse then barked into his microphone. Before he could reach the rear door it opened and John Farquarson fell to the pavement on his hands and knees, blood running from his scalp. Waving off the policeman, Farquarson pointed inside the vehicle. Leaning over Farquarson the policeman noticed a whimpering figure crouched in a ball on the floor. He shook Ismail Talawi's shoulder gently. "Are you hurt, sir?"

"Get away, get away." Eyes wild and dilated with shock, Ismail Talawi flailed at the policeman's outstretched arm. The policeman pulled back,

"It's all right sir, you're safe, it's over. You can come out." He turned back to John Farquarson and made the older man sit on the pavement. Reaching into his pocket for a large handkerchief, he wiped blood from Farquarson's face, then balled up the cloth, to press it over a jagged scalp wound. An ambulance screamed around the corner, followed by a police car with lights flashing. Somewhere from the direction of New Bridge and Fleet Streets sirens were adding to the rapidly increasing noise as more police cars arrived.

"Is Maggie badly hurt?" Farquarson tried to get up. "Where's Ismail? Is he . . .?"

"Please stay put sir, help is coming. The ambulance will get you to the Middlesex in a few minutes."

"Please help her officer. I can see she's hurt."

The Policeman shook his head. "I'm sorry." He lifted Farquarsons right hand gently and placed it over the cloth. "Hold this down hard. I want to check on your friend in the back. I think he's unharmed." He reached inside the Daimler and gripped Talawi's shoulder. "Let me help you. Are you injured?"

This time Ismail Talawi held on to the policeman's arm as he extricated himself from the Daimler. The policeman wrinkled his nose at the smell of excrement. He shook his head. Hell, who wouldn't shit themselves after being shot at?

§

Abbas Salameh mingled with curious bystanders as he walked slowly past the wrecked vehicles. A police cordon of yellow crime tape held pedestrians away from the wrecked motorcycle but Salameh saw enough to turn his stomach. He bumped into a woman standing on tip-toe trying to get a better look at the wreckage and blood-splash along the curb and muttered an apology. The adrenaline released into his system when he had activated the hit team had turned to nausea and now he felt real fear. Imam Basra had ordered the strike and he, Abbas Salameh, had hitched his star to the fiery cleric's rhetoric rather than obeying strict orders from Ayatollah

Albarrasan to do nothing but keep Talawi under observation. The failure would stir up a hornet's nest, not only here in Britain, but also in Iran. The wrath of Ayatollah Albarrasan was well known. He shivered. He would have to go to ground at once. Praise to Allah that he'd thought ahead. The safe house was unknown to the others.

Chapter 5

Corsica.

The *Izmir* rolled gently in a slight chop. The wind was
from the land and Ilyas nursed the throttle gently to
keep the motor sailer facing the rocky shoreline, black
and menacing in the pre-dawn darkness. Dragovic came
up the darkened companionway carrying a small
backpack over one shoulder. He stuck his head round
the wheelhouse door. "Thank you Captain, safe journey
home."

"Insh'Allah, *Efendim,* may Allah, *The Merciful, The
Compassionate,* also protect you." Ilyas turned, holding
out both hands. "Go with God and may he give you
success."

Dragovic clasped Ilyas's hands for a second, then
turning, stepped over the side into the waiting Zodiac.
Moments later the *Izmir* was a fading blur against the
gray-black of the sea. Dragovic did not look back.
Sitting on the floor of the Zodiac with a man behind
him and seeing nothing but the back of the man in front
he emptied his mind. There would be time enough to
worry about the future in the morning.

London – Edgeware Road

Abbas Salameh stared at the dark-faced man sitting on
the bed. "Koorosh? Koorosh Ghiassi. What . . . how did
. . .?"

"Know where your safe house was located?" The
dark face smiled, showing perfect teeth. "Abbas, try to
stop thinking like those revolutionary guard peasants."
The barb went home, for Salameh had spent two years
on Ayatollah Albarrasan's security detail before being

inducted into the Foreign Intelligence unit. "Did you
really believe that I was simply another disaffected
Iranian?" He rose, a short, plump fiqure in a smartly
tailored dark suit. Salameh looked towards the night
table; his Glock pistol was Velcro-taped on the back.
Following Salameh's eyes the man called Koorosh shook
his head sadly. "Even if you managed to reach it you
would still need this." He held up the Glock's metal gray
magazine, an exposed 9mm round-nosed cartridge
glinting dull copper in the overhead light. "Think man,
if we had wanted you dead I could have killed you as
you came through the door."

"But you . . .you were never . . ." Salameh stuttered, still in shock.

"Oh yes—yes I was. You and the others were not
party to the higher levels and with good reason I might
add. You're still operational and must return to your
office before the CID come around to question you.
Running will simply alert them. Do not underestimate
them Salameh, they would find this house in a short
time."

"But . . .They must know . . ."

"Why? You met Ahmed and Mashood at the
Iranian Club as we all did. Most of the members are
what they claim. Why should you be any different? Your
cover is sound and even if you were seen near the site,
which is unlikely; you were visiting the cinema. It might
be a coincidence that the cinema was right next to the
attack, but that might even count in your favour. A safe
house is the first rule that every agent is taught. What
makes you think you weren't watched? From the day
you arrived in England, we've had you under surveillance."

"But what did you think—that I would defect?"
Salameh's voice squeaked slightly but colour was return-

ing to his face. "I am loyal, have I not proved that?"

"Sit down please." The dark face did not change expression. "To answer your question, no—we did not think you would defect or that you weren't loyal to our cause. But understand this clearly, we do not take unnecessary chances even with those we trust. Now listen carefully, we do not have much time. You'll return to your apartment, and when you're questioned you'll answer truthfully that Ahmed and Mashood were known to you, but only as casual acquaintances. You'll express shock and offer full cooperation." Ghiassi reached into his jacket pocket to remove a flat silver cigarette case, from which he selected a cigarette and tapped it absent mindedly on the case. "Your strike was unsuccessful due to factors that were out of your control but it has been decided that another attempt is to be made." Putting the cigarette between his lips he lit it with a beautifully chased silver lighter and, drawing deeply, watched Salameh through half-closed eyes.

"But that's madness, the British will be ready for another attempt. It'll be suicide." Salameh's mouth had fallen open and he shook his head in disbelief. "How will you even find him? He will be hidden even as Rushdie is hidden."

"Have faith Salameh. Now go back to your apartment and wait for further orders." Ghiassi tossed the Glock magazine over to bounce on the bed. "We are much stronger than you can imagine, so have faith, your contribution will not be forgotten." Ghiassi walked to the door. Opening it, he turned. "The fact that you tried to escape the British authorities is proof enough of your loyalty. Tonight, the faithful will be saying prayers for your safety." The door closed with a soft click.

London – New Scotland Yard

"Do we have preliminary forensic yet?" Chief Superintendent Roger Ingram pushed aside the pile of reports stacked neatly in front of him and reached for the file Detective Inspector Basil Coulson was holding out.

"Yes, and for once we've had a stroke of luck." Coulson passed the file over. "The driver of the bike was decapitated when they hit the pole and his head rolled clear of the ensuing explosion. Both bodies were severely burnt and it would've taken forensic a while to come up with a possible ID."

Tapping the top sheet in his hand, which he'd been scanning while Coulson talked, Ingram raised his eyebrows. "But you've managed to identify the head this quickly?"

"One of the beat constables arriving on the scene identified the head as soon as he saw it. The constable is an amateur motorcycle enthusiast and recognised the man as a member of his club. The man's name is Mashood al-Barzani. An Iranian refugee who arrived in England from Syria about two years ago."

"Anything on record?"

"Nothing at all, not even a speeding ticket. He is—was—very popular at the club. A good sort apparently. Quiet, but sociable, and willing to pitch in as a volunteer for their various functions."

"Family, relations, any close friend's?" Ingram had a sinking feeling that someone who'd melted into the English scene so well would have left no strings which investigators could follow.

"A girl friend. A shop assistant at Purcells, the gloves shop. She's being interviewed at Tottenham station. From what I saw, before coming up here, she isn't going to be much help. She seemed totally bewildered and I suspect is an innocent—but," Coulson smiled grimly, "we'll find out." He reached over to take a sheet of paper from the top of the pile on the Chief's desk. "We think we have a fix on the driver." Scanning down the sheet, he grunted, "Here it is, Ahmed Agha, a friend of Mashood. They met frequently at their local club, a hangout for Iranian dissidents. We're busy interviewing all of their acquaintances. The remains of the assassination team, the backup crew, are loose out there. This was more than a two man job."

Ingram pushed his chair back. "Good work Basil, so what's the damage? Let's recap." Flipping through the pile of paper he grunted with satisfaction as he found the one he wanted and pulled it clear. "So we have two members of the assassination team down, the publisher's secretary," Ingram ran his finger down the list, " . . . Margaret Crossley and the driver of the Daimler, John Wilson, killed, John Farquarson injured and Ismail Talawi not a scratch." He snorted; "If the driver of the Rover hadn't reacted as quickly as he did…." He shook his head. "The Devil looks after his own, Basil." Ingram tapped the sheet with a stiff forefinger. "We're going to give the same protection to Talawi as we've given Rushdie." Ingram gestured towards his telephone. "Before you arrived the Assistant Commissioner was on the line. I've set up a meeting in about 20 minutes with Special Branch. I assume you've arranged temporary 24-hour protection for Talawi until we can fix a safe place for him?"

"Yes, that's taken care of. What's puzzling, if it's the Iranians, why they've not issued a *fatwa*? Talawi's book has been out for three months and there's been no Fundamentalist response at all. It's almost as if they wanted our guard down."

" And it was, Detective Inspector, and it was."

Ingram pulled his chair back, stacking the papers in two
neat piles. "We'll need to warn booksellers, publishers
and agents to be especially careful. I want a full profile
on this man al-Barzani and the driver, Ahmed Agha, and
all their friends, if possible by this evening. Do the
usual, but cast your net very wide." Basil Coulson
walked over to the window, staring down into the rain-
wet street below. "There is something wrong here Roger,
Talawi could've been assassinated in a number of ways
quite easily. Why such a splashy declaration of war? A
fatwa would have accomplished the same thing. I've a
feeling that this could be the work of a radical splinter
group and it could be no more than a small cell." Collecting his raincoat from the chair where he'd placed it
on entering the room, he spoke over his shoulder as he
opened the door. "Sometimes I think I'm getting too old
for this. I wish the bastards would keep their vendettas
at home."

Chapter 6

Tehran

Ayatollah Albarassan waited until Imam Basra was seated then reached over the coffee table to hand the Imam a folded newspaper. "Have you seen the headlines in today's *Daily Telegraph*?" he asked pleasantly, nodding to the servant to place the tea tray on the low table. Albarassan waited until the servant left the room and the revolutionary guard had resumed his position against the now closed door before leaning back in the ornate chair. Another, heavily muscled guard, stood by the curtained windows.

Imam Basra opened the newspaper, furrowing his brow in concentration. Albarassan knew Basra read English, but not well. Albarassan spoke softly, "It says there has been an attack on a vehicle carrying Ismail Talawi in London. It also states that the attack was unsuccessful, both of the attackers were killed." He pushed a china cup across the table. "You'll take tea, Said?"

Basra looked up; the dark bearded face hard. "Now the apostate knows he is marked. He will fear the judgement that has been placed on his head."

"Ah yes, indeed he will. But did we not agree that we would wait one full year before taking any action? It is barely three months since the council decided."

Basra growled deep in his throat. "I did not believe that to wait a full year was wise. Others will gain confidence and work with their filth to corrupt the faithful. We——." He paused. "There are others who feel as I do and I do not condemn their eagerness to take action."

Neat, very neat, Albarassan thought, sitting back and sipping his tea. The trick is to agree with the action but disassociate yourself from the players. He smiled briefly. "But Said my friend, we had a plan, a good plan, which has now been compromised. How can we hope to achieve our objectives if everyone has a different plan and breaks an agreement?" The voice was deceptively bland but Albarassan was seething. How dare this fatuous fool take it upon himself to wreck months of careful planning? "Your attack did not succeed and now Talawi has been hidden. What shall I say to those warriors who will now have a much more difficult task?"

Basra took the bait. Albarassan knew his ego would not allow him to deny involvement, even in a failed operation. "We will succeed. It is the will of Allah. His designs are beyond the understanding of men." Basra looked up, glowering. "We have struck a blow, which will give the unbelievers pause." He would have continued but his voice was cut off as the noose of thin wire dropped over his head from behind. Basra had not seen the barely perceptible nod that Albarassan gave the thickset man standing against the dark floor-to-ceiling curtains. His eyes bulged in shock and disbelief as much as from pain. This could not be happening, was he not Imam Basra, author of the *Nine Chronicles*, respected Imam of the Talifeq Mosque? Basra died still not understanding that the penalty for crossing ruthless men is always the same. Albarassan watched, emotionless.

"As arranged his remains will be found in the burnt wreckage of his vehicle on the road to Qum. Send a message to Corsica and advise that despite this setback we will proceed as planned." Rising from the chair, he ignored the small group of men who were lifting the dead Imam's body into a wooden box. He sighed as he walked to the door. Such a waste. The man had had a brilliant mind but no self-control.

Corsica

On the shore a small light flickered briefly and the
Zodiac turned a few degrees to line up with the flash.
Moments later they were scraping up the pebbled shore
of a small bay. Three men waited. One of the three
stepped into the Zodiac to replace Dragovic as
Dragovic stepped into the shallow water. The Zodiac
pulled back and with a slight surge of engine noise was
gone into the darkness. Not a word had been spoken
and now Dragovic felt a firm grip on his elbow as one
of the two remaining men pointed the way. His companion was already moving ahead into the darkness towards
a series of steps leading to the heights above. Hoisting
his pack more securely Dragovic followed the leader
toward the concrete steps.

The climb was steep and Dragovic could feel the
tightness in his chest as he climbed. Ten days at sea had
taken the edge off his conditioning and he would need
to start training as soon as he could. At the top of the
cliff a windswept meadow of short, stiff grass led to a
battered LandRover with a canvas roof. The leading
man climbed into the driver's seat, indicating that
Dragovic was to sit beside him in the front passenger
seat. The driver's companion sat on the bench seat
running fore and aft over the rear wheel well. The
LandRover started quietly, smoothly, taking Dragovic by
surprise. He'd assumed from the state of the exterior
that the vehicle was held together with bubble gum and
wire. He relaxed; these people were professionals, even
swapping his place in the Zodiac with the third man in
case they were seen descending the cliff with three and
returning with four. As the LandRover bumped over the
uneven ground towards a gravel road he wondered if the
man who'd replaced him had already created his new

persona and he'd be stepping into an existing identity.

They travelled north along the rocky coastline for thirty minutes as the sky lightened behind them then turned inland, heading west toward a rising landmass topped by a roughly shaped mountain that Dragovic estimated at about 2000 meters in height. The driver spoke for the first time, "There, Mont. L'Incudine." His French accent was rough, and Dragovic waited for him to continue but the driver didn't speak again until they were approaching a well-maintained coastal highway, then pointing north he spoke again, in French, "Solenzara, that way." Dragovic shrugged and wondered if the man assumed that he knew something of the geography of Corsica. Now the LandRover turned north again, joining the main road heading, Dragovic assumed, towards the town of Solenzara. After another thirty minutes the man in the rear grunted something in a dialect Dragovic could not follow, and replying in the same dialect the driver slowed the vehicle to barely walking speed, pulling well over onto the shoulder so vehicles behind could pass. Scanning the road ahead intently the driver grunted in satisfaction as he found the turn-off he was looking for. A short dirt road led off the highway to their left, ending in a rather rickety looking wooden farm gate.

The driver's companion, sitting on the rear bench seat, jumped over the tailgate of the LandRover. He lifted a rusted hoop of heavy wire from the anchoring post, and swung the gate open, waiting until they were through before speaking into a cell phone. He then closed the gate, replaced the wire and rejoined the vehicle. Dragovic noted the glint of what was probably an electronic plate at the point where the wire touched the post. No one would be coming along this road unannounced.

For another ten minutes they bumped over a

narrow potholed rural road before arriving at a large,
low, whitewashed stone farmhouse. The roof was of
terra cotta clay tiles. A large blue window box, filled
with brightly colored flowers, hung outside the window
nearest the main door. A large barn stood to one side,
joined to the house by a high stone wall covered in an
ivy creeper. Behind the house and barn, the ground, bare
of trees, rose in a series of low undulating folds towards
the foothills of the mountain. Critically assessing the
defensive position from a soldier's viewpoint, Dragovic
realised that the farm would be very difficult to approach undetected. Good fields of fire were available to
defenders and from his slightly elevated vantage point in
the Land Rover he could see no dead ground. The
farmhouse and barn formed a rough U shape, giving an
attack force no real rear from which to approach by
stealth. A plump, dark haired, older woman was waiting
by the door and smiled as Dragovic jumped down.

"Welcome—the Patron is waiting for you." She
spoke in clear unaccented French and looking at her
closely as he approached Dragovic guessed she could be
Greek or Iranian. Crows feet crinkled around the corners
of brown eyes and the dark hair pulled into a knot
behind her head was shot through with gray. Her smile
was genuine and holding out both hands she gripped his
hand. Startled, for a second he tensed, almost pulling his
hand back then realising what he was about to do,
relaxed. He nodded gravely.

"Thank you, it is good to be here." Dragovic
replied in French.

"Come, I'll show you your room and then you can
meet the Patron." She turned and led him through the
door into the house. Inside, the farmhouse had obviously been given a complete renovation. The floor, of
wide wooden boards planed smooth to a golden honey

colour and finished with a clear sealer, led from the
hallway. The walls were brilliant white but relieved by a
wide variety of paintings and wall hangings. Small,
woven woolen rugs scattered everywhere gave the
hallway and the great room beyond a cheerful, comfortable feeling. Ceiling lights had been replaced with wall
fixtures that gentled reflections. Turning a corner his
hostess led him along a short passage and opened an
oiled oak door. An open window showed that the room
faced the courtyard of the farm. It was small, but clean,
and considering the understated luxury he'd just wit-
nessed, a trifle spartan, which suited him fine. A single
bed along one wall, one pillow, and crisp sheets with the
bedcovers turned down. In the corner a pedestal sink
with a small mirror above and, leaning slightly away
from the wall opposite the bed, an ancient hanging
cupboard. Dragovic grunted and tossed his bag onto the
bed.

"It looks very comfortable." The woman seemed
relieved and Dragovic wondered why. She bobbed
slightly and said,

"If you're ready, we can meet the Patron now."

Dragovic inclined his head and followed the
woman back out of the room. His new room's heavy
door clicked into place as they departed. Dragovic
followed the woman down the passage. Moving with
short quick strides, her low-heeled shoes clicking on the
wooden floor, she led Dragovic into the great room. A
cheerful fire burned in the open fireplace, no doubt
because the air was chill at this elevation. A long polished table faced them as they entered. Set at the far end
of the table, three place settings and a huge bowl of
flowers arranged as a centrepiece were dwarfed by the
expanse of polished wood. To the right, facing the fire, a
large overstuffed sofa and half a dozen comfortable

lounge chairs were arranged in a rough semicircle. Several windows looked out onto the hills beyond. Dragovic noticed the heavy wooden shutters, partly concealed with curtains, flanking each window on the inside. A trim fiqure in a charcoal suit, his back to them, was looking at a map spread on the area of the dining table not set with eating utensils. The woman coughed, "Patron . . ."

Placing a book on one corner of the map the man turned to greet them. "So—we begin," he said, extending his right hand. Dragovic saw a middle-aged man; an unremarkable face topped with thinning hair. It was the eyes that caught his attention immediately. They were pale blue-green, alive with intelligence, humour and something indefinable. The man was shorter than Dragovic but the expensive suit he was wearing accentuated a slim athlete's fiqure. His grip bordered on painful and Dragovic wondered if he was being given a subtle hint of power in reserve. "Gip Lawrence." The voice, rich and smooth, pure BBC English startled Dragovic. Lawrence smiled. He'd obviously had this reaction before. Sizing up the younger man before releasing Dragovic's hand, he chuckled, "Yes, Mr. Dragovic. I'm English—English born and bred, and it's my job to make you an Englishman as well. It's fortunate that your parents insisted on your learning English as well as French." He pointed to the sideboard. " Would you care for a drink? I was waiting for you to arrive before having one."

Dragovic shook his head, "No, zank you." The English words coming from his mouth sounded harsh, uncertain. "It has been . . ." he struggled trying to place the words in the right order, "very long time before." He shook his head, "no—sorry—since, I spoken English."

"That's all right old chap, by the time you leave

here you're going to be as English as Churchill was." He placed an arm around Dragovic's shoulders. "Have a look at this," pointing to the map on the table. "This is a map of the farm and surrounding areas." He stabbed the surface with a well-manicured finger. "You must not go outside the perimeter which is marked as you can see. It's a large area so you should not feel overly confined, and we have a fully equipped exercise gymnasium in the barn. We have perimeter sensors in the ground and can track movement in and out. The perimeter guards have strict orders to detain anyone within 50 meters of the sensors." He looked at Dragovic coolly, measuring his response. Dragovic only nodded. "A lot of time and money have been invested in you and the plan, and we don't want you to feel you're in a prison, but security is paramount—you understand?"

"What plan?" Dragovic returned the look without blinking.

"Ah—of course, you've been at sea—but you've heard of Ismail Talawi the author of *Lunch with the Prophet?*" Lawrence frowned at the puzzled look on Dragovic's face. "You must be the only Muslim, or for that matter, non-Muslim who hasn't. Does Salman Rushdie ring a bell?" Lawrence stroked his face absently, while watching Dragovic carefully.

"Of course, the writer, the apostate, riten— sorry—written, *The Satanic Verses.*"

"Absolutely, well three months ago this man Talawi wrote a similar book, called *Lunch with the Prophet.* In it he questions the Koran and Hadith, mocks the faithful and insults the Prophet." Lawrence lifted his hands in a gesture of exasperation. "For reasons I'm not privy to there has been no action taken against this man. In this world Dragovic there are men who were born to the faith and now wish to destroy all that is honourable." His voice had risen and for a moment his pale eyes glittered strangely. "You've been given the task of cleansing this man from the world of the faithful. It's a great honour."

Dragovic laughed harshly, the sound odd, jagged, in this elegant room. "Please, not talk honour. I have seen what does honour. If it is required, I will kill this man. But not talk of honour." He looked at Lawrence, the tawny eyes cold. If this man tried to preach to him there would be trouble.

Lawrence, unperturbed by the sudden chill in Dragovic's manner, nodded as if satisfied. "Good, good. The Ayatollah Albarrasan decided that you would spend a full year training in preparation for your mission. No *fatwa* to be issued until the attack, no condemnation in the press or media for the blasphemy. That was the plan but now we have to adapt to changed circumstances." He walked over to a beautiful polished wood cabinet standing against the wall. Carved wooden clusters of grapes, leaves and vines entwined with plump cherubs cascaded down the sides of the cabinet to end in clawed feet resting on half globes. Bending, Lawrence opened a door, and removed a cut glass tumbler and a bottle from an internal rack. Dragovic made out the name Glen Morangie as Lawrence poured a large measure into the glass from the bottle. Taking a large sip, Lawrence turned back to Dragovic, who'd not moved. "Unfortunately another group, obviously not in touch with the Council, made an unsuccessful attack on Talawi two days ago." He shrugged, "Now, of course, Talawi will be given the same protection as Rushdie. Our task has become more difficult but not impossible." Raising the glass he took a deep swallow and immediately started coughing. Placing the glass down he patted his pockets as the coughing increased in intensity. Pulling a linen handkerchief from the breast pocket of his suit he dabbed his mouth. "Sorry." Another paroxysm of coughing. "Sorry—I said not impossible—difficult yes, but not impossible—we have friends in Britain."

Dispassionately, Dragovic scanned Gip Lawrence's face "How ill are you?"

"They told me you were quick. I have cancer. It's spreading, but the medical people tell me I have long enough to see you trained." A ghost of a smile drifted across Lawrence's face. "You disapprove of my drinking Dragovic. Now you know why. You'll be trained to hide such emotions and, like an actor, project those that will gain your objective."

Dragovic nodded soberly, remembering his first impression. That Lawrence was intelligent was obvious, crows feet at the corners of his eyes spoke of humour, but now he understood what had initially puzzled him. In the rear of the eyes where the soul lurked, there was resignation and sadness. Groping for something that would not sound trite, he spoke in French. "As Allah wills. May he give you peace and purpose for your journey."

Lawrence laughed out loud. "You have the tongue of a poet Dragovic. It's going to be a pleasure training you. We start tomorrow, and from tomorrow you are no longer a Muslim from Bosnia but, an English gentleman of the Anglican faith." He held up his hand as Dragovic opened his mouth to protest. "You have been given dispensation from the highest authority. Your faith is not in question. In your heart your faith will remain strong, but in order to achieve our objective, you have to become as one with your environment." He clapped Dragovic on the shoulder. "There is precedent—believe me. Now go and relax for the rest of the day. Walk around the property and familiarize yourself. Dinner is at six prompt and then you will meet Martin." Turning away in dismissal he picked up the book lying on the map and walked over to the fireside. Dragovic watched Lawrence lower himself into a comfortable chair and open the book

Chapter 7

London – New Scotland Yard

"Throw your case over there." The speaker pointed and turned to Sandy Flett. "It's all we could scrape up at short notice. Chief of Specialist Ops called us yesterday to say you'd be joining our little band of misfits and, as you can see, we're a little pushed for space." Sandy placed his new briefcase on the small desk jammed against the wall behind two large filing cabinets. The room held four other desks with barely enough room between them for one person to pass at a time. The room, originally painted in Civil Service cream, had long since faded to pale tobacco brown. Calendars and other notices were fixed, with drawing pins and tape, to most of the available space. A large whiteboard with unintelligible hieroglyphics scrawled in red marker pen, dominated one wall. Looking around with increasing interest, Sandy realised that this posting might prove interesting after all. He remembered vividly his conversation with Colonel Johnny Johnstone earlier, and his initial anger at being reassigned,

    "No Sandy, and that's final. I know that you think you're 100 percent recovered but that's not what the Medicos are saying." Colonel Johnstone pushed his chair back and stood, stretching his shoulders. He'd arrived in London on the morning resupply flight from Bosnia for an emergency conference with his superiors and had agreed to meet, for a few minutes, with his injured lieutenant. Sandy Flett was not only a member of his battalion but also the son of the man he'd fought alongside in the Falklands. Besides, he liked the boy. "Look Sandy, I know you think you can walk as well as ever but, a repaired knee, especially one so recent, takes time getting used to. No—" holding up his hand to forestall

the inevitable response—"listen to me. I've arranged for
you to spend a couple of months with Special Branch.
They're desperately short staffed and jumped at the
chance of getting a trained SAS officer into their diplomatic protection unit." He grinned suddenly. "And don't
for a moment assume it will be all cocktail parties and
embassy functions. Although frankly, if I was given a
shot at the class of champagne our diplomatic types
indulge in, I'd jump at the chance." He gripped Sandy
firmly by the shoulders. "Cheer up Sandy. It's only for a
couple of months and then you'll be back in the mud
and shit of Bosnia." Johnstone had walked to the door
before turning to face his subordinate. "I'd hoped to be
able to see your parents before I left but unfortunately I
have to catch the evening flight back." Glancing at his
watch he whistled. "God, where does time go? Please
explain to your father and make my apologies—and
Sandy—relax and enjoy." The door closed and he was
gone.

Now, as he studied the room and the young policeman who was showing him around, he began to feel
much better about his new job. This room clearly was a
working office, not some plastic and glass civil service
excuse to spend money. The policeman turned, sticking
out his hand. "Sorry, should have introduced myself, I'm
Tristam—Tristam Burns. The other two will be here any
second."

Gripping the proffered hand, Sandy smiled back,
"Alex Flett, but everyone calls me Sandy. When do I get
briefed?"

"Right now." A deep voice coming through the
open door, followed by a stocky man dressed in faded
corduroy trousers and a plain gray shirt open at the
neck, made them both turn.

"James?" Sandy stared at the new arrival. "Jimmy

Douglas? Well I'll be damned. Last I heard you were in Belfast." He leant forward awkwardly over the desk to accept the proffered hand.

"Transferred to the DPU six months ago. Blacked my book over the water, so being made to do penance with this useless mob." He laughed, an attractive chuckling sound. "What the bloody hell did you do to end up here?"

"Body damage—knee. Need recuperation, they tell me." Sandy still felt awkward at admitting his disability. If not being able to run as fast as usual was a disability, he thought sourly. "I'm here for R&R. I asked for the slowest crowd around."

Tristam Burns watched the exchange with a small smile. "You two obviously know each other, so let me introduce . . ." He lifted a hand to where a woman in a skirt and loose blouse was lounging against the door. "Meg, this is . . ."

"Sandy Flett, yes, I read the file. How's the knee?" She held out her hand but didn't smile. Sandy realised he was being weighed, but not for anything other than operational efficiency. With light from the brightly-lit passage behind her, the woman's face, framed with long dark hair that fell to below her shoulders, was in darkness. Her grip was cool and firm and for a second he was disconcerted. Catching himself he answered coolly.

"Better than it was—you have the advantage, I still don't know your name." The woman, who looked to be in her late twenties or early thirties, was now into the room, forcing James Douglas to move to one side to give her space. Sandy now had a good look at the face visible in the late afternoon sunlight slanting into the room from the rooftops across the street. It was a calm face, with strong, straight planes and a clear direct gaze. The hazel eyes assessed him and, letting go of his hand, she sat on the corner of a desk before answering.

"Meg Davidson."

Tristam Burns turned to James Douglas and broke the sudden awkward silence. "So what's the scoop boss? What's the mission for the morrow?" Tristam, coming out of Cambridge with a barely acceptable pass in classics, failed the Foreign Office exam and then, much to his stockbroker father's relief, found that he had an aptitude and liking for police work. Joining the Metropolitan Police as a constable, Tristam was earmarked for early promotion after his analytical skills helped solve a rash of arson attacks on East European companies based on the outskirts of the city. Due to his background and contacts it was felt that a stint in the Diplomatic Protection Unit would help his career and the force.

"Well, now that we've all been introduced, I'll tell you. Tris close the door, and if the rest of you will get to your desks I'll bring you up to speed." Douglas walked over to the whiteboard, picking up a soft cloth lying on Tristam's desk. Erasing the existing hieroglyphics from the whiteboard Douglas wrote in block capitals with a broad-tipped felt pen:

ISMAIL TALAWI. Protection team.

    1) Sandy

    2) Meg

    3) Tristam

    4) DPU staff on rotation.

Capping the pen he turned to face them. "Ok, you've all heard the news of the attempted assassination of our esteemed literary figure. Ismail Talawi, I'm told, is a difficult client. I hope the events of the last few days will have rendered him more amenable." He pursed his lips before continuing. "This, I suspect, is going to be much more difficult than looking after Rushdie. Talawi's protection detail have indicated that he's a royal pain in the arse."

Sandy Flett lifted one of the three folders that Jimmy Douglas had placed on a desk on entering. "Two questions."

"Go Sandy."

"I assume that this contains all the background. How much time?"

"It's RR, second question"

"Your name is not on the board."

"Sorry, not my doing. I'm to co-ordinate liaison with Special Branch. I'll be your controller—yes, Tris?"

"Sorry to be dense but what is RR?"

"Read on the run." Meg Davidson answered before James Douglas could speak. "I take it we are fully operational."

"As soon as I closed the door the clock started ticking. You'll find in the briefing notes that there is a whisper of a professional on call. The sniffers picked something up from Mossad." Douglas ran a hand through his hair and all banter left his voice. "Moshe Dobkins' contacts tell him that the two hits in Gaza on Arafat's men and the Rumayash strike on the Israeli reservists jeep all have the same signature." Douglas chewed his bottom lip thoughtfully. "There's more. Mossad managed to snatch one of the backup perps on the Rumyash hit—a kid called Hasid—who made the mistake of bragging to the wrong people in Beirut. Before he left this mortal coil he gave a detailed description to Mossad's forensic people. The photograph in your files is what Mossad has come up with."

"How long ago?" This from Meg.

"Three months. Despite some intense work Mossad has drawn a blank. Our man, if this is our man, has gone deep."

"You think he could have orchestrated the hit on

Talawi?" Meg had flipped open the file and was studying the photograph.

For several seconds Jimmy Douglas didn't answer, then he sighed. "That's the conventional wisdom from upstairs."

Sandy Flett looked up from his file, his forehead creased in a small frown. "You don't think so?"

"Read the summary in your file on the hits in Gaza and Israel. The man who carried those operations out likes to hit clean and leave no trace. The High Holborn swipe at Talawi was messy, too many bodies, too many possible problems—as happened of course." He paused but no one spoke.

"Sandy if you're asking what I personally think, then the answer is no—nothing fits. The Talawi hit was typical Hamas—lots of sound and fury. But—I've been wrong before." His eyes swept over them. "You'll report to Detective Inspector Basil Coulson once you've read your files. Usual security, nothing written leaves this office." He smiled for the first time since the meeting began, but it was the cold smile of an undertaker. "They are going to try again, of that we can be certain, so nothing, no matter how insignificant, gets ignored. We want this bastard and badly. An Arab fighting for Arabs I can tolerate but not . . ." he left the sentence unfinished. "OK people I'm on my way." He glanced at his watch and let out a low whistle. "Damn, late again." He hefted his scuffed briefcase and opened the door. Turning, he spoke. "Oh, Sandy, you're in charge on the ground—we connect every 24 hours—Cheers."

Chapter 8

Corsica

Dragovic stopped, and gasping for air rested his hands on his knees. Legs splayed, he hunched over. His heart pounded like a drummer on speed, his breath coming in deep rasping gasps. Perspiration slicked his body, clad only in thin running shorts and a saturated T-shirt.

The horse had dropped it's head to graze on the short stiff grass while the rider, in jeans and a thick check shirt, looked down at the hunched figure drawing agonised breaths. The rider spoke in lightly accented English. "Much better, mon ami, much better. You've cut your time by six minutes."

Dragovic looked up but did not unbend. He nodded, concentrating on restoring some semblance of normality to his trembling body. Finally, he straightened up, still breathing deeply. "Go ahead Martin, I'll walk back to the farmhouse."

The rider nodded, "As you wish Nick, see you at dinner tonight." He clicked his tongue and lifting his horse's head turned towards the white blip on the green carpet spread out far below them. A coil of smoke smudged the sky near the house where farm workers were burning summer debris. It was cooler now as autumn moved deeper into time's cycle. Watching the mounted man he'd called Martin move down the slope below him, Dragovic mused on the events of the last three months. His English was vastly improved; fortunately his schooling in England had been of a high standard, and he had an ear for nuance and tone. Gip Lawrence was pleased at the speed with which his pupil had adapted to the daily regimen. A 5-kilometre run on waking, then breakfast, after breakfast lectures on

everything English pertaining to his new persona. Lunch
at 1 p.m., a light snack followed by two hours of lan-
guage lessons. Between 4 p.m. and 6 p.m. he trained
hard with Martin, his close-quarter combat and survival
instructor. Martin had arrived shortly after Dragovic.
Like Dragovic, Martin did not refer to his own background. Once, after dinner, Gip had referred to Martin
as 'our Legionnaire' Dragovic knew that many Muslim
Algerians had served in France's famous fighting unit,
but Martin was of European extraction, his French was
flawless and his English nearly so. Often after a brutal
bout of survival combat in the gym hidden in the huge
barn Martin would reach into a small cooler bag and toss
Dragovic a can of beer. Both men would relax on the
plank bench while Martin analysed Dragovic's perform-
ance. He never raised his voice and never patronised the
Bosnian. Like all great instructors he recognised both
strengths and weaknesses in his trainees and quietly
chipped away to improve both. The two men were equal
in strength yet Dragovic knew that he would never
match the catlike grace and speed of movement that
Martin displayed under pressure.

A week ago, Martin had changed the regime to
what he called endurance exercises. A brutal 15km
course over the fields and then up into the mountains
before ending the run high above the farmhouse. Scattered along the route were fences, fallen trees and areas
of bog that sucked at Dragovic's feet. Dragovic could
feel the strength flowing through his muscles. His diet,
exercise and the fresh air had brought him to a peak of
fitness he'd never experienced before. He started to trot
down the mountain, surprised at how much he was
looking forward to a hot shower and dinner.

Gip Lawrence stood by the barn door. He'd followed the progress of two men, one on foot, one

mounted, through high-powered binoculars ever since the encrypted message had arrived as a flash burst from Iran 30 minutes before. Now he waited as Martin rode into the courtyard. The Frenchman vaulted lithely off the horse as one of the silent farmhands reached for the bridle. He patted the horse's flank as it was led past.

"A good run?"

Surprised, Martin raised an eyebrow. He and Lawrence usually reviewed the day's progress late in the evening after the others had retired. "Yes—a good run. He's a quick learner and his physical endurance is impressive."

" How soon before he's operational?"

Martin chewed on his bottom lip thoughtfully, his eyes never leaving Lawrence's face. For several seconds he did not speak then gave a slight shake of his head. "It depends on the degree of difficulty. If I accelerate the program I still need another 6 to 8 weeks to have him in perfect shape."

"You'll never change, you know that Martin? You're still the perfectionist." Lawrence gave a sour grin. "It's a quick in and out operation. We hear a member of the team that attacked Talawi without clearance, three months ago, is planning to go over to the British. The target is unaware his plans are known. I estimate one week away at most."

Martin shrugged. "His English is very good, but his French needs work to lose the Slavic accent. Physically he's in good, but not top shape. I assume the job is immediate?"

"Unfortunately yes, and he must use hand skills. I don't have time to insert equipment. How good is he at close combat?"

"Unless the target is very good, Nick can deal with most situations. How good is the target?" A light rain had begun falling, drifting in thin veils down from the mountain. Neither man noticed the change.

"Unknown—but surprise should give him all the advantage he needs."

"Ah yes, surprise. That is guaranteed then, Patron?" Martin's face had gone blank.

"Look, Martin I don't like this any more than you do. But we do as we are ordered. All I need to know; is he capable of a quick strike on a soft target?"

Both men were watching Dragovic, known to Martin as Nick Cartwright, trot up to the gate leading into the great field and the farmhouse. He was still 100 metres away but would soon be with them.

"Yes—he is capable." Martin exhaled in a sigh. "Do you want me in on the briefing?"

"Of course, you're going to be his controller for this mission. You'll base on Hayling Island near Portsmouth it's . . ." He stopped as Dragovic trotted up to them. "Nick, you look in tip-top shape. My God, what wouldn't I give to have your conditioning." He placed his arm around the younger man's shoulders. "We have a job for you, small but important. Go and clean up. We will talk after supper." He gave Dragovic an affectionate push.

Chapter 9

Retribution

Nick Cartwright, formerly known as Nico Dragovic, code name Cedar, looked out of the hotel window at the sun slanting off the sea. The hotel, facing the English Channel, whose gray-green waves slopped lazily onto the pebble beach, was set back across a paved road that ran parallel to the beach. The Isle of Wight could be seen dimly in the distance to the southwest. He flexed tired shoulders. The flight to Heathrow had been bumpy in the storm front coming off the Bay of Biscay. An Immigration officer had given his red Common Market passport barely a glance, but the nervous tension built up in anticipation had taken a while to subside.

Taking the tube from Heathrow Central to Leicester Square, he changed to the Northern Line. At Waterloo Station he caught the train to Portsmouth, travelling south through Guildford, Haselmere and Petersfield before finally getting off at Havant Station, one stop short of Portsmouth. Seeing an idling taxi and throwing his nylon carryall into the back seat, Nick directed the driver to the beachfront hotel on Hayling Island—the hotel arranged by Martin, who'd arrived days before.

The driver wanted to talk but Dragovic leaned back in the seat and answering in monosyllabic grunts, forced the driver into sullen silence. Paying him off outside the hotel, Dragovic added a generous tip with a half-apology, "Been a long day." Brightening, the driver gave him a broad smile,

"That's OK Guv, happens to all of us."

The hostelry, more a rooming house than a hotel, was comfortable in a slightly seedy, run-down way. The towels were fresh, and ironed, but untidy repairs to tears made by careless guests were evident. Stripping his clothes off quickly Nick stepped into the shower and, after adjusting the heat and flow on a circular wheel, endured the stinging hot water over his lean frame. He spun the wheel in the opposite direction, gasping as the water temperature swung from very warm to very cold. Gritting his teeth he counted slowly to fifty before shutting the flow to off. Towelling himself briskly with the small towel he felt his muscles relaxing. Rummaging in his carryall he found a slightly rumpled clean shirt and slacks. After dressing he descended the short staircase to the main dining room.

Martin, having arrived two days earlier, sat alone at a table set for two. Scanning the dining room Dragovic noticed that the only other unoccupied seat was at a table for four. He walked to Martin's table. "May I join you?"

"Please." Martin pointed to the empty chair.

Dragovic sat, holding out his hand. "Nick Cartwright." Martin, half rising, gripped his hand briefly over the table.

"Martin Dreyfus," releasing Dragovic's hand and slipping back down into his seat. A casual observer would have concluded that the two men had just met, and were sharing a table out of convenience. Dragovic waited until the waiter had taken his order and left before talking to Martin.

"Good flight?"

"Yes, and you?"

"Bumpy, but otherwise fine. You have the details?"

"Yes. I've been up to London." Martin smiled briefly, "Piece of cake. Just as Gip advised. Enjoy your meal, we'll talk later." The two men attacked their heaped plates following the first rule of undercover

work. Take advantage of every opportunity to fill up
with food. It could be days before either could eat
properly if a wheel fell off and they had to go to ground.

Chapter 10

Search

Sandy Flett looked at the notebook again. "It's some-where between number 44 and the corner." Meg Davidson, scanning the upper floors of the row of dingy shops that faced the right-hand side of Epworth Street, pointed with her chin.

"Look over the newsagent's. If you count the windows from number 44, it must be one of those." Wearing a scuffed leather bomber jacket and a short, tight black skirt, with a bright orange blouse, she was hardly noticeable in this predominantly lower working class district. Sandy, in stained jeans, dirty sneakers and a long-sleeved flannel shirt hanging outside his trousers, flicked the notebook closed.

"Yes, but where's the entrance? All of the build-ings in this street back onto the shops in Vauxhall Way. There must be a passage inside the newsagents. Let's check." He instinctively brushed his right hand over the hidden Sig Sauer under the bulky folds of his shirt. The two agents walked casually towards the newsagents, stopping to look into a window selling pastries. On the ground a group of black flies covering a sausage roll that a customer had dropped, then stepped on, rose in buzz-ing protest as the pair paused. Meg tightened her arm against the shiny black, imitation leather bag slung over one shoulder.

"I'll go inside first. Give me ten seconds to posi-tion."

Sandy put his arm around Meg's shoulders, giving her a quick hug, his mouth close to the glossy black hair. To any observers they were simply one of the many Saturday morning couples out shopping. "It's probably another dead end," he muttered. "This Salameh has no record of activism and has visited the Iranian Club on an infrequent basis." Feeling her stiffen under his arm he whispered, "OK—OK, I know—I know. Each of these is a potential. But think about it, we have interviewed— how many? Twenty at least, and CID have done interviews over the last three months without turning up anything." He sighed. "OK, I'll wait for you to get set." Working as a team over the past week Sandy and Meg found they had a lot in common. Meg had done her stint on the bloody streets of Northern Ireland in the super-secret women's unit known simply as 147.

Suspected and known IRA and Protestant Provisionals had, to their cost, ignored the dowdy, shabbily dressed housewives pushing strollers or hefting plastic bags of groceries who seemed to melt into the urban landscape. Sandy found, despite his reluctance to get involved with a working colleague, that he was attracted to this tall, unsmiling woman who rarely dropped her guard. He knew from reading her file that in Northern Ireland Meg had been surprised, when talking to the wife of a suspect, by two IRA gunmen arriving to punish one of their own for careless talk. After executing the man as he opened the door the gunmen had entered the narrow passage to kill the two horrified witnesses. Reaching into her shoulder bag to grip the hidden MAC 10, Meg blasted the two assassins back through the door onto the outside brick pathway. The second killer, hit in the arm, but protected by bulk of his colleague who'd taken the brunt of the automatic burst, lunged in desperation for his dropped pistol. Stepping over the twitching body of the first dying gunman, Meg coldly snapped a fresh magazine into the deadly machine pistol and blasted the top of the gun-man's head off as he tried to raise the pistol. The same

night she'd been airlifted to England and then spent
three months at the Army's psychiatric unit for trauma-
tised soldiers. Sandy knew from his own experience in
Bosnia and Ireland the terrible stresses that could surface after a tour of duty in those two sad areas of
conflict, and had watched Meg closely in the beginning
phase for any signs of weakness. She'd shown none.

Meg sauntered through the open doorway, parting
the multi-coloured plastic strips that hung down as a
deterrent to flies. Sandy casually scanned the street for
signs of unusual movement. Satisfied, he took a deep
breath and waited for a fat Asian woman, dressed in a
faded orange sari, hair coiled in a greasy, gray-streaked
bun, to enter behind Meg. Following the woman he
pushed the plastic strips aside and stepped into the dim
interior.

Two banks of flyspecked fluorescent tubing
illuminated the shop, each bank containing 4 tubes. In
one bank two tubes had burnt out and, from the layer of
dust adhering to them it had been a while since anyone
had given thought to installing replacements. Along the
left wall a rack containing magazines reached from floor
to ceiling. A youth, cigarette dangling from thick adoles-
cent lips, squinted through the smoke that curled into
his eyes while trying to appear casual as he flipped
through a girlie magazine. Sandy saw Meg standing near
the far wall looking at a rack of paperback novels next
to a pile of empty cardboard boxes. The Asian woman,
being served by the owner—a slight, swarthy Indian of
indeterminate age—was paying for a packet of cigarettes. The woman rummaged in a tiny purse and labori-
ously counted out coins as if the shopkeeper in frustration might lower the price just to get her out of the way.
Finally, muttering something about thieving traders, she
brushed past Sandy on her way out.

Reaching inside his shirt and holding his warrant

card so that only the owner could see, Sandy smiled at the man. "Mr. Abbas Salameh. Is he in?"

The shopkeeper turned a muddy shade of gray. He'd been selling marijuana under the counter for the last 6 months, and was convinced that the police were on to his operation. In fact, the local police had been aware of his trade for some time, turning a blind eye to what they saw as nothing more than a nuisance and not worth the court time. If in the future they needed to deflect media attention from a bungled police operation, or scandal, Mr. Patel would serve as a handy scapegoat.

Patel gulped, coughed to clear his throat and pointed to a blanket covering an opening at the back of the store next to the empty boxes where Meg was standing. "He's upstairs Sir—just returned Sir—thank you Sir." His voice was thin and high pitched

Sandy nodded amiably. "Thank you. Please don't call him. I'll give him a surprise." Sandy ignored Meg as he slid the curtain to one side; she would stay down in the shop covering his rear. He mounted the steep narrow staircase, its steps covered in frayed floral carpet. Reaching a short landing he rapped on the chocolate-brown door. For a moment there was silence, then a creak of bedsprings and,

"Yes, who is it?"

"Mr. Abbas Salemeh? I have a package for Mr. Salameh." Sandy transferred his warrant card to his left hand and closed his right around the butt of the Sig Sauer. The door opened slightly. Sandy held the warrant to the single eye the appeared around the door. "Police, Mr. Salameh, I wish to talk to you."

"Why, what is the matter? I have spoken to the CID several times."

"Yes sir, but there are some further questions and we would appreciate your assistance."

"I can tell you nothing. I did not know al-Barzani.

I spoke to him at the Iranian Club months ago."

"Can we discuss this inside, sir? It won't take long." Sandy looked back down the stairwell and motioned for Meg to join him. The door closed and Sandy could hear a rattle as the safety chain was unhooked. The door opened inwards and Sandy saw a sallow-faced, stocky man with thinning hair who matched the description he'd committed to memory.

"Sorry to trouble you, sir." Sandy half turned to indicate Meg, who'd stepped onto the landing behind him. "This is my colleague, Detective Constable Davidson. I'm Detective Constable Flett." The room, suprisingly considering the squalor outside, was immaculate. Salameh had obviously spent considerable effort to make the two rooms as comfortable as possible. A clean cotton mat lay on the polished tiles and a pine coat rack was screwed to the entrance wall. Inside the room a neatly made bed with a matching night table was placed against the far wall, under the window that Meg had seen from the street. In the middle of the room a glass-topped coffee table, covered in magazines, sat on a circular carpet of Oriental design. A worn easy chair covered with a white sheepskin and a half-opened newspaper showed that Salameh had been reading when disturbed. Through a doorless opening to the right, a second small room was divided into kitchen and washroom by a thin partition. The washroom curtain, hanging on large wooden rings, had not been fully closed. Sandy took in the entire area with a practised scan.

"This won't take long. If we can just go over your statement again Mr. Salameh. You stated that you met al-Barzani and Ahmed . . .?" He fumbled in his pocket for the names printed on a piece of stiff card.

"Agha, Ahmed Agha. Yes I have met them both. You must understand, I meet many Iranian refugees at

the Club. Some come infrequently, but others are more
regular. Agha and al-Barzani were not what I would call
regulars."

"How did you meet them?"

Salameh lifted both hands, shrugging. "I didn't
really meet them in a formal sense. It must have been at
least six months ago. al-Barzani was talking about a
motorcycle club and I overheard him talking to Agha. At
the time I was thinking of purchasing a cheap motorcycle and stopped to listen to their conversation. They
made it obvious that I was not welcome to interrupt so I
left. Frankly I would not have remembered them but for
that incident. I thought at the time that the whole
purpose of the Club was to make each other welcome."

"You never saw them again?" Sandy smiled amiably. "You do realise how important it is to be totally
honest."

Abbas Salameh felt a frisson of fear. This scruffy
looking man had, despite an outward appearance of
amiability, the eyes of a hunter. He swallowed, wondering just how much the police had uncovered. "Of
course, if they came back to the Club, I probably did. I
just don't remember them after that particular incident."

"Ah, I see. So apart from that particular incident
you probably didn't see them again at the Iranian Club
or outside the Club? Would that be a correct assumption?"

Salameh stared at the policeman, his mind frantically covering all the questions the previous CID officers had asked. Had he been seen near the assassination
attempt? What if the police had already questioned the
woman he'd bumped into? A thin film of sweat beaded
his face. He licked lips which had suddenly gone dry.
Sandy watched Salameh's face carefully. Something was
going on in the Iranian's mind, but Sandy's training kept

him patient. The man facing him knew more than he was letting on. He waited. The silence lengthened and suddenly Salameh burst out, his voice an octave higher. "I saw them once more." He looked imploringly at Meg, who stared back impassively. "But I didn't know it was them, not until later."

"Oh yes," Sandy's voice was deceptively casual, "and when would that have been, sir?"

Abbas Salameh shivered, suddenly cold. It was obvious they knew he'd been seen outside the Theatre. He began turning towards the Glock; Velcro'd behind the night table and stopped almost immediately, turning the movement into a shake of his head. It was too far; they would have him before he could take the two steps needed to get across the room

"On the day of the killings I was outside the Theatre. I was going to see the movie, 'To Taunt A Wounded Tiger' and was across the street when the shooting started. The bodies ended up about 50 feet from where I was standing. I was horrified and frightened and tried to get away but the police had blocked High Holborn so I walked past the bodies. By this time quite a crowd had formed and like everyone else I tried to see who it was."

"And did you recognise them?"

"No, as I said I tried, but the crowd was quite thick. I saw legs and parts of a motorcycle and left. I felt sick, the smell . . ."

"So how did you know it was them?"

"The Evening News. I saw the Police drawings of their faces on BBC1."

"So why did you not tell CID? Why tell us now?" Sandy's voice was neutral; his eyes fixed on Salameh's face.

"Because I was frightened. What would you have

done? I'm an Iranian, who knew, even if only slightly, both men. I felt sick and decided to not to say anything about being outside the theatre." Salameh reached into his pocket for a large handkerchief with which he wiped his face.

"And now?"

"Look." Salameh again lifted both hands waist high, palms outward. "I want to cooperate. I was stupid not to mention that I was outside the theatre when your colleagues asked me the next day. But please, put yourself in my shoes. I was being honest, until the BBC news I didn't know who the bodies were. I had no idea what was going on, all I could think of, who is going to believe me? Two Iranians, members of a club I attended, try to assassinate an Iranian dissident author. What would you have done?"

"What do you think of Ismail Talawi?"

"He is a disgrace to the faith of his birth. I detest what he has written and even if I don't agree with the attempt on his life, or the *fatwa* on Rushdie, I can understand why some would feel as they do." Salameh was breathing easier. He felt that unless the police had more evidence than what he had deduced he had nothing to fear. If these two had more information the questions would have been harder, more pointed. He relaxed slightly.

"You've read his book?"

"No, I have not. I've read reviews in the English and Iranian papers."

"Why not? You appear to feel strongly about Talawi's writing."

"I don't want to read it. Would you read a book written by a Christian that presumed to prove that Jesus Christ was a mortal man? That Christ was the product of an adulterous union and Joseph, a good and compas-

sionate man, went along with the fiction of virgin birth
to protect his own and wife's reputation? Why should I,
as a devout Muslim, read similar ridiculous allegations
about the Prophet Mohammed in Talawi's book?"

"Isn't that what Muslims believe?" This from Meg,
who spoke for the first time.

"We believe Jesus Christ was a great prophet, but
no, we do not accept that he is the Son of God. We
believe, as I'm sure you know, that Mohammed was the
last and greatest prophet." Salameh folded his arms
across his chest, tucking his hands under his armpits. It
would not do to let them see how his hands were trembling.

Sandy looked at Meg. She nodded slightly and
drawing a file from her shoulder bag handed him the
Mossad composite drawing of Dragovic. Turning back
to Salameh, Sandy held the 8 x 11 photofax up for
Salameh to see. "And this man? When did you last see
him?"

Salameh's bewilderment was too real to be faked.
"I've not seen this man." He took the picture from
Sandy and studied it intently. "This one I've never seen.
He's not a Club member."

"You're sure? You're not going to have an attack
of conscience the next time we talk to you?"

Salameh's face darkened and he hunched his
shoulders. " I don't know this man. I would remember
him, especially the eyes." While Mossad specialists
interrogated Hasid, Dragovic's companion in the
Rumayash explosion, an Israeli forensic artist built up
the picture of Dragovic from Hasid's description. Apart
from the shape of the face it was not a good likeness,
but the artist had somehow caught the flat dullness of
Dragovic's gaze.

Taking back the photofax Sandy nodded. "Thank

you sir, we'll want to speak to you again. Please advise us of any changes to your address or employment." He handed a card to Salameh. "Should you remember anything, anything at all, please call me or Detective Davidson at this number." Once again the amiable relaxed interrogator, Sandy smiled at Meg. "I think we have everything we need for the moment. Did you wish to add anything, detective?" Meg shook her head wordlessly. "Well then, I think that's all for now. Good day Mr. Salameh." Stepping back through the door Sandy closed it behind him and followed Meg down the stairs. They walked through the newsagent's to emerge into watery sunshine. They did not talk until they were around the corner. Neither noticed Dragovic watching the shop from across the street.

"So what did you think?" Sandy looked at Meg Davidson as he climbed into the driver's seat of their Volvo sedan.

Meg clipped her seatbelt tight and waited until the Volvo had entered the stream of traffic before answering. "I think he may be telling the truth. I can see why he didn't mention seeing the bodies. And he didn't try to hide the fact that he didn't like Talawi's writings."

"He probably assumed that we had spoken to other club members and were aware of his dislike of Talawi's writings."

"Yes, agreed, but he certainly didn't recognise the photo."

"No." Sandy slowed to let a milk float turn off the highway. "No he didn't recognise the picture. That's assuming the picture is a good likeness, of course."

Meg stared out the window. "Something is bothering me though." Sandy waited. Finally with a sigh Meg shrugged, "It's probably nothing, but did you notice his reaction when you told him how important it was to be truthful?"

"The half-turn towards the bed? Yes I noticed. You think he had something hidden?"

"It's a possibility. Something he didn't want us to see. Or, we could both be getting paranoid."

"Hmm, that's what they pay us for of course." Sandy flicked on the indicator and turned off the highway into the courtyard of a pub. "I tell you what. Let's have a coffee and make a plan. I could do with a sandwich. We'll go back and see Mr. Abbas Salameh after lunch. Maybe we can shake him up a little more. I'll get him into the kitchen and you can do a check of the bed and night table." Meg unbuckled her seatbelt.

"I think we would both feel better. Paranoia is catching."

"Yeah, and so is hunger. First things first." Sandy slammed the door of the Volvo shut before leading the way inside the warm interior of the pub

Chapter 11

A Simple Killing

Sitting in the grubby café across the street Dragovic saw
the man and woman he'd observed earlier walk away
from the newsagent's. Studying the building for the past
hour through several cups of bad coffee and pretending
to read the local paper, he'd seen Sandy and Meg arrive;
watched them embrace on the sidewalk but enter the
shop separately. He frowned. Could these two scruffily
dressed individuals be undercover agents? The briefing
notes Martin had given him warned that Salameh had
been questioned several times by the CID and the
possibility existed that he would be questioned further.
Dragovic could not see into the newsagent's window
and debated whether to walk across to check if the two
were bona fide civilians but decided to wait.

Twenty minutes later his patience was rewarded.
Meg and Sandy came out of the shop, Sandy giving a
quick look up and down the street, while Meg casually
scanned the shop fronts before they both moved down
the street and around the corner towards Vauxhall Way.
Grateful for the tattered lace curtain and grimy glass,
Dragovic leant away slightly from the window. They
were professionals.

He pondered his options. He'd planned to spend at
least two days watching his target before moving in to
kill Salameh but this development added a new urgency
to his operation. All he'd been told was that Salameh
was one of the men involved in the failed attempt on
Talawi and was a possible threat to his own future
strike. Salameh had been one of the men placed by
Ayatolah Albarrasan in England to assist Dragovic when
he arrived.

Had Salameh talked? Dragovic chewed on his

bottom lip thoughtfully. What had he learned? That what appeared to be two undercover CID agents had visited Salameh, all their actions indicating a desire to be unobtrusive. Did they expect Salameh to have visitors? Was a trap being set? Why not a phone call rather than a visit? He sighed. The permutations could be endless. Would the two agents return? Dragovic considered having another cup of the foul tasting excuse for coffee. Pushing himself away from the table he decided that now, while Salameh was unguarded, he would visit the room above the shop. His head bowed briefly, *Allah walk with me*, he prayed. Before rising he pulled the faded baseball cap low over his eyes, hunching his shoulders into the pea jacket. Walking over to the check-out till, where the counter assistant was flirting with a pimply male sporting an earring and a pony tail tied back with what appeared to be a piece of knotted string, Dragovic dropped enough coins on the counter to cover his bill.

Later, under intense questioning from Special Branch, the counter assistant would tearfully give a completely erroneous description, remembering only the slogan on the cap and that the man was dark skinned. Dragovic's skin had deepened to a mahogany tan on Corsica, and the girl could be forgiven for making what was an all too simple mistake.

Stepping into the street Dragovic waited for a gap in the light traffic before walking across the rain-slicked pavement. Pausing inside the newsagent's he allowed his eyes to adapt to the dimmer light. The shopkeeper Patel, busy with a local who had engaged him in conversation, out of habit looked up as Dragovic came through the door. Later, his recollection would be remarkably similar to the coffee shop girl's but with one important distinction. The man who entered, he would claim, was not of Middle Eastern or Asian extraction.

Resuming his conversation and distracted by two youths that entered behind Dragovic, Patel did not notice the Bosnian move towards the curtain that concealed the staircase. Dragovic's briefing had been thorough, and Salameh's room above the newsagents was well known to the eyes and ears of Ayatollah Albarrasan. Dragovic stepped through the curtain, still pulled to one side after Sandy's visit, and went up the stairs quietly. At the landing he tapped lightly on the door.

"Who is it?" Abbas Salameh, having checked his pistol, was bending over the night table reattaching the Glock to the Velcro straps, straightened up, the pistol in his hand.

"Police, please open."

Salameh stiffened. Why again, so soon? Why? He stared at the Glock in his hand. Perhaps they'd seen something. What, what could it be? Frantically he cast around the room looking for clues. "Wait please, I'm coming." He sucked his breath in deep gulps, trying to calm his suddenly racing nerves. They must have found something. He must deal with them. Reaching down he pulled the silencer clear of the Velcro fastenings and, screwing the silencer to the muzzle, approached the door. Salameh tucked the pistol into his waistband at the small of his back. Unlocking the door and pulling it slightly open he was stunned to see a man whose flat, dead eyes he recognised from the picture Meg had shown him just 10 minutes before. The picture only vaguely resembled the man in front of him, but the eyes were unmistakable. His mouth opened in shock and he gasped, "You! —You are not police. They look . . ."

Dragovic saw a small dark Iranian matching the photographs he'd been given. The man's face was shiny with a thin film of perspiration. Pushing the door fully open then pivoting on the ball of his left foot Dragovic

drove the stiffened fingers of his left hand deep into
Salameh's diaphragm and, as the man's knees buckled,
struck viciously with the blade edge of his right hand at
the exposed neck. Abbas Salameh was dead before
hitting the floor. Dragovic knelt and felt the Iranian's
pulse. Satisfied that the man was dead he straightened,
stepped over the corpse and grasped it by the ankles.
Dragovic pulled Salameh's body back into the room,
clear of the door. Salameh's Glock, loosened by the
tugging on his trousers slid out of his waistband and fell
to the floor.

Dragovic smiled grimly. His victim had obviously
been expecting a hostile visitor. Then he frowned;
remembering Salameh's startled look, and the brief
couple of words the man had uttered. Salameh had
recognised him, but that was impossible; he and
Salameh had never met. Was Albarrasan playing a
double game? He breathed deeply, slowing his pulse and
bringing his emotions under control. Something was not
right, somewhere there was a tear in the curtain that
surrounded him. Dragovic stepped out of the room and,
holding the doorknob with a handkerchief pulled the
door closed. Pausing on the landing, he listened for a
full thirty seconds, then walked quietly down the stairs.
He pushed through the plastic strips at the shop entrance, keeping his head down. Once again, luck was
with him. Patel was engaged in an acrimonious dispute
with the smaller of the two youths and all eyes were on
the mini drama at the counter. Dragovic stepped outside
and walked briskly towards the railway station and the
tube that would take him back to the heart of London.
The whole operation from start to finish had taken less
than 6 minutes.

§

Sandy pushed back his chair. "Well, that feels better. Give me a second to visit the men's room and we can go back to have another chat with Mr. Abbas Salameh."

Both had ordered fried fish and chips, washing the meal down with a pint of the local dark lager. Sitting in companionable silence they'd enjoyed their meal. Meg, surprised at how hungry she was, had attacked her food with gusto. She looked up, "I'll do the same" she chuckled, anticipating Sandy's retort, "visit the ladies, idiot, and meet you back at the car." She watched Sandy weave through the lunchtime crush around the bar and disappear into the next room, before wiping her lips on the paper napkin and pushing back her own chair. Fifteen minutes later they were strapped into the Volvo and driving back to Epworth Street.

"What excuse are we going to use for such a quick turnaround?"

"We need an excuse?" Meg raised her eyebrows. "I hardly think we have to make apologies for doing what we're paid to do."

Sandy laughed. "Indeed not madam, but you forget, I think, that we are not in Ireland now and we need inconvenient bits of paper like a search warrant. You know the sort of thing, big black stamps all over it." Meg punched him on the shoulder.

"Don't patronise me you SAS reject. You know perfectly well what I meant."

"Seriously, we are going to have to come up with some cover story." Sandy tapped the horn at a slow-moving sedan that seemed unable to choose a lane so straddled both. "I have a feeling that our man is savvy enough to call up a lawyer if we attempt to put pressure on him. How about we say that we've just had a call from HQ? The man, whose picture you showed him, has been seen in the area and we require him to call at once if he spots him. I'll take him over to the kitchen light to have a look at the picture and we'll have our backs to the room. You can have a quick shufti around the room."

"Sounds plausible. But you're going to have to keep him talking for a couple of minutes with his back to the room. I definitely want to look behind that night table and bed headboard." Meg studied Sandy's profile as he concentrated on his driving. They made a good team and she knew that he was attracted to her despite having received no encouragement. Turning back to stare through the windscreen she sighed. It was going to be difficult to keep their relationship on a purely profes-sional basis. She liked Sandy, found him to be quick, funny and very smart, but the feelings she had went no deeper. Sandy had invited her out on several occasions but she had always managed to find a plausible excuse for not going. Soon she was going to have to let him know it was not on, that she was not ready for any sort of relationship outside of the office.

"Here we are." Sandy swung into the parking area. A vehicle was backing out and he braked to wait for the empty space, causing another driver who had been cruising the lot for several minutes to honk and raise his hands in frustration behind their car. Having parked and waited for the irate motorist to move, the two detectives hunched over and checked their weapons before step-ping out into the weak sunlight that was trying to break through the thin gray overcast. Once again they entered the newsagents and acknowledging Patel with a brief wave went up the stairs.

Sandy tapped on the door. "Mr. Salameh? It's Detectives Flett and Davidson. Can we see you again for a minute? It's important." There was no sound from inside the room. Frowning, Sandy tapped again but moved clear of the door. "Mr. Salameh, please open up sir." He looked over at Meg who had her Webley up and was in a semi crouch covering the door. Sandy nodded, and then reaching down turned the doorknob. Finding it unlocked he pushed the door open and waited. Nothing moved, the faint hiss of traffic passing in the rain-slicked street below the only sound. Signaling his intention Sandy slid down into a prone position. Pulling his own weapon clear he peered around the doorpost, simultaneously swinging the pistol to cover Salameh's room. A waiting opponent expecting a hostile entry would have lost a micro second in redirecting their aim from middoor to floor and would have died in that brief span.

"Oh shit!" Sandy was staring into Salameh's dead eyes. "Meg, use your radio, we have a floppy." Coiling his legs underneath his body Sandy made a diving spring over the dead man, rolling as he hit the floor before bouncing up to cover the room. Slowly he lowered the pistol. The room was empty.

Chapter 12

Debrief

"He knew me Martin." The two men walked along the seafront, watching people lying on the pebbly beach trying to tan in the weak sun. "How? I've gone over everything since we arrived. Something doesn't fit. Did Gip say anything about giving Salameh my picture?"

Martin bent to pick up a small sea-washed pebble, examining it carefully before throwing it into the sea with a quick flick of his wrist. "What exactly did he say? Think carefully before you answer. I might spot something you have overlooked or missed."

"Exactly—exactly? Hell Martin I was in the full strike position." Dragovic's voice was calm. "I'm not sure, but it sounded like, 'You are not police. They look like . . .' or it could have been 'they looking'. But his first word was 'You' as if he had seen me before. I could see the shock in his eyes, but it was too late to stop the strike and ask him what the hell he meant."

Martin gripped his elbow briefly. "Don't reproach yourself. It may have been something as simple as mistaken identity." He raised his hands as Dragovic turned towards him in amazement. "I know—I know. It's far fetched, especially in our business, but there is no way Gip would have done something like that without telling you first. I've worked with him before and he's very methodical and meticulous." Martin turned to look over the sea, pursing his lips. "But you're correct. We have to assume somehow there is a leak." He looked at Dragovic thoughtfully. "Gip had intended for us both to stay here until the heat died down but I think you should leave tonight, we must assume that they have found the body by now. If that's the case they may be watching airports and ferries. I have a contact who has a converted fishing boat based in Bosham Harbour. Go back to the hotel and check out. Take a taxi into Havant and wait for me at that restaurant near the station."

"This contact. How reliable is he?"

Martin smiled grimly. "He runs a small hi-tech electronics company. Small boat radars and GPS systems. He also sells outside the normal channels, a greedy man. He knows the penalty for making a mistake. He'll run you across the Channel. It will be a night test of some new equipment if anyone asks." He snorted in sudden amusement. "I hope you don't suffer from seasickness. The last time I went over I spent half the journey flat on my back." The two men turned, retracing their steps slowly.

"You want to meet in France?" Dragovic asked.

"No, take the train to Spain as we originally planned then a flight to Italy and the ferry home."

Both men smiled at the Freudian slip. Home was a strange word for the Corsican farm, yet for both it'd become more than a simple training base.

"You know what this means?" Dragovic asked softly as he waited for a couple walking hand in hand to pass. "If I'm blown there's no chance that I'm going to get close to Talawi." He drew in a deep lungful of salt air. "We must find out what happened. The whole operation could be compromised."

"Yes, I know. I'll speak to Gip tonight and he'll check with his controllers. Don't leave Spain for a few days. I'll call you at the El Prado on . . ." He looked at his watch. "Today is Tuesday, let's say Friday—late Friday. By then we'll have run sweepers over the whole system. If there is a leak we'll find it."

Dragovic grunted. "Insh'Allah. For all our sakes I hope so."

"Gip will find the leak, if there is one."

Drogovic stopped, looking over the sea towards France, forcing Martin to pause. "You're not convinced?"

"It doesn't make sense Nick. You're far too important to the plan. The only reason to send us over here was to eliminate a possible source that could have compromised the main operation. I even argued with Gip that we should not use you but send someone else." He shook his head, the stiffening breeze off the sea flapping his lightweight jacket. Dragovic lifted his eyebrows but did not speak. "Gip agreed with me, he wasn't keen on using you either, but time was a critical factor, he couldn't risk Salameh going over to the British. Gip's controllers felt that Salameh was a weak link. Only a handful of top people are in on the details and there was no one else who could be trusted, especially over here. Remember it was a wildcat operation that tried to get Talawi. God knows what would have been the consequences of asking an unreliable in-place agent to dispose of Salameh." Martin sighed, spreading his hands expressively. "Seeing as we were overruled by Ayatollah Albarrasan we wanted to see how good your training has been. Tidy up any loose ends, polish the rough spots." He chuckled. "It's been good to see that there aren't any."

Dragovic scanned his controller's face carefully. He trusted Martin and what Martin said made sense. But still he felt a lingering sense of unease. He wondered at himself. He was not afraid to die; death after all, would be a welcome release. He looked down at his hands, hands that had killed mere hours ago—as a soldier he'd killed often, but this was different—and wryly realised that he still had the professional soldier's distaste for this murky world of half-truths and evasions. "As you say, it doesn't make sense. Perhaps . . ."

He hesitated, then shrugged and continued, "No, it doesn't matter. I think it's all too easy to become paranoid in this business."

"Paranoia will keep us both alive my friend, that's why you are going tonight by fishing boat. Caution never hurt anyone and, if we are wrong, nothing will be lost. I still cannot believe we have a leak, but . . ."

§

"Damn, damn it all to hell." James Douglas and Inspector Basil Coulson faced Sandy and Meg. "You said you left him, what? . . . half an hour before?"

Meg looked down at her notebook. "As close as we can reconstruct, a total of 43 minutes from the time we left him until we returned."

"Damn, to have missed the bastard by such a tiny margin." Jimmy Douglas struck the top of the table in frustration, then, annoyed at losing control, glanced across the room at Inspector Coulson. "Basil, do we have anything yet from Forensic?"

"Apart from apparent cause of death, nothing yet. The room is clear of prints. You found that Salameh had a set of Velcro clips to hold his Glock pistol behind the night table?"

Douglas nodded and turned to where Sandy and Meg sat facing the desk "Yes. That's what you said tipped you off, wasn't it Sandy? You felt he was hiding something."

"Both of us saw him start to look in that direction. But Meg thought more of it than I did. We discussed it on the way out and decided to go back after a bite to eat and check it out. The killer must have been watching and as soon as we left made his move."

"His?" Coulson's voice was soft, the Geordie

accent modified by years of living in the South.

"It had to be. A neck strike requires considerable force. Most women would have used a weapon. What puzzles me is that there was no sign of forcible entry. It's almost as if Salameh knew his killer and let him in. Have you checked out the café across the street?"

"It's being done. The whole area is being combed, and we are pulling in everyone who might have seen or heard something." A phone tinkled softly as Coulson spoke and Douglas lifted the receiver to his ear.

"Inspector Coulson? Hold on." He held up the telephone. "It's for you, Basil." Douglas waited until Coulson crossed the floor before handing over the phone and vacating his seat. Crossing to where Meg and Sandy were standing he dragged a chair around to sit, his arms hooked over the back. "I'll let you both get away in a minute. The Chief will want to read your official reports so you had better get started as soon as possible. Can either of you think of anything—anything at all you might have missed?" It was a measure of Jimmy Douglas's frustration, thought Sandy that he should even think to ask such a question. He bit back a sharp retort and Meg answered for him.

"We have gone over every minute, Jimmy. You know what we know. It's possible the people in the shop were scouts for the hit man. Only a proper investigation will—"

"A lone man, about six feet. Yes—yes of course. Good work Hamish. I'll be here for the rest of the afternoon . . . yes . . . no . . . OK." Coulson pushed the phone cut off button down sharply and immediately spoke into the mouthpiece. "Susan, call Central and tell them a composite will be on the wire from Hamish in a minute. Have it sent to all airports and ferries. Call Chief Superintendent Ingram and ask him to call me as

soon as he gets in. . . . What? . . . Yes of course . . .
Thank you." He put the phone down and there was grim
excitement in his voice. "We have a rough description,
it'll be here in a minute. Patel the shopkeeper saw our
man briefly. Dark skinned, about 6 feet tall, baseball cap
pulled low. He thinks European but isn't certain. The
man spent about an hour in the café across the street."
Coulson turned to Sandy. "You were right on that score.
Apparently he had several cups of coffee, read the
newspaper. The counter girl says he was very dark,
thinks he was an Arab. She claims he never spoke to her
beyond asking for coffee. She's a dimbulb of the worst
kind and I don't know how much use she's going to be.
But at least we know it was a man." He nodded in
Sandy's direction, "Right again Sandy, and we know he's
at or above 6 feet. Dark skinned. Ah—that must be our
fax."

The fax machine, balanced on a filing cabinet,
clattered briefly and a slowly moving length of paper
began to slide out of the machine into a wire basket
placed on a chair below the cabinet. Jimmy Douglas was
first to reach the paper. He waited impatiently as the
others crowded round. "Why in the hell do they always
come out upside down," he grumbled, tearing the paper
off as the machine stopped. He flipped the sheet over
and there was a collective gasp of disappointment.

"Not much to go on," Meg observed dryly. "I
doubt if we'll have a lot of success at the airports." The
picture was poor. Hastily done under extreme pressure
with information from two contradictory witnesses it
showed a dark, unremarkable face, half hidden in the
shadow of a baseball cap. A logo on the front of the cap
showed a circle superimposed on a triangle, the points
of the triangle extending beyond the circumference of
the circle.

Jimmy Douglas tapped the printout thoughtfully.

"I've seen that logo before. Sandy have you . . .?"

"I'm not sure—no, I don't think so." Sandy turned to Meg. "Where did you put the picture of our mystery man?"

Meg bent and delved inside her voluminous bag. She pulled out the folded picture and unfolded and smoothed it out before handing it over to Sandy. They crowded round as Sandy compared the two.

"You think it might be the same person?" Basil Coulson asked, frowning at the two pictures.

"I know that they don't look similar, and Salameh swore he'd never seen this man before. But what if our first picture is wrong. Maybe just enough to throw us off and maybe even Salameh. I'd lay money on the fact that he did not recognise the picture. What do you think, Meg?"

Meg looked hard at the two composites before answering. "I agree with Sandy. My take on Salameh was that he did not recognise this face—" she tapped the Israeli composite with a stiffened forefinger "—but I also think we have a professional out there and I think it may well be one and the same man in both pictures."

Jimmy Douglas stretched his arms behind his back, swinging the linked hands from side to side in an attempt to relieve the tension in his shoulders. "OK, you two get your reports started. I'll do a search on the cap logo. Basil you'll want to brief the Chief Superintendent." He pulled back his shirtsleeve and looked at his watch. "Can we meet back here at five? That gives us nearly three hours. Oh Sandy—I'll fill Tris in on what has happened. I think he's beginning to feel left out."

Sandy and Meg left the room, taking with them the fax composite and the picture of Dragovic sent by Mossad earlier. Detective Inspector Basil Coulson waited until the two had departed before picking up his raincoat.

"They make a good team." He said approvingly. "Young Flett has a feel for this kind of work and Davidson has a good mind."

Douglas looked up sharply. "Oy! You keep your Metropolitan hands off, old son. They belong to me. Poaching is the quickest way to screw up an investigation."

Coulson laughed, opening the door. "See you at five." The door clicked shut behind him.

§

The converted fishing boat rolled in a light swell, rubbing up against the polyvinyl bumpers protecting the paintwork. Dragovic waited while the man introduced only as Colin busied himself readying the craft for the short sea trip to France. Dragovic pulled the baseball cap out of his coat pocket and ran stiffened fingers through his short-cut graying hair. Dusk falling over the little harbour threw long shadows, and others working on their boats cast scarcely a glance at the two men obviously preparing for a trip. A man walking past greeted Colin, who obviously was well known down here, but beyond a brief nod ignored Dragovic. He hesitated to put the cap on. There appeared to be no need to hide his face from Colin and anyway the man had no idea of who or what he was. Martin Dreyfus had mentioned that Colin thought they were drug smuggling, hence the extra large payments of cash into a Cayman Island account for his services.

After leaving the newsagent's, Nick had intended to dump the cap at the rail station, but unable to find a receptacle, and pushed for time, had stuffed it into his pocket. It was time to dispose of the cap. Besides, he'd never been partial to this most American style of headwear. At the foot of the stairs leading down to the dock he'd seen a bin for waste. Dragovic looked around and apart from a small boy fishing off the upper dock he could see no one near the bin. Abruptly deciding, he walked to the bin and threw the cap inside. Colin was waiting for him as he returned to the boat and, stepping aboard, Dragovic helped push the vessel clear of the dock. The diesel engines muttered gently as Colin opened the throttles and the bow of the 30-foot ex-fishing boat lifted slightly as the twin propellers bit in.

It was nearly dark when Sam Dawood, the young boy Dragovic had noticed fishing, decided that it was getting too dark and he should return home. The fish were not biting this evening. He carefully wound in his line, unclipping the float and hook with it's untouched worm, and returned them to his tackle box. Wrapping up the remains of the sandwiches he'd prepared earlier he looked around for a disposal bin. Seeing nothing close, he dropped the bundle on the dock but, in a fit of conscience, plus he might be yelled at if someone else remembered seeing him eating earlier, recovered the fist-sized packet and walked down the steps to the waste bin Dragovic had used earlier. He lifted the lid and with a child's curiosity peered inside. He'd seen the tall fellow throw something there. The bin was empty apart from a baseball cap. The boy reached inside, his feet leaving the dock as he stretched for the cap.

"Hey, get out of there!" an angry voice came out of the near darkness. Sam, startled, grabbed the cap and pushed himself out of the bin.

"My cap fell in," he yelled into the near darkness as two men came into his view. "Look." He held out the cap for inspection. The leading man frowned down at him.

"Yeah, and what were you doing in there any-way?"

"Putting my rubbish in." The boy snapped defiantly. "Look for yourself."

"Get away home you little git, before I give you a thick ear." The man pushed him roughly. "Go'wan, git now."

Relieved, but angry, Sam scampered up the stairs, pausing only to collect his tackle, and trotted towards where he'd left his bicycle. He debated whether to yell obscenities at the two men now following his path off the dock and decided against it. After all, the cap looked in good condition and it was one of those that could be adjusted for any size head. Muttering under his breath he clipped his fishing tackle to the rear holder and swung his cycle towards home.

As Sam cycled home the evening news carried the composite picture the police artist had faxed earlier to Inspector Coulson. The logo was clearly visible and if the boy had been watching the news he would have immediately seen the match with the cap he'd found. His parents, drinking at their local pub, never even glanced up as the news broadcast flashed on screens across England.

Martin Dreyfus, sitting in the hotel lounge on Hayling Island, saw the broadcast and felt his stomach contract. Had Nick worn the hat on his return to Hayling Island? No, Nick had been bareheaded when the taxi dropped him off. But on the train? A stupid, stupid error, a mistake that could jeopardise a million-dollar project. Damn, the British were quick. He should have told Nick to ditch the hat, perhaps he had. It had never occurred to him to ask Nick about the disposal of easily identifiable clothing. After all, Cartwright was no fool and his training had been thorough. But still, Nick had been thrown by Salameh's recognition and it was possible that he'd forgotten to ditch the hat. The trail could lead here and once questioning started Martin knew, good as his cover was, it had not been designed for an in-depth investigation. Perhaps it would be safer to relocate to London. Martin knew the staff had seen him talking to Nick and perhaps they'd been seen on the promenade earlier. He weighed his options calmly. He had, as did Nick, two different identities. The present one identified him as Martin Dreyfus, a French account- ant with the firm of LaVoie et cie, boatbuilders. The other was as a Swiss businessman by the name of Emil Wasserman. Martin stood, brushing off a few crumbs from the biscuit he'd had with his coffee. He went to his room, packed quickly then called the desk clerk to make up his account and order him a taxi. He was very apolo- getic for the inconvenience, stating urgent business back in France.

Taking the taxi to Havant, Martin caught the train to Portsmouth and became Mr. Emil Wassermann, returning that night via Gatwick to Zurich.

Chapter 13

An evil son of a bitch

Ismail Talawi stared at the long smooth curve of the woman's back. She's just another groupie, he thought contemptuously, looking for another well-known scalp to add to her collection; even though she was the wife of a successful businessman and had money coming out of her ears. The woman, hearing him move as he sat up in the huge bed, turned over, smiling languorously, long honey brown hair falling across her naked breasts. "Hi there lover." She sat up flicking the hair behind her shoulders. "My God. What's the time?" Talawi reached for his watch on the bedside table.

"It's nearly three. What time do you have to be home?"

"Oh, Kenneth wants to take some Saudi tycoon out for dinner. I'll have some bloody desert Arab peering down my dress all evening." She shook her shoulders at him, the lovely breasts jiggling from side to side as she moved. Talawi grunted and reaching over grabbed one breast hard, his thumb and forefinger squeezing the nipple. The woman yelped.

"You forget Julie that I'm also a desert Arab."

Julie tried to pull away, tears springing to her eyes. "You're such a bastard Ismail. You know perfectly well what I mean. I hate these dinners where I'm supposed to be the pretty little ornament in a low-cut top." She shoved his hand away, and swung her long legs out of the bed. Striding toward the bathroom she tried hard to not let him see the tears. God, why were men such bastards. Her feelings for the handsome writer had flared like an exploding star and taken her totally by surprise. Meeting Ismail Talawi at a book signing shortly before the assassination attempt she'd, at first, been mildly amused by his obvious attraction for her.

Born to a poor Irish family, Julie McNulty found that her striking beauty opened doors, but she also possessed a quick and clever mind. Winning a scholarship to London University she'd graduated with a first in Economics. Meeting Kenneth Croaker, a rising star at stockbrokers Meredith, Barrett and Barclay, she'd been swept off her feet in a whirl of parties, flowers and attention. While others like Nick Leeson crashed and burned in the tricky world of derivatives, Kenneth Croaker, stepping adroitly through that minefield, made his first fortune by the time he was twenty-five. Cleverly anticipating Britain's rising prominence in pharmaceuticals, he invested heavily in drug manufacturing and, pursued by both Labour and Conservative factions in the government, was touted as a man to watch.

Brushing her hair in the full-length mirror she grimaced at her reflection. Yes, she had married Kenneth Croaker for security but also, she thought wryly, I was in what I thought was love. She shook her head in disgust. Kenneth wanted an ornament, a walking talking doll, for his dinner parties. In the circles they moved having the odd affair was not unexpected and Kenneth took full advantage of the numerous opportunities presented by nubile secretaries. The first time one of Kenneth's affairs surfaced, after 3 years of marriage, Julie, outraged and hurt, lashed back by having a forgettable affair of her own. She soon realised that despite the glittering, freewheeling lifestyle, she was still a convent-raised Catholic at heart and casual affairs were not her style. Julie was still in the emotional let down phase when she'd met Ismail Talawi and been captivated by his charm and interest. After confessing to the smiling, handsome author that she'd never read his novels, felt obligated to accept his invitation to a small gathering after the book signing. After they'd become lovers he'd told her that he'd never believed her professed claim of ignorance of his work and thought it merely a ploy to get his attention. Only later, when her initial amusement had been subsumed by a wave of love such as she'd never experienced, did she realise that he did not feel the same way. He was egotistical, selfish and self-centred. Tears pricked at the back of her eyelids. What was wrong with her? Why did she always pick the wrong men?

Talawi was dressed when she returned to the room, fussily trying out various ties to go with the light gray suit he was wearing. She watched him sadly. The affair was probably over. He had shown unmistakable signs over the last few weeks. At first she'd thought it was a reaction to the assassination attempt, but now it was fairly obvious that he'd found a new woman to stroke his ego. Julie Croaker was too smart and sensible a person to lie to herself, but God it hurt.

"I won't see you for a while." He turned to her smiling, holding up a brighter tie than she would've chosen for him. "This one OK?"

"Yes, it's fine. Another book tour?"

"What? Oh, not seeing you, you mean. No, not another book tour, thank God. I have to go up to Scotland for a week, then the Yard want me out of London for a while." He shivered. "They think the mad mullahs have a professional hit man here waiting for another chance."

Her stomach contracted. She remembered the terrible days following the assassination attempt when Ismail had been a frightened, nervous child. Then she'd been his rock and for a brief period had known real happiness. Julie wondered if seeing him so vulnerable had been more than his ego, once recovered from the shock, could stand. She had prayed for his safety and knew that she would do so every moment he was away. Keeping her voice noncommittal she asked, "What's happening in Scotland?"

"What?" Irritation sharp in his voice, as he critically examined another tie.

"You said a week in Scotland. What's on?"

"For God's sake Julie, you sound like the grand inquisitor. Stop examining every aspect of my life. If you must know, the Earl of Elgin has invited a small group of us to do some fishing in his stretch of water."

Julie bit back a sharp reply. It wouldn't do to fight, even knowing that he hated outdoor activities. The lie was obvious but a wrong step now could end it for all time. She drew a deep breath and went over to the chair where her clothes lay. Dressing quickly she waited until he had finished carefully arranging his luxuriant hair. Ismail walked over and kissed her lightly on the lips. 'Judas' she thought bitterly, but nothing showed on her face.

"I'll call you as soon as I know what's happening. It may be quite a while though."

"Of course. Please be careful." It took every ounce of willpower to resist throwing her arms around him. He looked at her, unsure, then his ego reasserted itself and with a small grin made a gun out of his forefinger and thumb, pointing at her.

"See ya kid." Trying to sound like a cheap Hollywood gangster. He tapped on the door and it was opened by one of the two plainclothes policemen waiting outside. Both had been assigned to guard Ismail. Mike, the older man, had developed a soft spot for Julie. He'd read the background reports on all Talawi's friends and was not impressed with most of them. Ismail Talawi might be a literary genius, but he was also a pompous prick who treated his minders with the casual contempt one gave to servants. The man was a fool, who treated the only good person Mike Hiscock had seen in his entourage of fluffy, politically correct egos with deceit.

The two men guarded Talawi on alternating night and day shifts, in rotation with six other plainclothes police, knew that he'd started another affair with Angela Burgess, the wife of a senior civil servant who fancied herself as something of a writer. Mike and Jeff Richards, his colleague, had been subjected to the brittle Angela's tongue. Hell, guarding Salman Rushdie had been a pleasure compared with this man. Mike lifted his hand in a small wave to Julie and gave her a brief smile as he pulled the door shut behind Ismail.

Julie waited until the door closed fully before slumping down on the bed, her shoulders heaving. Later, after washing her face with cold water to remove the puffiness around her eyes and putting on fresh make-up, she left the hotel. In a café across the street, Meg Davidson watched her leave and waited to see if anyone was tailing Julie. Satisfied, Meg folded her newspaper and, dropping change on the table, rose to follow. Sandy didn't look up as she passed and after waiting a few minutes he crossed over to the hotel. Entering the elevator he punched in the correct floor number and minutes later, with the help of a master key, entered the recently vacated room. Moving swiftly he reached behind the high, heavily brocaded, curtains to retrieve the mini video cam recorder. This part of their work made him uncomfortable and he wondered how Talawi would react knowing that every move was watched and recorded, even something as intimate as love making. Jimmy Douglas had been adamant when he and Meg had demurred.

"The man who killed Salameh, the Israeli reservists and, I'm pretty certain Arafat's men in Gaza, is a consummate professional. I'm convinced he's still in the UK. We're not going to leave anything to chance. Damn it all Sandy, you both know what the stakes are—a successful hit will cause all sorts of diplomatic tidal waves at a time when the Middle East is beginning to show signs of settling down." And so the level of hidden security racked up a further notch.

§

Dragovic, Martin and Gip Lawrence walked away from the farmhouse toward the main field, their shoes crunching the short grass. Gip stopped as a bout of coughing racked his body. Both men waited until he'd regained his composure. Wiping his lips with a handkerchief, Lawrence tried to smile, but it was obvious he was in some pain.

"We can go back to the house. I don't understand why you wanted to come out here anyway." Dragovic spoke with concern. He and Martin had returned to the farm in Corsica a week ago and, after an intensive debrief, resumed their regular routine of training. Gip had frowned when told of the surprise on Salameh's face.

"He can't have seen your face anywhere. The only person privy to this operation is the Ayatollah and he's as puzzled as we are. We have a contact at Scotland Yard. For obvious reasons we don't call on his services very often. He's very valuable as a long term asset but this is important." And so they waited while Gip flew to London and through a series of cutouts contacted his agent. Gip returned after two days and, looking worse than ever, had spent the morning lying on his bed. After lunch Gip asked the two men to forgo their training session and walk with him to the far pasture.

Now straightening up Gip shook his head. "No, I'll be fine. I need a bit of fresh air and some exercise." Gip looked over the rolling fields to the range rising beyond the forest edge. "It's beautiful here." Without waiting for an answer, he turned to face them. "I have the answer to your identification by the Brits." He drew in a deep breath. "Remember Hasid, the PFLP man you were given for the Rumaysh hit?" Dragovic nodded, a frown appearing. "Yes of course."

"Mossad picked him up in Beirut and he gave them an idea of what you looked like."

"How did they know who'd carried out the attack? Was there an informant?"

"The Israeli's are good, but not that good. No, your assistant couldn't resist bragging about his part in the operation, and Mossad has eyes and ears everywhere. They snatched him, took him back to Southern Lebanon and extracted all they could."

"But why were we not told? This changes everything." Martin's anger was apparent in the scowl on his face and the tone of his voice. "We could have been picked up as soon as we landed." Dragovic watched Gip's face intently. There was more to this than they had heard yet.

"The Israeli's were clever. They returned Hasid's body to Beirut and staged a car accident on the outskirts. Hasid had a reputation for reckless driving and his body was badly burnt. Our forensic people carried out an investigation, but I suspect it was perfunctory. After all, Hasid had not been out of contact for more than two days, and that was not unusual. It was assumed by the PFLP that it was a natural catastrophe." A fresh burst of coughing shook Lawrence's frame and he doubled over in pain. Dragovic moved swiftly to put an arm around the older man.

"Sit down Gip. Take a breather." He lowered Lawrence to the ground with Martin's help and then also sat on the short grass, facing his chief. Martin remained standing, his anger fading. It made sense, obviously they would have been told if anyone had thought there was the possibility of capture, but still . . .

"So what happens now? They have a picture of Nick. Hell no wonder Salameh thought he was seeing a ghost."

Gip Lawrence looked up, lines of pain cutting deep grooves in his face. He shook his head. "No—no. The good news is that the picture is only superficially like Nick . . . "

"Then how did Salameh . . ."

"Wait, let me finish. Salameh was shown the picture and he did not recognise the person shown, but said something about the eyes. I did not understand at first but when I saw a copy in London I understood what Salameh meant." Another paroxysm of coughing shook his frame. Dragovic looked up at Martin Dreyfus.

"We must get him back to the house. He should be in bed."

Gip Lawrence shook his head. "No, not yet." He looked over the fields back to the farmhouse. "Funny, isn't it. I'm not afraid to die, but I do want to see this operation succeed before I go. I was saying that when I saw a copy of the Mossad drawing I understood how he could have recognised you. By a stroke of luck the artist got your eyes down to perfection even though the rest of the drawing could be anyone. I suspect Hasid tried to throw them off as much as possible." He smiled at the two men. "Look at Nick's eyes Martin, what do you see?"

Martin frowned. He looked at Dragovic who

looked back calmly. "His eyes are not that unusual. No, I can't say I see anything that would make Nick stand out."

"Ah, you have been too long in this world of ours, Martin. Nick has the eyes of a killer. It doesn't show often but I've seen them change. " He patted Nick on the shoulder. "I've been thinking and what we have to do is soften the look. In town there is an optician I've used in the past. He will fit you with soft contact lenses, hazel coloured and without any magnification. It's the sort of thing they give movie stars when the script calls for eyes of a certain colour and the actor's eyes are different." He chuckled hoarsely. "Try to think kind thoughts, Nick, when you go through Immigration next time."

"It seems too simplistic, I—" Dragovic paused, then shrugged. "Perhaps that's all it was. So what do we do now?"

"Train and wait. Your target, after all, wasn't Ismail Talawi. And we've leaked through vague sources of the Iranian government's anger at the attempt on Talawi after President Rafsanjani expressly stated that the *fatwa* on Salman Rushdie was to be lifted. It will appear as if the government of Iran is disciplining dissidents within the movement for going after Talawi or Rushdie. The Western press with their usual high level of intelligence will accept such a story without too much difficulty. After all, it fits the facts." He held up a hand to Martin. "Help me up Martin." Dragovic rose and helped Martin lift Gip to a standing position. "We'll wait until the security is relaxed, and it will be. Martin said you needed a few more weeks of training, so we'll make good use of the time." The three men walked back to the farmhouse, each wrapped in thought.

Nico Dragovic had been born to the Muslim faith, and from what little Martin had told him, knew that Gip

Lawrence was a convert. But what, he wondered, caused an upper-middle-class Englishman to change, quite late in life, to the true faith. His arm around Lawrence's shoulders tightened slightly. Lawrence was a good man, and was showing courage in the face of his illness. Next time Martin and he were alone he would seek more information. There was much more to Gip Lawrence than showed on the surface. Martin, he knew, was an infidel, a mercenary who did what he did for money. Martin made no secret of his reasons for helping a cause he neither supported nor opposed.

§

Taking a long drink of water Nick wiped his face with a small towel, his muscles still trembling from the exertion of the past hour. Martin had just finished putting them both through an intense bout of close-quarter combat. Pointing the plastic bottle at Martin, Nick asked hoarsely. "What made you take this contract, Martin? You have no quarrel with Talawi. This is not your religion."

Crushing the beer can in his hands Martin threw it across the room, missing the wastebasket by inches. "A long time ago I fought for my country, saw friends die believing that their sacrifice was valued by those who sent them. Later, we were abandoned, told that orders we'd obeyed were wrong and were punished for the mistakes and lies of politicians and bankers." He pulled another can from the cooler and snapped the tab to open it. "So my friend, I decided to walk away from all the old lies, including, '*Pro Patria Mori*', and decided if money is what makes the world go round then I would accumulate enough of my own to give me a good retirement."

"But why this, why a Moslem cause?" Dragovic

watched his face carefully.

"It was an accident, but a fortunate one. I found that the people I work for keep their word. They honour their debts, one cannot ask for more." He took a long pull on the can, then, wiping his lips, turned to Dragovic with a grin. "Why so serious Nick? You think I will change sides if I'm offered more?"

Dragovic nodded. "Would you?"

Martin nodded in return. "It's a reasonable assumption, and a question I've been asked before. Let me tell you a story." He finished off the last of the beer and again aimed the freshly crushed can at the wastepaper basket. And missed again. "Damn. There was a time when I could hit something like that every time. Ah yes, where was I? I was in the USA and saw on the television an interview of a world champion boxer, I forget his name, a middleweight I think, and the reporter asked him how many more times he would defend his title. His answer made me think. He said, 'When I have 50 million dollars. That's the target I've set for myself.' The reporter said something to the effect that the champion was still a young man, and by the reporter's reckoning he must be close to that figure already. Did he intend to walk away from potentially much bigger paydays? The answer was a simple yes. He said that life was for living; he'd proved his skills and soon it would be time to move on."

"I'm sorry, I don't quite see how . . ."

"Ah Nick, you disappoint me. When I first signed up I told them that story. They understood right away that I was saying great wealth was not my aim, a bigger payday if you will. We agreed on the payment terms and the final amount. They've kept their word; there've been no lies, no deceit. I've also kept my side and reached my target, set 4 years ago, last December."

"Why are you still here then?"

"I was asked as a special favour, by a man I admire and respect, to do this one last project for them."

"And in return?

Martin reached for another beer, lifting the can out of the cooler before shaking his head and returning it to the bag. He frowned at Dragovic, then his face cleared. "We have trained you well Nick. No, not for money, that would break our agreement and in a way invalidate all I have just told you. That they understood. In return they gave their word that if I did this—train you and work with you in England—my records would be totally destroyed. That at no time in the future could I be brought back no matter how important the project. I have of course my own new identity but they have great resources and could have found me. So . . ." He stretched his arms upward; "when this is over I become a civilian, with enough money to live comfortably in a country where the weather is kind. And who knows, I might even find a good woman to share it with."

Dragovic shrugged, "Insh'Allah"

"Indeed, no one knows the future. Come on, we have an hour before dinner, lets see you run for thirty minutes."

"Before we go, tell me about Gip. Why does he help the cause? I've asked but he always brushes the question aside with a joke. It seems strange that an Englishman should be so dedicated to the faith."

Martin Dreyfus looked at his protégé for a long moment. Gip Lawrence had been his own controller on several missions but Nick had formed an almost father-son relationship with the man. It would do no harm to tell Nick the story. "Many years ago, Gip worked for a large multinational firm who sent him to manage a plant in Libya. He was there for several years and formed a

deep attachment to the country and people. In Libya,
Gip met and married the woman who became his wife.
She was a chemist who worked in the plant's laboratory;
and a Moslem. Gip was not religious, like most people
he'd given lip service to the Christian faith and was only
mildly interested in Islam. The company management
thought he'd become something of a security risk so he
was transferred with his wife to a plant in the States.
This plant produced special chemicals of various kinds
and Gip's wife developed a rare form of cancer, which
he believed was related to the chemicals.

Her treatment was very expensive and the company, six months after her diagnosis, did not renew her
contract. Gip believed, and he was probably correct,
that it was to save the expense of the treatment. When
Gip approached senior management he was warned, by
the company lawyer, that if he made waves his own
position was a possible candidate for downsizing and, as
Gip needed every penny for his wife's treatment, he
continued working. After a few months he'd sold his
house, cut back on every unnecessary expense and was
sliding deep into debt. Then there was an explosion at
the factory, accidental as it turned out later, but Gip was
targeted as the prime suspect. Finally he managed to
clear his name, but the atmosphere at work was so
poisoned that he could hardly get through each day.

One evening, a Libyan friend called to see them.
The friend, who'd recently been attached to the Libyan
UN mission in New York, was horrified at their desperate situation and made some phone calls back home. To
cut a long story short the Libyan Government flew them
back to Libya, paid for all the treatment under excellent
specialists, and made certain that Gip was looked after
in the weeks after she died. Gip felt that if members of
his own religion could behave so badly, yet those of his

wife's behave so well, then perhaps the Moslem faith was worth investigating. He studied, and like everything he does, did it well. A Libyan intellectual told me that Gip is highly respected for his knowledge of the law. Gip never forgot the kindness shown him and, although there was no overt pressure of any kind, converted to Islam. He offered his services to the Government and was attached to their Foreign Intelligence division. Over the years he's proved to be a very valuable asset. Ironic isn't it? They pull him out of Libya because they think he's a security risk and then by trying to save a few measly dollars proceed to make him one of the biggest threats to their security by stupid behaviour. Greed Nick—always beware of greed."

Chapter 14

False Assumptions

Sam Dawood trotted into the ugliest shopping centre in
England. Portsmouth could boast many old and beautiful buildings but this modern mass of monolithic gray
concrete would not win a prize even for utilitarianism.
He'd enough pocket money to buy a casting reel, money
carefully saved, money taken from his mother's bag
when she and the man he was told to call Dad returned
stumbling drunk from the pub. A lonely child, ignored
by his parents and with few friends, in fishing he'd found
something to make up for the lack of affection at home
and the often casual cruelty at school. The simple peace
and satisfaction of fishing from various piers in the area
substituted for the companionship denied by his peers.

Now wearing the cap he'd salvaged from the bin
on Bosham Pier a week ago, and a greasy windbreaker
two sizes too large for his skinny frame, he hurried down
a narrow passage leading into the open forecourt of the
shopping arcade. One hand deep in the pocket of his
jeans, he clutched the small bundle of notes and head
down did not see the two youths until a hand on his
chest abruptly stopped his progress.

"Watch where yur goin you little shite—hey Bert
lookee, he stood on me new runners." Shocked Sam
stared at his accuser, a much larger and older boy,
looking down at him. Another youth, smaller in size, but
still at least a year older than Sam, lounged against the
wall, smirking. There was no one else in sight, it was
early and because of his anticipation he'd forgotten that
the main shops only opened at ten a.m. Sam felt sick.
Being bullied was not a new experience. The two bullies
were unknown to him, probably out-of-towners in for a

day's mischief in the big city, and their intent was clear.
Sam stuttered out an apology while trying to pull back
from the hand that gripped the lapel of his windbreaker.

"Hey Bert, he says he's sorry. But I think he did it
on purpose." Sam was jerked back and forth violently.
"Yes, I think you did it on purpose you little shite." The
blow alongside his head made him see stars and tears
flooded his eyes. The baseball cap was ripped off his
head with a jerk. "Now where did you steal this . . . eh?"
Another slap alongside his head made his ears ring.
"Hey, it looks just like that one I lost at the
Mapplethorpe Fair last week. What you say Bert?"

Bert grunted assent. "Yeah, it's the same Marv,
maybe he's the one stole it." The lout called Marv,
releasing his grip on Sam's windbreaker, tried to fit the
cap on his own head.

Holding one hand to his swelling ear, the other
still firmly clutching his precious store of cash, Sam saw
his chance. Spinning round he sprinted back the 50
meters to the street and safety. Startled, the louts hesitated, and then realising that the boy might have a
parent in the vicinity quickly retraced their steps into
the shopping centre, Marv pushing the cap deep into his
jacket pocket. When he reached home he would wear it.
Marv would later come to wish he'd never seen the boy,
never taken the day trip into Portsmouth, never touched
the cap.

§

Jimmy Douglas rapped the desk with the clenched
knuckles of his right hand. His left hand held a cell
phone to his left ear. "Good work Max, this may be the
break we've been praying for." He looked at his watch.
"I'll get a squad car to bring us down. Yes, Keep him

incommunicado. What? Oh the usual. Helping police
with inquiries. Yes, you'll have to call her in, but lose
her phone number until we get there." He closed the
phone and looked at Basil Coulson, a broad grin breaking across his face. "A break Basil, a real break."

"Well, don't keep me in suspense man, what is it?"
James Douglas had dropped by Detective Inspector
Coulson's office minutes before and had hardly placed
his hat and coat on the chair Coulson indicated, when
his cell phone had rung. With a brief apologetic look at
Coulson he'd taken the incoming call.

"Remember the drawing from the Salameh crime
scene Bas? Remember me saying that the logo was
familiar? Well, I was wrong, it's not a common logo. The
closest match we came up with is the Civil Defence
badge." Douglas waved his hand in a swooping movement like someone flicking away a mosquito. "Probably
what I remembered," he said absently picking up his hat
and coat.

"Damn it Jimmy. What has happened?" Coulson
was half out of his chair.

"Get your coat Bas, the cap or one very similar
has turned up in Mapplethorpe."

"They're holding a suspect?" Coulson was out of
his chair, reaching for his raincoat in one movement.

"Not quite. A retired cop saw our broadcast and
this morning saw a kid wearing the same cap. He called
his old shop and the local police who know this young-
ster as a real candidate for Broadmoor in a few years,
picked the kid up. After first insisting it was his, the kid
broke down and now claims he found the cap in a waste
bin in the local shopping area."

"Oh Jesus." Coulson stared at his colleague. "That
means the bastard is . . ."

"Still around," Douglas finished for him. "He must
be a confident son of a bitch. Mapplethorpe is less than

30 minutes from Waterloo. My guess is that he saw the broadcast and ditched the cap."

"No." Coulson pulled on his coat. "No, this one is too professional to walk around in an easily identifiable cap. He probably pulled it off shortly after leaving the murder scene, probably after turning the corner towards the railway station. But now we at least have a direction." The two men walked quickly across the main reception area, Inspector Coulson ordering a squad car to meet them at the front entrance. Stepping into the light drizzle that had been falling all morning they waited at the curb for the squad car to arrive.

§

Marvin Bledsoe sat with his arms crossed defiantly across his chest. Fuckin' coppers, he though bitterly. The kid they razzed yesterday must've followed him and Bert from Portsmouth then called the cops. His brow furrowed. But where was the little fuckin' shite? Marv knew the coppers were looking for an excuse to have him in juvenile court again and he had no intention of helping them. Marvin Bledsoe at fourteen years old had been a running sore in the juvenile court system of Mapplethorpe since age ten.

The female constable watched Marvin bleakly. She wondered why the boy was here. A baseball cap, even if stolen, was no big deal; not contacting his social worker at once was, but something bigger than a cap was in the air. She knew that the social worker would go ballistic when she found out the boy had been held for two hours already and could be here a lot longer if the men from London didn't arrive soon.

"You want a drink Marvin?" She decided to make

sure the little swine couldn't accuse her of treating him badly.

The child sneered at her. "Yeah, a beer." He sniggered at his own joke. Constable Betty Small smiled back, containing her temper. "Tea, water or a soft drink Marvin, your choice." She rose, straightening her uniform. "I'm having a coffee." Her implication being that 14-year-olds don't get coffee. She raised an eyebrow at him and waited. Marvin fell into the trap as she'd expected.

"Yeah, gimme a cup of coffee." Constable Small smiled and went to the machine on the interrogation room table. She poured two cups and was just about to turn and ask what he wanted in his drink when the door opened and two men entered. She recognised Detective Inspector Basil Coulson from a seminar she'd attended in London, but the other hard-faced man was unknown to her.

"Ah that smells good." Jimmy Douglas took a cup out of her hand. "Black is fine, you people are certainly quick with your hospitality." Without waiting for an answer he turned to glare at Marvin Bledsoe. "Is this the suspect?" Marvin's jaw dropped. Something wasn't right here. Never before had he been subjected to such treatment. Being kept until the arrival of these two unknown men. The one in uniform looked important, judging by the way Constable Smart was standing. He felt a frisson of fear. Jesus he must've hit the kid hard enough to break something. Naah—it was just a slap, and the kid had run like the wind. What the hell was going on?

Basil Coulson took the other cup from Betty Smart's hand. "Stay here Constable and switch on the recorder."

"It's on sir. We haven't called his social worker yet."

"Ah yes, well will you please do so now. We want

to ask Mr. . . . " He glanced at the clipboard in his other hand. "Mr. Bledsoe, some questions." Jimmy Douglas had already gripped Constable Smart's chair and, reversing it, slapped it down in front of Marvin, before dropping his bulk into it with a thump. Coulson dragged a chair from the desk across the tiles to sit beside Douglas, who had the baseball cap dangling from one finger. Jimmy stared hard at Marvin and twirled the cap gently. "So tell me, where did you find this cap?"

Marvin's lip curled slightly. The man was trying to intimidate him, well he'd better watch out. "I tole the other coppers man, ask them."

The twirling cap flicked across his face with astonishing speed, it stung, rather than hurt, but the effect was considerable. Tears sprang from Marvin's eyes, his mouth fell open. Before he could speak the man smiled a grim smile. "Listen carefully sonny. I'll say this only once. This cap is part of a murder investigation in London, a serious murder investigation, and we need to know where you found it. Exactly where you found it and when." Douglas swung the cap as if to strike again and Marvin raised his hands to protect his face.

"I tole them, it was from the waste bin at the station. I tole them." He was crying now, thoroughly frightened. But his brain had already assessed that they knew nothing of the kid in Portsmouth. The man had said London.

"When?"

"Last night when I came back from Portsmouth. I saw it sticking out of the bin."

"And what were you doing in Portsmouth?"

"I went to see the football." Douglas grunted. A home game between Portsmouth and Southsea had been played in Portsmouth the day before; he'd listened to the results himself last evening. He nodded at Coulson.

"Let's go and see this famous bin. C'mon boy, you can show us yourself." Across the room constable Smart coughed,

"Excuse me sir, don't you think it better to wait for the social worker?"

Coulson shook his head. "No, Constable. Mr. Bledsoe, now knowing the seriousness of the situation, has volunteered to cooperate fully, haven't you sonny?"

The boy nodded jerkily. These weren't regular coppers. They didn't give a shit for his supposed rights that the social worker always went on about. Regular coppers wouldn't have dared to swipe him across the face. He felt his knee starting to twitch and that was always a bad sign. Both men rose and, leading Bledsoe, went into the main police station to advise their driver that they were ready to move.

§

"So . . .we checked the boy's story and it fits pretty well with what we already know." Jimmy Douglas stood in the briefing room facing Sandy, Meg and Tristam. "Which means, as you have already deduced, that our man is still circling. Waiting for another chance."

"Why kill Salameh?" This from Meg, leaning against the door.

"I suspect that Salameh was a weak link, and when our man saw two people who might be CID visiting decided that the time had come to plug a possible leak."

"We've checked the Iranian Club again. The files on all the club members are on your desk." Sandy held up a slim yellow file. "I've tried to assess which of the members might be possibles but everyone we've checked so far has a cast-iron alibi for both the hit on

Talawi and Salameh's killing."

Jimmy placed his hand on a stack of files piled on his desk. "Yes, I saw them Sandy, thanks. I'll ask Basil to do an independent check. But if our quarry is one of the club members he has very good cover. Yes Tris?"

"What are we going to do with Talawi? If he stays in London aren't we giving this fellow a chance for another shot?" Tristam looked embarrassed at the sudden silence.

"Well, well, Tris, you are a quick study. That's why I asked you all to be here this afternoon. Basil and I discussed the idea this morning. Basil is sounding out the head of SIS to see if they will give us some pointers. Their spy relocation program is pretty good. Bas will run that idea past Chief Superintendent Ingram and, if Ingram thinks it's viable, the final package will go to the FO for approval. The Foreign Office will need to smooth entry into whatever country is chosen."

Sandy laughed. "If it happens, and I have my doubts, I hope whoever makes the decision picks somewhere that has a decent climate."

A small frown of annoyance brushed across Jimmy Douglas's face. "You don't think it's a good idea Sandy. Why not?"

"Well for starters we have all the facilities we need right here in England. I've worked with foreign governments and it can be a bitch, as you well know; getting any coordination and support takes forever. Also—" he sat up straight and looked directly at Jimmy Douglas "we can use Talawi as bait to nail this clown. We've done it before."

Jimmy Douglas shook his head emphatically. "No, no no. This is not a black op over the water. This is a respected, world famous writer you're talking about. Imagine the consequences if we lose him. Jesus Sandy, you scare me. This fellow is the Tolstoy of our time."

Meg Davidson interjected quietly. "You both may have a point. We can move Talawi to a safe haven. Then get an actor who looks reasonably like Talawi to show himself sporadically, at selected venues, in the hope we can draw our man's fangs."

"The actor will know he's bait. How many actors do you think would be willing to take the risk? Do you know how much money is on Rushdie's head? At last tally, 2.1 million US dollars." Douglas scratched his arm, while squinting at Meg, his head cocked to one side. "But your point is taken Meg. I'll have someone look into that side of it."

Tristam spoke from behind Meg and Sandy. "I'll volunteer for that. I have friends in the Rep, and the Old Vic. I can frame a hypothetical question to see who'll bite."

There was silence, while Jimmy Douglas digested Tristam's words. "OK, but tread very, very carefully Tristam. If even a whisper of this gets out, the plan is useless."

Tristam nodded. "Of course boss. I'll get on it right away."

§

Detective Inspector Basil Coulson and Chief Superintendent Ingram walked through Green Park in the fading afternoon sunlight, two middle-aged men ignored by the few other pedestrians hurrying by. Coulson spoke quietly.

"What we don't know of course—is this fellow part of the original team, or is he operating on his own? If he's part of a team, how big is the support network? If he's a singleton we can probably catch him in time, but looking at the two who tried to kill Talawi and then this Salameh fellow it does appear that there is quite a network." Basil Coulson rubbed his neck tiredly. "I'm not sure that the cap proves much. Jimmy Douglas is convinced the hit man is still around."

"And you aren't?" Chief Superintendent Ingram paused to look at a row of flowers backlit by the sinking sun. In his spare time he was an avid gardener.

"Douglas is very competent and the plan suggested has merit. Frankly, I don't know what to think. If we keep Talawi in England and the next attempt is successful then the fallout will be vicious. But I've a gut feeling that we're missing something in this whole equation."

"Yes, early retirement is the least of our worries if we fail. I spent the afternoon with the Assistant Commissioner of Specialist Operations and Sir John Fowles of the FO and he made it very clear that keeping Talawi secure is a matter of national importance. He also told me that Cheltenham is picking up radio traffic from Iran indicating that the hit was to show Rafsanjani's displeasure at being made to look a fool after he'd publicly lifted the *fatwa* on Rushdie."

"You believe that?"

The older man laughed. "You're getting too cynical Bas. But to answer your question—no, it's too neat. It sets up the very conditions we want to avoid." Ingram stopped. "But we really don't have much choice do we?" He breathed in deeply, savouring the air, fresh after the earlier rain, before turning to face Coulson. "Very well, I'll give Sir John a call first thing in the morning and run the idea of an offshore hideaway past him. Has your team come up with a location?"

"Tentatively we have 3 possible areas. Obviously the USA; usual reasons, friendly relations, good intelli-

gence services etcetera. We've done similar favours for
them in the past so if we can sort out the details I think
that is our best bet. Canada is a good second choice
although their PM is not noted for his Anglophone
sympathies, but we have good ties to CSIS, their security
intelligence service. And finally the Antipodes."

"You can forget Australia or New Zealand."
Ingram shook his head firmly, speaking over his shoulder. "I know Talawi will flatly refuse, he thinks they're
uncouth barbarians who don't appreciate great litera-
ture. I recently read, in the *Sunday Times* literary supple-
ment, that an Aussie reviewer trashed one of his earlier
books and he's never forgiven the whole nation."

Coulson smiled sourly. "Ever wonder what it
would be like to have people jump to your every whim?"

"You don't like him much do you Bas?"

"The truth? No, I don't. I think he's a mean-
spirited son of a bitch. He enjoys hurting people. I
accept that he's a literary genius. I've tried reading his
stuff but it's not for me; not that that means anything, I
don't like Amis's stuff either but my wife loves it."
Coulson shrugged. "Hell, you saw the transcripts of his
affair with Julie Croaker. He screws around like a tomcat
. . ."

Roger Ingram studied his friend's face soberly.
"She's a married woman Bas. It was her call you know.
Talawi is single after all and I'm sure has lots of female
attention."

"Yes, I know, and I'm not excusing her behaviour,
but she is a nice woman, naturally kind and sweet
natured. I've met her socially and her husband is another
mean-spirited bastard. No it's not the affair, God knows
I'm not a Puritan. But it's obvious he enjoys inflicting
pain, especially emotional pain." The two men walked
in silence for a while then Basil spoke again. "I remem-

ber as a teenager we had a fellow in our boxing club, Michaels, Jack Michaels. He was very good, fast and an extremely hard puncher. He eventually had to leave the club—you know why? No one would spar with him. He was emotionally stunted, he boxed to inflict pain. I know that sounds odd, after all one would assume boxing is about inflicting pain. But it's not, not really. In a tournament I watched him keep his opponent, a vastly overmatched opponent, conscious when one clean punch would have ended the fight. It was like watching a cat torture a mouse. Talawi reminds me a lot of Michaels. I often wonder if he only wrote his latest book to piss off the Muslims."

"Hardly Bas." Ingram demurred gently. "I don't think any rational human wants to spend the rest of his life under a sentence of death."

"I know—I know, but the man is a nasty piece of work all the same. Still it's our job, and genius is genius eh?"

Chief Superintendent Ingram lifted a finger. "Hold on, I've just remembered something." He pondered thoughtfully for a second before speaking. "I looked through your staff files earlier today and Sandy Flett, the SAS officer attached to your team, has a sister in Canada. She lives in Vancouver, and is a doctor, a medical doctor. Vancouver might be a good place to consider."

Basil Coulson paused. "Yes, it might be. I know BA have a direct flight and we could probably find a good safe house in the surrounding country. They have excellent communications." He rubbed his jaw. "Hmm, it might be just the place for him to stay while we try to catch our killer here."

"I saw, according to your latest memo, that young Burns has found a likely person to impersonate Talawi."

"I'm damned if I know how Tristam did that. He claims this fellow is the same build and with good makeup could pass for Talawi. He spun some story about offshore work involving a little danger which entailed impersonating an Arab dignitary at a conference. The hook was a fat per diem and a big bonus." Coulson waited until a couple of teenagers had passed. "Of course we don't know if the deal will hold once our actor is told its Talawi he's impersonating. Tris seems very confident that this fellow will jump at the opportunity."

Exiting the park they reached the curb and Chief Superintendent Roger Ingram lifted his hand in a brief signal at the police cruiser parked in the no-parking zone. The cruiser moved toward them. "Right Basil. I'll run the preliminary plan past Sir John. No doubt he'll have to have it approved but I should have something for you by the weekend." The police car slid to a stop and a uniformed constable jumped out to hold the rear door open. "You're looking tired Bas, try and take some time off. That's an order by the way. " Ingram bent to enter the cruiser. "The graveyards are full of indispensable men you know. Love to Sara." The door closed and the police car pulled into the evening traffic.

Chapter 15

Another Country - Canada

"OK, we have a go. Sandy you'll fly to Vancouver. Your cover story is that you're going to see your sister. She's an expert on trauma injuries and you want her to have a look at your knee as well as having a chance to see her again. We've tentatively booked you into the Sylvia Hotel, but you'll sort out your accommodation needs once you arrive, I'm sure. The Sylvia Hotel is reasonably central with access to transportation. Spend the first week getting your bearings; rent a vehicle, the usual. You'll be there about two weeks before Meg and Tristam arrive. I'll be there intermittently, as I've been tasked to run Operation Tanglefoot at this end with Basil Coulson. As soon as you arrive contact the RCMP. Basil has names for you. We need a good safe house. Big enough to take Talawi, the three of you plus three Canadian security people." Jimmy Douglas turned to Meg. "Meg, starting tomorrow, you will attach yourself to Talawi. He has to be persuaded that this is not an option he can refuse. But gently, the man has the ear of some important politico's."

Meg Davidson looked puzzled. "Does he think the threat has diminished?"

"I don't know Meg. Our friend is a pain in the arse to deal with. He's already complaining about the level of security. Too obtrusive he says. Let him know that the threat is still very real." Douglas had no worries about Meg. Of his small team she was the most formidable. If Talawi thought he was going to patronise and push Meg Davidson around he was in for a nasty surprise. He sighed. Oh for a simple war. "Tris, you'll bring your protégé in and read him the Official Secrets Act, then we'll give him a proper briefing, before taking him off to Runnymeade House for training and rehearsals. He'll be incommunicado from his usual friends and family for at least six months. I take it you've advised him to place a cover story with his usual crowd?"

"Yes, he thinks he's off to the Middle East. He's told his friends that it's a documentary production and he doesn't expect to be back for the remainder of the year."

"OK. Small detail, Tris get your hands on a bunch of postcards from Qatar, Bahrain, Kuwait and Saudi and have our man write innocuous messages on each and postdate them. I'll leave that to you. Incidentally, you'll replace me as controller when I visit Vancouver so keep up to speed on all the details. I'm relying on your good judgement so don't cock this up. OK?"

Tristam Burns chuckled, "Sure Boss, I'm on my way." He levered his skinny frame from the chair and made for the door. "Do you want a ride home, Sandy? I'm going right past your place."

Sandy gave a start, "What?" looking at Tristam blankly for a second. "Oh, sorry, I was off woolgathering. Yes, thanks Tris." He stood, picking up the briefing file Jimmy Douglas had given each of them earlier. "Nothing else Jimmy?"

"No. Give me a shout once you've got your feet on the ground, usual drill. Your contacts, phone numbers and Canadian driving licence are in the file plus a little insurance." Jimmy grinned, "Not that I think you'll need it." Sandy flicked open the file, flipping through the stiff pages. He found the sheet he was looking for and grunted with satisfaction.

"Good. I'll remember you in my will old son." He snapped the file shut and picking up his windbreaker followed Tristam out the door. He turned to look at

Meg. "Luck with our friend, Meg." He waited, wondering even as he did so why he had to feel this way.

Meg looked up from her file, her face neutral. "Thanks Sandy, good hunting over the water." She smiled briefly and looked back down at the file on her lap. Sandy nodded and closed the door softly.

Jimmy Douglas watched the exchange with interest. Was Sandy falling or, had Sandy fallen for Meg? Not that I blame him he thought, but Meg doesn't seem that interested. He looked at Meg. "What was that all about?"

Meg stood, brushing down her skirt. "Sandy has a slight crush. It'll pass." She dropped the file into her bag

"He's a good man Meg. We did an op together, three years ago. My reading is that he doesn't go slight on anything."

Meg looked directly at James. "Jimmy, I could tell you to mind your own business but, you are our ops chief so for what it's worth there is nothing going on between Sandy and me. I like him, actually quite a lot, and yes, as you say, he's a good man. I figured that out pretty quickly, but there's no spark, I'm not interested in a relationship, not now, not ever. Sandy has received no encouragement from me and once he accepts that I'm not his type he'll relax."

Jimmy stuck his lower lip out thoughtfully. "As you say Meg. But, you know the rules." He cracked his knuckles before continuing "You are both too valuable to me for me to allow any distractions to get in the way." He was going to say more but stopped himself. She didn't need a lecture, not with her record. "OK Meg, we'll leave it there. Keep me posted on progress with Talawi. If he gets too difficult I'll have a word." He collected the papers on his desk. Meg hesitated, then realised the meeting was over. She had wanted to ex-

plain it wasn't her fault Sandy felt the way he did.
Damn, she didn't want to be taken off the case but
either she or Sandy would be reassigned if it became
obvious they were getting involved. She closed the door
behind her and made for the stairs. The sooner she met
Talawi the better.

§

Ismail Talawi ran stiffened fingers through his thick hair.
"No I will not go, and that is final." His voice, rich and
deep, mellifluous with the smoothness that only an
expensive education can produce, was in keeping with
the rest of the man she thought. Everything matched.
Not only was the man a literary genius, but he had the
build of an Olympic athlete and the strong, handsome
face of a Greek god. When favours had been granted to
mankind Ismail Talawi had been first in line. God did
have a sense of humour after all.

Meg smiled, in an effort to control her temper, are
all genius's such bloody-minded idiots she wondered?
"Mr. Talawi, this is not an option. You don't seem to
grasp the seriousness of your situation. A man has—"

Talawi cut her off in mid sentence. " Don't you
tell me what I do or don't grasp. I damn well am not
going to be jerked around. I can be protected just as
easily here as in Canada, probably better. Explain, why
is it so important that I move to Canada?"

Meg took a deep breath. "We've evidence that
leads us to believe another attempt is possible. It's been
decided at the very highest level that you would be safer
out of England for a while. We don't take these decisions lightly." She felt her temperature rising; who the
hell did this man think he was?

"Oh really, so you don't take decisions lightly,

even if it's going to fuck up my life completely. I've
been to Canada lady, and it's a terminal yawn. It happens to be the most boring country with the most boring
people God ever allowed to breathe. No, and again no.
You'll go back to your masters and tell them I'll not
consider Canada and that's final."

Meg's mouth fell open. She stared at the man in
front of her. Sweet Jesus did this self opinionated,
bombastic clown realise anything—anything at all? Her
mouth snapped shut into a thin line and the violet eyes
hardened. Talawi, looking away, did not see the subtle
changes taking place. "You pompous jerk." Meg stuck
her face inches away from the stunned author's face.
"You self-indulgent, pompous prick. You write a book
that pisses off hundreds of millions of people. You
caused the death of two people in your vehicle and the
death of a third we found later. There is a professional,
a very good professional, out there looking for you and
you have the nerve, the bloody nerve to tell us what we
can or can't do." She felt her pulse racing and fought to
remain calm.

Stunned, Ismail Talawi stared at her. Never in
recent years had he been spoken to like this, and by a
woman of all people. Something in the glittering eyes
facing him caused him to pause. His hands trembled
with suppressed rage but he controlled himself. "A third?
What are you talking about? I know nothing of a third
casualty."

Meg exhaled, feeling the tension flow out of her.
That had felt good, but it was probably the end of her
part in this program. Talawi would rush to complain and
Jimmy would have no option but to remove her. She
shook her head, the long, dark hair sliding like a gleam-
ing black helmet around the strong face. "No, and you
are not supposed to know. What makes you think that

just because you know a few people in power you are
privy to things beyond your competence to deal with?"
She sighed. "You may be a genius, only time will prove
that. Right now you are acting like an imbecile. Have
you forgotten that even the President of the United
States was assassinated?" She walked across the room to
retrieve her bag from the ornate sofa she'd left it on.
Looking over her shoulder she spoke quietly. "I apologise for my outburst. I will have someone senior come
down and have a word. Goodbye Mr. Talawi, I doubt if
we'll meet again." She was reaching for the door handle
when Talawi spoke.

"Wait, please." For the first time in a long time,
Ismail Talawi realised that he had behaved badly and
this woman was not like others he'd met in recent years.
If they'd sent a man perhaps he would not have spoken
as he had, but then perhaps he would've. She was right,
he was behaving like an imbecile. "Please, it is I who
should apologise. I beg your pardon. I have no excuses."
He smiled brilliantly. "Perhaps being treated with respect beyond what is normal gives one an inflated sense
of self importance. What did you call me—he rolled his
eyes at the ceiling—a self-indulgent, pompous prick?"
He laughed. "It's been years since someone has told me
truly what they think. Please Ms. Davidson sit down, I
promise no more outbursts, I'll listen to the plan."

Meg hesitated. The change was remarkable, the
man could charm the pants off—oh no mister, not me
she thought, grimly. He'd apologised though, that takes
character and he seemed genuinely contrite. She let go
of the doorknob and, keeping her face neutral, turned to
face him. "Mr. Talawi . . . "

"Ismail, please."

She nodded, "Very well, . . . Ismail. My partner
and I will be working closely with you for the duration

of your stay in Canada. It's critically important that you have confidence in our professionalism. If we ask you to do something you must accept that it is for your own good."

Talawi smiled broadly, "Now who is being pompous?" He lifted his hands in surrender as she started to frown, his head cocked quizzically to one side.

She tried not to laugh but failed. "Sorry, obviously you realise that." She drew a file out of her bag and opened it as she sat down on the sofa. "We have an agent, my partner, locating a safe house in or near Vancouver. He . . . "

"Thank God for small mercies. If one must go to Canada, Vancouver is the best. Montreal or Quebec City aren't bad, but the rest—ugh! It's like being sent to Leeds on a slow sunday afternoon." He raised his hands in surrender again. "Sorry, sorry, I won't interrupt again."

"As I said, we are actively looking for a comfortable safe house. The RCMP and units of CSIS are assisting." She noted his puzzled look and explained. "The Canadian Security Intelligence Service. Once we have a secure location we'll arrange transportation. We're assuming that your stay in Canada will be reasonably short, probably no more than three months." She flipped to another page. "Your present protection will continue with the existing support unit, until departure. Once you arrive in Canada the RCMP will assume those duties."

"And where do you fit in? You did say that you and your partner would be supplying aid, did you not?" Talawi was looking at her closely, and Meg answered without looking up.

"Yes, that's correct. Sandy and I will be co-ordinating liaison with the Canadian authorities and be continuously in touch with you of course."

"Good, I still prefer English spoken properly. This Sandy you speak of, is that short for Sandra?" He would accept one woman but two? He thought not.

"What? Oh no, his name is Alex, but everyone calls him Sandy. Afraid of having two women as body-guards Mr. Talawi?" She laughed, a soft throaty sound. "I've heard you're a bit of a chauvinist. If you hope to make genius category you're going to have to change."

Well, well, this woman was perceptive as well as tough. Talawi looked at Meg properly for the first time. He liked what he saw. Life in Canada might not be so bad after all.

Chapter 16

Agent in place

Gip Lawrence pushed his chair back, frowning. The message handed to him by a servant trembled in his hand. Puzzled, Dragovic and Martin Dreyfus watched him closely. Neither spoke.

"I have to return to England. Something critical to our mission has come up."

"Gip, you are not well enough to travel again so soon. What about Martin or me going instead." Dragovic's face showed his concern. For the past week Nick and Martin had noted signs of deterioration in Lawrence. The painkillers were no longer as effective and it was only through the exercise of sheer willpower that Gip Lawrence was able to function in a normal fashion. Dragovic looked over the table at Martin Dreyfus, who nodded.

"I agree with Nick. Let one of us do this."

"Thank you both. I appreciate the thought. But our mole knows only me. That's the way it was set up and he'll execute an immediate cutout should someone else be brought in. He's far too valuable to risk. I'm surprised he took a chance on contacting me through the network. Whatever it is, it must be important. Perhaps a clear shot at Talawi, I don't know, but we'll see." He stopped, panting slightly. Then continued. "In any event I need to see my surgeon in Harley Street. There are some new drugs the British have just developed. It will be a perfect cover, after all—" he smiled grimly "—I have a cast iron alibi."

Three days later, Martin and Dragovic watched through the windows as the helicopter hung almost motionless before touching down on the cobbles in front of the farmhouse. Two of the farm security men ducked under the slowly rotating blades and helped Gip Lawrence out. Holding his arms around each of their shoulders the two men half-carried, half-walked Gip into the building. The helicopter turbines whined slowly down to a stop.

Later, after Gip had a brief rest, the three men met in the great lounge. A servant handed drinks to Gip and Martin and a soft drink to Dragovic.

"Talawi is being moved to Canada. You'll be on your way to Canada tonight Nick. That is why the helicopter is standing by. Martin, you'll follow next week." He paused, his breathing laboured, the sound harsh in the quiet room. "The British are moving Talawi to Vancouver. We have a name." Again he paused to catch his breath. Dragovic watched his face. Gip was dying; that was obvious, and he felt a sudden wave of anger at the injustice of it. Gip was speaking again and they leaned forward to listen. "There is a doctor in Vancouver, her name is Anne Flett, Dr. Flett is a surgeon at St Paul's hospital. Her brother is one of the security team from England who will be protecting Talawi in Canada." He paused again, but this time, after regaining his breath, took a large sip of whiskey from the deeply cut lead crystal glass. Holding up the glass Gip smiled, "I'll miss this most of all." The Waterford crystal reflected the colour of the amber liquid across his hand and face from the light of the hanging lamp.

"You must arrive in Canada before he does, Nick. That'll ensure your bona fides. You must find a way to get close to the woman. My information is that she and her brother are close. He leaves for Vancouver on Friday. That gives you enough time to arrive ahead of him if you fly to New York from Rome tonight and then on to Vancouver. The ticket is in my briefcase with a supply of US dollars. There are also two credit cards in your name. Use your Cartwright passport. It's clean; there's nothing on their files in that regard. The file with details of your cover, as a businessman in Electro optics based in Germany, is with the ticket." The long statement seemed to exhaust him and he paused for a long time. Neither listener moved. They knew the answers would come. Finally Gip spoke again. "Go now Nick. Martin will follow in a few days. He will stay at the same hotel, the Hotel Vancouver, and his name will be Martin Dreyer, a Swiss businessman. Meet him there in five days." He held out his hand. "We will not meet again this side of Paradise, my friend. May Allah, *The Merciful, The Compassionate* give you success, and guide you and keep you. I've enjoyed your company and your friendship, and remember, Nick—Martin, even though an infidel, will protect you with his life." The smile was tinged with sadness, but the eyes and grip were firm.

Dragovic closed both his hands over Gip's. "As Allah wills, my friend. We are but dust in the eyes of the most high, yet I believe you have brought honour to his name. I will not fail."

"I know that Nick. I will die in peace. Go now, you do not have much time." Giving Gip Lawrence's hand a final squeeze Dragovic went to his room to pack the few items he would need to travel. Clothes could be bought once he arrived in Canada. He felt a great emptiness, not the sadness he'd expected. Perhaps, he thought, it was because he'd known Gip Lawrence was dying from the moment they'd met that he felt this way. He held his hands out looking for signs of trembling, but they were rock steady. Yet something was not right. Why had he surprised himself with that earlier wave of anger? Taking a deep breath before zipping up the soft

case he cast a last look around the room checking to see
that he'd forgotten nothing.

§

Anne Flett put the phone down; unaware that she had a
broad grin on her face. It was a typical early spring day
on the West Coast. A cold front moving in from the
Pacific Ocean bringing rain and a thick fog that tore
itself to pieces on the metal balcony railing around the
apartment.

"Sandy's plane is on time. I'm leaving now, are you
sure you don't want to come?"

"Annie, it's not due for another two hours girl.
Why must you go so early?"

Anne Flett looked at her husband sprawled on the
couch. He knew she hated being called Annie, yet
persisted in using the diminutive. She took a deep
breath. Nothing was going to spoil today. When Sandy
had phoned to say that he was coming over on holiday
and needed her to have an independent look at his knee
she'd nearly screamed with excitement. Only the pres-
ence of Sam MacGuire in her office prevented a yell
blasting down the hospital corridor. She'd planned to
visit England several times over the past month, now
that Sandy was working in London, but work always
intervened at the last minute. Now he was coming to
her. She smiled through the huge picture windows at the
gray mist outside the building. Nothing could spoil her
mood today; not even the female voice on the phone
that had asked for Mike then abruptly hung up when she
had answered.

Mike had been dismissive when queried. "Hell, I
don't know. Half the people I deal with in commercial
real estate think they work for the CIA. There is so

much competition right now that, whoever it was, he decided that even speaking to the wrong voice might give something away."

"It was a female voice Michael." Knowing even as she uttered the words that it was the wrong signal to send.

"So? Since when has my field been the exclusive preserve of men?" He'd looked at her crossly. "Grow up Annie. If I have a girlfriend, do you honestly think she is going to phone me at home—at the weekend?" Later when he'd gone through to have a shower before brunch she'd dialed the recall and copied down the number. Feeling slightly uncomfortable she decided that perhaps later she would check it. Lately there had been other signs, but work occupied her waking moments and that was probably the problem. Mike complained that he did not see enough of her. Yet when she rearranged her schedule to fit in with one of his requests they invariably ended up at some power dinner with various politicians he was trying to impress or win favours from.

Watching the fog she wondered if they were mismatched. Michael almost resented her work. He never asked how her day had gone. When she tried to talk about it he turned the conversation to something else. When they'd married, the second time for him, the first for her, he'd been a totally different person. They'd met a year after his early departure from Canada's Foreign Affairs Department. Mike Monroe had been on the fast track to a senior diplomatic position when the famous hostage-taking incident at the Empress Hotel took place, an incident for which he'd been blamed. Rather than see his career sidelined with a series of innocuous diplomatic postings until he retired, Michael left the Diplomatic Corps citing injuries sustained during the hostage taking. The Federal Government breathed a

sigh of relief and with uncharacteristic generosity
ensured he left with a handsome severance package.

Using contacts on the West Coast to start a commercial real estate enterprise, in the days when the West
Coast was awash with Hong Kong and Japanese money,
Michael Monroe was hugely successful. Even now, with
much less money available, Michael was still one of the
top brokers in the city. She smiled wryly at her reflection
in the glass. You had to give him that, he worked very
hard at everything he did and in the beginning he'd made
her feel like a princess. Was it partly her fault she wondered? Do people simply drift apart when their careers
take over? She turned to her husband. "Will you be here
when we get back?"

"Probably, although Sam Kwok of Leonid Developments mentioned that he might want a meeting today.
But," he levered himself upright, "unless he calls soon I
imagine the deal is on hold. Yes I'll be here. Do you
realise that the last time I saw Sandy was at our wedding?" He made a wry face. "God how time flies, has it
been six years already?"

Anne debated giving her husband a quick kiss but
as he made no move to rise she continued heading to
the door. "I'll call from the airport if there is any delay.
Could you put the coffee on at three? We have some of
that special Omitepe blend he likes." She waved and the
door closed behind her. Michael Monroe waited for five
minutes before picking up the phone and stabbing
angrily at the raised numbers.

"Jennie? Yes it's me. I thought I told you never to
call me at home. I don't care how important it is, Jesus
woman, can't you even think up a reasonable cover
story? Putting the phone down like that is just plain
dumb. Jenny . . .Jen . . . look, don't cry. Yes we can
meet." He looked at his watch. "In half an hour at that

coffee stop on Broadway in Kits. Yes, me too." Putting
the phone down he scooped up a leather case containing
his car keys, and went into the bedroom to pick up his
wallet and credit cards.

§

Dragovic stirred his coffee thoughtfully. His arrival had
gone smoothly, the Immigration officer barely glancing
at his red British EU passport and asking only a few
perfunctory questions before stamping it. Two 747s, one
from Asia and his from New York, had landed within
minutes of each other and no doubt the sheer volume
of humanity had something to do with his brisk transit
through Customs and Immigration. Taking a taxi to the
Hotel Vancouver, he'd asked the reception desk clerk, a
young woman obviously enamoured of his upper class
British accent, that he not be disturbed and, after a
quick shower, slept solidly for six hours despite the time
change.

Now he sat in the hotel coffee shop after a large
breakfast. It was a cool gray morning outside with
foghorns sounding in the distance. The first order of
business would be to find a rental vehicle. He'd been
supplied with both French and UK driving licences and
as an added precaution an international driving licence
was in his briefcase. He flicked through the tourist
brochure he'd picked up at the airport, giving various
rental agencies. Today he'd use his credit cards and draw
some Canadian funds in order to establish bona fides.
The thick sheaf of US dollars Gip had given him could
be converted into Canadian currency as and when
needed. Being so close to the American border and, with
the weak Canadian dollar attracting scores of American
tourists, changing US currency anywhere in the lower

mainland was a simple matter. Glancing at the weather outside he decided to purchase some warmer clothes and, catching the waiter's eye, asked for directions to a store where he might outfit himself.

Leaving the Hotel he was surprised at how mild the weather really was. The temperature must be above 10C he thought and, feeling well fed and rested strode briskly along the sidewalk stretching his legs. Finding the department store that had been recommended he selected a pair of warmer slacks and two turtleneck sweaters. The assistant, an older man, expertly sizing Nick up, offered suggestions and led him to the rack holding sports coats and windbreakers. Half an hour later looking at the pile of clothes lying on the counter, Nick smiled wryly at himself. For nearly eight years he'd been content with the minimum of clothing, the minimum of everything. Now he was in a city that shouted consumerism, blatant excess, from every shop window and he was indulging himself like a spoilt yuppie.

After Bosnia and his long convalescence in Libya he'd often wondered who was paying for his treatment and expenses, but his inquiries were always deflected with a gentle smile. "It is nothing Cedar, more is spent in a hour by a Saudi prince in Monaco. You've earned every dinar. Rest, recover—money is not your concern." He knew Gadaffi helped various Muslim causes and suspected that a large part of the money expended on his treatment had come from that source.

Paying with a credit card, Nick asked that the bulk of his purchases be sent to the hotel and, slipping on the newly purchased lightweight raincoat, set off to explore downtown. The tourist brochure in his hotel room described Vancouver as an attractive modern city, surrounded by breathtaking mountains and considered as one of the five most beautiful cities in the world.

Wrapped around Burrard Inlet with its stunning harbour
and set between the Coastal Mountains and Pacific
Ocean, even on a gray day, it's a spectacular city to visit.
The mountains were now visible as a cold front moved
through.

But Nick paid no attention to the scenery. He
wanted to get his bearings quickly and, looking at the
tourist map from the hotel was gratified to note that the
city is conveniently laid out in grid pattern. Striding
along West Georgia Street he turned down Howe to
reach Canada Place and the waterfront. Leaning on the
rail he watched a floatplane touch down and taxi up to
the dock. Looking across the Inlet at the North Shore he
could see houses gradually emerging as the low mist
burnt off. For the next two hours he criss-crossed the
inner city, memorising the main features of the downtown core.

Hailing a cruising taxi he asked to be taken to St
Paul's hospital. He wanted to see where Anne Flett
worked. As yet Dragovic was not sure how he was going
to meet her. Sitting in the back of the taxi he ran over
what he knew. Her husband, Michael Monroe, was in
commercial real estate; perhaps if he made enquires—
there must be a real estate organisation—central clearing house or something. He pushed the problem to the
back of his mind. Let it gestate he told himself; right
now getting his bearings was all-important.

§

Dragovic looked at the address the girl had given him.
The real estate office of Poseidon-G Developments had
been easy to find and his cover story of being an German manufacturer of hi-tech underwater cameras looking for a site to build a subsidiary plant brought immedi-

ate attention from the salesman manning the desk on a slow Saturday morning.

"No." Nick lifted his hand to stop the flow of sales talk. He'd realised quickly that the man was a relatively low-level employee tasked to man the weekend shift. What he, Nick Cartwright, needed was an introduction to meet Michael Monroe. "Please understand, I arrived yesterday and this is a very preliminary enquiry. I heard of your company from a colleague and wanted to do a reconnaissance before flying down to Washington State tomorrow to see what's available there. I'd hoped to meet with Mr. Monroe and perhaps discuss my requirements."

"Please, Mr. Cartwright. Let me phone Mr. Monroe at home. I'm sure he'll want to speak to you." The salesman was sweating. His job was on the line, this seemed to be an important client and Monroe would skin him alive if the man walked out and bought property in Seattle. He lifted the phone and punched in the number. He waited and, after several rings, the answering machine dryly informed him that Mike Monroe and/ or Dr. Anne Flett were not at home and to please leave a message. Stammering, the salesman, whose name was David Lincoln, gave the gist of what 'Mr. Cartwright' had told him earlier, giving Dragovic's hotel room number and the best time to contact him.

"Mr. Cartwright I'm certain Mr. Monroe will call you. I'll call him again this afternoon just to make sure he has the message."

"Very well." Nick, standing to leave, noticed a large photograph on the wall of the main office. A picture of two men shaking hands in front of an ornate gateway. He pointed with his chin. "What's that about?"

"That's the opening of our Squamish Country Club and Housing Estate project, Falling Waters. That's

Mr. Monroe and the Premier." Eager to impress the tall, unsmiling man he babbled on, not noticing the close attention Nick was giving to the photograph. "It cost nearly a billion dollars and it was completed just last year."

"Hmm. I take it this is Mr. Monroe." Dragovic pointed.

"Yes, that's Mike and John Halliwell."

"Well, thank you for your help, Mr. Lincoln." Dragovic walked to where he'd parked the rental Volvo, pleased to see that the parking meter still had a few minutes left. Once on the road he soon found a telephone kiosk and pulled over. Flipping quickly through the alphabet, he saw an entry for Monroe. M., Poseidon-G Developments, and recognised the office number from the salesman's business card. There was no other entry under Monroe. The man had an unlisted number. He flipped back through the huge directory to Flett. Dr. A., and alongside a note advising the caller to contact St Paul's Hospital. So, Nick grunted to himself, both had unlisted numbers. He thought for a moment, then dialed the number the salesman in the office had called. Dragovic had a quick memory for numbers, and watching Lincoln dial he'd memorised the numbers out of habit. As expected, there was no reply except the answering machine. He called directory assistance and explained, to the assistant on duty, his difficulty in getting through. The girl, disarmed by the aristocratic accent and that the caller knew the unlisted number, was helpful in advising how to locate Monroe's address. Smiling faintly, Dragovic went back to the rental car and opened the map he'd purchased earlier. The hi-rise complex where Anne Flett and Mike Monroe lived was located on False Creek. Looking at his watch, he decided he had enough time to have a good look at the building.

Dragovic found an empty parking bay near the

water and leaving the vehicle walked back towards the very modern complex, clad in stainless steel and green glass, towering above the banks of False Creek. Walking toward the entrance, a dramatic canopy of steel and glass suspended on cables, Nick saw a man coming through the door. The man spoke briefly to the door-man, who promptly bent to a microphone grill set into the wall, obviously ordering a vehicle from the parking garage below the building. With a start Dragovic realised the man was Michael Monroe and, turning sharply, retraced his steps, certain that Monroe had not noticed him among the other strollers heading to and from the building. Nick returned to the Volvo, started the engine, and waited for Monroe's vehicle to pass his position.

Later, in reporting the subsequent events to Martin Dreyfus, he was at loss to explain why he'd followed Mike Monroe to Broadway and taken a seat in the café where Monroe was meeting Jenny Lui. "I had a feeling, I don't know why, that I should find out what I could. Why so soon after arrival? Again I don't know. Perhaps having time on my hands helped. And yes, he could have seen me, but I was careful and he didn't."

§

Anne Flett watched the first passengers come through the arrivals gate. Impatiently she stood on tiptoe trying to peer over the man and woman in front of her. The man, sensing her closeness turned irritably then realised he was looking down at the top of Anne's head. With a grin he moved enough to let her slip to the front of the crowd. Anne smiled gratefully, ignoring the wife's bale-ful glare, and then nearly missed seeing Sandy pushing a trolley laden with two suitcases.

"Sandy!" She waved frantically and flinging her

arms out was lifted in a bear hug that nearly cracked her ribs.

"Anne, you're too thin." He held her at arm's length; a broad grin on his face as other passengers flowed past them. "Ah, but it's good to see you." He ruffled her short hair affectionately just as he used to do when they were teenagers.

She hugged his arm, not wanting to let him go for a moment. "How are Mom and Dad Sandy? Mom sounded tired the last time we spoke." She scanned his face, trying to register the changes that must have taken place after all the places he'd been. It was the same boyish, open-faced, Sandy. She remembered their father saying of Sandy years ago 'The face of a choirboy and the heart of a leopard. Sandy would make the perfect spy'. But there was a wariness in the eyes she'd not seen before, a tightness to the lips and she noticed his quick restless scanning of faces around them.

"Good, both in excellent health. I popped down to the farm to see them before flying over. Mom gave me a lot of stuff to bring you." He gestured to the second suitcase. "Why do you think I needed more than one? I have a letter in my briefcase as well."

"Put the trolley there." She indicated with a pointed finger. "I have a car outside. Oh Sandy it's so good to have you here. How long can you stay?" She felt him tense, then just as quickly relax.

"I don't know Anne, probably a month or two. I'll tell you about it in the car." He took a deep breath and, lifting both suitcases, said, "OK Sis, lead on."

Turning out of the car park on to the main road Anne Flett looked at her brother quizzically. "It's more than a holiday then Sandy? Are you here on a job? Can you tell me or not?"

"Not much old girl. Yes, it's a job, but nothing too

onerous, certainly not dangerous. Actually I've been sent
out here, I suspect, for a bit of R and R." He grinned
wickedly. "They don't use crocks for the heavy stuff so
you can relax."

She took a quick look at his face before turning
back to concentrate on the traffic. What he said made
sense, but she knew Sandy of old and he could keep
secrets. She remembered his award of the DSO for
something dangerous done in Ireland. For six months no
one in the family had known until Colonel Johnstone,
casually in passing, mentioned the medal to their father,
naturally assuming the old man knew. When asked why,
Sandy had shrugged and grinned. "Meant to, sorry—
pressure of work and all that." Oh yes, she thought, he
could keep secrets all right. Reaching across she gave his
arm a squeeze with her free hand. "Promise me you'll
try to relax. You're looking very drawn. You really need
a holiday. No mountain climbing or any of that stuff—
promise."

"No mountain climbing. The knee won't allow I'm
afraid. Although it's been getting better, hmm you've
just given me an idea . . ."

"Sandy!" A small fist hit his arm. "Don't even
tease me. I mean it; I'll have Ken Harmon the knee
specialist put you in traction for a while. You won't
even walk much less climb." His laughter filled the cab
and she smiled. He would never change. Sandy had last
visited Vancouver for her wedding six years ago and as
they drove back into the city she pointed out the new
construction around False Creek. She indicated her
apartment, sparkling in sunlight, which had finally
emerged from behind the cloud blanket covering the city
for the past week. It was a good omen.

"How's Mike? All well with the business I trust?"
Sandy and Mike were totally different in makeup. Where

Sandy had been born to wealth and cared nothing for money, Michael Monroe knew what it was to be poor and only driving ambition and brilliance had brought him the success he craved. Money to Mike was the key that opened doors, that gave him a luxurious lifestyle, but more importantly it brought the respect of the people that mattered to him. Sandy liked his brother-in-law and was slightly amused at Mike's obsession with having only the best of everything. For someone who had existed for weeks in the jungles of Borneo on a handful of rice and returned to base camp 10 kilos lighter, and enjoyed the experience, appearances were not a priority.

"He's fine." Watching the smooth lovely planes of her face tense slightly, Sandy wondered what the problem was. "The trouble is, we hardly see each other these days," she continued. "Both of us are working too hard. I think it's high time we took a week off our respective jobs and maybe your visit will be the excuse we need. He's at home now. I asked him to have the coffee ready." She swung the Range Rover down the ramp to the underground parking, activating the security gate with the remote clipped to the sun visor. Minutes later they were sliding up the outside of the building in the glass cage to the penthouse apartment.

"My God, what a view." The sun now fully emerged after the rain showed a sparkling vista stretching to the south. The horizon, washed clean of pollution by the recent rain, showed the distant mountains to the east standing hard and sharp against the sky. "You must love living here."

"Yes, it's lovely, isn't it. I sometimes feel guilty at having so much. The apartment is huge."

"C'mon Sis, you've earned it. And heaven knows that Mike has done his share. Don't be so Calvinistic.

The best revenge is . . ."

" . . .living well." She finished the phrase for him. "I know, but I see so much misery in my job that it makes one wonder about the justice of it all." She keyed in the security code and the ornately carved wooden door slid silently to one side disappearing into a wall pocket.

"Ta da. Please enter our humble abode." She dropped her handbag and coat on a low bench and called out, "Mike, we're here. How's the coffee?" She turned to Sandy, who looked around the entrance hall the size of a small conference room. Original paintings lined the walls and a lovely terra cotta sculpture of a stooping angel lifting a stick-thin child from the ground stood in the middle of the room. Anne noticed the direction of his eyes. "Mike bought that for our first anniversary. It's from the Vortex Gallery on Salt Spring Island. Mike commissioned it from Kathy Venter, the sculptor. It's wonderful don't you think? If we ever have to leave all this, that sculpture is the only thing I would not give up." Anne walked into the main sitting room. Puzzled, she called again. "Mike, where are you?" Leaving Sandy to study the room she pushed open the swing doors to the kitchen area, before turning to check the bedrooms and bathroom area. "He's not here. He said he would be here." Sandy saw her blink, her eyes brighter than normal, then her face cleared. "Oh damn, he said something about Sam Kwok of Leonid Developments calling him. Damn it. Now you see how work is interfering in both our lives. He can't even wait for his brother-in-law to get here. Oh Sandy I'm sorry."

"It's OK Anne. I know what it's like; you don't have to apologise. You don't run an empire by lying on the beach."

"For once, just for once, he might have tried."

§

The object of Anne's anger sat in a small coffee shop, on Broadway in Kitsilano, across the table from a smartly dressed woman who sipped from her cup. She had smooth olive skin and a composed, expressionless face framed with glossy black hair, smooth as a raven's wing, indicating her Eurasian background. Jenny Liu was one of Vancouver's most successful real estate agents, rumoured to have made at least a million dollars in two huge real estate deals on the North Shore. Her face showed signs of tears but when she spoke her voice was calm.

"What are you going to do?"

"I don't know. I didn't expect this, not from you. I thought you would be more careful."

"Me? What about you, why is it my fault? Damn you Michael." The tears started again.

"OK, OK. Hell Jenny no one reacts well to being blindsided like this. You say the test is positive but let's wait a week or two to be certain and test again. Are you sure you want to keep the child? You know how easy it is to deal with situations like this these days."

"Situation, is that what it is to you? Don't you have any feelings at all? You don't get it do you?" She shook her head sadly. "I misjudged you Michael. That's not something I do very often with people." She pushed her chair back and started to rise. "Don't worry, I'll handle this on my own. If I decide to keep the baby, you'll not be affected."

"Jenny, please. Wait." He gripped her hand. "Give me a few days. Hell I don't know how I feel. I never wanted kids and Anne has never made a fuss about not having any, but—now—" He lifted both hands help-lessly. "Damn it. I need to get my thoughts in order.

Look, we both agreed when we started this relationship that it would not interfere with either of our marriages."

"But it has Michael. I'm not going to stay with Reg, no matter what happens. He and I have been estranged for months. He'll know the child is not his and will press for a divorce. If I wish to protect myself and my assets I need to move quickly." She smiled bitterly. "Unlike you he is not a wealthy man."

"Jenny give me a few days, a week. I'll call you as soon as I've worked this through. After all it's not every day a man finds out he's going to be a father." He smiled tightly, the genesis of an idea forming in his mind. "Look, don't do anything for a few days. If we are going to . . . well leave it with me." He noticed the flare of hope in her eyes and thought for a second that he should simply put an end to this now. After all, she'd already said that she would handle the situation on her own. But damn it, she was exciting in bed, exciting and stimulating to be with. She understood the development game almost as well as he did. She enjoyed money and power . . . but love? He stood. "Look I have to get back. Anne's brother is arriving from England and I promised to be there." He threw some money on the table. "I'll call you after the weekend." He bent forward and kissed her gently. "See you soon." Jenny Liu watched him cross the street to where his flame red BMW sat. Her hands clenched tight under the tabletop. She knew she was in love with him. She also suspected he had no intention of leaving his wife for her. The tears started again and angrily she brushed her eyes with her handkerchief as she rose and left the café. She didn't notice the man sitting in the corner pay his bill and follow at a distance as she went to her car.

§

Anne Flett handed her brother a steaming mug of coffee. "It's that Omitepe blend you like so much. Whenever Mike goes over to Salt Spring Island he picks up a packet. There's a volunteer group on the island that brings the coffee in from Omitepe in Nicuaragua. They've adopted the Omitepe growers as a community project." She plopped down into a large black leather easy chair. "I wonder if Mike has left a message on the machine." She looked at Sandy affectionately. "You'll stay with us. I've organised the spare bedroom—would you believe this place has three—all with bathrooms en-suite."

Sandy took a sip of his coffee before replying. "No I'm afraid not Sis. The firm has booked me in at a place called the Sylvia on Robson Street. I'll need to come and go on an irregular basis and you don't want someone disrupting your lives."

Anne made a face. "I thought you might say that, but please, will you stay tonight? I've invited a few friends over to meet you. It's very casual and you can book in to your hotel tomorrow."

Sandy looked at her over the rim of his cup. "Of course, but only if you give me another half cup of coffee. I assume Mike is in agreement?"

"Yes, we spoke about it this morning. Speaking of Mike, let me check the answering machine." Anne walked to the phone set into an alcove and touched the play button. The first message was from a man called Lincoln at the downtown office asking Mike to call a prospective client. It sounded important. Then there was a second caller who did not leave a message. Anne frowned, was it that woman again? On a sudden impulse she pulled out the number she'd copied earlier. It was the number from the woman who'd put the phone down without speaking. Anne dialed the number. The phone rang several times, then an answering machine advised her that Jenny Liu and Reg Kipling were not at home and to please leave a message. She replaced the receiver, puzzled. The name Jenny Liu was familiar, then it hit her, of course the woman who'd pulled off two spectacular real estate deals with a Hong Kong billionaire and had made a lot of money in commissions. Her face had been on the cover of *BC Business,* a magazine that Mike subscribed to. Anne felt a wave of relief wash over her. Mike had been right; it had been a business call. She shook herself. Damn she hated feeling so suspicious and felt slightly soiled. Such behavior was not normal for her.

"You must tell Mike how much I enjoy this coffee. It was good of him to remember." Sandy was standing by the huge picture window looking over the city.

"Do I hear my name being taken in vain?" Mike Monroe walked through the entrance. "Sandy, it's good to see you again man." He gave Sandy a huge hug before pushing him back to look at him. Mike genuinely liked his brother-in-law. At the wedding he and Sandy had talked for a long time and found they had a commonality of interest in fly fishing and modern small arms. "How's the knee? Such a bummer that it happened, but I guess it could have been a lot worse. Anne says that it's almost back to normal."

Sandy chuckled, "Actually, it's been fine for quite a while but, I'm milking the disability thing for all I'm worth. Managed to get sent out here on a make-work project, which gave me the chance to see you two. How's the print-your-own money business?"

"Slow, very slow but we soldier on. Sorry I wasn't here to greet you but had an urgent call to meet a colleague. He's looking to unload some assets. Now—" he slapped his hands together "—let me get you a drink. I know it's not sundown yet but it's a special day after all."

Sandy hesitated, then shrugged, "A beer, any sort."

"Anne?" Mike turned to his wife. Anne looked at her husband with a puzzled look on her face. "You said he. Did Sam phone?"

"What, oh you mean this morning? Yes, he phoned just after you left. We had a coffee downtown. Now, what can I get you?"

"Oh, a glass of white wine. I think there's some left in the bottle in the fridge." She watched Monroe walk through the archway into the kitchen. Why had he lied? There were only two recent calls on the memory board, one from his office, and one that had left no message. His cellular had been in the Range Rover, she'd noticed it as she left to pick up Sandy and hers was in her purse.

"Here you go Sandy. It's a local draft from a microbrewery I have an interest in. Tell me what you think. Here's your wine, Anne. Now, a toast—to family."

Touching glasses they repeated, "To family." Anne, remembering, pointed to the phone. "There was a call for you on the machine, from your office, and it sounded important. The man sounded desperate."

Wiping beer foam from his lips with a napkin, Mike put his glass down. "Desperate you say. Well I guess I'd better call. Excuse me for a second."

Sandy wiped his own lips. "This is not half bad. A pity you don't drink beer Anne. Having a husband with a stake in a brewery sounds OK to me." He looked toward the window. "While Mike is doing business come and point out a few landmarks for me." He draped his arm over Anne's shoulders and listened intently as she indicated various landmarks, both old and new. A few minutes later Mike's voice caused them to turn.

"English businessman, just flown in from Germany, wants to look at industrial sites." Coming back into the room, Mike glanced at a piece of paper in his hand. "Fellow's name is Cartwright, Nick Cartwright. I managed to catch him at the Hotel Vancouver, just got in apparently. He's leaving for Seattle tomorrow morning. I invited him to come this evening." He glanced at Sandy. "I hope you don't mind. Thought it might be good to have another Brit in amongst us colonials."

Anne scowled at her husband. "Be honest, Mike. You thought you could do some business before he leaves."

Mike picked up his beer, draining it in one long swallow. He pointed at Sandy's glass. "Another for you—yes." He reached for Sandy's glass and grinned at Anne. "Of course I hope to do some business. I might even convince him to put off his trip to Seattle. Don't forget, darling, times are tough and the pickings slim. But, I did think that it might be good to have another Brit in the mix to welcome Sandy. Don't always assume the worst, love of mine."

Chapter 17

Lightning strike

The main living room easily accommodated the twenty plus guests that stood in small groups talking. A maid in a crisp white and blue uniform moved among the guests refilling empty glasses and handing out trays of finger food. The floor to ceiling curtains were drawn back and for a change the sky was clear giving a breathtaking view of the city lights, spread like diamonds on black velvet, below them. Dragovic sipped his Scotch, an 18-year or older single malt he surmised. Arriving later than most guests he'd been met at the door by Anne Flett.

"Mr. Cartwright?" Standing in the open doorway and backlit by the lights from the room behind her she'd greeted him with a smile. He remembered the sudden hollow surge that punched his heart making him catch his breath and could see nothing but the lovely face looking up at him. He nearly dropped the flowers he was holding. The room behind disappeared and only her face looking up at him seemed clear and sharp in contrast to the haze surrounding her. Taking a deep breath he steadied himself.

"Yes, I'm Nick Cartwright. You must be Mrs. Monroe." He held out the flowers. "You must forgive me I didn't have much time to choose."

"Oh, they're just lovely, thank you. Sarah—" she turned to the maid who'd arrived behind her "—please put these in the Chinese vase and put them on the main table." Her eyes had not left his face. She held out her hand. "Please call me Anne. Come and meet the others." Dragovic took a deep breath, what the hell was happening to him? First the rage at Gip's imminent death and now this electric jolt that ran up his arm as she held his hand. This was nonsense, he must be suffering the delayed effects of the Salameh killing and all the stress.

Anne, still holding his hand led him into a group near the window. She let go of his hand and smiled up at a stocky man dressed casually in tan slacks and open necked shirt. Dragovic recognised Sandy Flett instantly. This was the CID undercover man he'd seen leaving Salameh's apartment over the newsagents before he'd gone up and killed the man. Controlling his face with difficulty he forced a polite smile. Sandy turned from the woman he'd been talking to as Anne pulled his sleeve.

"Sandy, this is Mr. Cartwright, the businessman Mike dragooned to come this evening. Mr. Cartwright, my brother Sandy, also just out from Britain." She let go of his hand and standing on tiptoe looked across the room. "I'll see if I can spot Mike."

"Please, call me Nick." He held out his hand watching for signs of recognition on Sandy's face. Not that it was possible, Gip had said the Mossad composite, apart from the eyes, and general shape of the face, had looked nothing like him and even though the coloured contact lenses he'd tried in Corsica had been a total failure he felt comfortable in his carefully constructed persona.

"Sandy Flett. Good to meet you Nick. Did I hear that you are manufacturing underwater camera's?" Sandy cocked his head to one side appraising Cartwright carefully. The way the man carried himself spoke of a military background, and the eyes were still and watchful. An interesting fellow, Sandy said to himself, a man to watch.

"Not yet." Dragovic sized up the man in front of him. Ex SAS, Gip had said, injured in Bosnia. The face looking at him was frank and open, boyish almost, but it was the eyes. The eyes always gave one away. A man

like himself, a man who'd seen too much, a man of
secrets and as such to be feared. He spread his hands.
"Actually we're into Electro-optics but last year we
bought out a small East German camera company,
thinking that the synergy was good. It wasn't, but we
found their research department had been doing some
very good work on industrial underwater camera technology. As I'm sure you know, Vancouver has a reputation in underwater research and development, the Newt
Suit and such, so I thought I would do a little research
of my own." Dragovic's company did in fact exist.
Originally a front for discreetly moving Arab funds to
and from Europe it had recently acquired the East
German company and Gip Lawrence had cleverly fitted
Nick Cartwright into the structure as one of the Directors.

"Industrial underwater cameras? What are they
used for?" The comment came from a bank manager
standing to one side of the group. Before Dragovic
could reply the maid asked him his wishes for a drink.
He hesitated; he rarely drank, but Gip had said, 'If you
are going to drink, stick to one and stick to whiskey'. So
over the months on Corsica he'd allowed himself to
become immersed in the lore of scotch whiskey as
propounded by Gip Lawrence

"A Scotch, ice and a little water please." He
turned back to the banker. "Oil rigs, deep sea research,
that sort of thing."

"And you're planning on a plant here?" The banker
could barely hide his interest. Dragovic smiled and
looked out of the window, "What a wonderful view.
And where do you live in this beautiful city?"

Sandy watched the exchange with a half smile. As
he'd suspected, Nick Cartwright could look after himself all right. He saw his brother-in-law approaching

their group and Mike handed Dragovic a whiskey. "Glad
you could make it Mr. Cartwright. Anne tells me that
you've met Sandy. Have the others been introduced?"

"Nick, please call me Nick. Actually we were just
in the process of doing so." Gripping Nick's arm firmly
Mike introduced him to the banker, a retired oil company executive, and another real estate developer. The
men chatted about business for a few minutes before
Mike raised his hand.

"Let me show you something Nick—excuse us for
a moment people." He steered Dragovic past scattered
groups of people and opened a door into a room set up
as an office. A large plan table stood in the middle of
the room and along one wall a desk, executive chair,
filing cabinets and a computer. Hanging on the walls
were several framed pictures and photographs of build-
ings. Pushing a loose pile of plans to one side Monroe
unrolled a large plastic map of the Lower Mainland,
showing the area from Vancouver proper to the American border. He spread it out anchoring the corners with
leather covered weights. "Nick, I had a long chat with
the salesman you spoke to this morning and you know
why I invited you to come tonight. You're a businessman, and I'm a businessman, and frankly I know we can
give you a much better deal than the Americans can."
Monroe pointed to two areas on the map outlined in
blue. "Both of these areas have all services, both are
right on major transportation routes. And I can guaran-
tee financing. You were talking to Leo back there. He
has agreed to put the full support of his bank behind
any sensible plan."

"Mike, I have a meeting in Seattle tomorrow. Let
me get back to you when I return. As I told your man,
all I'm doing is a preliminary overview. Let me get some
more information before we sit down to serious discus-

sions. Remember, I've only been here a few days."

Mike Monroe lifted his hands shoulder high. "I'm sorry. It's just that I have a good feeling about your project. Look you said yourself that Vancouver is known internationally for underwater work and I hate to think of Seattle getting something like this. Remember our dollar advantage over the Americans, and UBC is turning out some very well trained graduates." He grinned at Dragovic. "All I ask is that you give me a chance to prove we can do a better deal for you than the Americans." He lifted his hands. "No more business I promise. Come, let's get back to the party. Maybe I can get you drunk enough to miss your flight." As they walked back into the room Anne, obviously coming to break up the business meeting, intercepted them.

"Shame on you Michael. Nick must have a dreadful opinion of Canadian hospitality." Smiling slightly Dragovic demurred.

"Not at all. As a businessman I fully understand Mike's desire to capture a client. I would've been surprised if he hadn't tried to discuss the project."

"I don't care, let me drag you away from the men and take you to meet an old friend of mine." Anne led him across the room to where an older woman was sitting sipping a long drink and chatting to a man in a rather loud suit. "Joyce, let me introduce Nick Cartwright. Nick, this is Joyce Caramanlis, an old friend. Nick has just arrived from Europe and already Mike is trying to snare him into a business deal." Dragovic bent to take the proffered hand, aware that the keen eyes were scrutinizing him carefully. Her grip was dry and surprisingly firm. Joyce patted the seat beside her. The man in the loud suit drifted away without waiting to be introduced.

"Sit down Nick, tell me all about yourself. Anne

don't go, sit." She indicated a chair, which Dragovic pulled across and held for Anne before sitting next to Joyce Caramanlis. For the next fifteen minutes he listened to the two women, prompting them to talk by asking the occasional question but deflecting questions about himself. He tried not to show his interest in Anne but caught Joyce looking speculatively at him when he talked to Anne about his work in Europe. The maid rang a bell to inform them that the buffet supper was ready and standing he waited for the women to fill their plates before moving forward with the men to help himself. Sandy Flett stood behind him and they chatted about sights to see in the city when work permitted.

Later, after disengaging from a group around him discussing golf and the stock market and not wanting to engage in more small talk, Dragovic pushed open the sliding doors to the balcony and leaning against the curved rail looked over the city. It was a mild night, a touch on the cool side, and he was glad he was wearing his lightweight all-wool sport coat. Staring over the city and trying to organise his thoughts he did not hear the doors open then close behind him. He smelt her perfume before she spoke.

"Don't you find it cold?" Since she was wearing a short, strapless black cocktail dress it seemed an odd question. He looked at her, light from the party inside causing shadows on her cheeks and forehead. Her dark hair cut short in a pageboy style glinted as she turned to face him.

"Don't you? After all, I at least have a coat."

She smiled and he again felt the sudden jolt that squeezed his heart. "Caught you. Do you know that every time you are asked a direct question you reply with a question? I watched you when Joyce asked questions. She likes you by the way."

"Ah, my apologies—it's an old habit. I didn't mean

to be rude." He made a vague movement with his hand. "I'm not very good at small talk, but in business it's a necessary skill. One I suspect is not top of my repertoire." Looking at her face the words jumped unbidden into his mind and he tried without success to banish them knowing even as he spoke that it was not a good idea.

"I have to travel to Seattle tomorrow. When I return could we have coffee somewhere?"

For a long moment Anne did not reply. He watched her face become grave and cursed himself for moving so quickly. He knew he'd offended her and wondered what he could say to retrieve the situation. Before he could speak the patio doors opened. Sandy and a blonde woman he'd met briefly before dinner joined them.

"Oh Anne, what a wonderful party." The blonde hanging on to Sandy's arm gushed, flinging her arms wide in a dramatic gesture. "It's such a lovely evening, it's been ages since we've had a clear night, look at all the stars."

Sandy grinned at Dragovic. "Beats the old office routine in London. A man could get to like this life."

Dragovic nodded, his face blank. "It has been a good evening, but I must get back. I have an early start in the morning." He held his hand out to Sandy, "I enjoyed our conversation. Perhaps we could meet for lunch before I return to Germany?" He inclined his head to the blonde and then looked at Anne. "Thank you for a very pleasant evening. If you'll excuse me I'll find Mike and say goodbye." He went back into the lounge angry with himself for being so presumptuous and wondering how he was going to salvage something from his uncharacteristically spontaneous request. Finding Mike talking to a group of men who all seemed the worse for drink he made the same excuse for his early departure but Mike insisted on seeing him out, walking with him to the hall closet to collect his raincoat. Nick promised to call as soon as he returned from Seattle and they were almost at the door when the maid, holding her hand to her ear, caught Mike's eye.

"Ah, telephone. Nick, don't forget, call me as soon as you get back. We'll do lunch." Clapping Dragovic on the shoulder Mike made for the office and his call. Dragovic folded the coat over his arm and looked for the electric switch that opened the sliding door when a voice came from behind.

"It's over here Nick." A slim white hand touched a panel and the door slid open. Anne stepped through into the elevator passage ahead of him. He followed and the door unbidden slid shut behind them.

"I want to apol . . ." He started to say, but she cut him off by placing a hand on his mouth.

"Please don't. It's very flattering to be asked. Are you married Nick? I never asked and Mike never said." He looked at her and she caught the sudden flicker of pain that crossed his face.

"A long time ago. She died." He took a deep breath. "I must go." He wanted to say more but the words wouldn't come. Blindly he stabbed the elevator button. The cage must have been parked for the door slid open immediately and he stepped in. All he wanted to do now was get away. Another minute and he'd have taken her in his arms and to hell with the consequences. He turned to face her as the door started to close.

"Call me, at the hospital, when you get back." She spoke in a whisper but it was as though she had shouted. The door snapped shut and he squeezed his eyes closed. This was not supposed to happen. This was insanity. He was here to kill a man, not to get involved with a woman.

§

Anne walked back into the room unaware Joyce Caramanlis had watched her leave with Nick and return smiling. As Anne walked past Joyce spoke softly. "He's a dangerous man pet. This is no lightweight like most we know."

The words caught Anne by surprise. "Good grief Joyce I've just met the man. Don't assume something that is not there. He's a very nice person, but—" She smiled at the older woman "—you mustn't read signs into common courtesies."

Joyce Caramanlis did not smile in return. "Anne I love you like a daughter. You know that and I try to give you good advice. Nick Cartwright is not what he seems on the surface. Oh, I know he's polished and charming but there is something under that façade. This is a man who gives nothing of himself away. There is an emptiness at his centre and he rarely smiles. I've always been wary of men who avoid answering simple questions."

Anne laughed. "Joyce I think you're letting your imagination run wild tonight. Come out to the balcony with me. It's a wonderful night."

Joyce rose with a sigh. "Sorry, you're probably right. It's just that once or twice I caught the look he gave you. Ah—that a man should look at me like that." She gripped the younger woman's hand and together the two walked out to the patio.

Chapter 18

The Stalkers

Sandy handed over the sealed envelope to the RCMP officer across the table. Both men, dressed casually in slacks and open neck shirts, had just ordered breakfast in the dining room of the Sylvia Hotel while watching the early morning joggers along Beach Avenue and looking over the placid waters of English Bay.

"You say he can be a bit difficult. In what way?" Sgt. Brian Kowalski sniffed at the appetising aroma coming from the kitchen. A long-serving veteran of the RCMP's undercover drug unit, he'd recently been transferred to the diplomatic protection unit. A change he wasn't happy about. The Brit sitting in front of him looked as if butter wouldn't melt in his mouth—that is, until you saw the hardness in the eyes or read the very sparse outline of his background which had arrived the week before. Kowalski was old enough and experienced enough to withhold judgement until he'd more of a feel for the team the Brits were sending over. He'd asked why Canada was being lumbered with the problem of Talawi and the answer given that the Brits had done similar favours for the Canadian Government in the past struck him as being untrue. He could not recall any cases in his, admittedly limited, DPU experience being shipped to the UK. America yes, and once to Mexico, but Britain? Still, it was possible he supposed. But this writer Talawi was by all accounts on the hit list of Iran's Ruling Revolutionary Council and that, as Rushdie had found out, was akin to being poised over a precipice with a large rock around your neck.

"Talawi seems to believe that as no *fatwa* has been

issued that the attempt on his life was an aberration by a splinter group."

"And what do you think?"

"We missed picking up one of the surviving hit team members quite literally by minutes. He was a warm floppy when we arrived. The rumour floated by Iran is that the leadership was annoyed at what was seen as a wildcat operation and sent a hit team to punish the perps."

"Sounds logical. Why don't you fella's buy into that?"

"Because it's just too pat. I hear you didn't buy into the *Mary Ellen* being just a private yacht in trouble when you did the big bust three years ago." Sandy smiled across the table as Kowalski's mouth fell open.

"Holy mother of God. You bastards have pretty good intelligence. My name never came up in the newspapers over that." He shook his head, "Man oh man I'll have to watch myself around you fella. But I see what you mean."

Sandy started to talk, then seeing the waitress approaching waited until she'd placed steaming plates of ham, eggs, sausage and hash browns in front of them. Coffee in large mugs followed and after checking that nothing else was needed the waitress moved off to serve another table. Without further ado both men started eating. Sandy, washing down a mouthful of food with a large gulp of coffee, pointed with his fork at Kowalski. "Brian I can see that bringing him over here causes a problem for your department but we do have a good reason. We have a plan in place to confirm or reject our theory but we need Talawi out of the way to execute it. All we need is a safe house where our friend can write his next magnum opus and some of us can maybe get a little fishing in. We don't anticipate any problems on this side of the pond."

"He won't be able to move around much. His face is pretty well known even here. I saw something in the *National Post* a couple of weeks ago with a full headshot of your man. How do you intend stopping him from getting out and about?"

Sandy, chewing on a sausage, swallowed. "We are not going to stop him moving around. Just limit his movements from the obvious centres. Our make-up people have made some simple changes, spectacles, different haircut and colour, that sort of a thing, but you'll be amazed at the difference it makes. That's why a good location for the safe house is important."

Brian placed his fork on the plate and wiping his lips with the napkin reached down into his briefcase leaning against the table leg. "We've come up with four possibles in the lower mainland and one further off. Check them out and tell me what you think. Now that we've talked I think I can see what you're after. I'll see if there is anything else available if those don't suit." He handed over a large brown envelope. "You'll find maps and real estate agents' addresses inside. Don't do any deals until we've had another talk, I'll want to look at it before you decide."

"Fair enough, I'll start this morning. Join me for a drink this evening?"

"Can't, my kid is playing in a hockey game. I have to be there, you know how it is." Brian pushed his chair back. "What made you choose this hotel?"

"My parents spent time here after the war. Apparently had a wonderful time so it was a natural choice."

"And how do you find it?"

"Well it has loads of character, which is nice, it's comfortable and the views from my room are worth any

disadvantages." Sandy stuck his lower lip out, thinking.
"If you've been to France it's at the French two or three
star level. No, more two star I guess."

"Hmm, well I've not been to France but my
wife's folks are due here next month and are insisting on
staying in a hotel. Which, guess what, I get to choose."
He sighed theatrically. "Let's talk tomorrow, same time.
They do a good breakfast here." He pulled out his wallet
as he stood. "I'll get today's, you can get tomorrows," he
lifted his hand in a half salute. "Don't get lost now."

Sandy watched Kowalski walk away then, draining
the last of his coffee, picked up the envelope. Leaving
the restaurant he sauntered through the doors to emerge
outside the hotel entrance. He paused for a moment,
getting his bearings, before striding off along the
sidewalk at a brisk pace. A short distance along his
route Sandy stopped and turned suddenly in the direction he'd just come as if he'd forgotten something
inside. No one came through the doors towards him.
Satisfied, Sandy walked back to the hotel and climbed
the stairs to his room. He tore open the brown envelope
and spread the photographs and maps on the bed and
spent the next twenty minutes studying the information.
Finally, sliding the pictures and maps back into their
envelope, he pocketed the rental car keys and went
down to the parking garage. His rental, a dark brown
Ford Explorer 4 wheel drive sport utility vehicle, sat
between a bright red Honda sport coupe and a silver-
gray Subaru Outback. Minutes later, steering the big
vehicle down Davie street and turning on to Granville
Street, he headed out of downtown over the Granville
Street Bridge.

The low, late afternoon sun glinted off towering
office windows when he finally headed back into the
city. It had been a frustrating day. The first two houses

checked were totally useless. They'd obviously been
thrown in to the mix simply to show willing. The other
two were better but neither had all the requisite conditions of quiet location, middle class neighbourhood and
restricted access that Sandy was looking for. The last
option was a house in Ganges on Salt Spring Island, Salt
Spring being the largest of the Gulf Islands group lying
between the lower mainland and Vancouver Island. He
would fly to Ganges tomorrow, a short 20-minute flight
from the floatplane dock downtown, and assess the
property. A scheduled floatplane service operated
between Vancouver city and Ganges, the main town on
Salt Spring.

Driving over the Cambie Street bridge he saw
Anne and Mike's apartment complex standing hard
against a darkening sky and on impulse punched in
Anne's personal number at the hospital into the cellular
phone clipped onto the console. He heard the phone
ringing for several seconds and was just about to cancel
the call when she picked up the phone.

"Hullo?"

"Anne, can you meet me for a drink? I'll pick you
up."

"Sandy, how lovely. Hold on." There was a short
period of muffled noise as she conferred with someone.
"Yes, where are you?"

"I'm just turning into Smithe Street and should be
outside the hospital in about five minutes. Come to the
Emergency door. Don't be long. I'll get a ticket for sure
if I'm here for more than a few minutes."

"I'll be there in a minute. If anyone asks you to
move tell them Dr. Flett is coming to meet you."

Ten minutes later Anne was sitting next to him as
he swung out of the hospital drive, heading back to his
hotel. At least there parking was not a problem. She

gave his knee a squeeze. "What did you think of the party last night?" He slowed behind a Mercedes hogging two lanes while the driver decided whether or not he was going to turn.

"It was interesting. You know some interesting people." He grinned, "Especially that blonde bombshell wife of the lawyer Mitchell. Does she always hit on single men at your parties?" Anne laughed.

"Yes, poor Eric has a hell of a time with her. I noticed how smooth you were in disengaging from her attentions."

Accelerating he made a push past the Mercedes who by now had decided that he was lost and slowed to a crawl while trying to read the street signs. "Mike seemed in good form and I saw that he managed to get Nick Cartwright into his office to push his properties."

"I know. Mike really doesn't know when to put the brakes on. I was pretty cross with him."

"Well Cartwright took it in stride. He was quite gracious I thought, and wasn't put out. I suspect he accepted the invitation expecting Mike to put the arm on."

"What did you think of him? Joyce Caramanlis says he's a dangerous man. She's quite perceptive when it comes to men. I suppose after two husbands that's inevitable."

"He's an interesting character. I didn't spend much time talking to him but I think he can look after himself; good listener, which is rare these days. Probably ex military, carries himself like a soldier. Why the interest?"

"No reason. What Joyce said intrigued me and after he left and I made a note to ask your opinion." She surprised herself and wondered why she'd held back from telling Sandy the real reason for her question. In the past she and Sandy had had no secrets from each other, but they'd been apart for many years now and had taken different roads. Sandy glanced at her curiously.

"Everything OK between you and Mike?"

"Sandy, don't put two and two together and get five. To answer your question—no, Mike and I seem to have drifted apart. I . . ." She hesitated, unsure if she should continue. Sandy waited. " . . . I picked up the phone the other day and it was a woman, asking for Mike. When she heard my voice she put the phone down. It was probably innocent, at least Mike's explanation made it seem so. I checked the number later and it was from a well-known real estate agent in the city."

"Well, I would think that Mike was probably right. He must deal with lots of people of whom a fair proportion must be women. Bad manners are becoming the norm these days." Sandy pulled into the parking bay and, picking up his envelope, got out of the vehicle.

Anne joined him and they took the elevator to the lobby. She glanced curiously at the brown envelope but made no comment until they were sitting at a table in the cocktail lounge and had ordered drinks. "Started work so soon?" She pointed to the envelope.

"Oh, this. Partly. It has some info on what I need while I'm here." He picked up the envelope and moved it off the glass table top, to a chair. "Now, talking about Mike, don't you think that you may be overreacting?"

Anne smiled at his obvious attempt to change the subject. Still it had nothing to do with her and she shouldn't pry. "Perhaps you're right and that's what I thought at first. But you know the strange thing is that Jenny Liu and I have met at several functions. And looking back at the most recent times, I've caught her looking at me speculatively when she thought I wasn't aware. At the time I didn't think much of it. Women are always eyeing each other; it's a feminine thing. You tell me why she didn't say something like. 'Hello Anne, is Mike around?' or something similar. Why put the phone down?"

Sandy looked at her somberly. Ever since they were children his sister had relied on his advice. Being the older brother he'd always tried to treat her often trivial concerns with grave consideration, but she was grown now, a successful surgeon and this was obviously a major problem. "I don't know Sis. The obvious answer is to ask her directly. I appreciate that asking directly is not always possible but there may be a different reason than the one you're assuming." The drinks arrived and after signing the bill Sandy clinked her glass. "Look, the only advice I can give is not to go off half-cocked. You know your husband better than anyone and I have to ask why any man with a wife as lovely as you would want to stray." He smiled at her before taking a sip of his drink. "Anne, I'm a great believer in intuition but also in making sure to have all the facts before acting."

"I know, and you're probably right. Let's talk about you for a change. How long do you think you'll be in Vancouver and, by the way, have you called Mom and Dad?"

§

"You surprise me Meg. It's not often that I meet someone who's had a classical education." Ismail Talawi looked up from the writing desk. Ten minutes earlier Meg, arriving to give Talawi the latest information relevant to his move, had found the author deeply engrossed in writing and was waved irritably toward a chair. Finishing up the chapter on his laptop computer Ismail turned to face her, "And what now, Centurion?" snapped sharply in Latin.

"The Legions protect. Caesar should remember

the Ides of March," she'd snapped back in equally perfect Latin. Meg kept from laughing out loud at the look on his face as he struggled to regain composure and dominance.

"Damn it Meg every time we meet you give me a lesson in humility. Where did you take Latin? It is almost impossible theses days to find it being taught anywhere."

"Cambridge. Now can I brief you on the agenda for our departure to Canada next week?" She snapped open the file on her lap. "One of our team is in place in Vancouver and is searching out various safe . . ."

"Cambridge, you're a Cambridge grad? What on earth are you doing in police work?"

She looked up. "Ismail, hard as it may be for you to understand, there are other people in the world who are as well and, in a lot of cases, better educated than yourself. I chose police work because it interests me. Just like you chose to be a writer. After all," she grinned at him, pleased to have found a chink in his armour, "look at the interesting people I get to meet."

"I've said this before. You're a very interesting woman Meg." Talawi looked at her speculatively. "I've an editor to read over my rough drafts and catch obvious errors but I need someone to read the manuscript cold. Someone who doesn't think I'm the next Doestoyevsky. We are going to be thrown together for quite some time and I wonder if you would consider doing that for me?"

Meg sighed. "Ismail I'm flattered that you would consider my opinion. I've read your previous novels including *Lunch with the Prophet,* and I must tell you that it is not my sort of reading matter."

"What didn't you like? Look I appreciate that books are a subjective experience. I have my own likes and dislikes and the new one is quite a bit different."

"You write wonderfully well. Your use of English is a pleasure to read but, and remember this is only my opinion, your use of metaphor, of continuous reference to obscure classical texts and arcane religious philosophies proves that you are well read but leaves the average reader wondering what you're getting at."

Listening, Ismail Talawi felt his temperature rising. How dare she. His novels were not written for the average reader, whoever that might be, but for posterity. Didn't she grasp that. Perhaps she wasn't as clever as he'd thought. Voltaire, Tolstoy and the other greats were read by the intelligentsia of their time but only now were they properly appreciated by the masses. A sharp retort sprung to his lips but he suppressed it. This woman had caught him off balance more than once. Turning on his charm he shrugged. "I appreciate your candor and I wish that some of my associates were so honest. But the request still stands. I would like to have your opinion. I probably won't accept all your criticisms but at least it'll be an experience for both of us." Until this precise moment the thought of getting Meg into his bed had not occurred to him. Not that she wasn't an attractive woman with what appeared to be a stunning figure under the casual clothes she wore but one did not consort with one's jailers. But, the thought intrigued him, just how difficult could it be?

Meg, taken off guard by the low-key response to her comments—she'd half expected an explosion for the man's ego was legendary—decided to agree. Perhaps she'd misjudged him; perhaps the outside persona was a front to protect the man inside. She took a deep breath. This wasn't in her brief but as he'd just said it could prove interesting for both of them. "As long as you don't take offence at what I say, yes I'll do it. Now can we go over the preparations for your journey?"

§

In an office on the other side of London Jimmy Douglas
looked critically at Tristam's protégé while Tristam
proudly surveyed the results of his creation. Wilfred
Blair's father had changed the family name from Al
Fawd when settling in England some forty years before.
Young Wilfred had gone to a good public school intend-
ing to follow his father's footsteps as an engineer but
found that he much preferred the theatre instead. An
accomplished actor, he'd progressed from local repertory
to smaller theatres in London. As a good character actor
he managed to carve a niche for himself playing Middle
Eastern and Mediterranean males. Now dressed in a
copy of Ismail Talawi's suit, his hair styled in the same
fashion, and sporting the neatly clipped mustache and
beard affected by Talawi, the result was startling.

"Walk away from me please Mr. Blair, then stop
and turn around." Jimmy signalled the technician to
keep the video camera running. "Good, excellent. Please
come back and sit." He waited until Blair had settled
himself, crossing his legs in a good imitation of Talawi's
gesture. "You have signed all the necessary documents
but, I must ask you one last time, are you willing to
carry out this deception? Tris has given you some of the
background and you understand that we need to keep
up the deception that Ismail Talawi is still in London
while we relocate him offshore." Jimmy didn't want to
mention the word bait, but that's what you are, he
thought dryly.

"No, I quite understand the plan. You'll provide
the same protection Mr. Talawi has and I'm to be seen in
selected nightspots from time to time." Blair shot his

cuffs in a fair imitation of one of Ismail Talawi's more
irritating mannerism's.

Jimmy grunted. The boy was really rather good.
God, I hope we're wrong about the hit man still being
out there, he thought. So far intensive inquiries had
failed to turn up anything significant. Even the cap had
eventually turned out to be a dead end. "OK, Mr. Blair,
as of now you are Ismail Talawi. Tristam will act as your
coordinator and I will arrange for the protection detail
presently tasked to the real Mr. Talawi to transfer to
your protection." He looked over to Tristam. "Tris,
that's something you can do today. Give Meg a call and
tell her to release the team around Talawi and have Basil
activate the fresh team to replace them."

"I don't understand, why not put the fresh team
on to me?" Wilfred Blair looked puzzled.

"Because, Mr. Blair, if by some mischance, one or
more of the protection detail has been identified by the
opposition they will be more likely to assume you are
Talawi than if we put fresh people with you." What
Jimmy left out, thought Tristam, was the fact that the
teams were rotated almost as a matter of course. It
actually made no difference unless 'Eyes', as they'd
taken to calling the hit man, had marked Talawi. In that
event the change was for Ismail Talawi's safety and
greatly increased the risk to Blair.

"Of course, how stupid of me. Well, let the
deception begin." Blair stood and followed Tristam out
the door.

Chapter 19

To kill a mocking bird

"When did you get in?" Dragovic dropped into the soft sofa seat across from Martin Dreyfus. Both men sat facing each other. The small seating area adjacent to the coffee stand on the echoing main floor of the red brick office complex housing elevators and the Hong Kong and Shanghai Bank's main branch at 999 West Hastings Street was empty at this time of the morning. Sitting they could look out of huge glass windows that looked towards the waterfront. A cryptic phone message left in his mail slot at the Hotel Vancouver had brought Nick to meet Martin.

"I came in on the late flight from London yesterday but thought it best to get some sleep before getting in touch. I have some news, but bring me up to speed with your progress."

Dispassionately Dragovic outlined his meeting with Mike Monroe and Sandy Flett. He gave a detailed description of Sandy Flett and described following Monroe and seeing Monroe's meeting with the Real Estate Agent Jenny Lui. "Monroe's wife is a doctor at St Paul's Hospital and I think she may suspect her husband. I've seen Monroe again and looked at some of the properties he is trying to interest me in. I've agreed to see him again after my next trip to the States, he believes I'm going down to Seattle. I've a tentative meeting with Sandy Flett planned, probably in the next few days. Flett is booked into the Sylvia Hotel. What I need is to get closer to Flett but there are no indications that Talawi is here yet." Nick stopped short of mentioning his plan to see Anne and wondered at himself.

"You have done much better than we could have

hoped for in such a short time Nick. Gip's had no further contact with our source in London so we don't know the departure schedule. The source will try to get a message through but don't count on it, our source is just too valuable to put at risk so we'll have to watch closely for signs of our friend's arrival. I'll book in at the Sylvia Hotel today and once I've identified Flett's vehicle I'll fix a tracker unit. Ha, I need a drink." Martin rose and went to stand for a two cups of coffee, Nick joined him and both men stood silently mixing the coffee with cream and sugar before returning to the seating. Martin slid a small envelope over. "A key to a locker in the bus terminal at the Via Rail station. Inside you will find your pistol and another tranche of money. The long gun is still in transit and will be in a different locker when it arrives. If I need to update information I'll use another locker and leave the key in an envelope with the concierge at the hotel. Remember that I'll be watching your back but lets not meet again unless it's an emergency or I have information that is critical to the success of our operation. If that happens I'll leave a message for you at the hotel. I'll be available to you . . . here." He reached into his jacket pocket and handed over a cellular phone. "It's been fixed to look like it doesn't work. If you try, it will give a low battery indication. However, if you push the pound key and the number 6 it'll activate my receiver and we'll meet in this restaurant two hours after you call. If the restaurant is closed I'll be in the lobby of your hotel. If you can't be there leave a message where you can meet with reception for me."

Dragovic turned the cell phone over. "I understand. For my part once the subject has been dealt with I'll advise you by activating this phone twice in quick succession. You'll know what's happened and you can initiate your own extraction plan."

"Good thinking mon ami. I'd a slightly different idea but yours is more elegant." Martin drained the last of his coffee and stood up. "Expect our friend to look different. I suspect that he'll have been given a make over and the first thing I'd do would be to get rid of the mustache and beard."

Dragovic scooped the cell phone and envelope up off the table as he stood. "Yes, we explored that possibility back at the farm. How's Gip doing?"

"As well as can be expected. He seems to be in partial remission. I think he wants to see us both back at the farm before he lets go." Martin made a wry grimace. "Ironic isn't it. We want him to stay alive while our mission is to take a life." He gripped Dragovic's arm fiercely. "Don't take chances Nick. Our opposition is very good and this hit will stir up a hornets nest."

"They won't be expecting trouble over here and it will take them a few hours to gear up after the hit. I expect to be a long way from the scene before they find a thread to pull on. But—as I said only a few days ago, the best laid plans of mice and men go astray and I've no intention of letting them take me." Nick's face had the cold, grim emptiness Martin remembered from the first days at the farm.

Martin grimaced. "Nick, don't even think like that. The hit on Salameh went like clockwork. This will also."

§

The two plain-clothes officers shook hands with Meg after she signed the official release form. The older man, whom she knew as Ron, folded the document before placing it into his inner coat pocket. "I can't say I'm

sorry to see the back of our friend. Lots of luck Meg."
Meg thanked them both then closed the door.

"What's going on?" Ismail Talawi came out of the
bathroom, a towel knotted around his waist, followed by
the make up artist. Meg's eyes widened. The mustache
and beard were gone, the brown hair now jet black and
cut unfashionably short made him look younger than his
40 years. She noted the extra layer of fat around his
middle. A pity that, she thought, for he had a good
physique otherwise. Good living and a sedentary lifestyle would do that every time. Noticing the direction of
her eyes Talawi coloured and pulled on the shirt he was
carrying. "What's happening Meg?"

"Changing of the guard. It's a precaution; we don't
want the old team to see your new persona. You certainly look different. Actually I think it's a vast improvement, you look years younger."

"Really." Ismail almost preened and turned to look
at himself in the long mirror. "I guess I could lose a little
weight though."

"If you wish we can organise a couple of fitness
machines for you in Canada."

"Damn you Meg, that's not the correct answer.
You're supposed to say something to the effect that, oh
no you look just fine." He scowled at her, "Am I always
going to be put down by you?"

"Ismail, you said it not me. Yes, you could lose a
few pounds, and if you want to it can be arranged.
Don't expect me to prop up your ego. You've lots of
lady friends willing to oblige." She turned to the police
make up artist. "Gerry, what else do you think he
needs?"

Gerry Smallwood shook his head. "There's not a
lot else we can do without special surgery. Keep him out
of the sun, a sun tan will darken his skin and with his

colouring he'll look like an Arab in no time, especially with that black hair. The voice is a dead giveaway so don't talk a lot Mr. Talawi, let your minders do most of the work. Oh, I've added a bit of height to his shoes. It is enough to cause confusion if someone thinks they recognise him. I will fly out in three weeks to retint the hair and make any other adjustments." He held out his hand. "Good luck sir."

Startled, Ismail took the hand. "Well thank you Gerry, not that I'm happy with the changes though." He made for the bathroom carrying his clothes that had been tossed on the bed.

"Most people aren't sir, but think of the alternative. Goodbye Meg, say hi to Sandy Flett for me."

"You know Sandy?" Meg's surprise showed. She'd only met Gerry Smallwood the day before. Smallwood's reputation had preceded him though for he was known throughout the undercover branches as a superb makeover specialist for special ops and witness protection programs.

"Northern Ireland, ask him to tell you about Ballyclana." Gerry gave a short bark of laughter. "Wonderful story." He snapped the small suitcase lying on the bed shut and straightening made for the door. "Good man is Sandy Flett." He eyed her speculatively, "A very good man. Well I'll be off then. Cheers." And he was gone.

"And who is Sandy Flett may I ask, a boyfriend, a lover?" Although Ismail had gone back into the bathroom to change the door was partly open. He came through in a clean shirt and slacks fastening a tie.

"Sandy Flett is my partner, and he's a highly specialised undercover operative. Right now he's in Vancouver setting up your safe house and protection." She sighed, "In my job Ismail there isn't much time for romance so relax, I'm not going to be seduced by the opposition or distracted by my own. Interesting though, that's the second time I've been advised what a good man Sandy is."

"Is he?"

"Yes Ismail he is. You're very fortunate in the calibre of protection around you. Now can we change the subject?"

§

Anne Flett wiped her forehead and dropped into her office chair. What a morning. The emergency room had been running at full tilt. Savouring a cup of tea drawn from the urn in the hall she sank back in her chair just as her office phone rang. Hesitating, she took another sip of tea. Enough was enough. The phone continued ringing until the answering machine cut in. Anne heard her own voice advising the caller to leave a message at the beep. For a second nothing happened then a distinctive English voice. "Dr. Flett—Anne, I'm sorry to have missed you. I'll try again later I've . . ." She reached for the phone, almost knocking her tea over.

"Nick? When did you get back?" She found her hand was shaking. She'd anticipated his call but not until much later in the day.

"About five minutes ago. I decided to fly back earlier than planned. I'm at the floatplane dock near Canada Place. Is this a bad time? I can call back later."

"No, it's fine. I've just finished my morning. I was thinking of taking a break and having lunch in the park."

"Stanley Park? That's quite near here. Is there a restaurant? Perhaps we could meet for lunch."

"Nick, I have to clean up first. Take a taxi to the

park and ask directions to Lumberman's Arch. I'll meet you there in . . . half an hour, say at twelve fifteen." She ran a hand through her hair, thank goodness for good hair that needed no attention. She went to the staff changing room and had a quick shower. Picking out a cheerful print dress from her locker she pushed her feet into sandals that had a slight heel, giving her the extra height she always envied on more statuesque women. Glancing critically at herself in the mirror she decided on lipstick and touched up her lips, something that would have surprised her colleagues. Anne Flett was known for her lack of make up at work, Matron once remarking to a nurse who commented on the fact that Dr. Flett never wore make up, "She is one of the lucky ones. She would look lovely in a flour sack in a tropical downpour." Picking up her bag and beeper Anne advised the reception desk that she would be gone for about two hours. "Call me, if there is an emergency. I'll be reasonably close."

The receptionist wondered if Dr. Flett, who rarely took lunch outside the hospital, was meeting her husband. "Enjoy your lunch doctor. I'll make sure that it's a genuine emergency before calling you."

Anne smiled her thanks. She felt the sharp tingle of anticipation, or was it nerves? This is ridiculous she told herself, it's only a lunch meeting, but even as she waited under the portico of the ambulance entrance for the taxi she'd ordered she knew it was more than that.

Dragovic sat on a bench watching the flow of people around the huge arch made up of three massive logs. The trip by taxi from the floatplane dock had taken ten minutes and glancing at his watch he saw he was early. The trip to Seattle had been necessary to establish a pattern of behaviour and a reason for leaving Vancouver after Talawi's assassination. He knew that once

Talawi was hit the roof would fall in. The Canadians and the Brits would react with total fury and he was counting on the fact that no one would question the English businessman who traveled regularly between Vancouver and Seattle. He'd return to Corsica via Singapore. A brand new set of identity documents sat in a locker at SeaTac International airport. Nick Cartwright would disappear while visiting the Mt Baker National Park and Dr. Anton Guiess would be airborne from Singapore to Rome.

So why am I doing this? Why am I meeting a married woman who is the sister of the man tasked to protect Talawi? Looking over the sparkling waters of English Bay he took a deep breath. Because you fool, he told himself, it is the best way to get close to Talawi. She is the key. And yet even as his mind reiterated the obvious reason he knew he lied to himself. Not since before Reena's murder had he felt like this. He saw Anne coming before she saw him and his heart leaped. The sun angling through the trees lit up her face and the shining helmet of her hair. She saw him then and waved, her face breaking into a smile that lit up her eyes. He rose as she approached feeling like a schoolboy on his first date.

"Anne, you look wonderful." His admiration open, obvious. "Where do you want to eat?"

"You know what I really would like?" She turned leading him towards the concession stand advertising Hot Dogs, Coffee and other quick foods. "I would love a hot dog and a cup of coffee and then to sit on the sea wall, while we eat." She smiled up at him. "This is one of my favourite places, and it's been ages since I've been back for a visit. I used to sit on the sea wall and eat my sandwiches during my probationary period at St

Paul's. You must have a favourite place, a place of good memories."

"Yes . . . yes I do. It's a farm on an island in the Mediterranean. I had good times there. One day, God willing, I will see it again." They had reached the snack bar and he watched as she ordered the sausages stuffed into a long roll and covered with a variety of relish and mustard.

"Nick, I'm going to put everything on mine. What do you want?"

Watching her enthusiasm at such a simple pleasure he felt his heart lift and he chuckled, "I'll go with your recommendation, after all, you're the Doctor." The vendor, a young woman working her way through college, thought what a handsome couple they made. The man looked a bit like Liam Neeson, her favourite actor, and the woman was just lovely. Paying for their food then picking up the two paper mugs of coffee, Dragovic followed Anne down to the seawall. A short ramp led to the exposed beach and a lower wall that curved around some rocks. Finding a smooth spot on the lower wall they sat down, legs dangling over the sand, their backs to the walkway that circled the entire park. Taking his hot dog from her hand Nick passed Anne her coffee and sitting in companionable silence they concentrated on eating the hot dogs without spilling food on their clothes.

Anne put her hot dog down to have some coffee and, swinging her arm in a wide sweep encompassing the bay and the land rising steeply on the opposite side, asked, "Isn't this the loveliest place to have lunch?"

"Sitting here with you on a day made especially for a lunch like this, there is nowhere else in the world I would want to be."

"Not even your Island in the Med?" She smiled at

him, "My brother tells me that some of the most beautiful women in the world live in Europe."

He looked at her quietly. "You realise what is happening to us Anne. We're not adolescents. I thought that I'd forgotten how to care." Squeezing his eyes shut he shook his head slowly before looking straight into her eyes. "It has been such a long, long time. I truly believed . . ." He shivered, "I'm sorry this is not fair to you. You know nothing about me."

Anne touched his hand gently. "You must have loved her very much."

Closing his hand over hers he stared over the sea, his face infinitely sad. "Yes, I did Anne. She was a kind, generous and lovely woman, someone you'd have liked and she you, but I've buried the past. Until we met at your apartment I believed I had made an accommodation with life." He gave a harsh bark. "The best laid plans of mice and men eh?" A fully laden container ship plowed across the water heading for the Lions Gate Bridge and the open sea. Letting go of her hand he placed both his hands on her shoulders and turned her towards him, oblivious to the looks of people skating by on roller blades. "Anne I did not expect to feel this way again. But I do, and pretending that I can go back to what I was is simply ignoring reality." He sighed. "I believe you feel the same. Yet we hardly know each other."

Anne drew his hands down into her lap. "Nick have you considered that you might be a very lonely man attracted to a woman who reminds you of your wife?" She scanned his face carefully and despite the mild temperature felt a shiver run through her. For someone who was almost obsessively logical her mind was totally confused. This quiet man with the gentle voice had touched something, a part of her that she

never imagined existed. She hugged herself tightly. Had
she ever been in love? Was this love or just a strong
attraction, a reaction to her recent feeling of living in a
vacuum? What about Mike? A few days ago she'd been
furious thinking he was cheating on her and was what
she was thinking now any better?

"I asked myself that question while travelling to
and from Seattle and the only face I see is yours. The
only voice I hear is yours. Since . . ." This was madness.
He had risked too much already. *Allah give me strength for
I am truly lost*, he begged as he struggled with his emotions. He touched her face with his fingertips. "Anne, I
only know that my heart sings at the sound of your
voice. That to sit with you here has given me more
pleasure than anything I've done through the long dark
years since she died." Abruptly he swung around away
from the water and dropped lightly onto the ramp running into the sand and water's edge. He held his arms
out to help her come down from the wall. "Will you
walk with me? In times when I need to clear my mind I
find walking a help."

Holding the bag containing the remains of their
lunch in one hand she gripped his arm with the other
and dropped beside him. Looking up at him she spoke
unsteadily. "Nick, this has all happened too fast. I'm as
confused as you are. I think we should both step back
and try to sort our feelings out."

He nodded somberly. "Yes, I agree. But—today let
us walk and pretend that we are friends who've been
apart. Such a day may not come again for either of us
for a long time." Walking together and looking at the
shoreline of this the loveliest of cities Nick spoke
gently. "There was a Persian poet in the sixteenth century who wrote, 'days are like petals, they bloom briefly,
their loveliness missed in the rush of men's useless

tasks, before they fade into the night of long regret.' I have too many regrets, too many days spent in useless tasks."

She touched his hand briefly. "Surely you must get satisfaction from your work. Sandy said that you're doing interesting work with underwater research. Don't you enjoy what you do?"

"It pays well, and it gives me something to do. The people I work with are good people but if I could leave tomorrow I think I would look for land here, breed horses, and grow grapes for my own wine. My family had a vineyard when I was a boy; I even studied viticulture before university. "

"I can't see you as a farmer Nick. Sandy said he thought you might have been a soldier." She didn't notice him stiffen slightly. "By the way he likes you and wants to see you again before you leave. But if farming is truly what you want why don't you?"

"Why? Because I owe——." He stopped. "I owe a great deal to the company, they helped me through the worst time in my life."

Puzzled she looked up at his face. "Surely others can run the company?"

"Of course. But, it's more complicated than I can easily explain. What made you swap England for Canada?"

"Oh, I'd just completed my medical degree at London University and decided to take a break. I'd always wanted to see Western Canada and the Rockies so I came here. I had a wonderful time and while skiing up at Whistler made friends with a doctor and his wife, Jason was resident surgeon at St Paul's. They persuaded me to do my internship here. It wasn't a hard decision; I'd fallen in love with the country and the life. Then I met Mike." She looked at him, gauging his reaction, but his face was impassive. "As the novels say he swept me off my feet. It was very flattering and . . . well, it was a whirlwind romance."

"Are you happy?"

"Now? That's an impossible question to answer. At the beginning we were very happy. But work in the last two years seems to have taken over both our lives. Oh it's not all Mike's fault, I'm as much to blame but we seem to be drifting steadily apart. Lately I seem to have been living in a vacuum. I eat, sleep and work and until I met you I thought I was happy, that is, when I gave it much thought." Catching his hand she stopped. "That's why we must step back Nick. I look at you and ask myself if what I feel is a reaction to the aimlessness of my personal life."

Turning they walked back towards the hot dog stall in silence and she had a sudden stab of fear, that he would leave and not try to contact her again. Before she could speak he spoke so softly that she strained to hear. "I've lived in the shadows for a long time and during the last few days thought I saw the sun again." His voice firmed. "I, of all men, have no right, none at all, to judge you, and you are correct. I'll not call you or try to see you again. I'll make certain that Mike and I conduct our business on neutral ground." They were back at the arch and turning to her he took her face in both hands then bent and kissed her gently. "I wish to have no regrets for this day and I wish you to have none either." Releasing her he studied her face for a long moment then, turning, disappeared momentarily into a throng of Japanese tourists arriving in a large group.

Through a film of tears she saw him reach the parking lot and saw a cruising taxi pull up.

"Are you all right dear?"

"What? Oh yes, thank you." Blindly she turned away from the elderly couple looking at her with concern. Her beeper sounded and without looking she took the cellular phone from her bag and punched the number for the hospital.

"Dr. Flett. You called?"

"Anne can you come back? It's Mrs. Singh, she's having trouble."

Brushing tears from her eyes, she took a deep breath. Thank God for work, at least that was a constant. "Yes, I'm on my way. I should be there in fifteen minutes."

Chapter 20

Love and Memories

Ismail Talawi carefully masked his irritation. He hated criticism, even justified, well meaning criticism. "Well, you certainly are making me rethink a lot Meg." God, she was attractive even if she didn't know bollocks about Egyptian pre-Pharonic religion and tried to pretend that it was his writing that was obscure instead of her knowledge. "So you feel that the passage is too complex with its references to the chaos of the underworld."

"Ismail, this novel is meant to be read and enjoyed by the general population. If I find it complex and, I'm a very average person, then don't you think others will also?" Meg, surprising herself, had taken considerable care with her appearance before arriving at the house in Lower Halliwell Green near Shepperton. The 16th century cottage, the final staging area while waiting for Sandy Flett's confirmation that a safe house in Canada had been arranged, was a mere 10 minutes from Heathrow Airport. The two undercover officers sharing the house had exchanged glances at seeing Meg arrive dressed in a crisp shirtwaister, hair brushed to a glowing shine and wearing elegantly simple sandals. The transformation had not been lost on Talawi. For the past week Meg had read through his rough draft without comment, stating that she would discuss flaws on the second pass. They had fallen into a routine of Meg reading quietly while he wrote for two hours. At 4 p.m. Ismail would put his pen down and going into the living room prepare ice-cold gin and tonics for them both. They would sit and discuss recent popular novels before Meg rose to leave at 5 p.m. Ismail, realising that Meg was relaxing in his company, made certain that he did

not say or do anything that would offend. He saw Meg
as a challenge, a worthy opponent after the string of
silly women he'd been involved with. The fact that Julie
Croaker had been genuinely in love with him and he'd
heard that she'd left her husband after their affair didn't
move him at all.

Meg's natural cynicism, blunted by the physical
transformation as much as the considerate attitude,
didn't notice that she was looking forward to their talks
with much more enthusiasm than she would have believed a few weeks before. He was an arrogant bastard
she told herself, but he had much to be arrogant about.
Around her, he was witty, gentle and considerate. He
didn't dig into her past, something Meg saw as considerate rather than Talawi's total lack of interest in anything
outside his immediate needs. A sexual predator with
long experience of women Talawi found the weak spots
in each of his conquest's armour, which he then
skillfully exploited. Actually, he didn't like women very
much. His own mother had been more of a servant,
bullied by her husband and subjected to petty unnecessary cruelties. Ismail was adored by his father and raised
to believe women were nothing more than chattels good
only for child bearing and male children at that. He
could perhaps be excused for his behaviour except that
from an early age he'd been sent to the best English
public schools, raised as a perfect Englishman, soaked
in the love poetry of Byron, Keats and Wilde. He had,
as Julie Croaker discovered, a cruel streak, a meanness
of spirit yet he also had great charm and could be
exceptionally generous. He smiled at her. "OK maybe it
needs more work. But right now I want to relax. How
about we go to the pub across the road for a drink this
evening and a meal. Let's test out the disguise."

Meg frowned. She and Jimmy Douglas had discussed the possibility of letting Ismail Talawi out and

she'd been opposed, using the argument that he could
have freedom in Canada where the chances of recognition were infinitesimal. Jimmy had been more relaxed
after the first successful outings of Talawi's *doppelganger*
Wilfred Blair. Despite stories of Talawi's temper and
refusal to comply with instructions he'd been a model
client. She hesitated. "After dark then, we'll walk across
to the Pub and find a dark corner. I still don't think it's a
good idea, but—you're probably right—a break will do
you good." Placing the manuscript on the table she
stood and brushed her skirt. "I'll ask Jack to go ahead
and Keith can follow after we leave the house. But,
please Ismail, don't do anything foolish like raising your
voice for example."

"Good, excellent I'll go and have a quick shower
but first let me make you a G and T." He bustled around
the room with sudden energy, fixing her gin and tonic
and making a joke about mad dogs and Englishmen
going out in the midnight darkness, before leaving to
change. Meg sipped her drink. Dusk was falling across
the roofs and in another half-hour it would be totally
dark.

Leaving the house just as the last light left the sky,
Ismail took her arm. "Let's pretend were an old married
couple. Adds to the disguise." Meg hesitated, her training rebelled, she needed both arms free should there be
an attack. Still what he said was true. The assassin
would be looking for a bearded, slightly shorter single
man. She relaxed slightly and allowed his arm through
hers to stay. The pub was a haven of light but fortunately the owner in a moment of rare extravagance had
changed all the outside and entrance lights to yellow
insect repellent bulbs. Everyone who entered looked
like a bad case of jaundice but as it turned out no one
took the slightest notice as they came through the door.

Finding a table against a rear wall Meg went to the bar
and ordered two glasses of the local beer. The evening
started slowly but as it progressed Ismail made her laugh
with stories of the literary merry go-round and his
schooldays at Charterhouse and Eton.

Later, wiping tears from her eyes, Meg lifted her
glass. "I can't have any more tonight. I have to drive
back to London. Do you want another one?"

Ismail shook his head, "No. I think not. Perhaps
it's time to leave."

Catching the undercover officer's eye she gave a
nearly imperceptible nod and watched him drain his
glass then rise and leave the pub. She turned back to
Talawi who was oblivious of the mini drama that had
been played out. "Have you ever thought, Ismail, of
putting those stories down just as you told them to me?
I suspect they would be very popular."

"Ah, you're very kind milady. But I'm very happy
with my own brand of magic realism. Come let us
depart before the Djinn find us and cast their snare."
Walking back down the winding street and across the
tiny green space in front of the house Meg realised he
was mildly drunk and it amused her. He held her arm to
prevent himself stumbling and when they reached the
cottage tried to persuade her to come in for a final drink.
"A cup of coffee then?"

"Ismail, I have a lot of paperwork to get through.
Reading the manuscript, and spending the afternoons
with you, however pleasant, eats into work time. I'll see
you tomorrow afternoon." In the cramped space of the
cottage entrance hall they were almost touching.

Ismail looked at her and his face darkened for a
moment then just as quickly cleared. "Of course, it's
selfish of me and you were good about this evening. It
was fun though, wasn't it?" He leant forward quickly

and kissed her full on the lips. "Thank you."

Stunned, Meg didn't move for a few seconds, then pushing Talawi back she reached for the doorknob behind her. "Ismail, lets keep this relationship on a professional basis shall we." She opened the door and stepped back into dark. "Goodnight." Without looking back made she for the alley where she'd parked her car. She heard Ismail call "See you tomorrow" after her. Crossing the small park she touched her lips. What was happening to her? The man was a womaniser damn it and a rotten human being to boot. She reached her car and, slipping inside, sat without starting the engine, as she tried to sort out her feelings. Her love affairs had always been brief, the men she went out with quickly realising that she was the stronger personality and unable to cope with a woman who was afraid of almost nothing usually ended the liaison after a short period. Sandy Flett was the first man in a long time she'd felt comfortable with but although she liked him a lot it was more the like of a sister for a favourite brother. She stared through the windscreen into the night. I hope, she lectured herself, that I'm reading this wrong and that I'm not falling for Ismail Talawi.

Standing in the darkened living room and watching her sitting motionless in the vehicle the object of her speculation smiled grimly in satisfaction. Whistling soundlessly he went to the drinks cabinet on rock steady legs. Pouring himself a good-sized Scotch whiskey Ismail Talawi sank into an overstuffed chair. It had been a good night and had gone exactly as planned.

§

"Your tax structure is a major stumbling block Mike. The Americans have some very good incentives to attract investment. I like what you've shown me so far but it's too soon to decide and I still have to discuss all the options with my board in Germany."

"Nick, I have access to some of the latest economic stimulation packages the government has put together. I know the premier personally and he'd be willing to have the government underwrite a soft loan."

Sitting outside the café in bright sunshine under a large umbrella set into the middle of their table the two men watched the tied fishing boats bobbing in the wash of vessels moving up the South Arm of the Fraser River past the Steveston fishing dock. Scattered on the table were the remains of lunch. Earlier in the morning Dragovic and Monroe had walked a piece of prime riverside property belonging to Monroe's associate Sam Kwok.

"Oh before I forget Nick would you be free for dinner tomorrow night? We're having a few people over."

Dragovic hesitated; he'd love to see her again. It had been a week now and he still had to stop himself reaching for the phone half a dozen times a day. Every time he returned to the hotel he checked his messages quickly hoping that she might have contacted him. This invitation was not from her. Mike wanted to keep him in play. Still, he would see her and perhaps they could talk. No, it would not work. Steeling himself he shook his head. "Thank you Mike but I have another engagement. Please apologise to your wife for me." He pushed back his chair. "I'll be calling Germany to set up a conference call and discuss this latest proposal. The riverside property is attractive for a variety of reasons. I don't like keeping you on a hook like this but two of our board are in the CIS at the moment and it might take a few weeks, but in any case I'll have to fly back to Washington State

Anthony Bruce

again." He looked at his watch. "I'll call you on Monday. Tell me is Sandy, your brother in law, staying with you?"

Puzzled, Mike shook his head. "Sandy, no. He's in the Sylvia Hotel. He'll be coming tonight. He's away right now. Why?"

"I must get in touch. We agreed to meet at your party and I've been rather busy. I'll call his hotel." Dragovic had known from the first day that Sandy was quartered at the Sylvia Hotel but Sandy must think that the information had come from an obvious source. He stuck out his hand. "Thanks for lunch. Until Monday then."

Mike Monroe watched Dragovic stride away before signaling the waitress to bring the bill. He scribbled some numbers on a napkin. If Sam was willing to take the Maple Ridge apartments in exchange for the riverside properties it might just work out perfectly. Pity about tomorrow night he thought, but still, the man was interested in the riverside lots, he'd seen Cartwright's eyes light up. The man might be a tough negotiator but unless the Americans could offer a lot more this deal was very much a go.

§

Nick was just about to enter the Hotel Vancouver through the Burrard Street entrance when he heard his name. Startled, he stopped and saw Sandy Flett approaching from the direction of the waterfront.

"Hullo Nick, this your hotel?" Sandy reached his side. "I'm parched, feel like joining me in a coffee?"

Nick smiled, his brain racing. What was Sandy doing outside his hotel? Was he blown? "Sure let's go inside, there are several places to choose from." He stood aside to let Sandy enter ahead of himself. "What are you doing down here? Were you looking for me?"

"No, glad I saw you though. I spent last night on a Gulf Island. An old friend invited me to visit so I took the floatplane. Just got back and thought I'd walk off all the food I've consumed in the last 24 hours." Sandy patted his stomach. "No wonder there are so many overweight people around."

Nick relaxed; it was a coincidence after all. The floatplane dock was in the direction Sandy had approached from and he remembered Mike saying something about Sandy being away. "I was going to call you. I had a meeting with Mike this morning and he gave me the name of your hotel. The Sylvia I think he said."

"Yes, that's right. Not as swish as this palace but nice and comfortable." Finding seats in the Griffin Dining room, which was filling with late afternoon customers, they ordered coffee for two. "How's the big deal with Mike going, or shouldn't I ask?" Sandy bit into a biscuit that had come with the coffee. He looked at Nick, who was busy pouring his coffee from a small silver jug.

"Oh, it's moving forward. Mike's very determined to get us into BC. You have to admire his energy and drive. Now it's just a question of seeing who comes up with the best deal." Nick took a quick sip of his coffee then after wiping his lips on the paper serviette, the coffee was piping hot, continued. "If it was my decision alone I think I'd choose BC despite the ridiculous tax structure. But Washington State has some very attractive options and I have colleagues to answer to."

Sandy nodded, "Yeah, he's a hard driving man. I guess that's what makes him successful in business at least."

"You're suggesting that he's not so successful in other areas? He has a lovely home, a beautiful, talented

wife in your sister Anne. I can't agree with you there."
Nick lifted his eyebrows wondering if Sandy would take
the bait.

Sandy laughed, "Bad choice of words. That's not
what I meant. I for one could never spend most of my
time engrossed in business. No, I'm sure they have
everything that you could wish for. And you, do you
spend all your time dreaming deals up?"

"No. I enjoy what I do but I'm not fanatical. I
believe in fate, what is meant to happen will and what is
not, will not. For example I asked Mike for your hotel
this morning as I intended to phone you and we meet by
accident several hours later."

Sandy taking a drink of his coffee, choked, then
coughed, finally clearing his throat to ask. "Seriously,
you base business decisions on fate? " His eyes sparkled
with humour. "You don't strike me as someone who
reads tea leaves."

Nick grunted. "If only it were so simple. No, I
apply the same criteria to any decision that most people
do. But, I feel that in many areas, whatever decision is
made, the end result is determined by actions taken long
before." He laughed at the look on Sandy's face. "It's a
harmless conceit Sandy, but a comforting one." He
drank more coffee and asked, "At the party Mike mentioned that you're a serving officer in the British Army.
Are you on leave?"

"In a manner of speaking. I injured myself while
with the UN forces in Bosnia and was sent back to
London for treatment. My boss won't have me back
until the knee is fully healed so I thought I'd take the
opportunity to visit Anne." Looking across the room at
a group of tourists just entering the restaurant he missed
the sudden tightness cross Nick's face at the mention of
Bosnia. Turning back he continued. "This is a guess, but

I take it you were in the forces at one time?"

Nick shook his head. "Not in Britain. I served in the Rhodesian Army until independence. After the cease fire I went to South Africa and eventually ended up in the situation I'm now in." He felt a sudden rush of gratitude for Gip's thorough training and cover story. To all intents and purposes he was Nick Cartwright, a former lieutenant in the Rhodesian Army's Light Infantry Brigade. Gip had insisted he read everything he could on the bush war in Rhodesia against Mugabe's guerrilla's.

"You fought well, your containment tactics were brilliant. But when the World is against you it's a pretty forgone conclusion." Sandy cocked his head to one side. Several members of the Rhodesian SAS squadron had, after the unit was disbanded at independence, been absorbed by the British SAS and he was curious to know what unit Nick had served in.

Nick didn't reply and finishing his coffee placed the cup down firmly. He looked up, an ironic smile on his lips. "Not all victories go to the best generals. They go to the best politicians." Lacing his fingers together and placing both elbows on the table he rested his chin on the point formed by his hands. "It was a long time ago Sandy. Tell me what was it like in Bosnia."

"Mud, endless acres of mud. Some good people, some incredibly bad people. Northern Ireland was a breeze compared to Bosnia. But let's change the subject to something more pleasant. Do you fish?"

Startled, Nick stared at him. "Fish, you mean fishing, fly fishing, trout that sort of thing? I used to, but years ago. I've probably forgotten how. Why do you ask?"

"Seeing as we're both visitors and this is supposed to be the best salmon fishing in the world it occurred to me that it might be a good idea to find a fishing charter boat and have a go. I can get Mike to set it up, you interested?" Sandy leant forward. "We'll both be back to the regular grind soon enough."

Nick regarded the younger man thoughtfully. It fitted in perfectly; he could track Sandy's movements without attracting attention. After leaving Anne in Stanley Park he'd decided not to see her again, in his bones he felt it would end badly, yet he knew that he wanted to see her and the arguments within himself were not resolved. He could offer nothing and it made his mission much more complicated—but—this way he might see her again. He hesitated, then seeing the expectant look on Sandy's face laughed. "Yes, I would enjoy that. But give me a bit of advance warning in case I have a meeting scheduled in Seattle."

For the next thirty minutes they chatted about various places they'd fished and what tackle was best suited to what area. Sandy discovered that Nick had been at school in Sussex and as a boy had fished several of the same rivers as Sandy had. This part of Nick's background was true. While based in London his diplomat parents, wanting their son to have the best education possible, made certain that the young Jugoslav Nicko Dragovic was turned into a standard English schoolboy. Sandy rose reluctantly. He enjoyed the older man's company but needed to see Sgt. Brian Kowalski of the RCMP again and confirm that the safe house on Salt Spring was acceptable. He promised to leave a message at the hotel once the fishing trip was organised.

§

Three hours later Nick returned to the hotel after checking the contents of the numbered locker at the Via Rail station. He'd carefully opened the oiled packet and checked the weapon wrapped inside while sitting on a cubicle in the station toilet. Satisfied that the pistol was the same Sig Sauer P245 he'd practised with on the farm, he rewrapped it and slipped it into his briefcase. The money, a large bundle of Canadian and US bills in varied denominations in a brown envelope, he also dropped into his briefcase and purchasing a *Vancouver Sun* newspaper from the kiosk walked across the small park to the Main Street Sky Train Station. Catching the three-compartment train fifteen minutes later, he rode as far as the Granville Street stop and walked the short distance to the Hotel Vancouver.

At the reception desk Nick asked if there were any messages and the clerk handed him an envelope with 'N.*Cartwright*' scrawled in pencil across the front. Stuffing the letter into his jacket pocket he rode the elevator to the third floor and his room. Opening the room door he heard the bedside phone ringing. Puzzled, he kicked the door closed with his heel and picked up the phone. "Yes?"

"Nick, its Anne."

Dragovic sat heavily on the bed. "Anne? Is everything all right?" His heart was pounding and he felt his chest tighten as if short of breath.

"Yes, yes everything is fine. Nick, can we meet? If you agree I can pick you up in 10 minutes outside the hotel."

"What's this about Anne?"

"I want to see you again. I have a free afternoon, unless—" He heard the tremor in her voice "—you're busy, of course I'll unders . . ."

"No—no. I'm not tied up" Nick cut her off quickly. "Are you sure Anne? You know how I feel."

"I'll be driving a dark green Range Rover. If you

wait at the pick up and drop off area, where the shuttle
bus and taxi's drop passengers, I'll collect you in about
ten minutes."

"Yes, I'll be there." Her phone clicked off and he
sat still for a long moment collecting his thoughts. What
was this about? He knew it was a mistake to see her but
he knew that he couldn't refuse. Hell, he couldn't help
himself. He, Nicko Dragovic, a pre-war captain in the
Yugoslav Army, combat survivor of the bloodiest ethnic
fighting in recent memory and now a proven, loyal
Muslim soldier of fortune for the Iranian hard-liners. He
Nicko Dragovic, the cold, emotionless, efficient killing
tool could not help himself. Staring into the mirror he no
longer recognised the man staring back. Shivering he
dismissed the thoughts that swirled around in his mind
and checking that he'd left nothing compromising on the
bed, left the suite.

Her dark green Range Rover came around the
corner and turned in as he stepped through the doors of
the hotel. She slowed as she saw him and stopping
leaned across to open the door. Quickly jumping into
the passenger seat he slammed the door as she pulled
away from the curb.

"Great timing." She gave him a quick smile before
turning back to concentrate on the traffic.

"What's this about Anne?" She was dressed in a
white blouse open at the throat and a short skirt in a
dark blue material that exposed a large portion of her
thigh as she drove. Her hair fell forward as she braked to
avoid a bus pulling out and he thought that she'd never
looked more beautiful.

"Mike phoned to say that you'd turned down
dinner tomorrow. Was that because of me?"

"Yes, was the party your idea?"

"No, Mike is determined to get your company into

the Lower Mainland. It's Sandy's birthday and he
thought it would be a great idea to combine his plans.
When he said he was going to throw Sandy a party and
invite you I knew you'd not come. I had lunch with
Sandy and he told me of your accidental meeting and
your plans to go fishing. He likes you." She turned along
Burrard Street heading towards the bridge over False
Creek and into Kitsilano. The traffic was fairly heavy
and Nick smiled as he watched her thread the heavy
vehicle past St Paul's Hospital where she worked and
over the bridge. Beating the traffic lights as they turned
amber at West 4th Avenue she turned West on 6th.
Crossing over train tracks and Macdonald Street, they
were suddenly in a quiet neighbourhood with shade
trees leaning over the street and sidewalks.

"Where are we going Anne?"

She pulled alongside the sidewalk, switching the
engine off. "We're here, come." She stepped out onto
the street and opening the rear door pulled an airline
travel bag from the seat. Bemused he followed her out
and heard the doors lock as she turned and pointed the
remote at the vehicle. She moved ahead of him down a
narrow path between an obviously new townhouse
complex and a large Victorian mansion. The townhouses
occupied the lot that had once been home to a similar
mansion and were designed to merge into the older more
sedate structures on either side. Speaking over her
shoulder Anne remarked, "This belongs to a friends of
mine who are travelling in Europe. I have the key to
check on their plants once a week." Reaching a door set
into the side of the building she fumbled for the right
key before one inserted to her grunt of satisfaction and
the door swung open. Dragovic followed her in and
Anne, reaching past him, pushed the door closed. Her
perfume swamped his senses and before he could move

she placed the bag on a low table and reached up to pull
his mouth down to hers. He stood stiffly for a moment,
undecided, then surrendering to her urgent mouth
reached around the slim body and pulled her tightly into
his embrace. They held to each other for a long time
before she pushed him back. He breathed deeply.

"Anne what—?" She placed a cool hand over his
mouth.

"I ached for you every day since the Park. I tried
to phone a dozen times and each time stopped myself at
the last moment. When Mike said he was asking you to
come tomorrow night I willed you to accept and when
you refused I felt . . .I knew then it made no sense to
stay away from you." She looked into his face, her eyes
shining. "You said that when you were away from me all
you heard was my voice and all you saw was my face. I
kept seeing your face, kept hearing your voice in my
head. Oh Nick I know it's wrong but I can't help myself." She was crying now, a tear trickling down her
cheek.

He pulled her into his arms, his voice muffled in
her hair. "Anne I missed you so. I missed you so." She
pulled away and picking up the bag in one hand pulled
him with the other up the stairs. "Come, our room is on
the second floor."

Later lying naked on top of the covers she traced
the scars on his chest and stomach with a soft index
finger. "Sandy said you were a soldier." She touched the
raised ridges; "You had good surgeons. This one must
have clipped your lung. Where did it happen?"

Hands behind his head and looking up at the
ceiling he sighed, "I was a soldier in a war that most
people have forgotten. I should have died and until I
met you I was only partly alive. Today, now, for the first
time in a long time I am whole. Let it be my love; I have

no wish or need to visit old graves." Rolling over to face
her he touched her cheek gently. "I will not lie to you
but there are certain things I cannot speak of." A shiver
ran down his frame as if a cold wind had washed
through the room and he fell silent. She waited, watching the shadows move across his face as the tree outside
the window moved in the wind. His hand traced the line
of her throat and moved slowly down to caress her
breast. *"You are lovelier than the telling of it, more graceful
than the singing reed. To my heart you are the eye of morning
and a memory that will not fade."*

She closed her hand over his and chuckled, a low
throaty sound. He felt her breast shake under his hand,
the nipple hardening as he moved his fingers gently.
"You say such lovely things. Did you just make that
up?"

"No, but I wish I had. It comes from a slim book
called *The Love Poems of Ba Anton*. That particular poem
has stayed with me, perhaps for just this day."

"There must be more, can you remember?"

He laughed. "Let's see what I can remember. It
starts, I think, like this—

You are lovelier than the telling of it,
More graceful than the singing reed,
To my heart you are the eye of morning and a memory
that will not fade.
But, an older tie has title and honour brooks no lies,
So I'll . . .' He stopped suddenly, an ice-cold clamp
gripping his heart. He could no longer hold. The words
"an older tie" resonated like a gong in his mind and at
that moment buried memories surfaced from beneath
the iron layers of will he'd covered them with. Crystal
clear, on a screen only his mind could see, he saw again
the bodies of Reena and Maia lying like broken bloody
toys scattered across the shattered remains of what had

once been a pleasant suburban house. His house pil-
laged by Serb irregulars, his family raped and tortured by
men from an Army he'd once been proud to serve. That
terrible day he'd sworn before Allah to avenge them and
had done so many times; again and again he'd knelt in
the mosque pledging fealty to his faith and praying to be
given the chance to purge his hate. Taking Anne by
surprise Nick sat up suddenly, hands clamped tight
across his face, knees drawn up and face buried so that
only the curve of his back and the top of his head were
visible. His shoulders heaved uncontrollably and then
the tears came. Like a great dam breaking the long
suppressed grief burst out and he cried like a child
without restraint.

Stunned, Anne knelt beside him, her arms
wrapped around his shoulders trying to comfort and
calm him, bewildered. "Nick, oh Nick my darling. What
is it, what's the matter?" She rocked him as mother
calms a frightened child and little by little the trembling
stopped. Finally he sat straight and drew deep breaths.

"I'm sorry my love, I'm so sorry and you should
not be part of this." He did not look at her. "For a long,
long time I've hidden my memories, buried them deep.
Today you've breached my defenses and as I recited the
poem I remembered things best forgotten. Hatred piled
on hatred. Things done that cannot be undone." He
gazed at a painting on the opposite wall, studying it
intently as if an answer could be found in the swirling
colours of the abstract image.

"Your wife?"

"And my little girl, and the men who killed them,
and were killed for it, and others who were innocent but
paid just the same." He took her face in his hands as
gently as if he were handling a precious piece of porce-
lain. "You must believe that I love you from the bottom
of my soul and that today I have been forced to finally

face the past." He kissed her gently, but she responded hungrily, her lips burning into his, her tongue darting like a small quick bird. His hands moved down her shoulders pushing her back and one hand reached down the curve of her back and over to the inside of her thigh to pull her legs gently apart.

Later, asleep, he lay facing her, his face relaxed and a deep rhythmic cycle of breathing lifting his chest with its irregular torn witness to a past life rising and falling steadily. Her arm underneath him was numb yet she did not want to move for fear of waking him. Studying his face carefully she smiled with pleasure and happiness. He was not handsome, but his was a strong face. He was gentle, surprisingly so for a man with so much muscle mass. Even during their wild lovemaking he'd been careful not to hurt her. Anne touched his face, her fingers barely brushing the skin, but he smiled in sleep and muttered something unintelligible. Nick rolled onto his back and seizing the chance she drew her arm out. He did not move. Naked, Anne rose and went down to the kitchen. Turning on the range then pulling a frying pan from the cupboard and several eggs and bacon strips from the refrigerator she began cooking. Singing softly to a tune coming from the radio attached under a shelf she didn't hear him coming down the carpeted staircase in bare feet. He circled her from behind, his hands cradling her breasts and his mouth finding the soft skin behind her ear.

Startled, she jumped, the frying pan clattering back on to the range. "Nick, you devil. I nearly burnt myself." She leant back into his naked embrace. " What are you doing up? I need more time to prepare our dinner."

"What about tonight? Don't you have to go home?"

" Michael is away in Victoria. He flew there after

lunch, and plans to stay the night. He called me from the airport with a few last minute details about tomorrow night's party. That's how I knew you weren't coming. Apparently he has an early morning appointment with the Premier. Is that something to do with your business deal?"

"Quite possibly. He mentioned that he might be able to get a soft loan from the government. Hi-Tech industry is all the rage these days so that's probably what he's after."

He gave her a squeeze that made her giggle, and said with mock anger, "You brazen hussy, you planned all this in a couple of hours?"

She squirmed in his embrace, her buttocks rubbing into his groin. "You must think me awful. But going back to the hospital after having lunch with Sandy when he told me how much he'd enjoyed your conversation then hearing later that you weren't coming I must've looked awful. Sam, that's the hospital administrator, took one look and told me to go home, said I'd been working ridiculous hours. That's true by the way, I tried to bury myself in work after our first meeting. I sat in my office for a long time trying to screw up courage to call you. If you'd not been there I'm not sure I could've tried again." She turned to face him, her hands locked behind his neck. "I love you Nick. You've bewitched me and I'm glad. I don't know what's going to happen and I don't care."

He bent and kissed her. "Let's take one day at a time. Neither of us was prepared for what has happened. I have to sort out my future but I know it has to include you." The letter he'd picked up the hotel, crumpled and unread lay in his jacket pocket lying with his other clothes on the floor of the bedroom.

Chapter 21

A carefully planned seduction

Condensation trickled down the outside of the glass and ice cubes tinkled as Ismail Talawi handed the drink to Meg. Outside, the last light of evening cast long shadows across the park and opposite houses. Taking a small sip Meg placed the glass down on a coaster. "I assume that you're prepared to leave at short notice?"

"All packed. I'm taking very few clothes along. I'll pick up what I need in Vancouver. Tonight I'll pack my laptop, backup discs and a change of clothes with my toiletries in the travel case that goes as cabin baggage." He lifted his own glass. "Cheers, let the adventure start. Did they tell you anything about the accommodation?" Dressed in a short-sleeved knitted shirt and dark, lightweight woolen slacks, his feet in Gucci loafers, Ismail dropped into the seat opposite.

Meg looked at him speculatively. He was an extraordinarily handsome man and he was obviously attracted to her. Working closely with him for the last 10 days she'd come to see another side of the arrogant, selfish, womanising rake. He could be very funny and considerate. When she'd arrived just after lunch to tell him that word had come from Sandy to say the safe house was ready he'd accepted the news without comment. They'd spent the afternoon in what was becoming routine; he working on his latest book while she continued reviewing the draft copy. Jimmy Douglas, convinced the hit man was still in England, wanted no problems with the real Ismail Talawi, encouraged her to keep to the routine. Thinking of Tristam riding shotgun on the fake Talawi she felt a pang of guilt. That should have been her job, she was better trained and had lots more experience than Tris. Still, she conceded to herself, I'm glad I got this detail.

"Of course not. The whole idea behind a safe house is that as few people as possible know the details. Even my boss has not been told. Once we're installed Sandy will have the RCMP inform SIS." She chuckled, lifting her glass. "Enjoy your last taste of luxury. Knowing Sandy's penchant for spartan living I think we'll be living rough."

Ismail Talawi gave a snort of laughter. "Not this time Meg. I fell for your teasing once before. But if you're correct we'd better enjoy our last taste as you say, so, this evening if you agree, I've ordered in a rather nice meal from the pub." Seeing the doubtful look on her face he held both hands out in supplication. "Come on Meg, I eat alone more than I want to and who knows what will happen when we get to Vancouver. I'll probably spend my time with some hairy, hockey playing, Canadian police officer."

Meg laughed, "OK, you've convinced me. I'm off duty from six but after dinner I'll have to leave in order to pack in case the call comes tomorrow. Jack will be back after six and Keith is keeping an eye on the house from across the street. What did you order for dinner?"

"Aha. Just you wait and see. I think you'll like what I've arranged. How's your drink?"

"Fine. You mix a good drink. The lemon slice is a nice touch." She leant back in the comfortable chair feeling very relaxed. Ismail watched her, a small smile playing on his lips; it was going exactly as planned. He lifted his own glass and after taking a sip asked,

"Have you had any success in catching the organisation behind the attack?"

"Some. We have a lead and that's why it's important you're out of the way. Your double is the bait."

"What's he like, this double?" Talawi was secretly

flattered that a stranger would put his own life at risk. "No doubt he's being paid well?" Before Meg could reply the doorbell rang. Picking up her cellular Meg was about to call but before she could speak Keith's voice crackled over her receiver from his observation post across the street. "A delivery from the pub. Did his Highness order in?"

"Yes, sorry, I should have told you. He only told me a couple of minutes ago. I'll collect." She put the cell phone down on the table and rose swiftly, putting a hand out to block Talawi.

"Stay put Ismail. I'll check it out." Meg went through the living room into the hall passage. The door had a frosted glass panel but on a 12" screen screwed to a wall inside the door to a minature video camera covering the outside entrance displayed young man she recognised as a worker at the pub. The man held a large tray covered with a white cloth. She opened the door with a smile. "Here let me take it." The tray was handed over and Meg backed through the door. "If you wait I'll get some money. How much is it?"

"It's been paid. Thanks lady." With a wink he turned and left. Meg watched the retreating back. So Ismail had assumed she'd accept his invitation. He must've ordered the meal several hours ago. Well why not? Maybe Ismail was right. After all being the target of a professional hit man backed with Iranian money must be rather grim. He needed to let his hair down. She sniffed appreciatively. Whatever was beneath the cover certainly smelt delicious. Entering the dining room she saw Ismail had laid the table for two and was busy lighting a centrepiece candle. A wine bottle dripped condensation in a cooler, but on closer inspection she saw that it was a bottle of rather good champagne.

"You've obviously thought this through. Is this how writers attempt seduction?" She handed over the tray, which he laid on the table, and with a flourish he pulled the cover clear. Two small circular bowls each holding a cut glass container filler with what appeared to be shrimp cocktail then two plates, the gold trimmed edges peeking out from under the cover of silver half globes. Carefully he placed each starter on the two table settings. The covered plates he put on to a warming tray on the sideboard. "When did you do all this?" she asked in amazement. Then remembered his frequent trips out of the study in the last half-hour. Ismail pulled the champagne from the cooler and with a sharp twist removed the cork quickly, pouring the bubbling liquid into her glass then his own. He returned the bottle to the cooler and spread his arms palms out.

"Shazam! And the meal is ready Madame." Stepping behind her chair he drew it back for her to sit on.

"How long have you been planning this?"

"Since about 1 p.m., the time you told me we're leaving soon. I decided that if we were leaving England for the colonies we would do it in style." He moved around the table to face her and sat down. "And to answer your question. Of course this is a blatant attempt at seduction but, knowing you, it has as much chance of succeeding as I have of writing pulp fiction. Now," he lifted his glass, "to the future. May it bring all we want."

Meg lifted her glass and touched his. The champagne was cold, sharp and lovely. The shrimp cocktail in a mildly spiced mayonnaise was delicious. Meg put her half-empty glass down and it was instantly refilled. She started to protest then decided to simply leave it untouched. Ismail rose and, going to the warming tray, lifted the cover off the first plate, and using a linen napkin as a glove carried the plate over to set in front of her.

"It may be a bit warm to touch so be careful,"

Ismail advised her as he returned with his own plate. Meg looked down at two medallions of filet mignon covered in a rich-smelling brown sauce. Shitake mushrooms were arranged around two roast potatoes and the balance of the plate was covered in lightly cooked baby vegetables. Her stomach growled. Lunch had been a quick sandwich hours ago. Waiting until Ismail was settled in his chair she began her meal. After a while she looked up.

"It's delicious Ismail. How on earth did the pub manage something as good as this?"

"I'll tell you a secret Meg. There are a lot of frustrated chefs out there. The money is in quickie pub meals, pies, egg and chips, that sort of thing but give a good cook a chance at something different and he'll jump at it." He took a drink of champagne. "My publisher gave me a couple of bottles of Mouton Cadet 98 when he launched *Lunch with the Prophet*. This is the last bottle."

Meg lifted her glass; it certainly was wonderful champagne. "What made you write a novel that you must've known would antagonise the fundamentalists especially after Rushdie's book?"

Talawi lifted his glass to the light, squinting through the champagne. "Have you ever considered how religion, any religion, but especially the main ones, have caused untold misery to the people it supposedly is meant to enlighten? Consider my own: female circumcision, the chardor, total male domination, tenth century punishments in the twentieth century. Yours, the inquisition, burning at the stake, drowning of supposed witches. I could go on but you get the message."

"I think it was Shaw who said the only problem with Christianity was that it hadn't been tried yet. So your novel is meant to bring about change? What made you believe, given what you've just said, that it is even remotely possible?"

"Ah, now that's just it. Every great change in human history has come about because one person refused to accept the status quo. I'm not an apologist for Hitler, but *Mein Kampf* changed the German people and history as did Marx's *Communist Manifesto*. Those two are poor examples I suppose, for the end result was misery, but the world was galvanised to find a better system. What I tried to do in my book was to show the main fallacy that underpins the Muslim faith and by doing so show that Christianity has similar flaws."

Meg wondered of he was trying to annoy her. Using Hitler and Marx as role models was a weak argument in any discussion. But, if she understood what he was trying to say, however obliquely, then his argument that a false premise could eventually have good results might hold water. She took a long drink of champagne and didn't object when he refilled her glass.

"You say that *Mein Kampf* for example forced people to confront their prejudices, but it doesn't seem to have worked has it? Recent examples in Bosnia, Kosovo and Rwanda jump to mind. I would argue that in fact such confrontational theories exacerbate prejudices, not diminish them." She took a sip of champagne and waited for the explosion.

He grinned. "I wondered what your reaction would be. Obviously the two examples I gave you are ridiculous but as examples of the power of the written word what I said still stands. However if we're talking religion then how about Luther's break with the Holy Roman Church? What about the various breakaway sects each trying to find the one true path and each one of those driven by an individual writing down his concept of God's word. All I'm attempting to do is force people to examine deeply held beliefs. The Moslem world has been held back by a religion that encourages rigidity of thought. We, after all, invented mathematics and astronomy, long before the flat-earthers of the Catholic Church persecuted Galileo the Arab world had conceived of a solar system in which the earth was not the centre of the universe."

"And then came Mohammed?"

"Exactly. Once religion became the state and the state religion, when men made laws based on false assumptions and imposed draconian punishments on those who would question, then pure thought died. You cannot have it both ways. If one looks to a divine authority for salvation and guidance then by extension one cannot have free will."

"You ignore the great truths of religion. Moses as a man was badly flawed but he brought down the Ten Commandments, which stand despite the vicissitudes of time. Perhaps Shaw's dictum with regard to Christianity could apply equally to Islam."

"You surprise me Meg. I would never have put you as a religious person."

For a couple of seconds Meg made no reply then, draining her glass, looked across the table at him. "I am what might be best described as a weak agnostic. My father and I had a similar argument before he died. His comment, which I have trouble with still, is that love is not a quantifiable quantity and neither is faith. One loves despite the illogicality of certain attachments and one has faith despite the assaults of scientific realism. He served in the Second World War and was a 20-year-old officer in the advance party that liberated Bergen-Belsen yet he never lost his faith." She stopped suddenly and looked at her watch. "Damn it, look at the time. Ismail I've had too much champagne. How on earth did we get into such a deep discussion?" She pushed her chair back.

"The coffee is ready. Let me get you a cup." He stood and walked to the ornate cabinet on which stood a silver coffee percolator.

"A quick cup Ismail, but I must get going. It's been a lovely evening. Thank you." She opened her cell phone and, checking a card from her handbag, dialed a number. "Yes, please send the taxi to lower Halliwell Green, it's the house facing the little park. I'll be outside." She added cream and sugar before sipping the coffee. "I wonder about you sometimes. It's almost as if you enjoy baiting people to see if you can get them to show their prejudices and when you began to find that boring you decided to bait an entire religion."

"You sympathise with the Moslem religion?" He was standing very close as she stood to leave.

"I know nothing of the Moslem religion beyond what I learnt at school and what I read in the papers. No, I'm neither for or against, one has to have knowledge of subject before one can judge. But . . ." she raised her hand to stop him speaking, "common sense tells me that you, a professed skeptic and, a man who has obviously a deep knowledge of his faith must have realised the reaction your novel would cause." She shook her head. "What puzzles me is knowing that you might be a prisoner for the rest of your life you still went ahead. You love the good things of life too much."

That Ismail Talawi was angry was obvious and the fact that he was fighting to control it was evident in the muscles of his jaw. He gripped her upper arms firmly but not painfully and gazing into her face spoke wonderingly. "God but you're wonderful even when you don't know what you're talking about." He pulled her forward and kissed her hard. For a moment Meg, slightly off balance and startled by Talawi's sudden move, relaxed in preparation to execute the kiu-ju move and break his hold. She felt the warmth of his body and found she was enjoying being held. Her arms started to slide behind his back when she realised what she was doing. She pushed him back firmly. "Enough! I think we've both had too much champagne."

He looked at her a long moment his face flushed and breathing faster than normal. "My apologies. I should not let my emotions take control. Whatever you think of my motives I cannot help myself. Please forgive me." He looked so contrite that Meg almost laughed.

"I enjoyed the evening. But it cannot go further than this. You must understand that if we ever got involved I would be removed from the case." She leant forward and taking him by surprise kissed him lightly on the lips. "That's to show there's no hard feelings. Now I must go."

He walked her to the door and helped her put her coat on. "Your taxi has just arrived." He took her hand and in a parody of a Prussian officer clicked his heels and raising her hand to his lips lightly brushed the knuckles with a kiss.

She resisted the temptation to ruffle his hair and turning away walked the few steps to where the taxi waited. She sank back in the cushions feeling lightheaded and happy. I don't want a relationship right now and especially not with this man, she told herself. She stretched luxuriously. But he could certainly kiss and was obviously attracted. She smiled into the darkness.

Ismail watched the taillights of the taxi disappear around the corner and smiling at his reflection in the glass spoke aloud. "You've breached the wall old son, now to take the castle," he murmured to himself.

Chapter 22

There are no simple choices

Nick laughed. "Imagine what would happen if I decided to come tonight. We'd give ourselves away in a flash. Don't you have to leave soon?" They had finished breakfast and, standing side by side, were busy washing the dishes. Early Spring sunshine reflecting off the house windows opposite illuminated Anne's face and hair as she bent over the sink.

"Yes, I'll drop you back at the hotel and go on to work. God I feel wonderful." She wiped her hands on a small towel hanging beside the sink and reaching up pulled his head down to kiss him. "I want you near me all the time but if you came tonight I think I wouldn't be able to keep from holding you." She looked at the calendar hanging on the pegboard on the adjacent wall. "I don't want to leave you but we'll have to wait until the day after tomorrow. I have surgery tomorrow morning and rounds after that and I can't cancel my afternoon clinic at such short notice." She nuzzled her head into his chest. "Can you exist without me for a day? I'll cancel all my afternoon appointments for Friday. I'll write the address down for you. What time can you get here?"

Putting down the last plate he circled her body with his arms, pulling her close and resting his chin on the top of her head. "I'll be here, no matter what, just after lunch. Now let's get you back to work."

"Wait." Anne bent over a small pad near the telephone and scribbled the address down. Nick pushed the slip of paper into his pocket and in doing so felt yesterday's unopened letter. Frowning he pulled it free and slipping a finger under the flap tore it open. A single piece of paper with the words, 'Meet me.' in Martin's handwriting. Anne, seeing him frown, asked, "What's the matter?"

"A meeting I should've had yesterday." He crumpled the envelope into a ball and thrust it back into his pocket. "It's business, and probably nothing that can't wait. I'll call when I get back to the hotel." He smiled but his mind was racing. Why would Martin want to meet? "Ok, I think that's everything. Let's go, you can drop me back at the hotel and I'll try to make amends for not being available for business yesterday."

"And what would you rather have been doing—hmm?"

"What a silly question.Working of course." He dodged her swing at his head and lifting her bag swung his other arm around her waist. "Back to work for both of us my lazy one."

Ten minutes after leaving the house Anne dropped him outside the Hotel Vancouver. Nick kissed her and jumping from the vehicle headed up the stairs to his room. Once inside he pulled the cellular from his suitcase and punched the pound key and then 6, the signal for Martin to meet him at the coffee stand area in the office complex housing the Hong Kong and Shanghai Bank. Placing the cellphone in his pocket and locking the suitcase again he returned to the lobby. After checking with the reception desk for messages he strode briskly towards Canada Place and the rendevous at number 999 West Hastings Street. Seated alone after collecting a cup of coffee from the Biega Coffee stand he opened a copy of the local newspaper It was 12:35 p.m.

"Been here long?" Nick glanced up; Martin dropped his jacket on the sofa and turned to the coffee stall. The wall clock now read 1:16 p.m. He waited until

Martin poured himself a coffee and was seated before
he spoke.

"About 45 minutes. Sorry about yesterday, I only
read your note an hour ago."

Martin glanced at him curiously and raised his
eyebrows but Nick added nothing further. Shrugging
Martin glancing round to check they could not be overheard then spoke in a low voice. "Early yesterday I
called the farm and was told that Gip's condition had
deteriorated rapidly in the last few days. He'd been
admitted to hospital the day before yesterday but,"
Martin took a deep breath, "Gip died in hospital last
night. I was assured that he was peaceful at the end.
He'll be cremated and his ashes returned to Libya to rest
on his wife's grave." Martin looked carefully at Nick and
saw a spasm of pain cross his friends face. "I'm sorry
Nick, to be the bearer of such news, but he was in a lot
of pain at the end. He knew long ago that this was going
to happen."

Nicko Dragovic looked down at the table. Even
though Gip's death had been inevitable he'd still received a jolt at Martin's news. A riot of conflicting
emotions surged and he wondered what he could tell
Martin about Anne. He decided to wait. The one truth
he'd learnt long ago was that decisions made in haste
usually ended badly. He looked up. "Insh'Allah. He was
a good man and I'd hoped to see him once more." He
expelled the air in his lungs in a long sigh. "I'll be glad
when this is all over."

Martin nodded; he felt the same as Nick. He
grimaced. "He was my friend too Nick, and I'll miss him
as well. We worked together on some difficult assign-
ments." For a while both men sat wrapped in silent
thought. Then Martin spoke quietly. "I also received
news that our subject is being moved soon. His flight

could arrive anytime within the week." Martin rose and walked to get another cup of coffee, then took a sip before returning. "Gip made some last arrangements before he went into the hospital. I've been told to tell you that two million dollars US has been placed in a Cayman Island account in the name of Shoemaker. The number is in the locker with the other equipment plus a full ID for Shoemaker. Read, memorize then destroy anything that can lead them back to us. The British and Canadians will cast a very wide net but our mentors know this and all our background will be eradicated on my signal of a successful strike. Your records, mine and anything else will be totally destroyed." He smiled grimly. "We will be born again my friend, this time to a normal existence."

Nick stared bleakly down at his clasped hands. "Tell me Martin, have you not asked yourself when is the killing going to stop? When do we finally break the cycle of revenge?"

Martin did not answer and looking up Nick saw his friend watching him with concern. Again Nick spoke softly, his voice weary. "I've had enough Martin. I'm tired of killing and I no longer want to stand on the bones of the dead, to wake in the night and talk with ghosts. For the first time in a long time I want to see tomorrow."

"This will be the last time Nick. We have no choice, you and I. Promises have been made and must be kept. Gip's death has been a blow and I understand how you're feeling right now but the operation is still running and when it is over we will disappear and it will be to a new life." He reached across to grip Nick's shoulder fiercely. "Talawi is nothing. This is not a man whose life is worth considering. You read the file. He chose his course and knew the consequences."

"No it has nothing to do with Talawi. As you say

Talawi is nothing." Nick sighed deeply. "Perhaps you're right. Gip's death has affected me more than I care to admit." He slid his chair back. "I will be at the Hotel waiting for your signal. When you go to the airport to see Talawi, remember we discussed how they may have altered his appearance."

"Of course, but Sandy Flett will be there and I've tagged his rental car." Martin had attached a remotely activated transmitter, no bigger than a packet of cigarettes to Sandy's rental car.

"The receiver is working?"

"Perfectly. I will reactivate the sending unit once Talawi leaves the airport. As soon as a pattern of movement has been established and the safe house has been located, I'll conduct a discreet surveillance and try to have a pattern for you to act on." Martin watched for a reaction, and seeing nothing in Nick's impassive face grunted. "It may take a while. I don't want the security people to see me around the area on a regular basis. Also I think you should take the opportunity, while I build a pattern of movement, to let people know that you intend to fly back to Germany and visit your firm. It will strengthen your cover."

"Yes, that makes sense. Have the principals been warned that I might visit? I've never met anyone from that organisation." Nick frowned, "Are they party to any of this?"

"Of course not. They're paid a very handsome retainer to have various partners who may or may not sit in at board meetings. They know your name and that you are an alternate senior director standing in for Gip Lawrence who has been on the board for 10 years. They also understand that you are looking for the location of a new factory planned for the American West Coast. Gip was very thorough, he assumed that you might need to

have a watertight story should anyone decide to check."
Martin smiled, "Don't look so grim, my friend, we are
going to win this time."

Nick didn't smile in return. "There are losses in
any victory Martin. And some that are never factored
in." He paused, considering, then spoke very softly,
almost to himself. "I promised Gip that I would carry
this through and I will." His voice firmed and looking at
Martin he continued, "Don't worry Martin. I'll not fail."
Rising, he collected their empty paper cups. "I've agreed
to go fishing with Sandy Flett. I like him, he reminds me
of what I was before the dog Milosevic came to power.
His career will be destroyed—I'm not used to this sort
of deceit."

"I know you're not and neither am I; from the
beginning it was meant to be a straightforward strike on
Talawi with no one else getting hurt. This complicated,
devious course was never intended and if Salameh and
the others had obeyed orders none of this would be
necessary. But, we agreed to the project, we accepted
the terms. I cannot abandon it now and knowing you I
don't believe you can either." He stood to face Nick and
punched him lightly on the shoulder. "There are worse
things in life than having to change one's career. Flett is
young, he'll recover."

Picking up the bill Nick walked over to the cash-
ier's desk and when he turned back after completing the
transaction Martin had left. Pocketing his change he
walked slowly back to the hotel deep in thought.

Chapter 23

A far country

Ismail Talawi rolled away from Meg Davidson. God, she had a lovely body but she was totally inexperienced in the nuances of lovemaking. He slapped her sharply on the thigh. "Go and make some coffee, woman."

Meg, lost in thought, jerked as if shot. She turned to her lover and smiled but her eyes were bright. "Hit me that hard again Ismail and I'll break all your fingers." Swinging her legs off the bed she walked naked to the window to peer through a gap in the joined curtains. "It's a lovely day outside. How about a walk to the shops?"

Talawi scowled. It was two days after the dinner with Meg in the cottage and he suspected that once again the move to Canada had been delayed. He was annoyed at her casual acceptance of their becoming lovers. This was not going as he'd planned. He'd thought that once he'd brought her to his bed she would be at his mercy like all the rest, but instead she behaved as though it was the most natural thing in the world. God, he disliked self-confident women. Bloody feminism he thought, scowling at her naked back. He was beginning to hate the enforced seclusion imposed by the security personnel and his mood was foul. Well, at least he'd used the time to good effect. He started to form a caustic remark when her cell phone rang.

" Yes, understood Jimmy. We'll be ready." Meg placed the phone down on the bedside table. She smiled at him. Still amazed at herself for giving in to his obvious seduction attempts. After the dinner and champagne she'd been driven back to her apartment wondering about her feelings. The following day she'd met him at the door of his safe house as usual and as the door closed Ismail had pulled her head to his and kissed her hard. She'd not resisted and that afternoon they'd become lovers. Meg knew the arrangement was wrong and if Jimmy Douglas found out she'd be off the case. Her training and experience told her to walk away from the obvious pitfalls of this relationship but she found to her surprise that she really was falling for the man. Meg pointed at the cupboard. "Start packing Ismail, we're on our way. The car will be here in two hours."

Stunned, he stared, all thoughts of putting her in her place driven out by a sudden gut-twisting jolt of fear. "Why, what's happened?" His voice high and sharp.

Puzzled, Meg frowned. "Nothing's happened. Sandy's finally firmed up the safe house. We fly direct to Vancouver on BA this evening. What's the matter?"

Realising how he must sound Talawi swallowed. "Nothing, even though I've been expecting the move it comes as something of a shock." He sat up on the bed. "No other news?—I mean about the professional killer—Is that why we're being moved at such short notice?" His voice wavered.

Meg shook her head and her voice held a touch of exasperation. "Ismail, we're off because that was always the plan. The delay in waiting was because Sandy wanted an absolutely secure safe house. These things can take time and no, Jimmy said nothing about the hitman but we'll all breathe easier when you're offshore." She went into the adjoining bathroom, leaving him sitting on the bed. "I'll put all your soaps and toilet things on one side of the washstand," she called through the open door. "Do you really want to take all these bottles?"

Without answering Talawi walked to the cupboard and began to lay clothes out on the bed. Buttoning his shirt as he dressed he saw that his hands were shaking. I bet she lied to me he thought. This is just too sudden, what the hell is going on? During the first weeks of their relationship he'd been so keen to bed the bitch that he'd not worried about the world outside and besides the new novel was causing him problems that were hard to overcome. Damn it! He noticed that he'd buttoned his shirt wrong, angrily started tugging at the offending buttons as Meg re-entered the room.

"Here let me help you." Meg swiftly undid then refastened the buttons and gave him a quick kiss. "Throw a change of clothes on the bed and I'll pack them in one cabin bag with my stuff." Ismail Talawi bit back a sharp retort. This woman and her team were all that stood between him and a messy execution, even if she wasn't that great in bed. He smiled, the practised charm overcoming his natural inclination to lash out.

"Stop babying me Meg. I can manage."

§

High over Greenland the British Airways 747 slid through the night sky. In the First class section Ismail Talawi, listed on his ticket as James Cross, sat beside Meg Davidson. Behind them in widely separated seats sat two other officers of the diplomatic security detail posing as businessmen. All were armed and the two accompanying officers would return to Britain once the RCMP had taken over security at Vancouver Airport. As Ismail dozed his head fell sideways onto Meg's shoulder. Gently she pushed him away and reaching over de-pressed the button that racked his seat back into the full reclining position. Ismail stirred but didn't move. Meg smiled, amazed that the motion sickness tablets had worked so quickly. The trip through terminal 3 at

Heathrow had gone smoothly, despite Ismail's nerves being on edge and seeing potential assassins behind every pillar. Looking exactly like a successful upper-income couple, Meg held his arm and dropped a few 'Darling's' whenever appropriate as they made their way through the Terminal. Mr. and Mrs. James Cross elicited not even mild curiosity in the hustle and bustle of the departure lounge.

Meg reflected on the events of the past few days and wondered why she found herself being drawn to the arrogant yet strangely insecure man she was tasked to protect. His behaviour today had been in character, yet she knew that despite her own common sense and knowing all the stories about him had he not attempted to hit on her she'd have been disappointed. Looking at his face relaxed in sleep she thought how much like her dead brother he was. Jeremy had been killed when she was 12 years old. Her parents and especially her father had taken the loss of their only son hard. Jeremy had also been over indulged and cosseted, yet despite all the attention he'd retained a gentleness of nature that was at odds with his often selfish behaviour.

The big jet droned on through the night and Meg finally lowered her seat back into a more comfortable position without being fully supine. Never a good traveler, she catnapped in short bursts.

§

Nick woke to the sun streaming through the open curtains of his hotel room. He swung out of bed. Today Anne was occupied and he should start planning his escape route, but until Martin contacted him he simply had to wait. Stepping into the shower he tried to compose his thoughts. The phone was ringing as he walked back into the bedroom toweling his hair. With a grin, assuming it was Anne, he lifted the receiver but before he could speak her name Sandy Flett's voice jerked him back from the brink.

"Well, it's nice that some people can sleep in. How do you feel about going out to sea this morning?"

"Sandy? Sorry I took so long to answer. I was in the shower. What's up?"

"Not what's up, but what's down. Remember I said I wanted to arrange a fishing trip?"

"You've organised a fishing trip?"

"Yes, a friend has a cabin cruiser moored at Galiano Island and has invited me and by extension you, on a fishing trip out to Active Pass. The salmon are running. If you're game I'll pick you up in 15 minutes and we can catch a floatplane from the terminal near Canada Place and be on Galiano by 9 am. It's a 10-minute flight. Feel up to it?"

Nick took a deep breath. This was unexpected. Damn, he wanted no more complications. He was about to refuse when Sandy spoke again. "Take a break, Nick. All work and no play—well you know the rest."

"What about tackle, clothing and so on?"

"All on the boat. All we have to do is turn up. We have to supply the beer of course."

Nick hesitated, then deciding, his mouth twisting in a wry smile. Why not? He still had to wait for Martin to identify the safe house and staying close to Sandy might help Martin especially if he knew that one of the protection team was accounted for, plus a day in the fresh air might help clear his mind. "I'll walk down to the terminal and meet you there."

"Good man!—See you in a few minutes."

Nick scribbled a message on a complimentary pad beside the bed and sealing it in an envelope called the desk. "I have a message for a Mr. Martin Dreyer. Send someone up to collect it. He'll be in later, please make sure that he receives it?" The message itself was innocuous but Martin would understand. Nick pulled the faulty cell phone out of his briefcase and keyed in the number for a letter pick-up.

§

The huge blue and white ferry, *Spirit of British Columbia*, swung through the twisting narrows of Active Pass. The surge of displaced water lifted the seven-metre cabin cruiser and Brian Kowalski gunned the twin engines gently to hold their position stationary. Sandy Flett, leaning back in a fishing chair bolted to the deck, held a salmon fishing rod clipped into a gunwale holder. His line with a fresh strip of herring bait trailed fifty metres behind the boat. Nick Cartwright sat on the opposite side of the cockpit, holding his own line lightly while sipping a cold beer handed to him by Brian Kowalski minutes before.

Sgt. Brian Kowalski had greeted Nick and Sandy on the Galiano Island dock and Nick had been startled to find that he was shaking hands with an off-duty RCMP officer. Flett and Kowalski insulted each other with the casual intimacy of men who'd much in common. At first Nick had found it hard to unwind, but slowly as the sun warmed the air and the gentle slapping of water on the hull relaxed his senses he found the bantering chatter between the two younger men amusing. Brian caught the first salmon, a nine pound Spring that fought fiercely before being brought close enough to the boat to be swung inboard in the landing net. For the next hour they all had fish strike but, apart from Brian catching a second smaller Pink Salmon, Sandy and

Nick were unable to set their hooks and disgustedly had
to haul in and check their hooks several times.

The day wore on and while idly chewing on a
cheese sandwich Nick felt an almighty tug on his line
and his rod dipped savagely. Brian yelled at Sandy to
pull in the other line to avoid entangling Nick's line that
was now screaming off his reel at an alarming rate. This
was obviously a huge fish. Gripping his rod firmly and
bracing his feet Nick struck hard, raising the tip of the
rod sharply upwards and setting the hook firmly.

"Let him run Nick, you have lots of line." Brian
Kowalskis face was flushed with excitement as he
steered the boat, making sure that the fishing line
streamed clear over the stern. "A couple of weeks ago a
tourist caught a 42.5 pound Spring Salmon using the
same white Hoochie you have on your line and at about
the same depth." Scrambling out of his chair Sandy
reeled in his own trailing line quickly, moving to the
edge of the stern to avoid getting in Nick's way.

Nick's mind emptied as he concentrated totally on
the fish that changed tactics suddenly and reversed
course. Winding in rapidly to keep the line taut and deny
the fish a chance to snap the suddenly slack line with
another change of direction he felt nothing but an
overriding desire to bring this contest to successful
conclusion. Time slowed, the sky seemed to darken, and
cradling the rod with his left hand, while he wound
frantically in with his right. Running the incoming sea-
wet line through his left thumb and forefinger he did not
notice the pain from an old cut opened by the sliding
nylon line. The first adrenaline rush subsided slightly
and he waited, every sense alive and quivering, as the
tension decreased on the line and the fish gathered it's
energies for another attempt to break free of the steel
barb. Sandy said something but he barely heard the

comment. This was a duel between him and the fish.
The line that connected them was 15lb test and if it was
even half as heavy as the fish Brian had mentioned he
would need every bit of his vaguely remembered boy-
hood skills.

The salmon exploded, running abeam of the
cruiser and again Nick slacked off the drag wheel to
allow the fish room to run, keeping just enough tension
on the line to tire his quarry and prevent a sudden, line-
breaking, jerk. "Watch him Nick. He's going to try to get
under the boat." Kowalski, anxious as a new mother
watching her child take its first steps. "You're doing
good. Just be careful, he's a wily one." Nick smiled
inwardly, why was it a 'he'? he thought irrationally. Now
the big salmon turned and for a second it flashed silver
on the surface before diving deeply and heading back
towards their boat. The sight drew a collective gasp
from the three men. "God, he's huge. Must be a fifty
pounder at least." The fish in a desperate attempt to
break the aggravation and outrage of the line tried to
slide under the boat and cut the line against the rough
edges and barnacles. Brian goosed the engines to push
the cruiser ahead and foil the salmon's attempt to go
under. Again it made a savage run to the stern but now
it was flagging; Nick could feel the tiredness in the fish
communicated through the line. He tightened up the
drag and began the slow careful process of bringing it
closer to the boat. Several times in the next 30 minutes
it made gallant attempts to escape but finally it surfaced
wallowing close to the surface.

"What a beauty. You lucky devil Nick." Sandy
slapped Nick on the shoulder. "I'll wait until its closer
then net it." Sandy held the landing net ready. Seeing the
boat the salmon tried to twist away but it was exhausted
and Nick pulled it in slowly until he was staring down at

the four foot long fish. A silver bright eye turned towards him and he was looking into a dark cave where a tiny spark of defiance glowed. The fish was done yet it emanated the anger and defiance of the truly free. It had fought bravely, had not surrendered, but been beaten by technology and the greatest predators on land or sea. Sandy dipped the landing net mounted on a long pole under the fish and was just starting to raise it when Nick spoke.

"Wait, I don't want to bring it aboard. Sandy, get the cutters and cut the hook."

Sandy Flett stared at him, his jaw dropping. "Are you mad. Nick, this is one of the biggest fish I've ever seen. I'm certain it will be a record. Brian tell him." Sandy turned to Brian Kowalski, who was eyeing Nick speculatively. "You're sure Nick? Sandy is probably right it could be a record."

"Yes, but I have no use for a huge fish. It would be a waste."

"Sandy, the cutter is under the seat." Brian smiled. "For a tourist you're a good fisherman and a pretty good conservationist Nick. A lot of people don't realise that the biggest fish are the ones that have the best chance of propagating good genes to the species. But still, it's hard giving up a trophy fish."

Shaking his head, Sandy reached over the side feeling down the line with one hand while with the other he closed the side cutter over the hook and with a sharp squeeze cut the hook and fish free. The salmon rolled slowly in the slight chop while still looking at the three men staring down at it then with a long tired undulation of it's tail slid down into the darkness of the sea.

Nick swung the line aboard. "I'll get you a new lure Brian." He placed the rod in a holder and stretched his shoulders before turning to Sandy Flett, who was stowing the landing net. "Sorry Sandy, but I couldn't bring myself to waste something so beautiful besides . . . . ." He shrugged, "Say it was an aberration, I really can't explain."

Sandy Flett straightened up and facing Nick, grinned. "Your fish old boy. But I think I understand." Sandy turned to Brian Kowalski and pointed at Nick's head. "No hat Brian, that's my theory." He punched Nick lightly on the upper arm. "Of course you realise that absolutely no one is going to believe us. Here catch…" Sandy pulled a beer out of the cooler and tossed it to Nick. The sheer excitement of the huge fish had left them all drained and no one objected when Brian turned for Galiano Island an hour later.

Back at the landing they thanked Brian and waited for the next floatplane while Brian sailed out of the harbour heading for his property at the North End of the Island.

Chapter 24

Salt Spring Island

Martin Dreyfus watched the small group of passengers walk across the parking lot to where Sandy Flett had parked two hours before. Next to Sandy's car was the unmarked police cruiser. Earlier, after following Sandy Flett's car from the Sylvia Hotel and parking several stalls away, he'd strolled casually behind Sandy and the burly RCMP officer he'd seen meet Sandy at the hotel several times. Martin, looking like just another person meeting the inbound flights, had checked the arrival board for the time of the British Airways flight from Heathrow then studiously avoided following Sandy and the Canadian policeman; he knew they would be in the arrival hall at the due time.

Now, exiting the arrival hall, hidden from view behind an excited family reunion, Martin watched the group of Sandy, the RCMP officer, Ismail Talawi and a woman he'd not seen before stroll down the steps to the open-air parking and the two vehicles. Martin had spotted the two British security men in plainclothes who walked across the arrival hall pretending to greet the man and woman who were obviously RCMP undercover protection. Martin smiled to himself; it was a nice touch using at least one woman. After talking for a few minutes with the Canadian officers the two Brits disappeared in the direction of the rental car desk. The two RCMP undercover agents waited until Sandy's group exited the arrival hall before casually following the group from a distance.

On arriving at the airport and parking near Sandy Flett's car, Martin had activated, by a radio signal, the cigarette-pack-sized transmitter attached to the

underside of Sandy's rear bumper. A hair thin black
wire, matching the black bumper was glued to the
outside face. Once the transmitter was activated Martin
could locate the vehicle with pinpoint accuracy.

Half an hour later Martin walked to his parked car
and strapping himself in he switched on the receiver and
waited as the liquid crystal screen hidden in the briefcase sized container warmed up. A map of the Fraser
Valley from North Vancouver to the American border in
the south became visible. The map went east as far as
Port Coquitlam on the Fraser River and to the bounda-
ries of Surrey and Langley. Martin rolled a small knurled
wheel enlarging the area where a blinking red dot was
visible. He frowned, as the area around the dot enlarged.
It was the airport and surrounding area. Sandy's car was
no more than two kilometres southeast from where he
sat. The red dot was stationary; Sandy had parked.

Vancouver International Airport sits on aptly
named Sea Island, a large delta barely above sea level,
encircled by the upper and middle arms of the Fraser
River. Starting his vehicle and driving out of the airport
parking area Martin stopped to pay his fee at the booth.
Leaving the booth he followed the main exit road, Grant
McConachie Way, and watched the distance plot begin
to widen as he turned northeast. Martin knew that
Sandy and party were south of his present position,
sitting somewhere along the bank of the middle arm of
the Fraser River. Taking an exit ramp he swung up and
over his previous route and found that he was now
travelling south down Russ Baker Way. The distance on
his Global Positioning screen shrank rapidly and ignoring the left turn over the Dunsmore Bridge he followed
Inglis Road directly ahead, flanked by the river on his
left.

Pulling off the road and coming to a stop he

rolled down the side window and was startled to hear a sudden roar. Peering through the windscreen he saw a Beaver floatplane lift off the river, water trailing like smoke from the pontoons. Martin grimaced. Of course, it made sense, there must be a seaplane terminal nearby. About 200 metres ahead he could now see Sandy's vehicle and the other escort vehicles clustered outside a small building on the edge of the water. A blue sign stated that this was the base of the Sea Air Company among others.

Starting up and heading towards the floatplane terminal he saw a sign on the right for Bendex Avelex and turning up Bell-Irving Road swung north away from the seaplane terminal. Finding an empty parking space he locked his car and walked back to the terminal building. As he approached, another floatplane took off and, with a former pilot's unfading interest, Martin stopped to watch as it lifted steeply and turned south. By the time he entered the small office the only people in evidence were two young attendants behind the desk.

"I wonder if I can get a flight schedule from you?" Martin smiled at one of the women who was busy collating a sheaf of papers.

"Of course." She reached over the desk and pulled a flyer out of the plastic stand. "This'll give you all our flights to the Gulf Islands and Vancouver Island."

Scanning the departure times Martin looked at his watch. He frowned, "I'm sorry, but as I arrived two floatplanes took off but I see no mention of a departure at this time. Have you revised your schedule?"

"Oh no. That was a special charter to Salt Spring Island." She noticed his puzzled look. "It's one of the Gulf Islands—the largest. We sometimes fit in special requests." She smiled, anxious to explain the aberration.

"It doesn't affect our regular schedule in any way."

" I see—well that explains it then. One has to watch schedules these days. It's no fun arriving 5 minutes after a plane has left." Waving the pamphlet he turned to leave. "Thank you, you've been very helpful. I'll talk to my wife and give you a call." Satisfied, he turned away from the girl and retraced his steps to where he'd parked his car. It'd been easier than he'd anticipated. The destination of Ismail Talawi's group was now established. Opening a map of the lower mainland and nearby Gulf Islands he noted that Salt Spring was indeed the largest and his map showed two different ferry connections to the island from Tsawwassen terminal south of the Airport. He would travel to Salt Spring by ferry and now that he had a visual on the protection surrounding Talawi knew that he would find their target without much difficulty. People after all had to eat and a local supermarket was the surest place to see the world go by.

Politics

Sir John Fowles sighed, "Of course we understand your position. But to shut down a perfectly legal newspaper would be to invite precisely the kind of criticism that my government wishes to avoid." He took another sip of the tea; why did they have to make it so sweet? Oh for a cup of something familiar, Ceylon or Earl Gray. Squinting over the rim he peered at Abajir Rafsanjani, the Iranian Foreign Minister. "Even if we could agree to your request it would probably have the reverse effect to the one you are seeking."

"Sir John, how can we remain indifferent to an organisation that spews out lying propaganda, incites our people to overthrow the legal government of Iran from its safe haven in England?"

"Consider minister, that the *Flame of Freedom* has, as far as we can ascertain, a readership of less than 1000. Her Majesty's government is of the opinion that such a small group constitutes no threat to the stability of Iran and of course, as with all such groups, we keep a close eye on their activities." He lowered the cup, watching in dismay as the uniformed servant hovering at his elbow instantly refilled it.

"Sir John, my government is working hard to improve relations with Great Britain and banning this propaganda sheet would be seen as a most favourable sign in the path to better relations."

Sir John Fowles suppressed a sharp response. Why did these autocratic regimes assume that the Western democracies could behave with the same impunity towards their peoples as dictatorships did to theirs? He took a deep breath, now for the counter punch. "Minister, Her Majesty's Government is concerned at attempts by opportunistic elements in Iran to harm citizens of this country." He saw a flicker of—what, fear? Surely not. "You obviously appreciate the effect on public opinion when a noted author and booksellers carrying his works are attacked on the streets of London. It would certainly assist our path to normalising relations if such attempts could end."

Rafsanjani grimaced. "You're referring to Rushdie and Talawi of course." He took a sip of his own tea before continuing. "Sir John, let me be frank; as you are aware no *fatwa* has been issued against Talawi. Since Ayatollah Khomenei issued the *fatwa* against Rushdie we have been, shall we say, more circumspect." He smiled thinly. "The attack on Talawi was not sanctioned by us. A dissident group acting out of religious fervor carried out the attack. As you said, opportunistic elements." He placed his cup down firmly, lifting a hand to forestall the servant. "Sir John, we are trying to rein in such ill-disciplined elements but it will take time. We don't have the same access to information as your police forces have."

An old hand at detecting the subtle nuances in diplomatic jargon Sir John heard the message. A sea change was occurring in Iran and both he and Rafsanjani were locked in an intricate dance to probe the others unofficial position. "You do know minister, that we have found one of the Talawi hit team dead in his apartment. An Iranian dissident called Abbas Salameh."

The surprise on Rafsanjani's face was genuine. The minister collected himself. "No, Sir John I must confess to total ignorance. You said dead. What was the cause of his death?"

"His neck was broken. He was struck on the neck by a person proficient in one of the martial arts. Our police team narrowly missed catching the perpetrator."

"Ah—I see," Rafsanjani nodded slowly, "and you assume that we ordered the killing." He lifted his hands palm outward. "Obviously I'll make enquiries on my return but I assure you that no one in my ministry has information on the man." He rose; he needed time to assess this latest bombshell.

Thankfully Sir John placed his cup down, rising as he did so. He held out his hand. "Thank you for your hospitality minister, I will pass on the details of our discussion. We cannot of course shut down any newspaper without proper cause but I'll talk to the managing editor about some of his more inflammatory comments." Both men understood that a trade had just occurred. The British wanted Talawi's assassination team in return for a clamp down on the vehement anti-

Iranian newspaper. Taking Sir John's hand firmly
Rafsanjani smiled.

"It has been a pleasure seeing you again Sir John. I
leave tonight for Tehran and will contact you once I
have more information."

§

The Iranian Foreign Minister Abajir Rafsanjani frowned
at the Ayatollah Albarrasan. The two men faced each
other across the minister's desk in his luxurious office in
the Ministry of Foreign Affairs building. "You knew of
the attack on Talawi?"

"No, not until after the event." Albarrasan kept
his face expressionless. "We had a plan but the pre-
emptive action by Imam Basra forced us to cancel.
Talawi, forewarned, has gone to ground." He shrugged,
"It was a good plan but . . ."

"You realise that we are opening discussions with
the British. They are at a very delicate stage. Any action
against Rushdie or Talawi will have a serious effect on
these discussions." Rafsanjani knew he was walking a
narrow line. The Ayatollahs were very powerful and the
revolutionary guards still a force to be watched. But
unless Iran could move towards a more liberal regime
progress in all fields would remain stagnant. People long
forced into an austere political system that held back
economic development were beginning to show signs of
restlessness, especially the students. His trip to Britain
had been because of the very real fear that the tiny
spark provided by the, *Flame of Freedom* newspaper could
ignite the tinderbox that was Iran. He looked up, a false
smile creasing his face. "The world is changing, Bahram.
The British and Americans came to the aid of the
faithful in Kosovo."

Albarrasan turned to stare out of the window.

Rafsanjani was right, the world was changing and he was intelligent enough to realise it might be time to change, there was probably advantage to be gained in riding this new wave. Still Talawi deserved to die, *Lunch with the Prophet* was much more of an insult than Rushdie's book. Without betraying the inner conflict he was experiencing, Albarrasan turned to face the Foreign Minister. "You suggest that those who plan Rushdie's and Talawi's punishment should suspend their efforts?"

"Bahram, neither of those two apostates would have received the attention they have, had we not placed a *fatwa* on Rushdie. All we've achieved, despite several attempts against Rushdie and now against Talawi is to equate Islam with terrorism. I know—I know—" he held his palm up. "—Those two are damned to eternity and in time an accident can be arranged, but for the present we need a period of calm. The British have a name." He looked down at the scrawled note beside his cup. "Abbas Salameh. I understand that you might have met him at one time?"

Albarrasan smiled without humour. "Your information is correct. But I meet many of our dedicated youth who decide without prompting that they must honour their faith."

"Bahran my friend, it might be constructive, in the short term you understand, if such dedicated youth be asked to return from abroad. Should you have the ear of someone who deals with these honourable ones we would be grateful if they could be advised to hold their anger in check."

Albarrasan looked out of the window into the deepening twilight. It was obvious that the original assassination cell was to be sacrificed to appease the British. But, the long-range plan to kill Talawi involving the Bosnian Muslim, Dragovic, and Martin Dreyfus was

known by only a few close intimates in the clergy, Gip
Lawrence was dead and he'd already given orders for all
traces of the Corsican operation to be removed. Anyone
trying to track the movement of his two killers would
find nothing but an abandoned farmhouse formerly
owned by an Englishman who'd died from cancer.
Anything that could indicate the purpose of the farm
had been thoroughly sanitized. So, he could betray the
broken remains of the cell in England, which would
give him a lever with Rafsanjani, and keep his own
operation in play if he wished.

The minister coughed.

Deciding, Albarrasan stroked his beard. "I agree. I
will see what can be done." Gravely he rose and, bowing
briefly, turned to leave the room.

Perspiration shone on the minister's upper lip. He
let out a long sigh of relief; it'd been easier than he
expected. But now he was in Albarrasan's debt and he
knew that debt would be called.

§

Instantly awake Nick rolled upright and swinging his
legs off the edge of the bed reached for his watch on
the night table. Glancing at the dial he let out a low
whistle. For the first time in a very long time he'd over-
slept his normal 5 a.m wake up. Running a hand through
his close cropped hair he reviewed the actions of the
previous evening. After arriving back in Vancouver from
Galiano Island with Sandy they'd walked slowly back to
his hotel, neither man ready to end the magic of a good
day. Saying goodbye, with a sardonic comment about
boneheads who don't know enough to keep a good fish,
Sandy caught a taxi back to his own hotel.

For a long time as the sky darkened Nick stood
looking down on the traffic outside his hotel. Twice he'd

pulled the Sig Sauer P245 pistol out of it's wrapping and staring at the oiled steel analyzed his rapidly narrowing range of choices. He felt nothing for Talawi for, as Martin had said, Talawi knew full well the consequences of his actions. He wished, sadly, that he'd never met Anne or Sandy, two people who were becoming major influences in his life. Leaving the hotel after dinner and walking without direction he tried to come to grips with the new and terrible complexities in his life. Could he defy Ayatollah Albarrasan? Had he not done enough? Could he kill Talawi and evade detection? Even as the thoughts swirled chaotically through his tired mind he knew the answers. He had no choice. Once Talawi's routine was established he'd have to decide on the method of execution and move close for a killing shot. It was almost a given that one or more of the security personnel would react and would have to be dealt with. What if the one to react was Sandy Flett? Could he kill Anne's brother? And what of the aftermath of a successful strike? If he escaped to reach the Caymans he'd never see her again. He'd allowed a woman into his life again and again it was going to cause him unbearable grief. And what would Talawi's death mean to Sandy? The young man impressed him as very few men had; he liked Sandy Flett and once Nick's false identity was exposed Sandy's career would be over. He'd be removed from his unit and sent to the Army's definition of purgatory.

After a light supper at a small restaurant down a side street Nick continued walking until in a dingy part of the East Side he'd walked into a bar. Ignoring curious glances from a few regulars and a couple of dirty teenagers obviously dealing in drugs he drank several large glasses of whiskey over a period of time. How long, he'd only a blurry recollection. Vaguely he remembered walking back to the hotel near midnight and the night clerk looking at him with apprehension. He'd undressed clumsily and fallen into bed naked, clothing scattered across the floor.

Now, awake, he felt drugged, sticky and annoyed with himself. Walking into the shower he scrubbed until his skin tingled then turning the flow to full cold stood gasping in the icy stream until he felt his head clearing. Wrapping the towel around his waist after drying himself he stepped out of the bathroom. Remembering the events of yesterday and needing a few answers he picked up the phone and dialed the Sylvia Hotel. Almost instantly Sandy answered.

"Flett."

"Sandy, it's Nick, just to thank you for arranging yesterday. It was a good day."

"No sweat, I certainly enjoyed it and I'm certain Brian did. I think all of us will remember that fish for a long time."

"I forgot to get Brian's address. Can you thank him for me? Is he an old friend of yours?"

Sandy laughed. "Actually he's a friend of a friend. I was asked to contact him when I arrived. He's a good sort isn't he."

Nick, looking at his own reflection in the mirror, saw himself nod. As he'd assumed, Brian Kowalski and Sandy Flett were colleagues tasked to guard Ismail Talawi. The phrase, 'friend of a friend' could mean government to government and if both could take the day off fishing it must mean Talawi was still in England. He felt a release of tension and realised grimly that he wanted the problem of Talawi to remain unresolved for as long as possible, yet he knew, the longer he remained in this actionless limbo, the chance of exposure increased exponentially. "Yes, I enjoyed his company. Do I owe you or Brian for fuel or anything else?"

"Nope. Brian refused payment. Claimed he was going fishing anyway and the case of beer you brought was quite adequate."

"Well thank him please. It was a memorable day." He hesitated but his training was too deep and chances like this were rare in the world he lived in. He needed to be close enough to Sandy to sense when Talawi was on Canadian soil and by a calculated set of circumstances had been befriended by the very man tasked to protect his target. "If you're free tomorrow evening how about joining me for a drink? The concierge tells me that there's a good English style pub in the vicinity. We could probably get a plate of bangers and mash." He waited. "Sandy?"

"Sorry, I was trying to think. I'd enjoy that, but tomorrow is a pretty full day for me and I might not be clear in time. I'd better not. Look, if things change I'll give you a call."

"Sure, I'll suss it out anyway and let you know how it stacks up to pubs back home. Well I must go; I have things to do. Speak to you soon."

"Yeah, good talking to you Nick." The phone went dead and Nick found he was gripping the receiver tightly, a sour taste in his mouth. A minute ago he was hoping Talawi would not come. Sandy's comment about a full day tomorrow must mean Talawi was arriving. He'd have to warn Martin to activate the tracking device.

Dressing slowly in corduroy trousers and a bleached denim shirt Nick pulled on a light sweater over the shirt, for there was still a nip in the air, and went down to the restaurant for breakfast. After breakfast he drained the last of his coffee and pocketing the keys given to him by Martin walked the few blocks to the

SkyTrain station at Burrard Street. ten minutes later he exited at the Main Street station next to the Via Rail terminal. Leaving the high level platform he walked down the stairs in a light drizzle and across the green space of Thornton Park before crossing Station Street and entering the Via Rail and Bus terminal entrance. The high ceiling of the central hall looked down on a tiled amphitheater, crowded with passengers, and made his way past the ticket booths to the lockers on the platform. Going through the automatic doors to the covered staging area outside the main building he turned left toward where the lockers were arranged in several rows. Checking the key number he found the one Martin had deposited his equipment in. It was behind the main bank and away from the gaze of casual passengers passing by, but mindful of security cameras he made no effort to approach the locker until he was satisfied that it was not under surveillance.

Opening the locker with the tubular key he found inside a large 70 x 40 x 15cm locked case made of a hard composite material adorned with various old and new stick-on hotel labels and a combination lock under the handle. The case, scratched and dented, showed signs of heavy use and looked every inch like a travelling salesman's battered display case. Which it was not. Nick lifted it clear of the locker, tensing his muscles for it was heavy, and closing the locker left the key in the lock. There was a safe in his hotel room with a personal combination that would do for the passport and papers and he'd not need the railway locker again. A man walking past bumped into his arm and a cold wave washed through him. Apologising with a smile the man moved away but it took a few moments for Nick to exhale and relax. He ordered a cup of coffee in the restaurant and sat quietly drinking while keeping a seemingly casual scan of passengers and greeters before being satisfied that there was no surveillance.

Back at the hotel he dialed in the combination and snapped the case open. A red British EU passport lay beside a sealed envelope, both of which rested on a pad covering the bulk of the interior. Nick opened the much-used passport and checked the photograph. His face wearing glasses and with dark hair looked back at him. Without thinking he touched his hair shot through with flecks of gray and gray over the temples, 'Silvertip' Gip had called him jokingly. No doubt under the pad with the weapon was a bottle of hair dye. He snorted wryly, not much of a disguise but it would do. Lifting both items clear he raised the flap. Packed securely in a series of foam cutouts lay a disassembled custom-made Walther WA2000 sniper rifle. He'd often wondered how Gip had managed to get the rifle. Only 72 copies of this exceptional rifle had been produced, in 2 variants. This one used the standard 7.62x51mm NATO cartridge. Nick ran his hand over the metal parts thinking of the hours he'd spent on the range in Corsica perfecting his skill. Always a solid marksman he could now put a 5 round group into a 10cm circle from 500 metres in less than 15 seconds. He would probably only need one shot and from much closer than 500 metres. Lost in thought he stared unseeing at a painting on the wall.

The phone tinkled softly, breaking into his reverie. Startled, he closed the case and turning the locking wheels under the handle, picked up the phone.

"Yes?"

"Nick?"

Dragovic exhaled softly, for a moment caught off guard by her call. All his thoughts far away from this lovely city and its spectacular scenery, away from Anne and the awakening of his soul from it's long bitter sleep.

He'd been walking through the memories of lying in the burnt grass of the Corsican farm putting carefully aimed shots into a man shaped-target 800 metres away across the valley. And coldly thinking then that the actual execution would be his call and he intended to be close enough to be certain. A long shot had not been in his plans then and neither had the possibility of capture. Then death in action would have been a welcome release. But now? Forcing himself back into the present he glanced at his watch before answering "Yes Anne it's me. What's the matter?" Her laughter brought a smile to his lips.

"Nothing, I just wanted to hear your voice and make sure you were still available this afternoon. I'll be leaving here in about an hour. At noon."

"I'll be there."

"Nick?" The voice was softer, deeper.

"I'm still here my love." Without thinking, the term of endearment slipped off his tongue and in a flash of self-revelation he knew that he was lost. He could not leave her behind, could not take her with. If he left her he would spend his remaining years a wealthy man in a gilded cage pursued by memories of what might have been. If he stayed he would end on a rope or worse: a life sentence in a cold Canadian jail.

"I love you." The phone clicked as she replaced the receiver into its cradle.

For a long time he sat still, holding the phone, until a disconnect signal interrupted his chaotic thoughts. He replaced the phone and walking to the window of his room pulled the closed curtains apart to look down into the crowded street below. Ideas came and were quickly discarded. Finally he turned back into the room. Perhaps he could talk to Martin. They had formed a friendship that might be strong enough for

Martin to understand his desperate dilemma. But that could wait. Turning back to the bed he picked up the passport and the still sealed envelope, placing them in the room safe. The gun case went into his suitcase, which he locked before sliding it back into the cupboard. Looking round the room he satisfied himself that everything was in order before locking the door and taking the elevator to the lobby. He did not notice Martin sitting in the coffee shop. Walking outside through the Georgia street entrance Nick hailed a cab, telling the driver to take him to the corner of Broadway and Trutch in Kitsilano. He never saw Martin exit from the same doorway to watch the taxi turn on Dunsmuir Street.

§

Turning off Broadway down Trutch street Nick's taxi crossed 6th Avenue before Nick saw Anne's green Range Rover parked outside her friend's townhouse. He leant forward touching the taxi driver, a fiercely bearded Sikh, on the shoulder. "Drop me off at the next corner, please." The driver nodded and pointed at the meter. Nick pulled a banknote from his wallet and, satisfied that it covered the cost and included a good tip, placed the note on the seat beside the driver as the taxi stopped on the corner.

Walking back towards the townhouse he re-hearsed what he had to say. Their affair had to end. In days he would kill the man her brother was tasked to protect. With luck he would make the Cayman Islands and reappear as someone called Shoemaker. He grim-aced at the thought, and then? And—what if—as so often happens in even the most carefully planned opera-tions, something went wrong? Nick looked down the pretty avenue with its overarching trees throwing dappled shadows across the sun-splashed pavement. He knew, deep within himself, that jail was not an option and if, through some fluke, he was exposed then he would die on the street trying to get the fool whose sacrilege had brought him here. Drawing a deep breath he stopped, shaking his head. This was the way to madness.

An elderly man walking his dog glanced curiously at Nick and asked in a soft voice, "Excuse me. You look lost, can I help?"

Nick, jerked out of the maelstrom of conflicting emotions, stared at the man without speaking. Then realising how strange he must appear forced a smile. "Thank you, but no. I know where I am." The man nodded and, in a gesture of old fashioned courtesy, lifted his hat before turning away. Nick sighed, accepting finally that there were no options. Talawi had to die. He could not ask Anne to become a permanent fugitive after the hit. She would, he knew, be horrified at what he had done. Such a deed would cripple any relationship. The half-formed plan to confess everything to Anne, abort the project, and run with her was a non-starter. Martin's comment that promises had been made and must be kept was more than a statement of fact; it was also a warning. The Ayatollah would have the world scoured for them both. Anne and those she loved would become victims of the punishment squads. He knew now what he had to do. He had to break the relationship today.

Anne opened the door almost as he pressed the bell. She pulled his head down hungrily fastening her mouth to his. Placing his hands around her Nick pulled her close. Finally he broke free and pushed her back gently. "Let me get into the hall. The neighbors will see."

"I don't care. Oh Nick, I want you so." Standing in the hall she looked so lovely that his carefully planned speech and thoughts of a clean break disappeared. Tomorrow was another day, another country, another time. He swung her off her feet and carried her up the stairs to the bedroom. Later, lying with her on the rumpled bed, he watched the late afternoon shadows move across the ceiling. She stroked his face gently. "I'm going to tell Mike that I want a divorce." She held her hand across his mouth as he started to protest. "It's not to pressure you my love. It's for my sake. Mike deserves better than to find out that his wife is having an affair. For all his faults he deserves the truth. He thinks my coolness is the result of suspecting him of having an affair. He's lied to me lately about incoming phone calls." She looked at him gravely, light coming through the window highlighting her dark hair with a metallic sheen. "I love you and whatever happens I cannot live a lie."

Pushing himself into a sitting position Nick placed his hands on her shoulders. "I want you to promise me something. I have to go first to Seattle then back to Europe for meetings. I want you to say nothing to Mike until I return - no." He shook his head as she started to speak. "I need, and you need, a period apart to put our feelings in order and I want to be with you when you tell him."

"Nick . . ." She tried to sit up, pushing against the hands holding her down.

"No—please—listen to me." His voice was firm. "I also have promises to keep. Promises that have nothing to do with us. I will be leaving very soon and . . ." He stopped, searching for the right words. "Anne you know that I love you more than life itself but I want you to have no regrets."

Gently she pushed the hands holding her aside and sat up, a puzzled frown creasing her forehead. "What is it Nick, another woman, someone in Europe? Is it Mike and the contract you're discussing?"

"No," he smiled sadly, "nothing so simple. Anne I can't explain right now. Just believe me when I tell you it's nothing to do with us." He brushed a strand of hair back from her forehead, stroking the smooth fall of her hair with the knuckles of his hand.

Watching his face she felt a premonition, a sudden stab of fear, a hollowness deep inside her chest. "Will you tell me what it is when you return?" she asked, a slight tremor in her voice.

"Yes. I promise that you'll hear the full story." He smiled. "Don't image for a moment that it concerns you or Mike."

"OK, mystery man, I'll keep my suspicions to myself." She placed her arms around his neck and nuzzled his chest. "As long as it's not another woman you'll be safe."

Nick pulled her head back and kissed her hard. She gasped as he released her. "My goodness it had better not be another woman Nick Cartwright."

Outside the townhouse long shadows were pulling the evening in as they left the building. From his rental vehicle, tucked tight to the kerb two hundred metres down the street, Martin watched them leave.

Chapter 25

The Big Break

A desperately tired Jimmy Douglas faced Detective Inspector Basil Coulson sitting across the conference table in Chief Superintendent Ingram's New Scotland Yard office. Coulson lifted the file off the table.

"You took an awful chance. What made you think he'd break?" Before Douglas could answer the door opened and Chief Superintendent Ingram burst in. Ingram shook off his rain sodden coat before turning to hang it over the hook behind the door.

"Sorry Jimmy, damned traffic crawling along whenever it rains. You'd think it never rains in London." He pulled out a chair and sat alongside Coulson. "The message said urgent. What have you got?"

Coulson spoke first, sliding the file across. "You remember the boy and the cap with the odd logo? The one that Jimmy and I went down to Mapplethorpe to interview?"

"Of course, the boy claimed to have found it in a waste bin at the local shopping centre."

"Yes he did, and we believed him. However, a teacher at the local school overheard our little thug bragging to his mates how he'd put one over the big shot coppers. The teacher called the local police who called Jimmy." Coulson looked over at Douglas. "Jimmy will fill in what happened then."

Douglas dragged both hands down the sides of his face before speaking. Outside the building, rain bounced off the windowsill, and slid in rivulets down the misted glass. The room was quiet except for a gentle murmur of voices outside the closed door. Both policemen waited.

"I interviewed the boy, Marvin Bledsoe, again.

This time he had a social service lawyer on hand." He paused, getting the sequence of events in order in his mind. "A young lass, going to save the world from civil-rights-trampling coppers, she was. Gave me a five minute lecture before I'd even taken off my coat." Douglas grinned without mirth. "I had to take her aside and explain a few details of the anti-terrorism act, the official secrets act and what happens to well meaning fools who step into the machinery." He sighed, "To cut a long story short, she and the boy found it advisable to cooperate. The boy did not find the hat in Mapplethorpe station as he originally claimed. He'd swiped it off a kid in Portsmouth. We found the kid in Portsmouth." The brevity of that statement was not lost on the two police-men. Both understood the intense, time consuming police work involved. Small wonder Douglas looked exhausted. "The lad, Sam Dawood, the original finder, took us to where he'd found the cap on Bosham pier. He also gave us a description of the man who threw the cap away."

"Our man—it fits?" Chief Superintendent Ingram's eyes were alight with excitement. Sometimes in the long dreary round of routine police investigations a sudden flash of clarity, a locking together of parts of the puzzle, makes up for all the disappointments en-dured. Ingram leant forward eagerly.

Jimmy Douglas's lips twisted in what could have been a slight smile at the excitement in the older man's voice. He continued. "Actually the boy only took a casual interest in the two men on the dock. According to young Sam the man who threw the cap away was tall, an Englishman from his accent. I showed him the com-posite photo but he was uncertain, remember it was dusk." Coulson, who'd read the file before Ingram arrived, saw the disappointment flush Roger Imgram's face and gripped his boss by the arm.

"Wait, Roger. There's more, a lot more."

Douglas continued as if Coulson had not spoken. "What young Sam did notice was the name of the boat that took our man out to sea."

"Holy Mother of. . . !"

"No," Douglas's voice was flat. "The *Marie Claire*, owned by a Mr. Colin Seymour." He paused. "We took him into custody. It seems our Mr. Seymour had a rather extravagant life style for a local businessman. He sold small boat radar's, GPS systems, that sort of thing. I had his tax records pulled for the last ten years and this fellow was living well beyond his declared income. But he was a hard nut. Refused to answer questions. I had a team going around the clock but he held fast until late Tuesday night." Chief Superintendent Roger Ingram glanced at his wall calendar and frowned.

"Why . . .?"

"Why didn't I advise you of Seymour's arrest two days ago?" Jimmy Douglas looked bitter. He took a deep breath. "Because Chief Superintendent there are things I do that you don't want to be a part of." He spread his hands and looked down at the table. "I needed answers, Seymour had them. You would've had to follow procedure. Seymour was much more afraid of his paymasters than he was of us."

"You keep using past tense. I take it he is deceased?" Ingram's face had hardened.

Jimmy Douglas nodded. "Look, Chief Superintendent, I don't enjoy doing this sort of thing but when we have high level assassination attempts, offshore hit men in the pay of the Ayatollahs and drug money used to fund terrorist cells then sometimes I can rationalise that the means justify the end." He raised tired eyes to stare at Roger Ingram. For a long moment neither man spoke then Ingram sighed.

"I understand, please continue."

"The hitman never gave a name but we now, thanks to Seymour, have a much better composite sketch. Seymour dropped our man off at Dieppe and through the DSDGE in France we've traced his movement through France by train to Spain. He stayed at the El Prado in Madrid for several days then flew out to Italy. Groupo V in Italy confirm that he landed at Leonardo da Vinci but he disappeared off the map at that point."

"Passports? You must have numbers and country of origin." Ingram realised that this operation had expanded dramatically and would require rethinking on everyone's part.

"One false and one stolen. This is a real professional." There was grudging admiration in Jimmy Douglas's voice. "Hell, he even used different styles of signature when purchasing travel tickets and rental cars." He pushed the file over to Ingram. "Everything we have is in there. We've lost some time but the next time he returns to hit Talawi we'll be waiting."

"What makes you think he'll come back? What if Salameh was a punishment killing? A warning to other wildcat operations, exactly as we've been hearing from our sources."

"As our man was leaving the El Prado he received a phone call. The receptionist heard him say to the caller that he was ready to go back to England. The caller said something and our man answered, as best she can remember, that *Gip is a walking dead man*. It stuck her at the time that the man seemed saddened. She assumed that it was about a relative. Now Talawi is of Egyptian descent and the old pejorative term for Egyptians is Gippo or Gyppo. I suspect that what he actually said

was '*The Gippo is a walking dead man.*' I'm convinced that
he'll be back and this time we'll have him."

For a long time the room was silent, each man
wrapped in somber reflection. Finally Roger Imgram
broke the silence. "I honestly can't say that I condone
your methods but . . ." Ingram sighed deeply, "Congratu-
lations are in order. What are you planning to do with
Seymour's body? You realise that questions will be
asked. I assume his family and friends know that he's in
custody?"

"No. We snatched him at the quay. He often takes
off without warning for days at a time; so at the moment nobody is asking questions." Douglas held up both
hands to ward off the inevitable question. "He was
found this morning lying on the floor of his car in the
harbour parking lot. Apparently dead from a massive
heart attack." Douglas pushed his chair back, the legs
scraping on the worn linoleum, as he rose. "I wouldn't
mourn for Seymour, Chief Superintendent He was a
thoroughly bad lot was Mr. Colin Seymour." He
stretched tiredly, nodding at the file lying between them.
"You'll find a lot of interesting information in there—
and now, gentlemen—I'm going to crash for a couple of
hours."

The two policemen waited until the door had
closed behind Jimmy Douglas before Ingram spoke.

"Speaking of Talawi, what's the latest news from
Canada?"

"Apparently he's not settled well. I spoke to Sandy
Flett last night and although our genius is obeying orders
and listening to Meg Davidson's advice at the moment,
he's getting irritable. The man is a difficult customer."

"Well it seems as if the plan to send Talawi offshore was correct. How's the *doppelganger* doing?"
Ingram referring to the false echo that U-Boat captains

used during the Second World War to evade destruction by destroyers circling in the sea overhead.

Coulson grunted. The term was apt. "Mr. Wilfred Blair, our Anglicized Arab actor, is performing rather well. Jimmy and Tristam have had him surface periodically at book signings and art shows and he's taken everyone in. They had a bit of a scare when Julie Croaker - you recall the abandoned girlfriend?"

"Yes, of course."

" Well she happened to arrive as he was leaving a play in the West End and tried to talk to him. Tristam nearly had a heart attack but managed to hustle our fake Talawi into a waiting car. The upside is that she actually thought Blair was Talawi, called him a heartless bastard, so it seems at the moment that we have a convincing substitute."

"D'you think Douglas is correct—the hitman is on his way back?"

"I think Jimmy Douglas is one of the best operators in the business so any assumptions he has, have to be taken seriously. What doesn't make sense is why did our hitman leave England if his primary target is Talawi? He could have gone to ground in England and waited his chance for a clean shot at our friend."

Roger Ingram looked up thoughtfully. "Yes, the same thought occurred to me. The more the killer moves about the greater risk of exposure. I'm still inclined to the theory that the hit on Salameh was a warning to other radicals." He pushed his chair back. From somewhere down the passage a phone trilled. Muffled conversation, a voice raised in anger, competing with the soft slush of rain on the window came through from the next office. "Word from the top is that our relations with Iran are improving. Both sides are being very careful to let nothing interfere with the political détente." Ingram locked his fingers together, stretching his arms full length. He sighed noisily. "I have to see Sir John Fowles at the Foreign Office this afternoon. Treasury are making noises about the cost of this operation and I have to decide how much weight to put on Jimmy's theory." He shook his head. "Whatever we recommend we are damned. Treasury will have our balls if Jimmy is wrong and we continue full airport and seaport surveillance at the present level. The Foreign Office will have them if we cut back and our *doppelganger* is hit. The media, in turn, will have a field day and the resulting fallout will set back détente for years."

Basil Coulson raised his eyebrows; "Surely Treasury can see the implications of scaling back the operation prematurely?"

Roger Ingram snorted derisively as he rose to his feet. "Treasury, Basil, is not a logical entity. Beancounters and bankers don't have to live with the end result of a bad financial decision. That clown Warwick has just been promoted after losing over a billion pounds in a botched loan deal with China and right now they would dearly love to have a distracting scapegoat."

"So what do you intend to do?"

"For the moment we'll stay the course." Roger Ingram grinned savagely. "I'm close enough to retirement and I'd love to see us nail the bastard if he comes back in. Still, I can't hold off the heavies forever. Tell Jimmy to increase our fake Talawi's exposure. It might precipitate action by the opposition." Ingram walked to the door. "I'm going to have some lunch. Care to join me?"

"No—thanks—I want to go back to my office and recheck some data. Something is niggling at the back of my mind. I've an uneasy feeling that we're overlooking something. I'll call you later."

Roger Ingram looked at his deputy thoughtfully. He nodded without speaking and stepping into the corridor pulled the door closed behind him.

§

Sandy Flett stared at his sister, surprise slackening the firm planes of his jaw. "Divorce Mike? But why? Ah . . . I get it . . . the last time we spoke I remember you saying that you suspected he was having an affair. Is he really having an affair? I knew you were angry with him but . . ." he shook his head " . . . hell, I had no idea you were contemplating divorce. Have you spoken to him? How is he taking it?" Brother and sister sat facing each other across the table in the elegant restaurant of the Pan Pacific hotel.

Anne smiled at her big brother. From childhood she'd always gone to him for advice. Despite promising Nick not to do anything until he returned from Europe she had to talk to someone and Joyce Caramanlis was away in Vegas for a few days. "Yes, I suspect he's having an affair but that's not the reason I want a divorce. And no, I haven't told him yet."

Perplexed, Sandy frowned, "Don't play guessing games Anne. What's going on?"

"I've met some one. For the first time I'm totally, hopelessly in love. That sounds so trite doesn't it? The cold professional surgeon talking like a love sick school-girl." Her eyes sparkled and Sandy realised with a start that his sister was bubbling with joy. He took a deep breath.

"Are you going to tell me how—why? You've just said that Mike's fooling around is not the reason for this decision. Forgive me but I'm a little confused."

Anne looked across the room. It was early and the place was, apart from a group of tourists sitting near the window, empty. She looked back at her brother and reaching across the table took his hand. "Don't be angry. He is so like you. You must believe me that we never anticipated this happening. Mike and I have drifted too far apart, I've suspected for some time that he was having an affair. Our sex life has been non-existent for quite a while."

"Don't you think that might have something to do with it?" Sandy asked, pursing his lips. "Anne, all marriages go through rough patches and you both have high pressure jobs. Don't you think this could be a reaction to your lifestyles?"

"That's what Nick said . . ."

"Nick, Nick Cartwright? —Our Nick?" The stunned amazement on his face caused her to smile.

"Yes Sandy—our Nick as you put it. He's flying back to Europe on Friday and wants me to think it over. If I still feel the same way when he gets back then we'll both go and speak to Mike." Anne gripped her brother's hands fiercely; "I love him Sandy. I really never understood the meaning before—I thought I did but, if he asks me to drop everything and go with him, I will—everything, you understand—Sandy he's so like you and Dad. I cannot imagine living without him." Anne released her brother's hands and sat back watching conflicting emotions play across his face.

"Anne, I like Nick. I like him a lot but, damn it Sis, what do you know about him? Hell, I enjoy his company. We had a great day fishing yesterday, he phoned me this morning—invited me to have a drink tonight. Now I wonder if he intended to sound me out."

"Are you going?"

"No, I have some things to attend to. I said I'd

phone him if I could get away." Sandy glanced at his watch, "Look Sis. I have to leave, It's important, but we need to talk some more. Standing, Sandy, still bemused by the news, kept his face expressionless but his mind was formulating a plan. He'd call Jimmy Douglas and ask him to check on Nick Cartwright. It was always possible that Nick was married. It'd be easy enough to check his background out, Anne need never know. He sighed. "OK Sis. I just hope you're not making a mistake."

Chapter 26

Closing the net

Nick read the cryptic message again. The desk clerk looked at him expectantly, but did not speak. Nick crumpled the paper into a ball. "When did this come in?"

"I'm not sure sir. It must have been in the past hour. We've been rather busy," he half apologised.

Nick nodded, and turned away. "Thank you," he called over his shoulder as he made for the door. Martin's coded note asked for a meeting at a major downtown bookstore at three thirty. Martin's note actually meant, meet me at the city library at two thirty. No one else reading the bland note could have extracted either the destination or time. Glancing at his watch, he realised he would have to take a taxi to get there in time.

Ten minutes later he sat facing Martin across a table in the courtyard of the new library complex. Around them sat office workers on their break and a group of students drinking coffee and loudly expounding theories in the self-confident manner of the young. No one gave the two middle-aged men a second glance.

Nick had greeted Martin with a brief nod and a quick handshake. Both men placed their briefcases on the two empty chairs of the four-seat table; to all intents they were businessmen meeting to discuss a deal over coffee. Nick raised his eyebrows. "You have information on the deal we discussed?"

"Yes, the package has arrived and its final destination identified. I'll need a few days to arrange a meeting between you and the principal." He smiled thinly, "To make sure we have all the information needed to close the deal." Martin glanced around casually before turning

back to Nick. "However, the reason I asked for the
meeting is to advise you that your successful project in
England is no longer as confidential as our principals
had intended. A trusted member of our head office
staff, you recall the gentleman who took you on a boat
ride? Unfortunately he's discussed details of your travel
arrangements with our competition."

Nick took a deep breath. This was not good.
"They are aware of our present location and project?'

"No. The only information they have is related to
our previous project in England and your travel to Italy.
Since the chairman's death our foreign branch office has
been closed and all sensitive files destroyed. They don't
have a lead beyond Rome airport. Also the belief in
their company HQ is that your trip to England was
meant to warn off other competitors."

Expressionless, Nick half turned to look at a
group of University students arguing about the slowness
of the latest inquiry into government wrongdoing. So—
The Brits thought that the Salameh killing was a warning to Imam Basra's group—Corsica would be a dead
end for Interpol but the English police now had a thread
and possibly more. Bleakly he turned back to Martin.
"You wish to accelerate our project here to avoid inter-
ference?"

"If we're to bring this deal to a successful conclusion I see no alternative, but one thing I've learnt in our
business is to make haste slowly." Leaning forward
Martin spoke softly. "I will have a good look at the
property, identify the downside and upside before letting
you in to close the deal. In a few days we should meet
again. I'll leave a message for you." Martin watched for
a reaction but nothing showed on the impassive face
looking back at him.

For a while both men sat in silence. Finally Nick

asked, "How certain are you of our information?"

"After the chairman's death I was asked to act pro tem. I had access to his confidential file. The source is solid. You must remember my money is sunk into this project as well."

Nick smiled grimly, "I was not questioning your integrity Martin. We know each other too well for that. Can we walk?"

Rising the two men walked down Cambie Street towards Victory Square where they dropped the pretense of being businessmen. "Do they have any more information on me? I'm thinking of the Identikit picture that was used originally, you'll recall I thought Salameh had recognised me," Nick queried as they strolled along an empty stretch of sidewalk.

"They have an enhanced description, yes, perhaps not a great improvement on the original. But, in any case, my friend, time is running out." Martin stopped as they passed a small alley and stepping into the shade looked closely at Nick. "What of the woman Nick? Is she going to be a problem?"

"No, I do not intend to see her again."

For a moment Martin didn't answer, then he looked up. "Nick, my task was to ensure that you weren't under surveillance. I saw you with her. I know that was part of your plan to gather information on Talawi's arrival but I think it has developed further than you intended. Am I right?"

Nick smiled grimly. "I used her Martin. Don't tell me I convinced you as well?"

Martin relaxed, he'd been holding his breath, "good, very good" he muttered. They resumed walking and speaking almost to himself. "I wondered about your feelings after our last conversation. She is very lovely and more than one operation has been ruined by a pretty face." He grinned suddenly at Nick, "In time Nick, you can if you wish, like Lazarus, rise from the dead."

Nick grunted, "You've too much imagination Martin. I've told her I'm on my way back to Germany via Seattle for discussions with the other directors. I'll be leaving Friday for Seattle."

"Keep your room at the Hotel Vancouver for your return. What about the weapons?"

"Back at the Via Rail terminal. I still have the long-term locker." Nick ran a hand through his short hair. "When it's over I'll dispose of the guns. Strange to think that we're almost there, after all this time." He turned abruptly and walked back the way they'd come. Martin watched the broad athletic figure move into a group of pedestrians and disappear. He sighed and spotting a taxi raised his hand.

§

Jimmy Douglas rubbed his jaw. "How did you get the tip Bas—how? I need to know the source."

"That's the strange thing, it came from Sir John Fowles office. Someone in Iran is not happy with the attempt on Talawi's life and is leaking names to one of Sir John's contacts."

"But this fellow?" The paper dimpled as Douglas stabbed at the file. "Koorosh Ghiassi? According to this, the man is a Harley street surgeon. Why would some one who is as well connected be involved with the Iranian hit squad?"

"Why not? Hell's bells Jimmy there's plenty of precedent. Remember Burgess, McLean, Aldridge and the others?"

Jimmy Douglas chewed thoughtfully on his lower lip. Deciding, he sat up. "OK, Bas, I'll pull in the others

but I'm going to leave Ghiassi in place for the time
being and I want all reference to him removed from your
files. I don't want some Yard hotshot thinking we've
slipped up on this investigation and rushing in to muddy
the water. I'm convinced that Talawi is still a target and
for all we know this could be a ploy to throw us off the
scent."

"A sprat to catch a mackerel?"

"It's worth a try. Will you sanitize the file?"

"Of course. I'll let Roger know that you've made
a direct verbal request."

Douglas grunted. The old civil service dictum,
'cover your ass at all costs,' still applied even at this
rarified level. "Thanks Bas." Rising he pushed the chair
back. "I'll be in touch." Hesitating at the door Jimmy
wondered if he should mention Sandy's request for a
scan on a Nick Cartwright. Sandy had added that it was
a low priority request. Still, he'd better check it out.
Lifting his hand in a half-wave he left the room.

Back in his office he punched in his personal
security code and the desktop computer blinked rapidly
then steadied as the taskbar illuminated. Jimmy typed in
a series of encrypted codes and immediately the screen
filled with dozens of names from A. Cartwright to Z.
Cartwright. He frowned; Sandy's message had included
the phrase 'underwater cameras/research/optics'. Jimmy
typed in a separate search box 'business/profession'
then immediately 'underwater cameras'. Again the
screen blinked. He waited. The screen began scrolling
slowly and he read.

N. Cartwright
Director: Inforlag AG. Hamburg

A series of phone, fax, and e-mail addresses followed.
Jimmy grunted in frustration. If he went back to the
main menu he could spend all day trying to find the right

Nick Cartwright. He mused, chewing thoughtfully on his pencil, then reached for the telephone. He punched in the main administration office number for Inforlag AG and waited.

"Yes, Guten Tag, I'm trying to get hold of Mr. Nick Cartwright. Is he available?"

"Wait please." The voice was female, young, probably an executive secretary. He heard the click as he was transferred and then a male voice, older, heavier, with a strong German accent,

"Ja, you wish to speak to Mr. Cartwright. What is your name and about what please?"

"I understand Mr. Cartwright is involved with your underwater camera division. I would like to discuss the technology with a view to purchasing some units. My name is James Douglas and I represent several oil companies that are looking to upgrade their underwater surveillance capability around offshore oil rigs."

Jimmy heard a sharp intake of breath and then there was a long silence. Puzzled he asked. "Did you get that?"

"Ja, I'm sorry, I was thinking. Where did you hear of us? We do not advertise, you understand."

"I have a friend who knows Nick and your firm was mentioned as a contact."

"Ahh- Ach so. You must understand Mr....?

"Douglas, James Douglas."

"Mr. Douglas, Mr. Cartwright is not available at the moment and it may take some time to get in touch. Can you leave me your number?"

"If you can give me some idea when he'll be back I'll call again. Perhaps his wife can help?"

"Mr. Cartwright is not married, and it may take a few days, if you would give me your number I'll see that he gets your message."

Jimmy wondered why a casual inquiry could cause

such obvious consternation. Perhaps the technology was secret? He shrugged; at least the man existed and wasn't married. Two of the markers Sandy had given were correct. He gave his cell phone number and thanked Mr. Keibel for his time. Replacing the phone he scribbled a short note to himself before switching off the computer and levering himself out of the chair. Jimmy reached for his raincoat and made his way out the door. "Going home, and unless it's nuclear war don't ring me." he called out to the two front desk receptionists. The door to his office closed slowly on stiff springs. The note lay face up on his desk

Call Jeff, Min of Def, re undwtr cams-Inforlag AG

§

Stretching luxuriously Jimmy Douglas opened his eyes to see the sun streaming through the bedroom window and lighting up the far wall. Marilyn had pulled the curtains back and he could hear the clink of utensils as she did something in the kitchen. The smell of fresh coffee drifted into the small room. He looked at the bedside clock in disbelief before throwing the covers back and swinging his feet out on to the carpeted floor. It'd been the most refreshing sleep he could remember.

"Hey, love why didn't you wake me?" he called as he made his way to the bathroom. "I'm going to be late." His wife called back but the words were lost in the rattle of the extraction fan as he turned the shower on and stepped into the glass-sided stall.

Twenty minutes later, showered, shaved and dressed for the office Douglas sat eating the huge break-fast his wife had prepared. Marilyn Douglas watched with satisfaction as her husband devoured his plate of bacon, eggs, fried tomato and toast. Lately, his hours had been erratic to say the least. He was losing weight and she knew that he was not eating properly, but after 20 years of marriage she'd learned nothing would change her husband. Talk of the English Bulldog, she thought. But Jimmy was more like a terrier, getting a fierce grip on a case and hanging on tenaciously until the myriad pieces began to form a recognisable pattern. She sighed. He didn't want to acknowledge that age could slow him down, and still tried to maintain the pace of his youth when as a young SAS officer he'd done everything at full throttle.

"Now, what's on your mind eh?" Jimmy looked up at his wife. "I know that look. What are you going to say?" He smiled and reached for his napkin.

"Jimmy, try to eat regularly, please. I know you're busy but it worries me that you look so thin. They can't begrudge you a few minutes' break for a meal."

"Thin? My goodness Mare, I could do to lose a few pounds. OK, OK," he lifted his hands as he saw her face darken. "Bad joke, I'm sorry. Yes, I promise to slow down and chew my food. Actually from the way things are going I think I can honestly say that I'll be home on time tonight. Hey," his face brightened, "Why don't you get tickets for the new play, Silver and Gold I think it's called? We can have dinner at the Greek place across the road from the theatre." He rose, reaching for his briefcase, and giving his wife a quick kiss made for the door.

Arriving at the office Jimmy stopped to chat with the receptionist, a retired Royal Marine, and collecting his overnight mail headed into his office. Dumping his briefcase on the floor next to his desk and dropping into the swivel chair he began to read his mail. He was busy slitting open the third letter when the phone rang and with a grunt he placed the half-open letter on top of the memo he'd left on his desk the night before.

"Douglas . . . Oh hullo Basil . . . When? . . . Of course, give me about 20 minutes."

Chapter 27

Safe House

"Thomas Aquinas believed that Hell was a wasteland of ice and snow but I never thought it could be wet and green." Ismail Talawi stared out the huge picture window at the mist-thin rain drifting in fine clouds across the neatly mowed lawn and driveway. "Purgatory can't be any worse than this."

Salt Spring Island, tucked in the Strait of Georgia between the mainland of British Columbia and Vancouver Island, had been the final choice of Sandy and RCMP Sgt. Brian Kowalski. The safe house, set in three acres of woods and pasture, had been rented from an American businessman who, in a burst of enthusiasm while visiting Salt Spring several years earlier, had purchased the modern log home on a quiet road only minutes from the main shopping centre. Finding that he could only spend a few days every year in his dream cottage but determined to hang on to his acquisition as a retirement haven, the businessman arranged for a local property management company to rent the house. Brian Kowalski heard of the property coming vacant through a friend of his wife's who was moving back to Vancouver after the sudden death of her husband. Brian arranged to examine the property with Sandy Flett and the two agreed that it was ideally suited for their purpose.

A rental agreement was quickly signed and arrangements made to install Talawi, Meg and the female RCMP officer while Sandy booked into the nearby Seabreeze Motel so that he could keep a discreet eye on any movement near and around the safe house. Sandy would liase with Brian Kowalski in Vancouver using the scheduled floatplane service for meetings.

Irritated, Meg looked up from the novel she was

reading. Since their arrival three days ago Ismail Talawi had produced a long litany of complaints. She'd tried to convince him that Sandy had chosen the best possible option but on their first meeting the two men had taken an instant dislike to each other. Meg suspected Sandy could see that her relationship with the author had progressed far beyond what was allowable or acceptable on a mission but he'd made no comment when Ismail draped his arm around her shoulders in an ostentatious display of possession. She recalled Ismail Talawi sneering at Sandy's choice of a safe house in a rural area on this quiet island. "I'm not a farmer—I don't want to look at a bunch of bloody sheep." The stocky SAS officer smiling briefly when Talawi demanded an Internet connection to, as he put it, "Remain in touch with the civilised world". Sandy answering with a perfectly straight face. "The hot water not working then sir?" She'd felt uncomfortable and tried, shortly after Sandy's departure, to make Ismail realise his behaviour was counterproductive. The author had turned on her in fury. "D'you honestly believe anyone would follow me to this godforsaken place? Why couldn't we be in Vancouver where at least they have a semblance of culture?" Placing her novel down and holding her anger in check she'd gone into the kitchen to speak to Gloria, the RCMP officer, who was busy organising the delivery of meals.

Impervious to the beauty of the island and bored, Ismail stopped writing, claiming difficulty with the end phase and demanded to be let out of the house. Meg, desperate to keep the peace and despite her irritation, understood her lover's frustration, finally agreed on this third day to make a tour of Ganges, the main shopping centre. Now they stood outside of Mouat's, the main general store, looking across the road to the Vortex

Gallery and being totally ignored by people moving around them. Gloria loitered in front of the Salty Shop watching their rear, but it was very obvious that Ismail Talawi in his present disguise was another unremarkable tourist in a town that saw far too many in the course of a year.

"Ah, let's see what bric-a-brac the local intellectuals produce as art." Ismail strode ahead of Meg, crossing the street to where the gallery sat on the corner of Grace Point Square. Pushing open the glass door behind Ismail Meg caught her breath. Facing her a large multipanel painting of a naked man in mixed media dominated one wall. The artist had used the technique of sgraffito, a difficult method where even the slightest error of judgement in execution could ruin days of work. She heard Ismail grunt in surprise, "Well— well, what have we here?" Life-size terra cotta sculptures of young women in various poses were spread throughout the gallery. Having taken art as an elective at Cambridge and, while not gifted herself, Meg could recognise and appreciate what she was looking at. Captivated, she ignored Ismail and devoured the stunning array of works by a variety of artists. Blom and Onley she knew, Shadbolt was vaguely familiar, but Venter was new to her and it was his work that drew her back to stand in admiration. Ismail, irritated by her absorption, reluctantly followed her around, listening with a bored expression as she pointed out the nuances of the large and small works that hung on the walls.

"First Latin and now art. You continue to surprise me Meg. Come, let's find a place where we can have a cup of coffee. I'm sure Gloria is tired of standing on street corners."

Meg frowned, and bit back a sharp retort. His allusion to the RCMP undercover officer annoyed her.

Gloria was certainly lovely, with long blond hair and hazel eyes, and Meg had watched with mounting anger as Ismail turned on his formidable charm. At first she'd assumed it was to punish her for siding with Sandy but then realised with dismay that he was on the prowl again. Gloria, to her credit, had shown complete professionalism in all her dealings with the author but Meg knew from her own experience that resistance simply acted as a spur to Ismail Talawi's determination. "We've hardly arrived. Don't you want to see what's upstairs?"

"No. I'm thirsty. Come." He turned and was opening the door before she could protest further. With a last reluctant look at the painting she joined him.

§

Sitting on a bench outside the Canadian Imperial Bank of Commerce Martin Dreyfus watched Ismail Talawi and his companion exit the Vortex Gallery. Martin waited as they disappeared into Grace Point Square and grunted in satisfaction as the blonde in jeans appeared from the direction of the parking lot. Two days of patient watching had finally borne fruit; Ganges town was, after all, very small and compact and he'd easily identified Talawi, despite the alterations to the authors face and height. He acknowledged with professional detachment that the Brits had done a reasonably good job and a casual observer would have ignored the author and the dark haired woman at his side. He'd identified the blonde as part of the security screen with Sandy Flett at Vancouver airport and despite careful cross-checking had not noted any further protection around the author.

Martin felt certain that there must be more. Where was Sandy Flett? Arriving himself by ferry from

Vancouver three days ago, the same day he'd seen Sandy meet the author at Vancouver's International Airport and take the floatplane to Salt Spring, Martin had caught a brief glimpse of the SAS man exiting the Bank of Montreal in Ganges. Now Sandy had disappeared. It was possible he was back in Vancouver, but it was also possible he was watching for threats to Talawi from a position Martin had not identified. Martin felt a ripple of uncertainty lift the hairs at the nape of his neck. The SAS were not a unit to be taken lightly. He stood, glancing around as if uncertain as to where he should head, then turned away from the direction that Talawi and his escorts had taken and sauntered toward a row of single-storied shops and boutiques opposite a gas station.

Two days later he had what he needed—the location of the safe house and aerial photographs of the house and surrounding countryside taken from a hired light aircraft, the pilot believing he was a taking a European tourist keen on unusual shots of Ganges town and local area. He had extraction routes, ferry and floatplane schedules and a wealth of detail. After a final stroll through the town he arrived back at his vehicle in the car park behind a popular coffee shop. He stretched and slid onto the driver's seat. After spending a total of four days on Salt Spring it was time to leave. If Flett was in the area it would only be a matter of time before the SAS man would start noticing someone who always seemed to be in the vicinity of Talawi or his safe house. Martin looked around. He liked this place, and it had a good feel—his accommodation at the little Bed and Breakfast in the Fulford Valley had had the charm of a more leisurely age. Perhaps after? … He snorted with amusement at his meandering thoughts. Anywhere connected with the Talawi hit would be forever off

limits. Shrugging, he started the car and turned toward
the ferry terminal at Fulford Harbour.

   After he'd passed on all the information, the
final phase would be Nick's responsibility. Nick should
be back in Vancouver today after his final trip to Seattle.
Once he'd briefed Nick he'd be on the Cathay Pacific
flight to New York and would reappear as Monsieur
Henri Dumont, a French businessman heading for
Lisbon on TAP the Portuguese national airline. Once on
the ground in Europe Martin Dreyfus would disappear,
never to surface.

§

Martin watched Nick exit the taxi and enter the dingy
bookstore. He waited, motionless, checking for any tail,
but the traffic flowed past. It was a good place to meet.
He could see down the street for a long way and the
bookshop backed onto a larger building so surveillance
from the rear was impossible. Satisfied, he cut across the
street towards the bookstore. The door jingled as he
entered and a gaunt, sad looking man with a scraggly
grey beard looked up hopefully.

   "Can I help you?"

   "Browsing," Martin grunted shortly as he pushed
past into the dim interior. He'd located this shop earlier
as one of several possible meeting places. It sold a mix
of; astrological, new age and whatever second-hand
books the owner could pick up from estate sales. Martin
had chosen it mainly for the location, but it had the
added advantage of a greatly varied clientele so an
open-necked shirt would be as normal as a suit or Indian
cotton pantaloons. He saw Nick leafing through a book
and moved around several floor-to-ceiling racks before
reaching him. He smiled and said softly, "My car is

across the street. The dirty silver hatchback. Meet you
there in ten." He moved away and from the next aisle
heard Nick pay for the book he'd been reading and leave
the store. The tinkle of the bell echoing as the door
closed.

Martin waited another few minutes then left the
store and walked down the pavement to the recessed
entrance of a thrift store selling used clothing. He could
see, reflected in the glass, Nick sitting in his car reading
the book. Martin took a deep breath. The end phase of
any operation was always the most dangerous. Everything converged—the hunted, the hunter and let's not
forget the gamekeepers, he thought grimly. Nothing
moved down the long street except a Transit bus, which
hissed past grumpily looking for passengers at the stop a
hundred metres on. He walked back to the car and,
slipping onto the driver's seat, started the car. Nick did
not look up until they were into the main stream of
traffic heading towards Route 99 and the American
border.

"All set?"

"Yes. There is a parking lot in the mall coming up
on your side, we'll talk there." Martin maneuvered
across two lanes of traffic and turned into the huge
parking lot of a mall and allied shops that stretched for
several hundred metres. Richmond, a suburb of Vancouver in the flat delta lands of the Fraser River, seemed to
Nick to be made up of nothing but enormous shopping
malls spaced at regular intervals. Martin found an empty
slot a good 300 metres from the nearest mall entrance.
There were several empty spaces around them at this
end of the parking area. Most of the cars following
cruised close to the main entrance looking for recently
vacated slots. Nick turned to face his controller as
Martin switched off the engine and began rummaging in

a briefcase on the back seat. With a grunt of satisfaction
Martin brought out a large brown envelope.

"Here is the information you'll need. I've
planned your strike on the assumption you'll use the
rifle. I've marked two positions that will give you a clear
shot at Talawi from the woods surrounding the house.
The distance from either position to the house is about
300 to 350 metres. The best time will be early evening
at dusk, or a little later. You'll be shooting over a road,
so if you shoot as a car goes past it might create enough
confusion to give you extra time. There are no dogs and
as far as I could determine no in-ground security. Once
you've fired, leave the rifle and head through the trees
to the driveway of the empty property where you must
park the rental car—here." Martin dug into the envelope
and extracted a set of car keys. "The rental is a small,
used Toyota, ubiquitous, very forgettable. I rented it
from Victoria and parked it in the All Saints Anglican
Church parking lot on Salt Spring. I had a word with the
rector; told him I had to return to Vancouver by
floatplane on urgent business for a few days and offered
to pay parking there while I was back to Vancouver. He
kindly dismissed my offer and even showed me the best
spot to park it. I told him I'd have it picked up soon. It'll
excite no comment." He pointed to another dot on the
map and clipped to the map was a photograph of a
brown Toyota Corolla, the license plate visible.

"After you've picked up the car, drive around
and get a feel for the distances you'll be travelling in the
dark. Once you initiate the operation, leave the car
facing down the driveway on the empty lot off Long
Harbour road so you can roll down towards the road
before starting it up. There are so many trees between
you and the house that they'll not hear you. I could

hardly hear the traffic on Long Harbour Road when I did my recce."

Nick nodded. Martin had been totally thorough and had taken risks to establish the best line of retreat. Martin pulled a folder piece of paper out of the envelope and flattened it out.

"I've included this schedule for the Long Harbour to Vancouver ferry and the Fulford Harbour to Vancouver Island ferry. Leave it under the seat as if you forgot it, so if it's found, the search will concentrate on the Ferries. Now, there seems to be a steady stream of traffic heading both ways along Long Harbour Road in the early evening. With a little luck, you'll not attract any attention. When you hit Long Harbour Road turn back to Ganges and the Marina." Martin took a deep breath. "OK so far?"

Nick scanned the carefully drawn map marked with red dots indicating the salient points Martin was making. He frowned, "There are a lot of variables in this Martin." It was a statement not a question.

Martin sighed. "I know. I'd have preferred to hit Talawi in Vancouver but Flett and his team realised the advantages of Salt Spring as a hideaway. Yes, from our perspective it's more difficult but also there are advantages. Security is fairly relaxed, remember they've allowed Talawi to walk around the town. I doubt if he'll be recognised during the time that they have him there." Martin slid out a rental form. "I've rented a medium-sized cabin cruiser from Sydney on Vancouver Island which you'll pick up tomorrow in Sydney and motor over to Ganges. It's about 35-40 minutes travel at full throttle, but you can make your own assessment. I've rented a berth for you at the Ganges marina for a week. Since you're listed as a European tourist on a fishing holiday, they'll expect you to come and go unpredictably. Once you've arrived and tied up, walk to the church and collect the car. After the hit park the car here." Martin pointed to a parking area behind a building he'd marked *coffee shop*. "People come and go at all hours. Walk to the marina and board your boat. Return to the Sydney marina, dispose of all your previous documentation at sea on the return to Sydney." He stopped and looked quizzically at Nick. "I assume you've collected the documentation for your new personas, Drayton and Shoemaker, from the locker at the Via Rail terminal?"

"No.— Not yet, I'll start preparations once we finish here."

"OK, once you've moored the cruiser, remember it's on a two-week rental so no one will bother you for payment. Walk up to the center of Sydney and go to this address." Martin smiled at the look of surprise on Nick's face. "He's one of the faithful, been there a long time in deep cover. I activated him before we left Gip's place. Make the changes to your appearance at his house and he'll drive you to a small private airfield outside of Victoria. Ali will arrange the charter plane that will fly you to Abbotsford Airport in the Fraser Valley. There's a return ticket for Mr. Drayton to Toronto on WestJet Airlines in the folder. From Toronto you can pick up a flight to Europe. There is a real Mr. Drayton living in Toronto, just in case they start checking passenger lists."

Nick took the envelope and studied the photographs of Talawi, Meg and Gloria without comment. He studied the map of Salt Spring Island with the location and photographs of the safe house. "I don't see Flett's photograph here." He looked up at Martin.

"Oh he was there all right. I saw him three days ago. He has either returned to Vancouver or is keeping a very low profile. His vehicle has moved from the sea-

plane terminal to the Sylvia Hotel. That's where it is
now."

Nick took a deep breath, expelling it in a long rush
of air. "You've done everything I could expect Martin,
but this is going to be a bitch to walk away from. Every
road, air and sea movement will be clamped. Hell,
leaving Ganges in a cruiser will itself attract attention."

Martin stared ahead, his face blank. "I know, damn
it. I know. I've been going over everything in my mind
until I can't think straight. But, from the strike until you
board the cruiser should be no more than 15 minutes
and there is bound to be a lot of confusion at first. Also,
there is always a lot of boat traffic in Ganges Harbour,
you'll not be alone in moving around. The flight to
Abbotsford is a well-used irregular operation serving
businessmen in a hurry who are prepared to pay for the
convenience." He turned to face Nick. "I don't think we
can watch and wait for a better chance. Delay now
increases the risk to us. The Brits have that composite
sketch and knowing them they'll play with variations on
the basic outline. We're living on borrowed time, Nick."
He spread his hands in a typically Gallic gesture of
frustration. "I've told Albarrasan we're in a position to
strike. I expect the funds to our accounts and the saniti-
zation of records are ready to go—look, if you want
more time I can let them know we are going to delay. It's
your call."

For a long time neither man spoke, then Nick
smiled grimly. "We both know that time is critical." He
sighed. "Very well. I'll pick up the cruiser tomorrow
afternoon. I want to see what it's like to travel between
the islands before the light fades." He held out his right
hand, "We'll not meet again. I've enjoyed your friendship, Martin. Stay alive to enjoy your retirement."

Martin took the proffered hand, bringing his left

hand round to grip Nick's elbow. "And you also Nick, it's been good working with you. Gip would be pleased." He hesitated, as if to say more then squeezing Nick's elbow pointed to a taxi rank across the road from the parking lot. "I'll be at the hotel until late tomorrow afternoon. You can contact me by cell phone until four p.m. Good luck Nick."

Nick opened his door, "Insh'Allah, my friend. As God wills." The door slammed shut and Martin watched Nick cross the traffic towards the taxi rank. Martin shivered; Nick was right, they'd need more than a little luck. Taking a deep breath he started the car and headed back to the city.

§

Ayatollah Albarrasan watched Foreign Minister Abajir Rafsanjani escort the Swiss chargé d'affaires to the door and smilingly bid the diplomat goodbye. Albarrasan waited as the two men chatted briefly, then Rafsanjani was walking towards him. "Bahram, my apologies for keeping you—an unexpected interruption." He inclined his head in the direction of the departing Swiss diplomat. "Please, come inside." Rafsanjani stood aside to let Albarrasan enter. Gesturing, Rafsanjani pointed to a large sofa and several heavily brocaded chairs clustered around a low table. As they crossed the floor a servant was removing the coffeepot and cups from the previous interview. "More coffee please Hamid. And some cake, you know what the Ayatollah prefers." The servant bowed, withdrawing silently on slippered feet. Rafsanjani dropped heavily into a chair. "Ah, for a quiet trip to the mountains. Much is happening Bahram. As you see we are in the process of negotiating a further loan to cover our external debt. At last we are being taken seriously in the financial capitals."

Albarrasan nodded. He'd wondered at the urgency of the call to meet with the Foreign Minister. Surely it wasn't to discuss finance. He waited without speaking as two servants busied themselves placing small china coffee cups and a long-stemmed silver coffeepot with a tray of date cakes on the table. "Your call said the meeting was urgent. How may I help the Foreign Minister?"

Rafsanjani waited until the coffee was poured and the servants had withdrawn. Then, after sipping from his cup, he looked at the Ayatollah and Albarrasan was puzzled by the grim look on Rafsanjani's face.

"The British have rolled up Basra's network in England." Rafsanjani took another sip before placing his cup down.

"Yes, I know. As we agreed."

"What of the others Bahram?"

"Others?"

"Please, Bahram. You and I are too old for this kind of fencing. Can you call them off?"

Ayatollah Albarrasan shook his head slowly. Someone must have talked. But who? As he lifted his own coffee cup, his face was impassive but his mind was in overdrive attempting to form a suitable reply. Rafsanjani interrupted his racing thoughts. "Libya is an old friend, Bahram, and Gip Lawrence was much respected. Sending his ashes back was admirable but a mistake. Tell me about Corsica."

"Ah, I see. You know then that we had an operation pending."

"Bahram, I'd hoped, and I still hope to see you taking a much more active role in the changes that are coming." The Foreign Minister paused. "If you haven't shut down Corsica you must do so now. At this juncture

Iran cannot afford adverse publicity. I thought we'd
agreed. In fact when you gave me the names of Basra's
team I recommended to the President that I be allowed
to ask you to fill a senior position in the government. Is
Corsica under control?"

Albarrasan stared down at the table. Corsica had
been sanitized. The reports were in a locked safe in his
office. The files on 'Camerone' and 'Cedar,' codenames
for Martin Dreyfus and Nicko Dragovic a.k.a Nick
Cartwright, were in the same safe in a thermal box.
Should the box be tampered with it would instantly
incinerate the contents. He looked up at the minister
and made his decision. "Corsica has been shut down but
two agents are close to Talawi. They are in position to
strike. It may not be possible to abort the mission."

The minister's face paled under his tan. "What are
you saying Bahram? You're telling me they are out of
communication?" He leaned forward, his face suddenly
tense.

"They initiate communication. Camerone's last
message, received yesterday, was that they were in the
final stages of the operation and would not communi-
cate again until they had achieved success and were
clear."

"Bahram this is disastrous, you must contact them
and cancel their mission, at once."

Albarrasan did not reply. So close to achieving his
goal it was a bitter pill to swallow. Resignedly he decided to salvage what he could from this new turn of
events. "I will try—I have a man in the vicinity who may
be able to contact one of the agents, the one we code-
named Camerone. Camerone will advise Cedar."

"You must—you must. What assistance do you
need from the government?

"Give me 48 hours. If I have not managed to

contact them in that time we may have to warn the
British to return Talawi to England."

"I see. So, Talawi is hidden in another country. I
assume you intend to expose the identities of the men
you call Cedar and Camerone to the British."

Albarrasan stifled an angry reply. "No, we cannot
do that. Sacrificing Basra's group in England can be seen
as punishment for disobeying orders but to expose our
own agents will have long term negative effects on other
agents. These men have served our cause well."
Albarrasan rose stiffly. "Two days Minister. I'll advise
you as soon as I have word."

"Another hour love, I'll be finished shortly." Jimmy
Douglas glanced at the clock as he put the phone down.
He'd enough time to finish checking the last of his
correspondence before going home. Tonight he did not
intend to let his wife down. Ten minutes later, after
finishing a taped reply to the last memo, he tossed the
letter and hand Dictaphone into a wire basket for the
night secretary to collect. Stretching his shoulders, he
marveled at how completely a good sleep could refresh
a person. Glancing down he noticed the memo to himself he'd scribbled last night. Frowning, he hesitated. It
could wait. Then with a wry grin Douglas decided to
clear his desk completely. Picking up the phone he
pushed a number on the speed dial.

"Jeff? —Yes, — can you do a quick check for me?
— I don't know, now do I? —That's why I'm asking
you. Here it is then—can you run a trace on Inforlag
AG. Hamburg. They make super-secret underwater
cameras or something, the sort of thing you warlike
types like to play with. I need to know how kosher they
are, directors' backgrounds, that sort of thing. How
soon— Oh no panic, tomorrow will do—. Thank you,

young man, I'll mention your invaluable assistance to the PM." Grinning broadly Douglas replaced the phone and settled back in his chair as Tristam Burns entered.

"Trouble?"

"No." Tristam looked puzzled. "You asked me to report in periodically. Blair is resting so I thought I'd pop in to see if there was any news from the front line."

"Nothing that concerns you Tris. All is quiet. How's the film star?"

"Loving every minute. Talawi should hire him permanently." Tristam dropped his lanky frame into the hard chair facing the desk.

Douglas waved a forefinger at his subordinate. "Don't get too comfortable. Tonight I'm off on the dot. Have me a date with the missus, so if all is proceeding to plan you can go back and nursemaid our charge."

Tristam laughed but didn't move. "I'd hoped to hear of dramatic developments from across the pond. Something that'd require my unique skills to resolve."

Jimmy cocked an eyebrow. "Sandy'll be glad to hear of your concern. I read your repo . . ." The phone rang sharply. Douglas lifted the receiver, "Douglas— What? No I don't have more information. It was a request from a field agent, why? —What're you saying Jeff? — BundesPolizei—What sort of flag on Inforlag?— Political?—Shit, you're sure?—Sorry, sorry, of course. Look Jeff, fax all the info on the secure line including headshots if you have them on file. I know it's late— tomorrow—Yes." Douglas slumped back into his seat, his face thoughtful. "Tris I'm going home in a few minutes, could you contact Sandy?" Jimmy Douglas reached behind to pull a slim file from a rack and open-ing it scribbled a series of numbers on a pad, which he turned round to face Tristam. "There's Sandy's contact phone and also his e-mail. Ask him for a photograph of his sister's boyfriend. A clean headshot if possible."

"What's up, Boss?"

For a few seconds Douglas didn't reply, massaging his jaw between the thumb and index finger of his left hand. Tristam noted how the scar tissue on the hand seemed to flow with the movement. The older man stared past him, lost in thought. "What?— Oh I don't know— probably nothing. Sandy sent in a level three request. Wanted a trace on a man that his sister is seeing. It now appears that the company this man is a director of, is under active investigation by German security, they have a political watch."

"I can't see Sandy asking for info on something unimportant but a level three request is pretty mild." Tristam looked puzzled.

"Hmm. I know. He wanted to know if this fellow was married, didn't want his sister getting in too deep if he was. Not the sort of request we normally process but Sandy and I go back a ways. Now it seems as if he may have picked up on something more. Still," he flexed the skin of his jaw again, "If this group are into specialised underwater technology it's possible that they're selling to unsavoury elements and yon boyfriend may be hiding something. German security is paranoid after nearly missing the nerve gas sale to China—not that I blame them mind you. So, young feller, get in touch and have that picture on my desk by nine tomorrow." Douglas levered himself upright, a smile erasing the thoughtful look of moments before. "The privileges of high office, young Tris. I'm off to the Opera while you look after the security of the realm. I'm confident it's in good hands." Chuckling he escorted Tris out of the office and together the two walked to the stairs leading down to the street below.

Chapter 28

The End Game

Sandy read the de-encrypted message again. The e-mail had arrived on his laptop computer during the early hours of the morning. Tris had sent 'Subject photo req'd' and the terse message puzzled him. His request for a trace on Nick Cartwright had been irregular, investigations using bureau staff for personal reasons were strictly forbidden. It happened of course, but if an audit revealed such a request had been executed the perpetrators could expect sanction. Jimmy knew that, so why was Jimmy involving Tristam? Sandy shrugged. Jimmy must have a good reason or maybe was simply under pressure of other work and had asked Tris to follow through. He remembered Mike taking snapshots at the party where he'd met Nick Cartwright for the first time. Picking up the phone he dialed Mike's office number.

"Mr. Monroe, please—Yes, tell him it's his brother-in-law." Sandy waited, listening to muzak coming in to the earphone.

"Sandy, sorry to keep you waiting. I'd a couple of salespeople in for the morning briefing. So what can I do for you?"

"Mike, remember the party, the day I arrived from Britain? As I recall you were busy taking snaps of people all evening. Anne even nagged you about the flash going off in peoples face's."

"Yes, I wanted to finish off the roll. I had a series of industrial shots taken earlier that needed processing the following day and thought to clear the camera, why?"

"Did you manage to get one of Nick Cartwright?"

"Cartwright? Nick Cartwright. Hmm—I think so,

give me a second, they're here somewhere. Oh yes, here—we are." Sandy heard the phone being placed down, a scraping sound, then, "Yes, a rather nice head and shoulders shot of Nick talking to you, actually. You want to tell me what this is all about?"

"No doubt you've heard about our famous fishing trip. I want to scan the picture into my computer and manipulate the photo to show Nick pulling a whale out of the water. Bit of a lark really. Can I pick up the print?"

"Of course. Hang on—the bicycle courier is leaving the office in a few minutes, I'll have him drop it off at the Sylvia. I assume you're calling from there?"

"Michael old son, you're a gentleman and a scholar." Sandy replaced the phone, a thoughtful look on his face. He'd scan the photo in and, attached to an e-mail, it would be in England within the hour. With luck, Jimmy and Tristam might still be at their desks.

§

Reinvigorated by another full night's sleep James Douglas arrived early at his office and decided to have another look at the Salameh file. He punched a number on the internal phone line. " Who's the Duty Officer today? Yes put me through." He waited, then, "George I need to look at the file on the Salameh killing. And a package should have arrived from Jeff Outerbridge at the Ministry of Defence—it has—good. Can you bring both round?"

Switching on his computer he noted several messages waiting in the electronic inbox, one from Sandy in Vancouver. The photo he needed was attached with a query from Sandy asking for clarification. Jimmy smiled. Sandy wanted to know what the hell was going on. Jimmy touched the print button and an 8x11 colour print slid out. Picking the print up Jimmy studied it carefully but could see nothing remarkable about the face. The picture showed Cartwright listening to something Sandy was saying and the man's head was cocked slightly sideways. A strong face, deep wrinkles around the eyes, no facial hair. Jimmy grunted and placed the print to one side as the duty officer stopped at the open door. "The file on the Salameh killing and your parcel from MoD, sir." He placed the cardboard file box and buff envelope on Douglas's desk and held out the receipt book for signature.

"Ah, thank you George." Jimmy signed the receipt and waited until the DO had left his room before cutting the tape that sealed the box. He decided, suddenly, to clear up Sandy's problem first, and pushed the Salameh box aside, opening the package from the MoD. Several sheets of foolscap and a collection of grainy photographs shook out onto his desk. A memo attached to the top sheet in Jeff Outerbridge's scrawl caught took his attention.

Re yr. enq, no photos on file. It appears as if Cartwright is a silent partner. Bkgrd info unavailable. Tried BundesPolizei on yr behalf. Nada. Sorry,'

Jeff.

Jimmy massaged his chin, puzzled. What the hell was going on? First the strange hesitation by Keibel at Inforlag AG, then nothing on Cartwright, even the BundesPolizei had nothing. Something was not right. He reached for Sandy's photo and studied the face with more interest. There was something familiar, but what? A thought crossed his mind and with an oath he pulled open the Salameh file and flipping through the documentation found the latest picture the forensic artist had made of Salameh's killer. Holding both the photo and drawing at arm's length he felt his heart lurch. It was not possible, it could not be the same man, the match was not perfect but he knew deep in his gut that somehow the opposition had penetrated their security and he was looking at the man who'd killed Salameh and was now poised to kill Talawi. Jimmy grabbed his phone, realising with a shock that his hand was slick with sudden perspiration.

"Basil, get over here right away. It's fully urgent." Slamming the phone down he punched in the number for Sandy in Vancouver and waited in mounting frustration as the number rang unanswered. He tapped out a rapid e-mail to Sandy. "Suspect Cartwright is match with Israeli composite and our enhanced pic. Move Talawi now. Get RCMP to hold Cartwright on unspecified charges. Call ASAP!" He encrypted the message and stabbed at the send button. Once again he tried Sandy's cellular phone number and when it rang unanswered, called the Duty Officer.

"George, I want you to drop everything and start calling these two numbers until you get a reply. Once you have contact, call me. I must speak to Sandy. This is status critical. Log the time, starting now." He gave the DO both the Silvia Hotel and Sandy's cell phone numbers. Now all he could do was wait for Basil Coulson to arrive.

Chapter 29

A lie to comfort the dying

Sandy parked his car in the driveway of the safe house, leaving his overnight bag on the front seat. The cellular telephone lay next to his bag. Sandy stepped out of the car and made for the front door.

Watching him through a side window Gloria called out, "Meg, Sandy's arrived." She opened the door with a smile. "Hullo Sandy, good to see you. We have a problem."

"Problem, there's no such thing in our profession, only challenges. Did they miss out that part in your briefing?" Sandy gave her a broad grin and stepped inside as Meg came down the stairs.

"Sandy, Ismail is sick." Her face was creased with concern. "I don't know how seriously, but he's had the runs for a couple of hours and looks like death."

"Show me." Sandy followed her up the staircase to the master bedroom. Talawi, fully dressed, sans shoes, lay stretched out on the huge bed. His face was waxen and perspiration beaded his upper lip. Sandy put his hand over the author's brow, noting how hot the man felt. "Can you stand?" he asked.

Talawi's eyes flashed for a moment. "I suppose you'd like me to run around this pestilential island. The blasted food here is what's caused this." He closed his eyes before speaking again. "I want a doctor brought here at once."

Sandy looked across at Meg and shook his head in refusal. "Have you or Gloria had any symptoms?" Both officers shook their heads. "It's possibly his appendix." Sandy leant over Talawi. "Have you had your appendix out?"

"Since when are you a qualified doctor?" Talawi's

breathing was rapid but the voice was as waspish as ever. "For your information I had it out years ago."

Sandy held out his hand to Meg. "Give me your cell phone. I've left mine in the car." Keying in a series of numbers he waited expectantly. "Dr. Flett please." Holding his hand over the mouthpiece he spoke to Meg. "I don't want him seeing a local doctor here. We'll fly him to St Paul's in Vancouver and Anne can have a look. They'll have better diagnostic equipment there and we can isolate him in a separate ward." He looked over at Gloria. "Can you check if the charter floatplane is available? If it is we want it right away."

Gloria nodded. "I'll get the local phone book." She left the room quickly as Sandy turned back to his phone. "Anne, its Sandy. I'm bringing in a friend with stomach pains. No." He hesitated. "Look Sis, this is business and I need a secure private ward. Can you fix?" He listened intently to the other end. "Anne, this is important, keep it to yourself—I know what I said, you can give me a bollocking later—Yes, we're leaving right away. If a plane is available we should be at St Paul's in 40 minutes." He handed the phone back to Meg as Gloria called through the open door.

"The plane is available and standing by."

"Good, Meg you come with me. We'll take your vehicle, it'll be more comfortable for Mr. Talawi. Gloria you stay and hold the fort, I'll call you from the hospital. You call Sgt. Kowalski and advise him what we're doing. Ask him to meet us with transport at the floatplane dock in Vancouver. OK people, lets get moving."

Outside, lying on the passenger seat in Sandy's car, the cell phone rang continuously for a full minute then stopped. Ismail Talawi, despite his protestations, was able to navigate the stairs from the bedroom and apart from lines of tension around his mouth, managed to climb into the large family van parked in the circular driveway ahead of Sandy's car. Sandy and Meg helped Talawi into the van through the sliding side door and as they started the car Sandy's cellphone rang again, but by this time they were moving down the driveway. In London a frustrated Jimmy Douglas was calling the Duty Officer with instructions to get hold of Sandy.

§

Nick stared across the waters of Burrard Inlet, his back to the giant logs of Lumberman's Arch, the delicate tracery of the soaring Lions Gate Bridge over the First Narrows on his left. A sparkling white cruise liner, tiered like a mammoth wedding cake, slid through the water in front of him heading for the docks at Canada Place. He stared unseeing at the panorama of ship and seabirds, joggers and cyclists. For several hours after leaving Martin he'd checked the plan for flaws and confirmed what his gut instincts had told him initially. He would kill Talawi, that was a simple matter, but escaping the certain wrath of both the British and Canadian security services was another altogether.

A hit in Vancouver with its sprawling urban area and diverse population would have given him a high chance of escape. But escaping a small island? An island, totally dependent on easily monitored ferries and floatplanes with choke points everywhere? Martin's use of a cabin cruiser was, at best, only slightly less of a gamble. With Talawi down, the Coast Guard, police helicopters and possibly military would be scouring the area like wasps from a nest prodded with a stick. Once he pulled the trigger he'd need at least 90 minutes to get from the ambush site to Sydney. If, and it was a big if, the cabin cruiser could cover the distance in half that time. What if, as sometimes happened, something went awry? Blocked fuel filters on the boat, a broken shear pin on the propeller? Long ago Nick had found the old soldier's formula; 'estimate the time required, then double it' was true. He'd need more than luck. This time, he'd need a miracle.

Strangely enough he felt no fear. The die was cast. He'd made peace with his God in the privacy of his hotel room an hour ago. But not to see Anne again, not to touch her face or hear her voice was an agony he could hardly bear. At last he stood. This was where Anne and he had walked on their first meeting. Running his hand gently over the stone wall he tried to harden his heart, bring back the terrible memories, hatreds that had brought him to this place and time. But those grim memories were fainter, the hatred purged to a sadness of knowledge that an eye for an eye was the antithesis of life. But the choice was no longer his to make. If he refused, after swearing fealty to the cause, his life and the lives of those deemed to be responsible for his failure were forfeit. Despite the mild air, he shivered, remembering how he'd executed Salameh like a dog without a thought to the man's guilt or innocence; the Israeli soldiers had died despite, or perhaps because of, his detachment. What had Martin said? Promises that were made must be kept. He could not complain, not now, for he'd known from the beginning the consequences and rewards.

Turning to look for the last time at the lovely scene in front of him he sighed, remembering, his father telling him as a boy about an old Lion, toothless, sick and scarred, excluded from the tribe by a younger male, watching the circling Hyenas close in.

"The Lion knew the time had come for one last battle, a battle that could not be won, but he would go down fighting. It is always better, Nicko, to keep fighting." Nick grimaced. So much for platitudes. He would give anything to walk away from this last battle, but then . . . he straightened, resolve hardening his features, and made for the parking area and his vehicle. He must not see her again but even as he walked the path he knew he must.

§

Martin stopped packing his small suitcase when a knock on the door made him look up. He frowned, puzzled. "Yes?"

"Camerone it is Ali."

Martin's jaw dropped. "What, the hell . . ." He strode to the door and, peering through the peephole, saw his deep-cover contact from Sydney on Vancouver Island. The man he'd told Nick to contact was standing in the passage. Checking to see that the man was alone he opened the door and pulled Ali into the room with an oath. "What the hell are you playing at? You know you should never make direct contact unless I initiate."

"I have a message, an urgent message from home. I tried to call you, but you were out for a long time. It was imperative I pass it on to you. You must abort the mission. You must do nothing to the apostate, that's the message and I have orders to confirm that you have understood and obeyed."

"What!" Martin stared at the man in amazement. "From who—? Who would expect us to abort now?" Martin's mouth hung open in total surprise. "I've launched the arrow, he is travelling, on his way. Once the strike is over, he'll be heading to you as planned. You must return, he'll need your help."

"Camerone, understand. Albarrasan himself sent

the message. It is absolute. You must abort the strike. Can you reach Cedar?"

"I don't know. It may already be too late. I'm leaving on the six p.m. flight to London tonight. Cedar has been launched . . ." Martin sat down on the bed. "Go back, if it is too late you must still help Cedar. I will try to intercept him but . . ." Martin shook his head, wrestling with the disastrous news. "Go Ali, I'll call you when I have more news, go."

Ali stood, uncertain, then he placed a hand on Martin's shoulder. "May Allah, the merciful, the compassionate, give you success. I will await your call." He left the room soundlessly. Martin stared at the phone. It might be just possible that Nick was still at the Hotel Vancouver. He dialled the number and waited tensely as the desk answered.

"Is Mr. Cartwright still in the hotel?"

"No sir, Mr. Cartwright left about two hours ago. He made me check his mail box for messages."

"Did he take any luggage?"

"Yes, he had a bag and a case."

"Case, what kind of case?"

"It looked like a case for carrying plans in, a hard case, sort of silver colour."

Martin sighed in despair. The case containing the sniper rifle was with Nick, it must mean he was on his way. "Thank you," he said, replacing the phone as the receptionist asked, "Can I get him . . ." The only place to find Nick now was at the convergence point, the ambush site. He felt cold, every instinct told him to leave, he'd done what he could and going to Salt Spring would increase the level of danger astronomically. Martin walked over to the mini bar and pulling a minature bottle of brandy out from the rack, unscrewed the cap and in one fluid movement tilted his head back, gulping down the contents. Directly above the bar was an ornate tinted mirror and as he lowered his head he saw his reflection staring back. Remembering the betrayal that had driven him away from his former life into working with Gip Lawrence and the fundamentalists, he knew he could not betray Nick by abandoning him. Picking up the phone he called the floatplane service and booked a seat on the next flight to Salt Spring. Scowling at his reflection in the mirror he muttered, "Fool," before leaving the room and locking the door behind.

Nick listened to the phone ringing. The receptionist had been hesitant until he'd mentioned that he was Dr. Flett's brother. "Of course Mr. Flett, I'll track her down." The ringing ended abruptly and Anne spoke, breathless as if she'd been running, "Sandy, what is it?"

"Anne, it's Nick, sorry but I had to speak to you and the receptionist was going to brush me off."

"Nick—? I thought that you were going straight on to Europe from Seattle. What's wrong— what's happened? You sound dreadful."

"I must see you before . . ." He hesitated. "Anne it's vital, can we meet? I've very little time."

"I can't leave the hospital Nick, I'm waiting for a patient coming in from one of the islands. Can you come here? We can meet in the cafeteria on the fourth floor. It's not very private but I don't care. I'll tell the desk to page me as soon as you come." She laughed. "Use your real name."

Staring at the handset his lips twisted and closing his eyes he emptied his mind. He went back to the car. In the trunk the Walther sniper rifle in it's battered composite carrying case and his bag with a change of clothes and makeup lay under a blanket. He felt the

bulk of the 9mm Sig Sauer under his windbreaker,
tucked into a waist holster. Starting the car he drove
toward St Paul's hospital. Crossing Davie Street he saw
an empty parking space and braked sharply, ignoring the
outraged honking from the car behind. After locking the
car and placing coins in the meter he strode rapidly
along the sidewalk, waiting impatiently at the crossing
for the lights on Davie and Burrard Street to change. At
the hospital he followed the signs directing patients to
reception and waited while an elderly man at the desk
was processed.

"Yes, can I help you?"

"Dr. Flett. My name is Cartwright, she's expecting
me."

The receptionist gave him a cool searching look.
"If you'll wait sir, I'll page her."

Nick went to row of seats against a wall. He sat,
picking up a magazine and was leafing through, not
looking at the pages when he saw her coming through
the doors. Her face lit up as he rose and Nick felt the
breath catch in his throat. Anne stretched out a hand
and pulled him back along the passage she'd arrived
from. "Nick, what's the matter? You gave me a such a
shock, you sounded awful."

"I'm on my way in an hour Anne. I need to talk to
you, can we find a quiet place?" His eyes pleaded, his
hand in hers trembled.

"Of course, come into my office. Nick what is it?"
Her brow creased with concern.

"I'll explain, but not out here." Wordlessly she
scanned his face then turning led the way to the elevator. Their elevator was crowded and standing silently he
looked down, avoiding the questions in her eyes, until
they reached the third floor. A short walk brought them
to a door with her name painted on a plate in black

letters on a white background. *Dr. Anne Flett* the plate
stated. Pushing the door open she ushered him in then
turned and closed the door. Nick waited, arms hanging
loosely, unsmiling. Anne took a step towards him but he
held out a restraining palm. "Wait, wait until I've told
you. Sit down Anne."

Anne's face dropped and sitting behind her desk
she whispered, "For God's sake Nick, what is it?"

Taking a deep breath, Nick spoke quietly. "I came
to tell you that I'll not see you again." He shook his
head as she started to rise, her face draining of colour,
ashen. "No, please Anne, wait. I had to see you for the
last time. I love you and I'll always love you, but I have
promises to keep and a journey . . ." he hesitated " . .
.from which I'll not return. I want you to forget me." He
smiled sadly. "For the remainder of my life I'll not forget
you."

"You have a wife in Europe?" Anne's eyes were
bright with sudden tears.

He sighed, "Ah, if it were that simple. No,
there's no one else, as I told you, my wife and daughter
were killed long ago. I'm not married Anne. I did not lie
to you about that, nor about my love for you. But . . ."
He searched for the right words, his heart aching at the
look of loss and confusion on her face. "I'm not what I
seem to be. I have a debt to pay, a debt that . . ." Again
he struggled with the words. "I cannot tell you more."
He raised his hand slowly to stroke her cheek, brushing
the tears aside. Through her tears Anne watched him
turn at the door, his face sadder than any she'd ever
seen. He spoke for the last time. "Find it in your heart
to forgive me, my love. Whatever you hear, whatever
others say, if you believe only one thing of me, believe
that if I had any choice, I would stay."

"I don't understand, what is so important. . . "

She held out both hands beseechingly but the door had closed behind him. Anne dropped into the chair, her shoulders shaking and tears trickling through her fingers. Finally she sat upright and, searching for a tissue, began to clean up her eyes and cheeks.

Meg's cell phone tinkled as Sandy helped Ismail into the unmarked police cruiser driven by RCMP Sgt. Brian Kowalski and parked at the top of the ramp leading to the Vancouver floatplane base. The floatplane, having just landed on Burrard Inlet after a twenty-minute flight from Salt Spring Island, bobbed gently in the water alongside the dock. Ismail Talawi, despite a litany of complaints and shrugging off Meg's solicitous arm in a fit of irritation, had managed to move up the ramp to the sidewalk from the sea-level dock under his own power. Meg flipped open the cell phone.

"Davidson—Yes Gloria,—What!" The exclamation brought Sandy's head up sharply, stopping his movement toward the front passenger seat.

"Trouble?" he snapped at Meg.

"Gloria had a flash message from London, on your cell phone—here, speak to her yourself."

"Gloria it's Sandy. What's happened?" Listening to Gloria's rapid report Sandy's expression changed to one of stunned amazement. Brian Kowalski was out of the car now and watching the two agents carefully. He waited as Sandy thanked Gloria and handed Meg her cell phone back.

"Tell me." Kowalski realised the incoming message had badly shaken both agents and felt the hairs at the back of his neck rise.

Looking at him with disbelief still written all over his face, Sandy spoke jerkily, trying to process the information. "Nick Cartwright—Nick the man you

fished with—Nick—Nick Cartwright is our hit man.
London has an arrest on sight request to your division
going through right now. They've been trying to get hold
of me. Gloria heard my cell phone going off repeatedly
on the seat of my car on Salt Spring." Drawing a deep
breath Sandy straightened, professional training taking
over. "We must get Talawi to St Paul's and that secure
room. Brian can you arrange for more plainclothes
officers at the hospital to provide additional support?
Meg, sit on the left side next to Talawi. Make sure he
keeps his head down. You cover the traffic side; I'll
watch the sidewalks. Brian will watch for ticks. Our
departure from Salt Spring was unscheduled so I'm
certain no one is aware that we're in Vancouver but, this
man is very good—Nick—of all people." He shook his
head, still in shock. "How did he know—? How the hell
did he breach our security?"

"Those sorts of questions can wait. Let's get
Ismail to the secure room." Meg slid in next to the
author who having listened with mounting fear, gripped
her arm fiercely, his fingers biting into her flesh.

"Get more police—get more police. This is how
they tried in London—Oh God, Oh God, why did I let
you talk me into coming here?" Ismail Talawi was
frantic with fear. Easing Talawi's hand from her arm
Meg pulled him close and pushed his head down into
her lap.

"Stay down, as Sandy says you are probably safer
here than on Salt Spring." Meg tapped the shoulder
holster under her jacket. She debated removing the
pistol and having it ready in case of an ambush then
decided that the sight of a firearm would probably give
Ismail a heart attack. Kowalski pulled away from the
flight pickup area past the parked cars and turned into
the flow of traffic moving along Canada Place Way.

Now everyone in the vehicle was on high alert but, as they turned up Burrard Street and as Brian barked instructions into a dashboard-mounted microphone, the tension eased slightly for there seemed to be no obvious tail. Sandy's comment that the unsheduled trip would have thrown any stalkers off the scent relaxed the protection detail slightly. Kowalski maintained a steady speed up Burrard, catching the lights turning green at each intersection. Crossing Nelson Street he called over his shoulder.

"Meg, St Paul's Hospital is coming up on the right, you'll see it once we're past St Andrews Church and the Century Plaza Hotel. Leave Mr. Talawi in the back and come around to the sidewalk before letting him out. I'll watch the traffic. Sandy, shield Talawi as he exits the vehicle. I have squad cars on the way but it will be a few minutes before they get here." The distant wail of a siren came through the open window as Brian slid the car to an abrupt stop outside the hospital.

§

Joining a group of visitors leaving through the main entrance Nick pushed through the door. Blinking in the bright sunlight outside the entrance he walked down the slight ramp and stopped to draw a deep breath, trying to clear his head, letting the crowd flow around him before continuing to the short flight of stairs leading down to the sidewalk. Disinterestedly, he saw a large sedan slide to a stop and a woman exit into the flow of traffic then come around in a crouching run to the rear door.

Alerted by her action Nick noted that the woman's hand was inside her jacket. Without taking her eyes off the few pedestrians crossing the intersection at Comox Street she pulled open the rear door before turning to face the way the vehicle had come. Eyes widening in amazement Nick saw Ismail Talawi step uncertainly from the vehicle. A disguised Talawi, the hair was darker and the beard gone, but after studying every possible adjustment to Ismail Talawi's photograph for months on Corsica he knew his man without hesitation. Then with a jolt he saw Sandy clamber out of the front passenger door.

The main body of people leaving the hospital with Nick had thinned out and not ten feet away Ismail Talawi stepped towards him. Their eyes locked and time slowed to a crawl; Nick slid his hand to the spring-loaded holster and the Sig Sauer 9 mm pistol jumped into his hand. Through a clear bright tunnel he saw the mortal fear in Talawi's widening eyes, the man's mouth opening in shock. The policewoman with Talawi, in trying to get her weapon free, had snagged it under her jacket. She was shouting, her mouth working, but he heard nothing and felt his pistol coming up cleanly, the safety catch snipping off under his thumb.

Knees bent, both arms extended in the classic shooter's crouch Nick started taking up the first trigger pressure. The policewoman—he recognised her now, she was the one who accompanied Sandy the day he'd killed Salameh—abandoned efforts to free her own weapon. She knew, in the space of a heartbeat, that Ismail Talawi was doomed—unless—then, without hesitating, she stepped in front of Talawi, who'd covered his face with his hands and was sinking to his knees, blocking with her body the man she was tasked to protect.

Nick hesitated. In another life, at another time he'd have shot through the woman, the steel-jacketed .45 ACP bullet punching her clear over the crumbling form behind. His next shot would have killed the author. A brief smile flickered around the corners of his

mouth acknowledging her courage. He began lowering
the Sig Sauer as Sandy's bullet took him high in the
chest and the second from Brian Kowalski threw him
back against the low wall flanking the walkway.

Nick tried to raise his hand but it was strangely
unresponsive. He coughed and the metallic taste of
blood filled his mouth, a great silence surrounded him.
From what seemed a great distance he saw Sandy coming closer and kicking at what he recognised as his
pistol. Something was wrong with his eyes, Sandy was
standing in a cone of light. Nick coughed again, bubbles
frothing over his lips. Sandy said something and was
yelling at the man behind. People were running; Nick
noticed his right hand was trembling as if with the ague
and he could not stop it.

"Nick, Nick can you hear me?" Sandy was kneeling beside him, wiping the blood off his jaw. "Hold on
Nick, a doctor is coming. You're going to be okay. Chest
wound, not too bad, I've seen worse, you'll survive.
Hold on now." The sound came and went and he tried
to smile at Sandy but the light was fading, which was
strange, as it was only midday.

In the hospital Anne Flett walked back to the reception
area. Sandy and his patient from Salt Spring were due
shortly and she should check with the admitting clerk
that they were ready. Hearing a series of sharp cracks
she wondered briefly at the noise but the turmoil of her
meeting with Nick drove all other thoughts from her
mind. She touched her face with cold fingers—why?
What could be so terrible that it could drive him away?
Reaching the main reception lobby she was almost
knocked down as a man burst through the doors from
the walkway outside.

"We need a Doctor—outside—there's been a

shooting right outside." His eyes were wild with excitement and his voice at an impossibly high pitch.

For a moment Anne stood stock still trying to absorb the import of the words, then training took over. "Get a stretcher," she snapped at an orderly staring in amazement at the visitor. Running, Anne was through the swinging door in four strides. The scene stopped her like a brick wall. Sandy was bending over Nick—her Nick. A woman in jeans and a polar fleece jacket stood over a huddled fiqure. The woman had a pistol in her hand and was covering the street. Another man on the sidewalk was barking into a hand-held radio. The whine of police sirens coming up Burrard Street was getting louder.

Stunned she saw bright pink blood bubbles burst from Nick's mouth. Dropping to her knees she pushed Sandy aside. Nick's eyes were filming over and in desperation she called his name over and over even as her fingers probed the wounds. Nicks eyes flickered then slowly brightened and he smiled. He tried to speak and more bright bubbles flecked his lips.

Anne gasped with relief. "Don't talk Nick, you've a lung wound. We'll have you inside in a minute. Stretcher—where's that stretcher?" Anne stared around, swinging back to Nick as he whispered.

"No . . .Sandy . . .knows. He tried . . . a lie to comfort the dying. Good man . . . good ma. . . . Re . . . member . . . what I . . . told you."

Cradling his head Anne watched in despair as the light faded from his eyes then Sandy was gripping her shoulders and lifting her clear of Nick's body as the stretcher bearers arrived. Burying her face in Sandy's chest Anne sobbed inconsolably like a lost child.

Debris:

Glancing at his watch for the tenth time in as many minutes Martin sat waiting for Nick to arrive and claim the vehicle that had been left in the Anglican Church parking lot in Ganges. Sitting in the nondescript vehicle meant for Nick's use on Salt Spring Martin had an unobstructed view down the long southeast reach of Ganges Harbour. He could see past Goat Island that partially protected the marina and as far as Second Sister Island at the mouth of the inlet. Nick should be visible soon, steering the cabin cruiser up the inlet from the direction of Swanson Narrows and Vancouver Island.

Earlier the rector, passing on his way to the church and noticing the lone occupant in the vehicle, had stopped for a brief chat. Dismissing, with a smile, Martin's thanks for allowing the use of his church's parking area he readily accepted the explanation of waiting for a delayed friend. Returning the priest's wave as the rector disappeared into the church office, Martin had grimly settled down to wait. Twenty minutes later a sudden break in music and an excited voice coming over the car radio caught his attention and brought him bolt upright in the seat as he turned up the volume.

"*We interrupt for breaking news. This just in, an attempted killing was foiled minutes ago outside St Paul's Hospital in Vancouver. The lone attacker was shot and fatally wounded by undercover police protecting a man being taken to St Paul's for treatment. Information is still coming in and we'll update you as more becomes available.*" The music resumed, then abruptly. "*CBC news confirms that the man under attack at St Paul's hospital was Ismail Talawi the British author under sentence of death by radical Islamic fundamentalists. The lone gunman was shot by undercover police from Vancouver's elite diplomatic protection unit, and died at the scene. We are going live to Carol Oates our correspondent on the scene—Carol?"*

Martin started the car. He had time to catch his alternate flight. It would be tight but if he took a floatplane from Salt Spring to Seattle he could be clear of North America before the hounds picked up his scent. The radio was a babble of words and reaching down he punched it off. He felt ice cold and hoped for Nick it'd been quick.

Ayatollah Albarrasan read the flash message from Canada once more, then kneeling at the safe he pushed the destruct button on the thermal security box containing details of his two agents, Camerone and Cedar. He smiled thinly. The outcome could not have been better if planned—a failed attempt, by a non-Arab assassin kept the Iranian-British talks on track. The hardline radicals within the clergy would assume that he, Ayatollah Albarrasan, had been responsible for the attempt and would support his nomination. Rafsanjani and his backers in the government would assume that he'd compromised his own agent to the British and Canadian authorities and would be duly grateful. Camerone deserved to disappear.

Tristam Burns stuck his head round the door. "You wanted me Boss?"

"Come in Tris. You know Basil Coulson and this is Mike Dunlevy. Mike is a code and cypher expert from Cheltenham." Jimmy Douglas pushed his chair back and stood stretching his shoulders. His face held a strange expression. Reaching to a slim orange file on his desk he held it to Tristam. "Close the door and have a look at this."

Tristam took the file obediently and flipped it

open. He gasped and the file fell from suddenly nerve-
less fingers. "Oh—God, how long have you known?"
He sank into a chair and buried his face in his hands.
His voice was muffled and his shoulders shook. "I'm
glad it's over."

"Known—known, since yesterday—you little
shit." Jimmy Douglas was moving around the desk, his
control cracking. "We could have lost Talawi, Meg and
Sandy—I should—." Basil Coulson held out a rigid arm
blocking Douglas's path to his lieutenant.

"Steady Jimmy, Tris is going to tell us why, aren't
you Tris?"

Tristam looked up, his thin aristocratic face
streaked with tears. "I had a homosexual affair, just
once. Actually hated it." His voice was suddenly bitter.
"But it was a set up. I was at a party at the home a
Harley street surgeon—"

"Koorosh Ghiassi?"

Stunned, Tristam stared at Basil Coulson, "You
know him?"

"Yes Tris, we know him, carry on, you were saying
you attended a party at his house." Tristam gazed across
the room, eyes blank, his mouth twisted in a bitter line
of self-disgust.

"Yes, anyway I had too much to drink, snorted a
line or two of cocaine and found myself in bed with a
fellow—someone took photographs. The next day I was
told they would go to my father unless I passed on the
odd bit of information. I was promised that nothing
against HMG would be asked of me."
Tristam stared down at the floor, silence permeated the
room; the wall clock ticked loudly and the clack of
shoes walking past in the corridor resonated in the
silence. "But when the attempt on Talawi took place I
was instructed to keep my control fully informed of our

progress in tracking the man they called, Cedar." He stopped, and looking directly at Jimmy Douglas said quietly, "I'm sorry Jimmy. I should have—."

Jimmy Douglas turned away in disgust, his face working, then suddenly he spun round. "Who the hell cares if you're gay or straight? Where the hell have you been living the last ten years? This is treason—don't you get it, you stupid, stupid child. Men have died—one of them by my—"

"Jimmy!" Basil Coulson's command was sharp, unequivocal. "That's enough. Not everyone here is sanctioned for full disclosure." He turned to Tristam. "Jimmy has a point. You must know that being homosexual is not an impediment to any occupation—"

"But I'm not—don't you understand? I'm not." Tristam worked his hands together. "My father—." He stopped, then in a rush the words spilled out. "He won the MC at Bir Hakiem and a bar at Nijmegen with the Canadians. He thinks sodomy is disgusting—he's not a bigot, but he'd not understand you see? My mother died when I was twelve and he raised me. I'm his world—he was so proud of me being in the service—he's been ill for a long time. Seeing those photographs would've killed him." Tristam looked at Basil Coulson, an agonised plea in his eyes. "I'll cooperate fully but can you keep the pictures from him?"

Coulson turned to Jimmy Douglas. "Burns will be debriefed by a full team from counter intel. Most of what will come out will be classified. Providing he cooperates fully I think we can keep the sordid details out of the gutter press."

Jimmy Douglas, in control of his emotions once more, nodded in agreement and pushed a key on his telephone. "Ask security to come in now." Douglas turned to Tristam and Coulson would later remark that

he'd never seen such sadness. "You know Tris, had you
come to me I could've seen your father and shown him
how easy it is to fake photographs. I'd have told him you
were undercover and that the opposition was trying to
pass disinformation along in an attempt to discredit you.
You see it would have been so easy." He walked to the
door as the two security officers knocked. "Bas, Mike, I
need a drink. Will you join me?" He stepped into the
passage to wait for his companions.

Epilogue

18 months later

Sand blew in under the tent flap. Swirling gently it lifted the flap before subsiding into concentric circles of fine sand. The sound of sobbing, wafting on the hot air, came from where the latest batch of refugees sat in listless silent bundles of exhausted humanity. Probably another starving child had just relinquished its tiny, tenuous hold on life.

Cradling a cup of tea in both hands Anne Flett watched the project pilot, Martin Dresseur, and Chanda Ndege, the UNHCR representative, walk towards her over the baked ground. She smiled tiredly at the two men as they plopped down beside her on the wooden bench.

"Good flight?"

"Ha!" Ndege spat on the dirt floor. "Going to Addis is never a good flight Anne, you know that."

Martin laughed. "Chanda hates it when they point their rifles up at the aircraft as we fly in. He wants a steel plate to sit on." He stood, propping the canvas mailbag on the bench. "I need a beer—Chanda, you?"

"See if there's a cold soft drink in there. If not I'll have a beer." Chanda Ndege mopped his face with a large cotton handkerchief. Anne knew Martin never drank during the day and Ndege was a Moslem from Malawi to the south—it must have been a rough trip.

"Did our drugs arrive?"

Chanda scowled across to the medical tent past the shuffling lines of refugees to where Drs. Raoul Desbottes and Michel deMaregy were working their shift after replacing Anne Flett and Tomas Pulay. "Some." He took a deep breath. "Most of what you begged from St. Paul's survived, but the antibiotics from

London—." He lifted his hands. "What are we doing
here Anne, when the very people we're trying to save are
stealing us blind?"

Anne reached across to touch his arm, but the
grizzled head of the big black man turned away. With a
snort, he rose and stumbled out of the tent. Anne
watched the broad back disappear in the direction of
the main office. She sighed. It was a good question and
unanswerable. They were all here because they believed
it mattered, that it did make a difference. Since joining
Médecins Sans Frontières a year ago she'd come to realise
that what she'd seen as an escape from the intolerable
depression in the months after Nick's death was not an
escape from despair but a journey into a far greater
despair. Being wounded herself she understood the
enormity of the tragedy paraded daily in front of her
and her companions in this sun bleached waste of sub-
Saharan Africa. And because it was so terrible she found
from somewhere deep inside the resources to rise like a
gale-battered ship to ride out the storm in her soul.

"Chanda gone?" Martin put two cans of beer on
the table and sat across from her. "Poor bastard. They
gave him a rough time in Addis. He takes it so personally."

"And you Martin? How do you remain so calm?
I've never seen you lose it like the rest of us and yet
you've been here nearly as long as I have."

Martin took a long pull on the beer before wiping his lips and looking directly at her. "Losing it, as you
put it, is a healthy sign and soon you'll have to decide
on renewing your contract or returning to the real world.
During this past year I've seen you slowly come back to
life and it's been good to see." He raised the can for
another drink.

Anne smiled at him affectionately. "From the
day you arrived you've been my safe haven, my shield.

It's almost as if you were sent here to watch over me."

Martin sputtered, coughing as he lowered the beer can down. "Damn it Anne, don't say things like that or I'll start believing I'm almost a nice person. Let's change the subject shall we. I noticed a letter and parcel for you when I collected the mail." He reached over to rummage in the bag, "Ah, here we are," and handing her a thin letter and a bulky parcel watched carefully as she turned the letter over.

"It's from Mike." She seemed reluctant to open it.

"Your ex-husband?" Martin opened his Swiss Army knife and handed it to her.

"Yes, I wonder what he wants." Anne looked at him as she took the knife and slit open the flap. Her hand trembled slightly as she pulled out the single sheet. She read it silently before handing it to Martin.

"You're sure you want me to read this?" He held the letter face down on the table. Anne nodded silently, staring out of the tent opening. Martin took a deep breath before turning the letter over.

Vancouver, B.C.

My Dear Anne,
It has taken me this long to get up the courage to write to you. I spoke to Sandy last week. He's based in Kosovo, as I'm sure you know, and was passing through Vancouver attending a seminar or something mysterious. We had dinner and talked for hours. Your brother is a wise and generous person. He's forgiven me for turning you away. I know I do not deserve such generosity after my awful behaviour. Blaming you for my own guilt is something I cannot forgive in myself. There is nothing worse than a hypocrite.
Jenny lost the baby in her third month and we separated before you left the clinic in England and your parents' home. My

letters were returned unopened and your parents refused to tell me where you were. Sandy made it clear that they wanted to protect you as much as possible. He agreed to address this letter to you and post it for me.

I've been concentrating on work and despite having what most would consider a very successful year I come home to an empty apartment to sit and stare at your portrait on the wall. To say that I miss you would be the greatest understatement of my life. If this letter reaches you and you can find it in your heart to forgive me please reply. If we could meet anywhere in the world I'd fly there tomorrow.

Mike

Martin folded the letter carefully and handed it back. "You are going to have to decide. As I said your contract comes up for renewal next month. You should think about returning to the real world."

"The real world, Martin? I recall hearing you call it 'Camelot on the sewer.'" She placed the letter back into its envelope. Lifting the second packet a puzzled frown crossed her face. "This was posted in Nairobi. Why didn't the sender simply mail it to us here, we're still in Kenya after all?" Martin shrugged,

"UNHCR and MSF have offices in Addis, I guess they assumed it was the central collection point."

Still frowning Anne tore open the flap and a small battered book fell onto the table. She lifted it then gasped, "Oh God." Her face drained of colour yet her eyes lit up with sudden delight.

Martin came around the table fast to grip her shoulders from behind. "Easy Anne, what is it?"

"Nick—Nick quoted a poem to me. You remember I mentioned the poem and book to you. It was so lovely and I asked if he'd made it up but he said no; it was from a book called *The Love Poems of Ba Anton.*

After he—after he died I tried to find a copy but it was out of print and eventually I stopped trying. This is the book. But who—who apart from you knows the full story? I never even told Sandy about the book."

Holding her shoulders firmly Martin spoke over the top of her head. "Anne, Nick had support, a man, a friend who tried to save him at the end. No—" he stopped her from turning to face him "—listen to me." Anne sat looking straight ahead but her hands came up to touch his. "Long ago, like others, I fought in a country that no longer exists in a war that no one remembers. Men like Nick and myself belong to a small fraternity, men who have no allegiance except to each other. When you told me of the book I made inquiries and called in a debt. The man who sent this no longer exists but he knew Nick and wanted you to have it."

Anne turned under the strong fingers to look up at the calm face. "And you Martin? Did you know Nick? Is that why you followed me here, to cancel your debt?"

Martin laughed, "If it comforts you to think that, so be it. I came here because it was the only job open to a washed up freelance pilot. I stayed because I met the kind of woman a man dreams of meeting if he's lucky." He brushed a strand of loose hair back off her face. "Anne, don't dwell on the past. You are young yet and have a good life ahead of you. Go home and regain your life."

"And you Martin? Are you going to renew your contract?"

"Me—of course—who's going to keep Chanda from exploding, if not me? Anyway, until my wealthy aunt in Paris dies, I cannot afford to retire."

Anne stood, a small smile playing around her lips. She reached on tiptoe to brush his lips lightly with her own. "Well, Captain, you're going to have me to put up with for another year as well. Come, I think the cooks have goat a la thornbush as the main course. You can provide the wine from your secret stash." Hooking her arm through his she led him toward the mess tent. The sun, a crimson disc, was sinking fast now and the sobbing from the refugee group had stopped. A drum tapped softly in the distance.

FINIS 01

If you've enjoyed reading this novel please tell your friends and acquaintances how much you enjoyed it and perhaps suggest your local library or bookstore order a copy. If you really want to give me a boost call your local radio station and mention you've just finished a great West Coast thriller.

I'm a small, struggling, independent Author/Publisher and every bit of support you can give helps. I neither receive nor request government subsidies.

As a reader your judgment and comments are of great interest to me. Should you have suggestions, criticism or helpful advice please send them to my e-mail address.

E-mail: glendambo@saltspring.com
web page: www.anthonybruce.com

If you have enjoyed reading this novel you may wish to order copies of Anthony Bruces' previous novels.

To Taunt A Wounded Tiger. A diplomatic hostsage drama set in Victoria, B.C. and Isla Del Sol: Trade Paperback Price $16.95

The East Wind : An adventure set in the burning wastes of the Namib, the oldest desert on earth. A man marked by a bitter war: a woman lost between duty and love: A spoilt, indulged youth learning late that money cannot buy life or reverse the wheels of fate.
Trade paperback: Price $18.95

Order by Fax, e-mail or phone to:

Glendambo Publishing
151 Saltair Lane
Salt Spring Island, B.C.
Canada.
V8K 1Y5.

E-mail: glendambo@saltspring.com

Phone: (250) 653 4449

Fax: (250) 653 4419